RIPPING
ABIGAIL

a Quilted Mystery novel

Barbara Sullivan

10 digit ISBN: 146351137X
13 digit EAN: 978-1463511371

QuiltMyst Publishing.

Printed in the United States of America

ACKNOWLEDGEMENTS

Grateful acknowledgement is extended to the many friends and family members who have supported my writing. Their feedback has been an invaluable asset in my continuing efforts to improve my craft.

A special thanks to daughter Sue Sullivan for her expert and professional editing, and for the generosity of her words; her sensitivity and sensibility nurtured my creativity. I am likewise thankful to my son-in-law Steve Sedam for his beautiful cover artwork. And to daughter Cynthia for her invaluable insights into Latino- and Hispanic-American culture and history.

Dedicated to my Marine.

List of Characters at end of book.

"Though youth must only wait,
While age can only fear,
Love at first a fate
Is last a feeble tear.

Oh love, my heart is yours
From youth's deflowered field
O're life's imperiled moors
My heart will never yield.

And now I ever cry."

From the Latter-day Poems of Ruth McMichaels, 1934-

PROLOGUE

The twitter.com entries of John Shaw, Pinto Springs High School graduate, allegedly transcribing the last words of his six classmates. Timestamps and content captured by a following dorm friend Wednesday, Oct. 22, 8:15 a.m. and later reposted on the friend's blog. The entries are reversed in order for clarity.

They left the phone on cause I was sic and couldn't go. I listened all nite. Was supposed to be a punishment. Was the worst.
2 hours ago

Fell asleep once or twice, so began recording. We were best buds. We were the Magnificent PS7. Here are the last words of the other 6.
2 hours ago

It's the whole horse thing of Pinto Springs. That's why we were the Magnificent Pinto Springs 7
2 hours ago

I begin their words: Jimmy Winters says, "Hey, Ratface, wake up. Wake up man. Hey, Rats, we're lost."
1 hour ago

Rashaad (Ratface) Maloof says, "What? How?"
1 hour ago

Ricardo (Ricky) Rodriguez says, "What's happening Bro? Where the freak are we?"
1 hour ago

Winters: "I don't know, Ricky. Rats was supposed to keep me on track, but he fell asleep an hour ago. I must have...I don't know, taken a wrong turn."
1 hour ago

Maloof: "Don't blame me."
1 hour ago

Leopold Cooke says, "Okay, calm down. How lost can we get on the California interstate system, people?"
1 hour ago

Cooke: "What is this, 5, 8? James my boy, how can you not know which freeway you're on?"
1 hour ago

Winters "If I knew I wouldn't be asking you, Leopold my boy, would I?"
1 hour ago

Cooke "My pins are falling asleep, my boy, sit on Baker for awhile. I'm going crippled."
1 hour ago

Rodriguez: "Okay, okay. You know, this looks like 8, out by freaking Chula Vista. Maybe we missed the turnoff to school."
1 hour ago

George Baker says, "Hey man! What the hell?
1 hour ago

Rodriguez: "Your turn to carry my sweet-ass load, Baker baby."
1 hour ago

Winters: "No. We're not on 8. We're not on 5. I don't know where the crap we are, guys."
1 hour ago

Cooke: "Don't panic, Jimmy my boy, Cooke to the rescue. A sign will come up soon. Go back to sleep my people. Jimmy and I have got the helm."
1 hour ago

Winters: "Not a good idea, Leo. This is like.... Sweet Jesus, my eyes won't stay open."
1 hour ago

Baker: "Ricky! Stop wiggling your butt. You're making me hot."
1 hour ago

Rodriguez: "Eew, you like my freakin' brown ass, eh Black Boy?"
1 hour ago

Baker: "Keep wiggling, you'll find out how much."
1 hour ago

Have to break. Tears and tears.
1 hour ago

Rodriquez: "Hey, like maybe we've entered the freakin' Twilight Zone. Doodoo-doodoo, doodoo..."
48 minutes ago

Kim Lee says, "Shut the f*ck up! I'm trying to get some shut-eye back here. Least I can do in this hole you call a third-row seat."
46 minutes ago

Rodriquez: "Ratface, you're the great navigator, where the freak are we?"
45 minutes ago

Maloof: "My name is Raashad, Ricky. You better start using your real names too guys, if you want to get anywhere in the biz world."
44 minutes ago

Baker: "Let me see. Hmm. Trees and more trees. We're in the woods."
44 minutes ago

Cooke: "Helpful, my boy, very helpful."
43 minutes ago

Lee: "Hey, Rats, you can't rename yourself now. We been calling you Ratface since you were six years old. And you still look like a rat..."
31 minutes ago

Maloof: "Stay on the road, Jimmy!"
29 minutes ago

Winters: "What? Oh sh*t, I fell asleep again! My brain is mush. What the f*ck did they give us in TJ?"
28 minutes ago

Cooke: "You mean what the f*ck did you take in TJ? Nobody spoon fed you, Jimmy my boy."
26 minutes ago

Lee: "Wait a minute. Woods? Do we know these trees? Like from three trips from Pinto Springs High to TJ last year? Is this..?"
24 minutes ago

Baker: "Sh*t! We're on 13! You've got us heading back home, Jimmy. No can do, guys, my dad..."
23 minutes ago

Cooke: "The Reverend..."
21 minutes ago

Baker: "...will excoriate me if I show up stoned out of my mind..."
19 minutes ago

Rodriguez: "Smelling of Mexican pussy."
18 minutes ago

Baker: "...he'll drag my ass right off campus and back home..."
18 minutes ago

Maloof: "STAY ON THE ROAD, JIMMY"
17 minutes ago

Winters: "Huh? Crap, I'm really spacing here, guys. And it isn't funny Ricky."
17 minutes ago

Lee: "Maybe we can crash at somebody's house. Maybe your house, Winters. Your old lady won't mind."
16 minutes ago

Maloof: "Jimmy! What are you doing? You can't do a U-ie in the middle..."
16 minutes ago

Cooke: "WATCH OUT!"
15 minutes ago

I tuned in the news and heard the report. All dead. They're all dead. A header with a sixteen wheeler. And now I join them.
9 minutes ago

PART ONE

stitch in time

Chapter 1

Friday, October 24, 9:30 am

My name is Rachel Lyons and my husband Matthew and I are private investigators working our late life second careers in and around San Diego, Cleveland and Imperial Counties. Our California company is called LIRI which stands for Lyons Investigations and Research, Incorporated. LIRI is currently housed in our home and Matt and I are the principal owners. We have two full-time apprentices helping us with the growing security and investigative needs of the area. We've been in business for three years now.

Some of you like to see the characters you're reading about, and you'll be reading a lot about Matt and I, so I'll describe us. Of course you must remember this is all from my point of view.

Or POV as some of us writers like to say, although I'm really a journalist. That's one of my duties with our company, keeping records of our day's activities, often in the form of a journal, and also doing most of the research for our business.

Okay, here goes the description part again. I'm in my early fifties, with an accent on the early, I color my hair mostly in shades of blond, and some people consider me pretty. I'm about average height and we aren't discussing weight here. Or anywhere.

Matthew Lyons is a hunk. He was born a hunk—I have his baby pictures to prove this. Dark brown hair, Paul Newman blue eyes, muscular, six two, and the girls gasp when he enters the room. Even now that he's in his mid fifties. And that's all I'm going to tell you about my husband--except, he's mine, so hands off.

Matt takes care of all the dangerous stuff in our private investigating business, and he manages the two male apprentices currently associated with LIRI.

At least he used to handle all the scary stuff. Last month I started redefining my job description, kind of by accident, as I found my way into a lot of bad scary stuff.

But I'm convinced that was an aberration. More about this later, back to the here and now.

I was cooling my heels outside Principal Edward J. Forsyth's office at Pinto Springs High because I needed to speak to him about a recently enrolled student. That student was Abigail Pustovoytenko. I initially met Abigail three weeks ago at the first Quilted Secrets bee I attended. I met her mother Gloria doing some investigating I completed ten days ago. Gloria P. is head nurse of the Cleveland County Hospital Intensive Care Unit.

At the moment, Principal Dr. Forsyth, as his nameplate on his door listed him, had more important things to attend to because the six boys in Wednesday's horrendous early morning accident had been graduates of Pinto Springs, and a constant stream of worried parents, students and teachers were cycling in and out of his office.

The school was planning a "Grieving Service". The city of Pinto Springs, California was in collective mourning and the Grieving Service was to be one of the many opportunities the powers-that-be intended to offer the community for expressing their grief.

The fatal accident had occurred only fifty-three hours ago. Five of the six CSUSD college freshman died within hours of the crash. The sixth, driver Jimmy Winters, was hanging on by a thread according to rumors. The car the boys had crammed themselves into for a night of heavy drinking in Tijuana was broadsided on the right by a heavyweight, refrigerated HappyFoods truck as Winters tried to do a u-turn in the middle of I-13.

Interstate 13 is the main north south freeway feeding Cleveland County.

The boys had been friends since early childhood, as well as being recent graduates of PSHS. Needless to say, the parents were devastated, and the community was distraught.

The whole world now knows about this accident, thanks to a Twitter account of the conversation leading up to the accident posted by the seventh of the boys, one John Shaw. Shaw, also a freshman student at UCSD, had missed the trip to TJ due to a bout with the flu. I read his Twitter page yesterday, when all of this hit the regional news like an avalanche moving at warp speed. Chilling. Especially his opening line that he was preparing to join them.

Fortunately, John Shaw's parents were phoned by a dorm friend and warned. They retrieved him from the University of California, San Diego around ten that morning and sped him home just as an army of reporters were zeroing in for interviews. No one knows where his parents are hiding him at the moment.

What a terrible thing, to lose five of your life-long friends all at once. Maybe six.

By the way, Pinto Springs High is centrally located on the mile high Cleveland County plateau, situated east of our home in Escondido.

Which brings me back to why I was cooling my heels.

Chapter 2

As I've said, my mission this sad morning concerned one Abigail Pustovoytenko Beardsley and her recent enrollment at the high school. Thirteen year old Abby was one of the Quilted Secrets gals I sewed with last month at my first ever hand quilting bee.

Beardsley is Abigail's father's last name. She elected to drop it when he and her mother separated. I don't know when this separation occurred.

Her mother and primary guardian, Gloria Pustovoytenko hired me early this morning to retrieve Abigail from the school and bring her home. Early this morning was when Gloria first got wind of the fact that Abigail had been attending classes at PSHS. A remarkable fact given this was her third day.

According to her mother, the girl was illegally enrolled at PSHS. Gloria's reasoning was that the homeschooled Abigail is enrolled in a charter school already, the Stowall Academy of the Arts.

Don't bother looking it up on your Blackberry. It isn't listed anywhere. I've searched. In simple English, Gloria is fighting Abigail's desire to attend public school. *Nothing is simple or we'd skip this existence altogether and move straight into heaven*, as my mother used to say and I often repeat to myself.

So here I sat, wondering how I would bring this retrieval thing off. Public school systems aren't happy about homeschooling to begin with, so when a homeschooled child decides to up and enroll herself in a public school—with or without her legal guardian's permission--I suspected that said public school would fight like crazy to keep the student on their rolls.

Abigail P. was sitting in a classroom somewhere on campus at this very moment. I wished she wasn't. I wished I wasn't here to do what I suspected could well be illegal.

I wasn't unaware of Abigail's feelings in the matter. She'd complained about being homeschooled all through October's bee. However, the general consensus of the other women in attendance--those who had known Abigail for far longer than I--was that she was better off staying home. According to them, Abigail was a very special student and a brilliant artist.

And Gloria had assured me that Abigail's education was above par, with input from tutors and a variety of field activities with other homeschooling parents.

California law has been fairly supportive of homeschooling. I say fairly, because up until recently there was no actual law allowing homeschooling. But there has never been one against it either.

But to make the issue even more secure, a recent ruling by the California Court of Appeals Second Appellate District has declared that *"California statues permit homeschooling as a species of private school education."* It currently appears there is no further appeal expected.

In the wake of this decision, and perhaps because Abigail was becoming increasingly rebellious about the issue, Gloria and many of her fellow homeschooling parents quickly formed and registered a PSP, or Private School Program. This was done on October first--the first day authorized by this new ruling. (This would be the illusive Academy of the Fine Arts already mentioned.)

The supportive part also comes from the fact that as of this date none of the "teachers" registered as "working" in this "private school" need be certified by the state as such. This may change. Also, the instruction, though necessarily in English, and necessarily covering several branches of study required in all public schools, could be fulfilled in large groups or small, at any locale, and with no defined curriculum as long as a record of "attendance" was kept.

A trip to the zoo with mom or dad therefore could constitute a biology lesson, as long as mom or dad wrote the date and time down in a log.

Consequently, Gloria believed her grounds for sending me to the school to retrieve her daughter rested with the truancy laws of the state, and that in effect by not "attending" the homeschool classes she'd been scheduled to attend this week she was skipping school. Truant.

AWOL.

I hoped because the school was so involved with the deaths of the five recent graduates from PSHS I might just pull this off...at least for today. This would give Gloria P. time to get her act together and hash things out with her daughter.

She needed to start talking with her daughter and meeting her personal needs—instead of talking *at* her daughter which I suspected she was doing. I suspect this because I have in my fairly long time on this planet observed this behavior in relatives, friends and yes, even in our own efforts at parenting.

And Gloria needed to keep in mind that it might not be long before the *Forces to Liberate Kids from the Tyranny of Their Parents* would gather themselves around Abigail's cause. Reminding her of this probable complication was to be my second task for the day.

Maybe she already knew it.

The principal whizzed by me for a third straight time. I almost reached out and grabbed his pant leg in a desperate effort to grab a few seconds of his time. Instead I smiled a weary smile at the secretary whose hawk eyes were drilling into my own disapprovingly. Public schools were very protective of their territory, which included every living child on U.S. soil between the ages of five and eighteen.

Secretary Chrissy Prichard, with her own nameplate, clearly didn't side with me on the homeschooling issue. Either that or she was a naturally disagreeable person.

The principal whizzed back into his office and growled over his shoulder, "Show Ms. Lyons in."

I stood and whizzed right in after him—not waiting for Ms. Prichard to introduce me.

"Dr. Forsyth, thank you so much for taking the time

to speak with me...."

"Sit down!"

A spurt of anxiety filled my chest, some leftover emotion from my own adolescent days, no doubt. "Of course, sir," I answered politely, and took a deep breath.

I began telling the principal why I was there, but he cut me off mid-sentence.

"Let's get something straight, Ms. Lyons, Abigail Pustovoytenko has every right to attend high school here if she so wishes. In fact if my schedule weren't filled to overflowing with grieving students and parents, and a press conference scheduled with the mayor for noon, I'd argue the point with you until school let out at two-fifteen. But it is, so I can't. You and your so-called *client* Gloria Pustovoytenko are dead wrong in your insistence that this poor child be forced to continue with a fake education because of her mother's personal paranoias and prejudices."

He'd actually pronounced her last name correctly.

I still wasn't sure I could.

Chapter 3

He had cleverly just introduced what I knew could be one of the statewide challenges made to homeschooling sooner or later, that of racial prejudice. Maybe even nationwide. In other words, he was intimating that the hidden reason Gloria P. and others like her didn't want their children attending California's public schools was to keep them separated from some ethnically inferior group of children.

I sidestepped this hot potato.

"But sir, she's currently enrolled at the..."

He waved an impatient hand to silence me.

"I am required by law to accept this phony school of yours..."

"Not mine, sir. The homeschooling mother I represent has enrolled..."

"...but I don't have to respect the insulting lie that is underlying such a so-called *school*. And I doubt seriously there really is one at all. From my experience, these so-called schools are nothing but fronts for parents who are denying their children the right to a decent education, one that includes proper instruction in *all* of the basic subjects a public school offers..."

He was yelling now.

"...and doing so for purely selfish reasons, because they'd had bad experiences themselves, because they want to keep their children with them like little Peter Pans, never allowed to grow up. How does this mother know her daughter might not thrive in school? How does she know what Abigail might be capable of learning in a formal educational setting unless..." He waved an impatient hand again, this time at his own digression.

"At any rate, at this point I have no time to argue with you. Abigail will be retrieved from her classes as soon as we locate her. You can wait outside."

"Locate her..?"

Three parents were ushered in by the secretary who, still glaring at me, indicated haughtily that I should follow her. My two and a half minutes with the *Prince* were over.

This time I was deposited out in the hall by the nurse's office to do my waiting--where I imagined secretary Prichard hoped I would catch something contagious. Instead, I sat listening in as a young girl asked for her weekly supply of condoms. Nurse Janet Kaplan—according to the sign next to her door— proceeded to explain how to slide it over his member.

"I already *know* how to use it Ms. Kaplan. Like, you told me all this junk last month, remember?" Nurse Janet was a sweet faced gray haired lady on the edge of retirement. I imagined she was as comfortable about handing out condoms as I would be if I had the job.

As in *not*.

I'm a prude.

"Humor me. I'm required to read these instructions to you..." I heard her mumble.

Definitely more than I wanted to know about today's world. I settled back in my comfy new waiting chair, a metal on metal folding device no doubt meant to discourage students from wanting to see the nurse too often.

Chapter 4

A half hour passed during which I'd struck up a reasonably friendly conversation with school nurse Janet Kaplan about the sad events of the day.

She asked me about my neck brace, which I'd become so accustomed to I'd forgotten I was wearing. I told her briefly I'd been in a car accident of my own just eleven days before, one in which fortunately no one had died. That my car had been rolled on a different freeway (and on what felt like a different dimensional plane) and I'd suffered a severe neck strain as a result.

I was almost done with the pain, but talking about it reminded me I still hurt a little. My doctor was insisting I keep the brace on for a full month or suffer the return of the mind blowing pain I'd first experienced. I was trying. But I have to avoid mirrors all together before leaving the house.

What I didn't tell her was that the accident had been no accident. That someone in a white truck had tried to kill me, someone who had not yet been identified.

I also didn't tell her that this was the first day since the accident that I'd been out driving around on my own. Before this morning Matt had chauffeured me everywhere. Matt had another court case to testify at this morning, so he was unable to assist me. Our two apprentices were likewise busy.

I've decided not to tell my doctor that I was driving again.

Matt was the natural choice to do court testimony for our little company, on two counts: one, Matt's thirty years' experience as an officer in the Marine Corps made him a very credible witness, and two, my former career had been as a librarian.

Librarians are not really known for their public speaking skills. Not that mine were bad, I just tend to say too much. It's the Freedom of Information thing that librarians have at the center of their brains. You ask, we tell--or find a book that will do the same thing.

Okay, maybe it's not about being a librarian. Maybe I'm just too loquacious. Or...maybe I have this big need to sound like I know stuff.

That would be because I was a second child, and the first child was very intelligent. And pushy. It's called second child syndrome. But I'm giving you way too much information.

Anyway, whenever our business became involved in any work that was to be used in a trial case, Matt did that work so he could testify.

My mind drifted back to the mild anxiety I was carrying around over Abigail's reaction to my doing her mother's dirty work. Our relationship was through the Quilted Secrets bees as I've already stated, and I needed that relationship to stay friendly. Consequently, I'd made up my mind that if Abigail refused to accompany me I would just leave without her and tell Gloria to deal with her daughter when she got home from work.

Problem was, Gloria was head nurse of CCICU and often did overtime. This morning when she'd called she told me she'd been working twelve- to fourteen-hour days since the accident on Wednesday and she didn't expect that to let up anytime soon.

Aside from dealing with the deaths of the five boys, three of whom made it into her ICU, she still had Jimmy Winters to deal with twenty-four seven. And one of the dead boys' fathers had been delivered to her with a heart attack mid-day yesterday.

That had been George Baker's father, a local Baptist pastor and an African American. Two health strikes against him, in my book. George Baker senior had a very stressful job as a pastor. And my knowledge of health issues for African Americans included high risk for heart disease, especially if they were overweight. Gloria told me Baker was carrying an extra fifty pounds and the prognosis was iffy. They weren't sure he would pull through.

The now dead George Baker junior was his only son.

So my thoughts were that Gloria deserved all the help she could get. I could never deal with the deaths of five young men the way she was now doing. And frankly, I liked Gloria P. a lot. She has spunk.

And I also thought that Dr. Forsyth wasn't the only one with an overly full schedule, and if Gloria could have been here she would have done a masterful job at defending her decision to homeschool Abigail.

She would have pointed out the hours of endless boredom that constituted much of the public school day.

She would have pointed out the clear evidence of failure of the mass produced education system that has evolved today, a public school system nothing like what it once was a hundred years ago.

She would have cited dropout statistics, the increasing incidence of school violence in recent years, and the eight-foot-high fencing surrounding the school campus to keep terrorists out.

She would have pointed to the over-sexualization of our young people that was spreading like a disease through all American public schools. And the superior test scores of homeschooled children as compared with public schooled children.

But she wasn't here, and I wasn't eager to get into any debate of this nature. I just wanted to retrieve Abigail and be done with it.

Another young pimple-faced female arrived to see Nurse Janet—this one looking like she was experiencing menstrual cramps, and my sore backside and restless nature drove me off the metal chair and out into the main hall in search of interesting displays.

Chapter 5

In between the grease stains and almost washed off graffiti on the institutional green walls there were several glass fronted cases lining the main hall. Most of them were filled with sports trophies. I finally found one that celebrated last month's academic excellence award, with the catchy title, "September's BraiNerd" and the winner's photograph.

He looked like a BraiNerd. I was willing to bet most of the students would die of humiliation if they found their own picture on this wall display.

I smiled and continued to ponder the situation with Abigail while perusing several more trophy cases. I have to say, trophy cases are a complete waste of space. At least they broke up the monotony of filthy walls. But why not try to teach something in this space?

I did learn that Pinto Springs had a pretty good football team. But its baseball and basketball teams could use some improvement. I had yet to find the soccer team's trophies at all.

A bell rang, reminding me of a fire drill I'd practiced centuries ago, and the halls of knowledge filled with disorderly, rude, weirdly dressed, large and small, tall and short, young people. They trailed a peculiar odor behind them. I clung to the piece of grimy wall I happened to be at when this river of youth had flowed out of the classrooms and prayed I wouldn't accidentally be swept up and carried into a room when it was all over. I had learned from my own years at high school so many moons ago that there was no getting out of those rooms once the doors closed.

Lockers opened and slammed back shut. Girls screeched and giggled, boys slunk their way down the hall, some of them desperately clinging to their pants which were clearly too large. You get the picture.

At one point I remembered why I was here and began searching the faces of the kids swarming around me, but I didn't see Abigail anywhere.

Another siren rang and the torrent of teens was sucked into the rooms again like water down a drain and the noise ceased as abruptly as it had begun.

I was a visitor from outer space and this was the first thing I was learning about the life forms on this particular planet. I wasn't staying long.

The odor dissipated, my brain tried to identify it, drugstore perfume, sour clothes, cigarette smoke, urine and sweat...well, you get it.

I was alone. For several seconds I savored the calm in the hallway until I was reminded of the events of this week. I casually pushed myself off the sticky wall, pulled down on the hem of my short jacket, straightened my hair a bit and continued my stroll.

Two young girls rounded a corner ahead of me, probably from another hall, one I hadn't explored yet. They were bawling their way toward the nurse's office. The near-hysterical sobbing echoed off the tile and plaster walls and somehow ushered in a small knot of kids through the double doors at the other end of the corridor. They were carrying black ribbons over their arms. I watched for a moment as they began attaching them to a couple of classroom doors.

This brought my attention to the closest classroom doors and the decorations hung on them. The doors already had a sprig of flowers of one type or another hanging from them and some small phrase expressing grief--no doubt decided upon by the homeroom class for that room. The nearest one said, "To Leo, Rats, Ricky, Kim and Bro. We will never forget you." I followed the signs further away from the main offices of the school, reading as I went. I felt like Alice in Wonderland. Another proclaimed, "DON'T DRIVE STONED FOOLS!" A third said, "Death is NOT glorious. It's just *dead.*"

Dead was written in blood red ink.

Obviously the teachers had directed some of the messages. The preachy signs outnumbered what I felt were the students' actual feelings, namely shock and grief.

Teenagers were emotional anytime, half estrogen driven, half testosterone, and all borderline crazy with their frightening life-change. The introduction of mass-grief into this chemical witch's brew had the potential to be dangerous.

A memory flitted into my brain and out again, of a study I'd read in one of the many colleges I attended over the years in hot pursuit of a workable degree. The study was on teen suicides and the contagion of emotions. Within that study was a simile of the transition children go through during their teens. A simile for those who don't know is a form of figurative language. This one was something to the effect, *What would it feel like to wake up one morning in the body of an octopus?*

For me, this simple simile had summed up adolescence in one short sentence. Until now. By the time this event with Abigail was over I would have a new definition of adolescent stress forever lodged in my brain. Like a permanent splinter.

Chapter 6

Along with his five friends, Jimmy Winters' car crash had claimed another life. It wasn't the truck driver, he survived but he was in bad shape mentally. The other victim was a hapless driver who had gotten caught up in the deadly dance between Jimmy's car and the HappyFoods sixteen wheeler. A father of three on his way to his second job in the early morning hours, the poor man died at the scene.

Anonymous had already posted pictures on a popular internet site showing the aftermath of Jimmy Winters' fatal error in judgment. I won't elaborate. They were gross. So is Anonymous.

It seems to me the human race was growing less sensitive to each other's pain and agony with each passing day thanks to modern technology—if indeed it had ever been truly sensitive. The Romans certainly showed little sensitivity toward the gladiators.

Maybe *in*sensitivity was more our true nature, and only with the aid of religion and other educational efforts did we learn to relate to each other's suffering.

But enough philosophizing. I return to the reason I was here. In the middle of all the high emotion of the past three days, Abigail Pustovoytenko had decided to make her dash to freedom. She'd enrolled herself using her mother's work as an excuse for not having a parent with her. In a matter of minutes, she'd filled out and signed the forms, was quickly sent to a counselor's office to select a curriculum and was sat right down in her first class. I know all this because Abby bragged to me about it much later.

She has spunk, too.

So now she was officially registered as a freshman at PSHS, despite having no record of prior formal education, despite having no parent with her, *just sign here little miss, no questions will be asked.*

What a stunning legal world we live in today.

The PSHS school officials didn't care about parental rights. What they cared about was adding another student to their decreasing rolls so they could bring in more money and keep their jobs.

I didn't know if attending public school was a good idea for Abigail Pustovoytenko or not. What I knew was that at the tender age of thirteen she was an accomplished artist who appeared to know as much about history as I did. And I had a bachelor's in the subject. Of course that was decades ago. My excuse for being impressed.

She'd done the impressing at that first bee I keep telling you about, where she spent hours regaling us with her knowledge of early American history and the history of quilting. It helped pass the time.

Abigail even had her own website, one that she'd actually designed and that a fellow homeschool student had launched online for her. I'd seen the site and it was beautiful.

These homeschooled kids were no dummies.

Aside from discussions about American history, we'd collectively done a lot of *sharing* about our early childhoods at the bee. Each of us had shared a story we remembered about ourselves as an exercise intended to introduce me to the others in the group. I was the *new-bee* after all. Pun intended.

I blame all this sharing business on the Internet. I blame a lot of things on the Internet, including the near demise of public libraries, but that's another story for another time. The libraries have survived by adapting, as we all have.

The reason I bring this up is that Abigail shared a poignant tale about her father. Joseph Beardsley suffers from chronic kidney failure.

Beardsley and Abigail's mother are now estranged. I don't know whether the split was caused by the stress of his disease. I just know that he now lives somewhere in south San Diego County and that he has pretty much withdrawn from his fatherly duties.

Gloria Pustovoytenko emigrated from the Ukraine late in her teens. Once here in the United States she finished her nursing degree, and met and married Joseph Beardsley.

In the early part of their marriage, after Abigail was born, Gloria brought her mother over to live with them. Abigail's grandma was called Nana—which I realized also means grandmother. I had no other name for her and really didn't need one since I didn't expect to ever be talking with her.

I should also say that I can barely understand Gloria because her Ukrainian accent is so thick. Life in the Pustovoytenko family must be very interesting with Abigail speaking only English, Nana speaking only Ukrainian, and Gloria speaking some bastardized combination of both languages.

I don't know where Joseph Beardsley is at this point in time. I also don't know what his feelings are about his daughter Abigail attending public school.

Matt and I had mulled all this over this morning and Matt left a message for one of our apprentices—Marvin Luis Lewis--to take on the task of finding him in case the issue over her education went in the really bad direction we knew it could.

In that event, Joseph Beardsley--whatever his current health--could well be dragged into this business.

My feeling was, if Gloria just accepted this detour from homeschooling for a little while and let Abigail experience the monotony and general turmoil typical of the average American high school, Abigail would quit on her own, and return to the much richer environment she now felt she needed to escape.

But Gloria P. was in a snit-fit over her daughter's rebellion, and she wasn't inclined to accept anything. Gloria explained to me this morning that she just wanted time to work things out with her daughter.

Chapter 7

As if Anonymous' grainy photographs of the fateful accident weren't bad enough, then the words of John Shaw were found by the world. The entire transcript of what the boys said to each other when they thought no one was listening had been instantly slammed to approximately two billion Chinese, Indian and European email accounts.

This other half of the world, the Eastern Hemisphere, learned about the boys' deaths before we Americans did. The sun wasn't up here yet.

My immediate reaction to the email when I read it was that privacy had joined sensitivity at the bottom of our list of important things.

Again I scanned the hallway, now wondering when the principal or his aides would finally cough up Abigail.

The contrast between the many expressions of grief in these halls and the bloodlust sometimes found on the internet was disturbing to me. It left me wondering what precipice the human race was teetering off. And, what dichotomous coupling had produced our bipolar human race.

Perhaps God was a woman and the Devil her husband, and we were their offspring.

Of course some guy somewhere had the opposite theory. We were probably both wrong.

My wondering came from my formal study of history and my lifelong observance of human behavior. The lessons contained within these two activities taught me that these behaviors—simultaneous grief and bloodlust-- are a symptom that usually precedes great human turmoil, as in war. As in the downfall of great empires and the chaos then ushered in.

Five young, intelligent boys and one devoted, hardworking father dead, and also scavenged to feed our amoral lust for entertainment.

I hated that I was also a watcher.

"Not much being accomplished in the classrooms today."

The voice over my shoulder startled me out of my dismal reverie and I turned to see a short, heavyset man somewhere in his fifties leaning against a door jam. Behind him was the school's media center.

"I can imagine," I said. "You must be Stephen Norton, the librarian."

"Right. And you are?"

"Waiting for a student," I answered. "My name is Rachel Lyons."

"Why do I know that name?"

I returned his stare, wondering if the recent events in Cleveland County had made me famous or infamous. But he didn't make the connection and we moved on.

"Mind if I take a look? I used to be a librarian." I motioned toward the interior of his library.

While showing me around his media center our conversation continued.

"Not at all. Come on in. I'm just waiting for my next class to arrive. Where were you a librarian?"

"North Carolina, a few years ago now. This is nice. Quite good-sized."

"Not for a high school with over three thousand students, but California doesn't have the money it should for its support buildings--science labs are even worse off."

I nodded my head. The media center was basically the size of four regular classrooms, and separated into four different spaces by low cases. The section just to the left of the door was a well equipped computer center.

A closer look revealed that the machines were five or six years old. Wires twisted everywhere beneath them, dirty fingerprints stained the sides of the monitors and the keyboards were almost illegible. The books in the room looked tidy, though. I caught Norton giving me the once over, caught him while his eyes were mid-chest.

"Still have many readers?" I asked.

"Every class that comes in. They're required to check a book out every week, whether they read it or not. Whether they return it or not." His face turned slightly red. I noticed his shirt collar was grimier than the school walls.

The phrase burnout came to mind. My librarian's heart went out to him. My women's lib heart wanted him drawn and quartered for sexual assault. Speaking of dichotomies.

The awaited class arrived at Mr. Norton's door and I slid by them back out into the hallway, waving a little goodbye to him as I went.

The kids were staring at my sponge-wrapped neck as I wriggled by their sloppy line. I thought one of them was going to grab it. The collar began to feel like a lifesaver's ring, heavy and bulky. White on my decidedly orange jacket.

I headed back down the hall to see if any progress was being made on "finding" Abigail P.

There wasn't. I sighed and sat myself back down on the torture chair and continued my musings.

Gloria's discovery of Abigail's rebellion hadn't come until last evening. The fool girl didn't bother to return home until well after five yesterday—several minutes after her mom. So mom started making calls.

Mom said she still didn't know where Abigail had been from mid afternoon on, Thursday. Abigail wasn't telling. Nana was feigning indifference.

Maybe grandma was a co-conspirator.

Abigail had made no excuse when confronted. She just mumbled something clearly made up on the spur of the moment, and climbed the stairs to her bedroom. Slammed her door and locked it. Refused dinner.

Gloria had told me all this at least three times this morning, each time asking, where did she eat? *Where did she eat?*

As if that was the whole issue. Abigail had eaten somewhere other than her mother's kitchen.

And now Gloria wanted more time to talk with her

rebellious child.

I imagined Gloria and Abigail weren't communicating so much as slinging epithets at each other these days, if only figuratively. Thirteen, a wonderful year to discover your mother has it all wrong.

Thankfully, I'd raised boys. Matthew the Marine had done all the tough stuff, keeping our boys out of trouble. I began wandering again, in an effort to control my wondering. I was getting a headache. *Where the dickens was Abigail?*

I passed a row of metal lockers badly in need of paint. A few of them were so dented by what I assumed was roughhousing that they wouldn't even close anymore, certainly didn't lock. They offered the protection and privacy of cubby holes. But at least cubby holes would hold papers and books. Here everything was spilling out into the halls.

Things were certainly different from my own high school days. I couldn't imagine such damage left unattended back when I went to school.

Budgetary restrictions or administrative apathy?

Pavlov's bell rang again and the classroom doors sprang open like mouse traps in reverse. A flood of noisy mice cascaded down the hall toward me and I scooted back toward the metal chair. I began practicing saying Pustovoytenko over and over. My lips were even moving in anticipation of pronouncing the difficult name perfectly. Now I was really attracting stares.

Chapter 8

"Uh-oh," the school nurse mumbled as she moved from inside her office.

I looked at her as if to ask *what* then followed her line of sight to catch an official looking woman as she slid around the corner into the Admin offices.

"Latisha Harper from Social Services. She's a nice enough lady if you don't argue with her. "

My blood began to boil knowing that the Principal had been lying about not being able to locate Abigail. I'd been cooling my heels for close to an hour so he could line up a social worker visit.

But I took the nurse's advice and put on my most agreeable face as I was called back into the principal's office.

Latisha was a super-sized black woman, very middle aged and wearing a formal dark suit—brownish--with an emerald silk shirt underneath. Her oversized leather purse and briefcase matched each other, more shades of brown. Definitely dressed for fall.

She stuck a large, dry hand out forcefully and I took it. We shook. It was soft and warm. I immediately regretted not dressing more formally. My jeans and casual-though-expensive sporty jacket were outclassed.

"I felt for the school's sake we needed to involve Social Services in this event..." Dr. Forsyth began smugly. But the Social Services woman cut him off.

"More to the point, Ms. Lyons, for the sake of Abigail, Dr. Forsyth felt a family advocate needed to be brought in from Social Services. I need to see your identification again, and I need you to fill out these." She had a mild Southern accent she was controlling nicely. She slid several sheets of paper across the corner of Forsyth's desk toward me. "We can't just let you take her away from school, even with a letter from her mother.

Especially since we have yet to actually meet Mrs. (she glanced at her notes) Pust...er...voo-tanko." I smiled blandly.

"I think she goes by Ms. actually. Her married name was Beardsley but after the divorce she changed it back."

"Oh? And Abigail took her mother's maiden name?"

I didn't explain why. "Yes."

"I see. How well do you know Abigail?"

"Well, if we could bring her into the office I think she could better assure you than anything I might have to say. Have you found your newest student yet, Dr. Forsyth?" I was bluffing. I had no idea what Abigail's reaction to me was going to be.

"She's lost?" Latisha Harper said sharply.

"No, not really. I just felt it best..."

"Of course," Harper said dismissively and returned her attention to me. "Ms. Lyons..."

"Actually, I prefer Mrs."

Okay, I was getting on the wrong side.

She stopped and stared at me.

"Or, just Rachel is fine."

"Rachel, then," she smiled the warm smile of a hungry hyena. I returned in kind. At least now we understood each other.

"These forms are a mere formality." She tapped the papers with a painted nail of her heavy right hand. The color was the dark red of freshly drawn, extra iron-rich blood.

"Of course. I wouldn't have it any other way, Latisha."

She pulled back in her chair, and folded her hands in her lap.

I began filling out the paperwork, one of which was a release form from the school, the other a general informational form about Abigail and her family and my relationship to them. In the background I heard Latisha suggest *Edward* go ahead and bring Abigail into the office to confirm my identification personally. He didn't move.

"I understand Abigail's mother works days. And

where is Mr. Beardsley?" Harper asked me.

I glanced at my watch as if it held the answer and thought fast.

"Probably having his thrice weekly dialysis right about now." Of course, I had no idea where he was or when he received kidney dialysis.

"He's on..." Harper caught herself. The father having a disability might not help the principal's cause, which I assumed was to keep Abigail in his school against parental wishes.

She tried another tack. "Are there no other relatives?"

I dodged. Always do a one-two punch with a misdirecting jab in the middle if you can. It helps undermine your opponents' confidence.

"Interesting. This form asks for the name of the school Abigail is transferring in from. Since she's not actually transferring--that is since her mother hasn't authorized a transfer from her current school--do you want me to list the other school's name anyway?"

"What other school? I thought you said she was being homeschooled, Ed..er...Dr. Forsyth." Latisha's intelligent brown eyes turned toward the principal. He made a whiney face and started to protest. Then he visibly switched gears and began gently educating the social services woman on the recent changes in the new laws governing California homeschooling.

He was making a grave error. Latisha Harper's dark face darkened even more. He was humiliating her with a patronizingly simple version of the new ruling. I almost felt sorry for him.

I waited until the embarrassing moment played itself out. Then always being helpful, I answered Latisha's question about the other school.

"Her regular school, the one her parents have enrolled her in, is the Stowall Academy of the Arts." *Or was it Fine Arts?* But it didn't matter. Stowall was a powerful name in these mountain parts. Why not use it.

I didn't let the fact that the Academy was a front for the homeschoolers stop me. And I wasn't far off in adding Stowall to the nom de guerre of the fictitious school, as the two main families who drew up the paperwork for it were local Stowalls.

The principal and the social worker straightened their spines in response and looked at me with fresh eyes.

"The father is related to the Stowalls through the Beardsley family tree," I added innocently.

The Stowalls were a historic, once-wealthy, still powerfully connected family in this part of Southern California, and I was still exploring how far those connections spread and how much dysfunction they have managed to cover up over the years. But in this case, mention of their name added credibility to my task.

I filled out another line on the school's release form then answered the social worker's way-back-when question, when she'd asked where Abigail's mother was.

"Gloria Pustovoytenko (it slipped *wonderfully* off my now practiced lips) is the head nurse at Cleveland County Hospital Intensive Care Unit. So I'll be dropping Abigail off at the Academy of Arts once I've finally retrieved her."

Triple Whammy! Yes!

"There is no such..." Spittle flew from his churlish lips. His face did a presto-chango and he was once again a mature adult.

He'd caught himself, way too late. I raised my eyebrows in response and waited for him to shove his foot deeper down his throat. Of course there was no physical "school"; none was required by the new homeschooling laws—which he'd just baby-talked his way through. Oh, I was so winning this verbal battle.

But Latisha was still back at Gloria's place of work.

"Cleveland County Hospital. That's where they are caring for the Winters boy." *The sole survivor of Sunday morning's crash.*

I returned her shocked with my solemn and soulful.

"Yes. And she's very busy right now caring for him."

Her eyes had doubled in size. I thought I heard Edward groan.

I bent to fill out more of the form. My concentration

was on connecting with Latisha. My face wore the mild mask of bureaucratic compliance. I had at least learned that trick with during my many years as a public librarian.

After a few minutes I reached down in my own briefcase, brown leather that unfortunately didn't match my blue paisley purse. However the purse contrasted nicely with the beaded and embroidered orange jacket. My shoes were, well, my shoes. I handed Latisha a form of my own.

"Would you like to make a copy of Abigail's registration form at the Academy?"

Thank heaven I'd stopped to pick this up from Nana after my talk with Gloria.

"Oh. Yes, that would be helpful." Latisha smiled the warm smile of a proud lioness admiring another lioness' performance and took the registration form out to the secretary.

I kept my head down, continuing to work on the papers she'd given me. When I finished, I placed my calling card and ID on top and turned them toward Latisha Harper, matching her proud smile and raising her one perfectly innocent one.

"Rachel Lyons, Private Investigator..." She looked up at me as her brain light went on. "Aren't you the woman who recently shot that suspected child molester?"

She was referring to my encounter with Eddie Stowall, the deeply damaged man-child of the Stowall clan, who seems to have rescued a kidnapped child from her abuser--though the circumstances were suspicious, to say the least.

"Yes, I am."

Latisha's eyes slid down to my Styrofoam collar.

"Turned out he may not actually be a molester..." she murmured.

"Yes. It did." I agreed, humbly.

"But he shot you first, I believe I read."

"Yes. Unfortunately. He was terrified."

"Yes. Very unfortunately. An unfortunate situation all around," she murmured.

"Yes. It was."

"Is he still missing?"

I nodded my head, sadly.

"But you're okay, are you?" Latisha's eyes had softened to downright motherly, even though I was assuming we were around the same age.

"Yes. I'm fine."

"You're a very brave woman, Ms...ah, Rachel. He certainly could have been—dangerous, and that poor little girl.... But I hear she's doing okay."

"Yes," I agreed.

Dr. Forsyth forcefully cleared his throat.

Chapter 9

As we left the principal's inner office to await Abigail's arrival, not arm-in-arm as you might have thought but close, Latisha said, "Nice necklace. Where'd you get it?"

I picked up the large blue cloth covered beads that draped around my neck on a thin rope—just below my medical collar and fingered them gently. "Online at Clearwater Creek. I believe they were handmade in Kenya. Aren't they nice?"

"Yes, they are lovely. Clearwater Creek, hmm? They match your bag very nicely."

"Oh, thanks. I actually feel half dressed compared to you, Latisha."

"Nonsense. By the way, that Eddie Stowall man, the one that shot you, if and when he's found he may be able to use my boyfriend's help." She handed me two calling cards, one of her own and one with the name Jason Milkstone, Attorney at Law embossed in silvery blue on it.

I wasn't interested in helping Eddie Stowall, but she didn't need to know that. He frankly gave me the creeps. I frankly haven't made up my mind about the disturbed and disturbing Eddie.

"And if they ever catch the bastard that rear-ended you and gave you that pain in the neck Jason might could help you with that, too, honey."

We were down. I smiled.

Over her tall shoulder I noted that Abigail was wending her way toward us. Her face lit up as she spotted me and waved. She had no idea why I was here.

The social services woman saw her happy greeting and said, "Okay then, it seems everything is in order, Rachel. If you need any further help on this matter you just call me. I really can help Abigail and her family if need be. But it looks like you may be able to help her family work things out just fine, at least I hope so. It was a pleasure meeting you. You keep up the good work, you hear?"

A thought popped into my head. What had turned Latisha into a "sister" of mine?

"I will. You too, Latisha." She walked away, slinging her large pocketbook over her shoulder and swinging her heavy briefcase as if it only weighed an ounce.

Maybe she changed her feelings about me because of my obvious brilliance.

Maybe she liked the way I dressed.

Maybe she just bonded with me because the Prince was such a fool.

Whatever.

I returned my attention to the pony-tailed Abigail, who had just about caught up with us, and quickly decided where we might best discuss what was about to happen with her.

"Hi, Abigail."

"Hey, Rachel! How are you doing? How's your neck?"

I directed her out the front door of the school, making small talk as we went. The lunch crowds were still milling around in groups, some of them eating outdoors despite the threat of rain again today.

"What's going on?" Abigail asked, as realization dawned on her that I was here to see her, not the other woman I'd been talking to.

"I like your hair that way. Makes you look really cute. Why don't we sit for a minute over here?"

The redirect wasn't going to work. Her face fell to anger.

Abigail was my height, five foot eight, and had flawless alabaster skin. Her thin blond brows questioned me over her dark green eyes. Her Betty Boop lips were threatening to protest. I moved quickly.

We took a vacant cement table among the other students eating lunch. I was thinking we might be able to talk more calmly with others around us. Her face changed to stone.

"Your mom is scared for you, Abigail," I said as quietly as I could. "She wants me to retrieve you and deliver you to Mrs. Fillmore's house. She said you could direct me there."

Abigail just stared at me, a wild array of emotions at play just beneath the hardened surface of her porcelain face. I changed my mind about sitting among other students.

"Would it be better if we just went to my car?"

"Yes." She bit the word like it was a sour lemon.

"Okay."

We rose and walked in silence across the grassy lawns of the school. Another lunch bell rang and the kids on the grounds filtered back inside while others streamed out. My heartbeat stepped up a bit.

"I'm going to be late for my next class."

Abigail had stopped in her tracks. She was thinking through her options and I didn't like the one she seemed to have landed on.

I quickly looked away and unlocked my car thinking for sure she would turn on her heels. But no, she slowly began walking again and finally slid into the passenger seat a minute after I did. And then I saw why.

I started my engine and risked another look at her face. Tears were streaming down her cheeks.

"Oh, hon..."

"Don't! Just get me out of here!"

Right. *Don't play with my emotions.* "Okay. But I want you to understand I'm on your side on this issue, Abigail."

"Oh, sure!" She choked back a sob.

I decided not to take her directly to the Fillmore home—where she was supposed to be schooled today, and pulled off the road into a local dog park instead.

Chapter 10

I parked and turned toward her again.

"Let's take a minute to calm down. Maybe a walk?"

"No! What did she do, hire you?" She wiped furiously at her face, very embarrassed.

"Yes."

"I have *rights*, Rachel!" She was speaking barely below a shout. I could hear the constriction in her throat as she fought to control her anger and humiliation.

Abigail was feeling a complex soup of emotions— not only frustrated and thwarted by her mother, but also betrayed by me. After all, I had met her first at the Quilted Secrets bee and had gotten to know her there before I'd ever met her mother, and now her mother had waltzed in and hired me to forcibly remove her from school. I could understand her emotional firestorm and I worried that this errand would jeopardize our friendship.

"Of course you do. And this will be resolved to your satisfaction. What we're in right now is what's euphemistically called a "process". It's not a bad word, really, for how this will all play out. It's just...well, in my own experience with *processes* I've come to dislike the word. It's really just another word for a *timeout* for adults, like you might give children who've lost control."

"I'm not a child!"

"Of course, you are, Abigail. Legally. But that doesn't mean you are powerless. It doesn't mean your needs aren't real. And we are playing a very adult game now. Besides, in some ways we're all children here, you, me and your mother. Because this is new to us and we're learning as we go."

She quieted--still swiping at her leaky eyes angrily.

I continued. "Emotions demand immediate gratification. What we need here is careful thinking."

She took another ragged breath. I had to get

through to her, get her to open her mind to an honest discussion with her mother. So I appealed to her love of history.

"A process is a democratic invention--and you are in a democratic disagreement right now, a political arrangement with your mom where you two can't agree on an outcome. Democratic disagreements take time to work through."

She looked at me, a little more thoughtfully. I was also appealing to her exceptional intelligence. Something Gloria couldn't do at the moment because she was feeling too threatened by her daughter's rebellion. But then she used her intelligence to argue my decision.

"Okay, fine, a democracy. I vote we turn around and go back to school, *now*."

"And your mom has voted no."

"So, we have a stalemate--you think? And I'm not telling you how to get to Mrs. Fillmore's because I'm not going back there—*ever*."

I began to wonder if something had happened within the homeschool group.

But at the moment she had the upper hand and I debated whether I should call Gloria for the directions to this Mrs. Fillmore. Gloria's work at the ICU often made her difficult to reach. And I needed to connect with Abigail.

"So, what? Are you going to break the tie vote between my mom and me?"

"No. I don't have a vote in this issue. Matt and I are just involved to hopefully bring the disagreeing parties to a calmer place where they might be able to find a solution that meets both their needs."

I was thinking about the divorce cases Matt and I were often involved in. I was using the same kind of language. The thought scared me a little. Children and their parents shouldn't be on the brink of divorce.

"Oh? Like what? War or peace? My way or the highway? Do you have any idea who my mom is?"

"Don't go there, Abigail. That's not necessary. You've already selected an ally for your side of this argument, the school administration. Now your mom has hired us. But I want you to understand, we are not really her ally in this matter. We're neutral. We're just bringing two disagreeing parties to the same table...to discuss their differences."

Maybe I was copping out. Maybe I was a little too afraid of what this difficulty might do to my relationship with one of the Quilted Secrets members.

"You think you can change her *communist* mind?"

I stifled a smile. *Communist.* I thought we'd killed off that word. Switched it for a softer sounding term. Another euphemism, socialism.

"What I think is that things have gone beyond her simply being able to tell you what to do anymore." I paused, letting her digest the thought. "She hasn't necessarily come to realize this yet but the ball is in her court, and this is because you've lobbed it back to her successfully. Can you see that?"

"So now it's tennis." She turned to stare out the side window.

I sighed. "So now it's patience. Step back, slow down, let...things continue at a safer pace and see how long it takes your mom to realize she must work through this problem with you in a way that makes you *both* feel safe."

A couple of students drifted by. The thirteen acre neighborhood dog park was popular with the students during lunch break. It was a short half block away from the school. I was wishing we could stroll through the park too.

Abigail muttered, "I've been talking *peacefully* with her for months! And why wouldn't she feel safe? I'm the one whose whole life is being..."

"Emotions," I murmured, then instantly regretted it. That was a caution I should reserve for a client. Abigail was not my client.

She stopped herself. Breathed deeply and wiped the tears off her cheeks.

"I know what you're saying, Rachel, but humans are at least half emotions. And we both know at my age emotions hold sway. I'm not wrong here just because I have emotions. I've tried to reason with my mother, but...but she was born and raised in an Eastern Block country, for crying out loud. She can't relate to me. She thinks all she has to do is put her foot down and what she wants will be done. The *discussion* with her so far has been all one-sided!"

"And she left that formerly communist country so she could be free. Somewhere inside her is the...rebel, if you would, who ran away from her native country at a very young age."

A couple of raindrops hit my windshield. Maybe telling me I was in dangerous territory. But I couldn't seem to stop from going there.

"What you need to think about is your endgame, Abigail."

She looked at me with cold eyes. Thirteen-year-old cold eyes are a frightening sight.

"I have."

Chapter 11

Suddenly a group of boys raced around the edge of the parking lot from the direction of the high school. The boy leading the pack was running as if for his life. It wasn't until he was brought down almost directly in front of us, and three of his pursuers proceeded to pin him down while a fourth straddled him and began whaling away at his face with his fists, that we realized what was happening.

"It's the Pintos!" Abigail said. "They're the baddest gang in Pinto Springs High. Gangsters. *Bastards.*"

She spat the word out as if it was poison.

Her vehemence startled me, but never for a moment did my eyes leave the awful sight on the ground no more than twenty feet away.

I almost missed Abigail's reaching for the door handle—almost missed her opening the door.

"Hey! Stop that!" I heard her yell as I finally broke free of the spell and lunged for her. I caught hold of her arm and pulled her back into my car just on time.

Three of the boys turned their attention on us. A nasty grin slowly spread on the lead boy's face as he took a few steps toward us.

Abigail was opening the door to confront him!

"Abigail! You can't stop them. They aren't thinking right now." I locked the car doors. "It's probably some kind of gang initiation."

I was punching numbers on my phone, calling the Pinto Springs police, starting my engine, throwing my car into reverse, and trying to turn my vehicle so we could get out of there.

Then I saw the look on Abigail's face.

"Now you're a coward?" she yelled.

I shot back angrily, "Now I'm responsible for your safety. The authorities will take care of this." We pulled away and back out onto the main road. I didn't even think about the fact that I was breaking the law using my cell phone.

Somehow I was driving my car, giving the details to a Pinto Springs PD dispatcher, and keeping an eye on Abigail all at once--with Abigail's raving voice as a backdrop.

"You're a coward! You're leaving that poor boy to be beaten to death!"

Finally I closed the phone and put both hands on the wheel. I could hear sirens in the distance. The boy would be saved.

"Where are we going? Where are you taking me?" Abigail cried.

I couldn't take it another minute and I pulled off the main road down a side street that I didn't recognize as the street she and her mom lived on until later.

"And now I supposed you'll tell my mom about the terrible violence going on at the school, won't you. Now you'll give her another reason to fight this even more."

Frustrated at her continued anger, my own emotions at a peak because of the gang initiation I imagined was still continuing in the park behind us, I found my own angry tongue.

"So now I'm not just a coward, I'm a snitch? Nice, Abigail." I stared her down and she shrank into herself against the window and returned to sobbing.

Great.

Great, great, great!

I'd just torn any and all hope of connecting with this young thirteen-year-old because my ego was hurting.

This wasn't about me.

I calmed myself, and placed both my hands on the wheel again, looking around at where we were.

At least I'd remembered to get directions to Gloria's house before ending this morning's phone conversation, and I finally realized I was heading toward there already. We were only a dozen houses away.

The Pustovoytenko home was in the Pinto Hills Condominiums complex, perched on rolling hills southwest of Pinto Springs High.

From the top step of the front porch Nana made brief eye contact with me I couldn't interpret, and then closed the door silently between her crying granddaughter and me.

Just wonderful.

Now my taut neck muscles were on high alert. I drove home telling myself if it hadn't been for Abigail's presence I'd have taken on the whole rotten gang.

Chapter 12

Nine year old Abigail watched her mother Gloria drive away toward the hospital in the gathering dusk. She turned away from the front window and stared at her foreign-born grandmother, Nana. Her nine year old brow was wrinkling. She could feel it. She wanted her grandmother to see her continued displeasure.

"Vona volia buty pizniy teper."

She will be late now.

Translating the peculiar words and responding at the same time, Abigail said, "Speak English, Nana."

"Niyakyy. Vy navchaty Ukrayina."

No. You learn Ukraine.

Even though she understood Ukrainian fine Abigail firmly believed she had to force her grandmother to learn English, so she never spoke the ancient language.

Her Nana believed she should force her granddaughter to learn Ukrainian, so she never used English even though she knew enough to understand most of what was said around her and could probably speak it if she wanted.

Abigail thought about how Ukrainian sounded, like it was a language spoken in reverse, as if it were being played backwards on a tape recorder. It was more than peculiar, it was magical.

Abigail's mother was going to be late to work because they had argued--again.

She was bored, always staying at home, never spending time with other kids. Only occasionally seeing the other homeschoolers. And her tutors. Work, work, work, that was all she did.

What harm would it do for her to attend a class or two at the local school? She could easily handle both. Her homeschooled friends could be interesting, but they were also kind of weird.

Abigail didn't want to be weird. It was *Gloria* who wanted her to be weird—only she called it *special*.

Pooh. Abigail turned away in disgust and sat down briefly at her computer. Maybe Skywalker was online. He was the only cool guy in the whole bunch of their group. He was very cool. Really smart, and really cute.

But Marjania liked him, too. *Marjania* the fake *Albanian*. Marjania whose real name was probably Mary Jane or something stupid like that. Marjania who had real blond hair, while Abigail's looked like she'd been washing it in the *pukey* liquid left behind after doing the dishes.

Behind her Abigail heard Nana take another noisy sip of her evening cup of tea, and then she heard her grandmother's dress slipping and sliding over her underclothes as her grandmother moved toward her downstairs bedroom to watch her little television.

That had been the room Abigail wanted for her studio. She turned to look at her retreating Nana—still wrapped up in the anger from the argument with her mother—and she watched as the ancient woman slid her door until it was almost closed, her small dark eyes sunken in the purple folds of her aged flesh, staring back at her from within a bright yellow light until the contact was finally broken by the swinging door. Leaving only a little light shinning out onto the foyer. A few strands. A glowing flow.

From where she sat, facing the front window adjacent to the front door, Abigail saw that the little light sneaking out of Nana's bedroom splashed up onto the first risers of the staircase like an ambitious brook trying to flow uphill. But it couldn't. Rivers were supposed to flow toward gravity's down. So after only a few steps up, the stairs moved on without the little light, climbing up alone into a dark oblivion that Abigail couldn't see from where she sat. The dark oblivion held her father's bedroom.

But Abigail could see how the light changed colors in its attempts to defy the down gravity. The light slipped from a warm yellow to a charcoaled purple as it went, as if losing its strength, as if growing sickly with the effort to climb, as if her grandmother's aging wrinkles had poisoned the light from the start.

As if the sickly man in the room above the stairs was making the light sickly, too.

She noted that the meager light never moved toward the front door only a few feet across from the stairs— through which her mother had made her escape. The dark wood of the front door remained an enigma without the rays of the light, like a slab of cold granite.

A painting grew in Abigail's mind, perhaps an Edward Hopper.

But the vision also reminded Abigail that the old woman wasn't good with stairs anymore which was why she'd been given the little room Abigail wanted for her artist's studio. Nana's hips were bad.

And the vision reminded her she needed to remember to give her father his meds at eight o'clock. Only forty-five minutes from now.

And Skywalker wasn't online. No one was. She was bored with World of Warcraft, anyway.

Chapter 13

Abigail sighed and left her computer and walked toward the sun porch off the side of their condo. She deliberately bypassed the dinner dishes that still needed her attention. The sun porch served as a small den, and also as her painting room.

The den was a good room to paint in, plenty of light in the daytime with all the windows, but the kitchen was often noisy and she had trouble concentrating. And at night it could grow cold. Not good for her fingers.

It would have been a better room to paint in if it had doors to close. The double wide entrance connected directly with the family's other living spaces, which meant she had to paint while they talked and argued, and listened to the other small television in their condo.

That was what she and her mother had fought about this night. She wanted double doors installed so she could close them out. She'd found some French doors at Home Depot that she wanted to use her allowance to help pay for.

How could she concentrate on her paintings with all the noise only a few feet away.

Anger rose in her child's breast again.

Her mother said she couldn't shut herself away from her dad. She needed to be able to hear him call if he needed anything.

It wasn't fair. Her whole life wasn't fair.

And from the disappointing discussion of the doors they had moved as usual to her repeated desire to join the other neighborhood girls at the elementary school just around the corner.

Nana should get the hip surgery so she could go live by herself. Then they'd have more room.

Using both hands, she pulled her skimpy dishwater blond hair behind to the nape of her neck and secured it with the hair band on her wrist.

She threw the wall switch and a bank of lights her mother had recently installed bathed the den in a smooth glow. As if the lights had infused it with life, her partially completed painting jumped out of the darkness at her. Whites and lavenders and greens danced on the canvas in excitement like little puppies happy to see their mistress. She smiled.

She would finish the lily tonight.

She didn't want to be Georgia O'Keeffe, but she knew she could learn much from the female American artist's style of painting. So she was reproducing another of O'Keeffe's most famous works, using different colors and a coarser brush, even a palette knife in some places to smooth the background. An O'Keeffe knockoff, but with Abigail Pustovoytenko-Beardsley twists.

What she loved most about the American artist was her abstract representations of flowers. O'Keeffe managed to paint flowers as if they were music for the eyes. Abigail reached for her headphones and secured them to her ears. Tonight she would paint lilies like Mozart.

The Mozart's baroque fugue flowed into her ears, trying to still her angry thoughts. Only occasionally did her mind return to the evening's argument.

Nana liked to remind Abigail that life was never fair. That Abigail had the best childhood in the world. That she was born in America, the greatest country in the world. Homeschooling was the price Abigail paid to be an American to Nana's way of thinking.

But how was she an American if she wasn't allowed to attend American schools?

Abigail suddenly realized she'd made the stamen too orange. Now she had two reasons to be angry.

She sat back on her stool and breathed deeply, listening to Mozart's reasoned rhythm. Then she scraped her mistake off the canvas with her palette knife so she could begin again. But her mind took her elsewhere.

Gloria thought public schools were incubators to raise the devil's spawn. Nana had said something in her backwards words that Abigail didn't catch, but to which Gloria nodded her head in agreement. It only made Abigail angrier.

They didn't trust anything American. Shopping malls. Public parks. *Libraries,* for crying out loud.

Her mother Gloria hadn't arrived in America until she was almost an adult, so she was as foreign in her thinking as Nana, who'd lived her first sixty years in the old country.

She picked up her paintbrush again, softened the orange paint, took another deep breath and finally slipped into the Elysium that only creative people could enter while here on earth.

Hours later, she placed her brush down. She was never completely happy with her work. It should be better. It should be more, more...*Georgia.*

But it wasn't bad.

Her mother had forbid her to throw any of her works away, threatening to take her headset away if she did, threatening to ban television entirely from the house, threatening...well, *everything* that made life worth living. So she accepted the level of work she was doing, and began to clean up, piling things up neatly into a pyramid. With stairs.

Stairs.

She looked at her watch, her heart leaping into her throat. *Ten!* She was two hours late with his medicine!

She raced from the den, scampered through the kitchen and passed her grandmother's now closed bedroom door. She took the stairs two at a time.

"Dad! I'm here dad!" *Oh no*, she'd forgotten the meds, they were still downstairs.

But the thought was driven forcefully from her mind by the hideous view before her. Sprawled on the floor on his back, her father was motionless, his eyes half open, his face blue.

She'd killed him! Her painting had killed him! She raced to his side, now terrified.

"Daddy! Daddy!" She lifted his wrist and took his pulse as her nurse mother had taught her. She couldn't find it!

But he was still warm and she leaned forward and felt for his breath with her cheek. A pale breeze stirred the small hairs on her face.

"I'll get your meds!"

But how would she get the insulin pill down his throat?

"Yakyy ye tse?"

What is it?

Abigail screamed at her grandmother as she raced back down the stairs for his medicine.

"Call her. Call mom! He's dying."

She found them and started back up the stairs.

Her Nana might not understand her!

Completely panicked now, Abigail began to wail as she knelt beside him and forced the small pill between his clenched jaws.

It wasn't going down, it wasn't going down.

She'd killed him!

Finally, she remembered what her mother had taught her about CPR, and she began pounding on his chest and breathing for him--his fetid breath a poisonous accusation of her crime.

It took forever for the ambulance to arrive. It took forever for them to finish what she had started and reclaim her father from the terrible grip of Death.

It would take years for little Abigail to make peace with her terrible mistake.

Chapter 14

Wisdom stood attentively listening to his brothers the wolves. They were telling him to liberate himself, *give up the soft life, roam wild and free over the hills.*

He was giving the idea his full consideration.

I was feeling sad, for the wolves who no longer roamed freely and for Wisdom whose ancestors had joined us in the cave long ago. My German shepherd Wisdom wasn't healthy.

He was on the back deck of our Escondido home watching the eastern darkness swallow the western twilight. I stood a few feet behind him, observing his deliberations--waiting for him to make his choice, and sipping a hot cup of tea. I knew whatever he decided, I'd go with it. He was my beloved pet but his life was his own, especially now.

My Wisdom-watching had been tinged with melancholy for close to a year. Our beloved pet now carried his death on his nose, a growing lump of bone cancer just beneath his left eye, which was wedging itself further into his nasal passages with every passing day.

We'd seen the vet; the choices were ugly.

Wisdom was ten years old and we couldn't bear to see him suffer through human medical care for cancer. Our choice was to make his final months the best we could. We take him out for an ice cream cone a couple of times a week and continue his daily walks. I've always spoiled my dog with fresh protein with every meal, but now I was probably overdoing it. Why not?

He stopped his deliberations to briefly scratch at his ear. He glanced back at me long enough to tell me he knew I was there then returned to his vigil.

I guess he'd decided to stay with us. Besides, the wolves were in the San Diego Wild Animal Park around the corner, not exactly free.

A cool breeze hurried the change from light to dark, moving a couple of clouds over the setting sun.

Matt and I had purchased our Escondido upside-down, two-story house back in 'eighty-three, when he did a three-year stint at Camp Pendleton Marine Base. I say upside down because our house is built into a hill and the main living areas are upstairs. The downstairs, a walkout basement, holds an extra bedroom and a large game room our three boys used to play in.

Back when we first bought the house, then Major Matthew Lyons had worked in the First Marine Division Headquarters. Our three boys were young then, attending elementary school. Thankfully we'd kept the house when we were sent off to another duty station. We knew we would miss Southern California when we left and that this was where we wanted to end up after he retired.

Now our sons are married and have children of their own and their families are scattered across America living in three different states.

I wished my grandchildren lived two houses over, but we visit them every chance we get, and they return to the California of their childhoods whenever they can.

The best part of our eighties-style hillside home is that it sits on an acre of precious California land and is pretty much surrounded by redwood decks.

My dog and I often listened to the wild conversations from the Park while waiting for Matt. Just last night we'd heard the zebras having a quarrel with the giraffes--probably over territory.

Wasn't it always over territory?

"Hi. How's our boy doing?"

I turned and kissed my man and said, "How was your day?"

Wisdom rushed to greet his master. It was a guy thing. Well, come to think of it, it was a gal thing, too. We both cheered up when Matt arrived.

"Good. What's for dinner?"

I smiled. "I thought Chateaubriand would be nice, with a side of radicchio-pasta salad served with mustard dressing and topped with fresh ground black pepper. And I thought we could finish off last night's bottle of D'Alessadro Syrah, you know the Italian red?"

"We didn't have an Italian red last night. We had a fine Two Buck Chuck cab, as usual. But tell me we're having the Chateaubriand and radicchio-pasta salad and I'll settle."

"How about a juicy steak, salad-in-a-bag and a baked potato for you?"

"Sounds more like something I can afford. Anymore sneezes?"

"No, but he hasn't eaten his dinner yet. I think it's hurting him. He doesn't howl as much anymore either."

He nodded his head. Wisdom had returned to his vigil. "But he's still listening."

Matt and I moved toward the open sliding door arm in arm.

"Start the grill while I take a quick shower."

"Sure."

We share our nightly kitchen chores, but since the kitchen wasn't spacious we split the workload. I defrosted, Matt cooked, and I cleaned.

After thirty years of cooking for a family dominated by kids' taste buds I'd lost my sense of chef. And in the end, I'd been reduced to a short order cook.

One night I came home exhausted from my work at the library and took a look at my husband stretched out on the couch--Matt was already retired, the kids out of the house--and I said, "If you want to eat tonight, you can get up and cook."

Astonishingly, he did. And I took his place on the couch and promptly fell asleep. Thirty minutes later he woke me for a delicious meal and he's been Chef Matthew ever since.

Who knew?

That had been back in North Carolina, our final duty station. And it had been another of those cataclysmic moments in life where you realize you've been living by the wrong rules, someone else's rules.

And now we were back in California and living in the house we'd bought years ago--on our second tour of duty here--and kept as a rental.

Matt never overcooked the meat, he made the best tossed salads in the world, and he was into presentation, an important skill that cooking for kids on the go didn't allow me to develop. Most nights now I feel as if I'm eating at a fine restaurant.

He took a sip of fine cab and said, "What happened at the school today?"

I brought him up to speed, including the mess at the park. I let him know the boy at the park was found by the police alive and badly bruised. He was treated at a local clinic and released to his parents.

"They're probably gang members, too."

"Who?"

"The parents. Did you attend the memorial service?"

"You mean the Grieving Rally?"

He looked at me questioningly.

"They renamed it a Grieving Rally, I think because the planned pep rally for this weekend's football game had been canceled and they didn't know what else to do with all the scantily clad cheerleaders roaming the halls."

"Isn't it cold up there by now?"

He was referring to the fact that Cleveland County was a mile high.

"Yes, especially in the late afternoon. I sure didn't jump around in a bikini when I was a cheerleader in high school."

He smiled that smile. Really more like a leer. I'd sprouted a vision in his head.

I took a bite of salad, and a sip of red.

"To answer your question, no, I didn't attend it. After retrieving Abigail I came home and brought us up to speed with some paperwork. Later I listened to the news, and according to channel eight, school authorities decided the word *service* would have been a violation of the separation of church and state. I can't tell you if the cheerleaders cheered or prayed."

He shook his head, a gesture of disgust.

Wisdom nudged my leg, urging me not to eat all my steak. Of course I wouldn't. I would put some of it on top of his dinner to encourage him to eat.

But Matt was back at the cheerleaders.

"Scantily clad, huh? Maybe we should attend some of the games this year."

"It's a long drive." Cleveland County was east of us. We could see the plateau from our back deck.

"Could be worth it."

Wisdom slumped to the ground with a disapproving groan. "I concur, Wisdom. He's a rude lout."

"So you haven't heard any more from Gloria."

"Not yet. But I'm afraid we probably will."

Which was when the phone rang.

Chapter 15

I swallowed a last bite of salad and reluctantly rose to stifle the mechanical scream in the kitchen. I stepped onto the kitchen porch, holding the phone to my ear.

"Rachel, she's out of her *mind*..."

At least I thought that's what she said. Gloria Pustovoytenko's accent was as thick as Ukrainian barley pudding. I'd been hoping it was one of my three daughter-in-laws. Or maybe even a son.

"Hello, Gloria."

"She won't listen to reason. She told me she going back to school again Monday. What can we do?"

We? I turned it around. The way it really was.

"What do you think you can do, Gloria? You and Abigail."

"I don't know, I don't...but...she even started talking about how I left Ukraine, ran away when I was young. She's *threatening to run away now?* She's a baby. She's thirteen! She doesn't know a thing about the world. Besides, I was almost legal when I found my way to America!"

So my attempt to connect mom and daughter had backfired. Wonderful.

"Did she actually talk about running away, Gloria?"

"No. But she *meant* that."

Gloria continued to complain while I tried to get her to focus on why she felt so strongly about public schools.

"They're violent! The teachers unions have ruined them. Any loser can get a teaching job and keep it forever no matter what they do wrong. The kids are exposed to drugs...sex, you name it. I remember school in Ukraine. I remember the thugs who used to roam our halls. Only they were called *party* members. Here, they are *gang* members. There's no damn difference.

"I'm scared, Rachel, I'm afraid she'll run off...like I did. But she won't end up in a beautiful America, she'll end up in a...."

"She won't. She won't leave her art, Gloria. Children who hit the streets are running away from a dangerous situation. Your family is loving...."

I was hoping to calm her using gentle words.

"Yes. But Abigail is even more headstrong than I was."

Probably not.

"Isn't it mostly talk, now?" I suggested.

"She wasn't here again today when I got home. I called Jeannette, the mom she was supposed to be with, and she told me Abigail never made it to her house. What happened? All my mother will say is she was meeting you for the grief...what do they call it? A...grief rally? What is that?"

Uh-oh. I suppose I should have tried to reach Gloria and let her know I dropped Abigail off at their home, but with what was going on at the hospital, I didn't.

"When did she get home?"

Gloria sighed loudly. "Not until after six. I don't know what to do, Rachel. She's out of control. It was after dark! I'm having apoplexy."

It came out sounding like apple-proxy and I realized I was still hungry. She finally wound down and I asked a difficult question.

Was I pouring oil on a hot fire?

"Why did you decide to do homeschooling, Gloria?"

"First off, we are *eclectic* homeschoolers, and it doesn't mean Abigail isn't receiving schooling, it means she's receiving it in a relaxed atmosphere and tailored to her interests and abilities."

"And if she goes several months telling you she does not want to learn math, that's okay?" I asked.

"Well, to an extent. Eventually she has to cover the subjects but she has much greater flexibility than she would in an *institutional* setting. She's in charge of pacing herself."

"She's in charge..." I tried my old leading ploy. Of course it backfired.

"Don't play psychiatrist with me, Rachel. I'm the nurse, remember? In my country the State was all! Even after we revolted, the State had full control of our lives from the time we woke in the morning until the time we were finally allowed to sleep at night! I was not raising my family like that."

"You hated *Communist* schools, Gloria. American schools are...." I paused to let her fill in the blank. It took a nanosecond.

"Worse! Much worse. They control every moment of a child's life but they don't even teach! Or they teach the latest political ideology. *That's what Communist schools do,* they teach dogma from the mind of some power-drunk dictator! These American schools are teaching *chaos theory*, now.

"You think American kids are learning anything about the world? They did away with geography a few years back. Before that they reinvented math. Now it's not just groups of ten, it's groups of three and four and any fool number at all. I have ten fingers on my hands! That's why it's groups of ten! *And history!* History is one big lie. I study the curriculums. There's no music! There's no art! These schools teach American children that they are bad and that their glorious history is nothing but a road map of imperial domination.

"Now the idiots in charge are doing away with grades! *Even some colleges*. It's all madness.

"Pretty soon your doctors won't need to have degrees anymore because degrees are too judgmental. I don't want my child to learn this empty nonsense."

"Wait. Do, umm, *eclectic* homeschoolers grade their children?"

Silence radiated from my phone until my ear caught fire. I switched the phone to the other side of my head.

"I'm confused, aren't I Gloria?"

"No. Not you, Rachel..."

She was thinking. I waited.

"Okay, that was the Communist heart still feebly beating in my chest. You are right. I have problem with these ideas, still, even though I agree intellectually with them, part of me is wondering where this will all lead. Part of me is afraid."

Good. Thinking slowly and carefully is always a good thing. Maybe.

She sighed audibly. "But those schools, Rachel.... I know what you are implying. I know you are saying Abigail is driving her education toward a public school. But those schools..."

I had to admit to myself that I had been surprised by the open display of gangs in the hallways of the Pinto Springs high school, but I let her do the talking—or rather yelling. Besides, she wasn't talking to me, she was talking to Abigail, who was probably on her bed covering her ears with pillows.

I had great respect for Gloria Pustovoytenko. She had left a country that spoke and wrote in a radically different language and managed to attend college to become a nurse, all in English. Our two languages even have different alphabets.

Time to move on. I asked another burning question.

"Gloria, do you know of anything that might have happened in the home schooling group that Abigail meets with? Maybe something to do with the other kids? Maybe..."

"No. She's never had a problem with the kids," Gloria was quick to reject that idea.

"She only meets with them once or twice a week. We realize we have to do something to get our children out of the house and together with their peers. Usually they're off on some field trip. And we share.

"Just last month I had the group over to the hospital, taking them through pediatrics, discussing the medical professions available to them. The others do the same. They share their work place or their area of special knowledge. We have a chemist who regularly teaches them, and a writer who works on their English. Or maybe we take them to the museums and zoos. The local colleges have classes for homeschooled children too. It's always something new, then when we get them home to our own houses we build on that experience to teach primary skills at whatever level they are."

It sounded great. I wished I'd had that kind of schooling.

"One family I really love, they have a seven acre farm, about half the size of Hannah Lilly's. But they have goats and horses and chickens everywhere. We spend a lot of time going there to learn animal husbandry. And gardening. I regret not having a garden here. And chickens. We always had chickens back in Ukraine."

Hannah Lilly was another of the Quilted Secrets bee women. The Quilted Secrets group has been in existence in Victoria Stowall's family for hundreds of years, dating as far back as the Colonial days. I learned this at the first bee I attended, early this month.

She prattled on for another half hour. By the time I got Gloria off the phone, I could actually understand her, she was so relaxed.

There was nothing more I could do but urge her to work it out with her child. It was a process.

Chapter 16

I was back in the dining room sipping the last of my Two Buck Chuck and listening to Matt flip through our favorite cable news stations--doing news hopscotch, trying to find something he agreed with.

Suddenly, Matt said, "So how's Gloria? She married a Stowall too, right? Have you gotten over being related to them yet?"

He'd had more than one glass of wine.

I didn't answer. I didn't feel like arguing with him about my new Quilted Secrets friends. I got up to clear the table. What Matt was referring to was the fact that I'd been given a Stowall genealogy at the end of the last bee (my first bee with the group) and it turned out one of my distant relatives was on it.

It was scary thinking I was step-cousin to a group of people who were frankly weird, especially Victoria Stowall's branch. But I feel the need to add here that I am a twelfth cousin to Victoria Stowall. Through several marriages. And I take after my mom's side of our tree. My connection with Victoria is through my father's side. Just so you know.

Why did this feel like I was saying I was only a distant relative of the human race? Because if we follow either of the current theories on where the human species came from it all leads back to one profound beginning. So we're all related.

At any rate, it turns out all of the women who sew together at the Quilted Secrets are connected to the powerful Cleveland County Stowalls. And, that fateful bee had led to my most dangerous case to date, unraveling the genealogical and genetic secrets that Ada Stowall had stitched into her mysterious quilt. I still didn't know who ran me off the road in a big, white truck during that assignment.

On the other hand, being related to Victoria Stowall and her mixed up brood also meant I was related to Hannah Lilly and Geraldine Patrone, two great gals. And Gerry was Marshall Patrone's wife, the billionaire owner of the San Diego major league soccer team.

And Matt was a major soccer fan. So his next question fit.

"Have you gotten an invite to dinner with our cousins the Patrones, yet?" I grinned. Then I LOL'd. That was the first time I'd realized we were related to a billionaire.

"No, but I'll keep working on it."

I bent down to place my empty glass in the top rack of the dishwasher and rediscovered my neck didn't want to go in that direction anymore. I cried ouch and sucked in a deep breath as I tried to absorb the lightning bolt that had just electrified my brain.

Matt came up behind me and straightened me up.

"How's your pain level? Maybe you should go back on something stronger than Ibuprofen."

"No way. I just need to remember..."

I didn't finish the sentence, another pain struck. Matt took my elbow, and moved me down the hall where I laid down on our bed to take the pressure off. Prone was good.

"You have to tell those women you aren't going to sew next month, Rache. No way I'm letting you..."

I let him ramble, reminding myself that Marines talked like that.

Sometimes I would engage and argue, but right now all I wanted to do was stop the pain in my torn cervical muscles. It radiated from inside my weary brain all the way down to my shoulders, and then spread out from there into an upper body dull ache.

Matt had been campaigning for me to leave the Quilted Secrets group ever since the evil white truck first tried to drive me off the road three weeks ago.

And the next bee was only a week away. I needed to heal faster. I didn't want to miss it.

You might think I'd want to skip it, in fact all of

them, after what I'd just gone through because of those women, but I was eager to sew with them again. They were...my new family. They were exciting, and female. That second item is important when you are working in what is essentially a male world. Private investigation is dominated by males, just as crime is. And I missed being immersed in the library world—my last career, one that I'd worked in for more years than I can remember before taking an early retirement to follow Matt west to train in PI work and eventually open our own company.

"Here. Take these." Matt was attempting to shove a couple of white horse pills in my mouth.

"What are they?" I grabbed the pill bottle out of his hand. "*Oxycontin!* Where'd you get these?"

"I called the doctor, told him how Gloria had thrown your pills away. He wrote another prescription."

I just stared up at him from the bed. He was close to spilling the glass of water.

"Matt. What are you thinking? I was almost addicted to these."

He was thinking nurse Gloria had interfered with my medical care. I was thinking nurse Gloria had saved me from drug addiction. We'd had this conversation already.

"I'm thinking you should be lying flat on your back for at least another month. And so is the doctor."

"The doctor said I should stay flat on my back?"

He glared at me. I gently pushed the pills away.

"Throw them away, Matt. They're dangerous. I'll be okay. The pain has already subsided. I just get tired at the end of the day. Besides, I just finished a glass of wine."

He straightened and withdrew his offering with a sour look on his face. "I'll take over with Gloria and Abigail. You stay home and I'll have Will and Luis help me." He was really freaking out, poor dear.

"I'll be fine in the morning, Matt. But we need to talk about how you feel about my new friends."

He left to channel surf. I closed my eyes and the next thing I knew it was morning.

Chapter 17

Saturday, October 25

I don't want to leave the impression that Matt and I are having marital problems. This tug-of-wills war game has been going on since before we married—thirty-three years ago this summer. So this isn't exactly a fly-by-night relationship. It was the real deal. We would work things out. But sometimes I had to work around him.

So when Abigail called me this morning--this being Saturday, the day after my miserable attempt to connect with her while spiriting her away from school—I didn't turn her over to Matt.

This was women's business. She was one of my sister quilters. Matt would have to forgive...again. Besides, he was off with Will spying or something.

"Rachel? I need...you said we could talk. Anytime."

"Yes, I did, Abby. And I meant it. Anytime."

I heard sniffles and a heavy sigh. "This isn't gonna work for me, Rachel."

"I know, hon. Can you tell me why? Can you explain to me why you need to go to public school?"

There was a pause. It went on until I thought we'd slid into the void.

Finally she said, "I need friends my own age *and* my own intellect. Most of the kids in the Academy are...well they're smart and all. I like that about them a lot. But...they're..."

The void grew closer, I waited.

"It isn't fair to call them nerdy, but that's how they make me feel. At least the boys do."

"Boys are always slower to mature Abigail. I'm sure you'll find this to be true at the high school as well," I said, hoping I was sounding neutral. But of course I was sounding motherly. I felt motherly.

"Freshman boys are. But I don't really belong in the

freshman class. I guess, well they want to test me...next week. You know, a placement test. I'm thinking maybe I should be in the junior class. Junior boys are...."

I filled in the blank. Sexy.

"Any particular junior boy?"

The void gained some more ground. I hoped it didn't swallow our call up entirely. She needed to talk. I needed to hear.

Another deep sigh. At least she wasn't sniffling.

"I have to meet them, of course," she said.

That wasn't an answer. So move on.

"When's your birthday, Abigail?"

"December. Why?" Defensive.

So she was almost fourteen. "Planning my calendar. Are you online? I mean are you on Facebook?"

"Of course not. That's over. I tweet, on twitter.com"

Over? I'd just joined. Bummer. But Luis would need to know what social media Abigail was on. He was our resident IT geek, one of our two apprentices. So I lied again, telling her I was on twitter.com too, and asked her what her ID was. Fortunately she didn't ask me for mine.

Luis' formal name is Marvin Luis Lewis. (His parents thought they were comedians.) But he hated the name Marvin so he was making the best of what was left, Luis Lewis, by inventing catchy online IDs. *Louie-Louiee* was the one I liked the best. Lewee-Lewee was another version. And Lou-Lou was another. His girlfriend Sandra, who we have yet to meet, didn't like the Lou-Lou one.

But my current concern was that even if Abigail wasn't crying anymore, she sounded really down. I was hoping he could find and follow her on Twitter and see what she was telling her friends.

Then it hit me.

"Hey, Abby. I've got an idea. Do you want to go shopping? You know, get out of the house a bit?"

The void withdrew a bit.

"Maybe. That is if *Gloria* will let me out of prison. My grandma is watching me right now, but we can't even communicate so I just tell her what I want and she believes me."

Grandmas and grandkids were often familial co-conspirators. If I lived closer to mine I'd be in a heap of trouble with my three daughter-in-laws.

"Think it would be best if I cleared it with your mom."

In the background I heard a gravely voice.

"*Just a minute Nana.* I gotta go. Let me know if the Ukrainian Lioness says I can get out of my cage." And the void swallowed her.

So maybe they could communicate. Maybe the teenager Abigail didn't want to admit she could talk with her Nana because the other kids didn't think it was cool for her to have a foreign born grandmother. Kids could be like that.

I called Gloria, and when I'd finally connected with her in ICU she groused the whole time about how Abigail was due to go on a field trip to "the farm" today. I reminded her she wanted me to connect with her daughter and she finally relented.

Chapter 18

Worried about Abigail's state of mind, I decided to bring Hannah Lilly into the loop with a quick call. She of the chocolate voice.

She was Zen. And she was a New Age farmer living in Vista with her husband Peter and three small children.

Last month, Hannah and Gerry Patrone had joined me in my search for Ada Stowall's killer. Ada Stowall was the quilter whose place I'd taken in the Quilted Secrets group after her death. Initially I'd been hired to research her quilt and study her genealogy. At least that's the way I saw things. But ultimately it all got tangled, quilts, genealogies and murders.

To cover Hannah and Gerry under my private investigator's license, I hired them each for a dollar--and they surprised me by accepting. This was after I'd been hired to investigate the death of Ada Stowall.

During the course of that investigation I learned that Hannah's mother Ruth was Victoria Stowall's sister, while Ada Stowall had been Victoria's daughter-in-law. I point this out here so that you know that Hannah is also related to the mysterious Stowalls. And she appeared to be as uncomfortable with her fairly close relationship with them as I was with my distant one.

Gerry Patrone, as it turned out, was another relative. Like every other member of the Quilted Secrets Sisterhood, she too was related to the Jake and Victoria Stowall clan. Her maiden name was Beardsley, which was a branch of the clan.

Another line of the Beardsley branch of the Stowalls married Gloria Pustovoytenko, and thus Abigail was also related to this enormous and very weird family. I had yet to figure out the kinship of the others who sat with us at the once-a-month bees. But I was working on it.

The genealogy they'd handed me at that first bee

the beginning of this month—October--ran across one whole wall of our spare bedroom, and partially onto the next. It was still hung for me to ponder whenever the mood enveloped me—a bit like a heavy fog.

As I've said, I have very mixed feelings about being related to these nut-cases.

Just how weird the Stowalls were was vividly illustrated to me last month when Hannah's mother Ruth was brutally beaten a few days after the last bee—likely because she assisted me with my research into Ada's death. The unknown assailants bent on keeping the Stowall family's darkest secrets secret were still at large. The county and Pinto Springs city detectives are working at it, or so they tell me.

That investigation not only led to the discovery of who killed Ada, but also to the fact that Ada and her equally mentally disturbed and disturbing husband Luke had imprisoned their son Eddie in a small chamber of horrors in their basement for decades.

Most of the events of the Ada investigation had spun out atop Cleveland County plateau, between San Diego and Imperial counties. A mile-high county, its size and isolation from the rest of Southern California made it a force to be reckoned with in California politics--but more about that later.

But back to my call to Hannah: with all Hannah had on her plate now, which included taking care of her comatose mom at home, I didn't feel I could enlist her help to any great degree, but a chat shouldn't hurt.

It had been only two days since Hannah had brought her mother Ruth McMichaels home from Cleveland County General hospital.

I'd first met Ruth at the Quilted Secrets bee and I'd really connected with the cantankerous old woman. She wore Crocs, my favorite casual shoe, and L.L.Bean exercise clothes. And she was happily irreverent—which I thought of as a state of rude wisdom I might achieve one day if I lived long enough.

So I was doing my own grieving over Ruth's suspended state, and wouldn't have bothered Hannah

and her family at all except that Hannah had once
worked in a child psychiatrist's office and I was hoping
she'd gained some on-the-job insight into teens and
their concerns. I wasn't disappointed.

"How's your mom, Hannah?"

"Better."

I pressed my luck, and probably her comfort zone.

"Is she responding?"

Hannah sighed deeply and said in her darkest
chocolate voice, "Not that you'd notice."

*So, what? She was responding clairvoyantly?
Telepathically? Psychically?*

Okay, I understand this is *my* problem. There was
really zero proof that Ruth McMichaels was anything
magical. I just needed to believe she was. It some how
rounded out my world.

*And she sent me a dream once...from her almost
grave. Not to mention answering my unspoken questions
time and time again.*

"I really feel responsible..."

"Stop it, Rachel, okay? How could you be
responsible? Because we asked you to research Ada's
death and my mom called to give you information? And
because of that, bad people came and attacked her. Or
because you were attacked too and ended up in the
hospital and under heavy medication for a week? Or is it
because you know who the bad guys are and are
refusing to tell us?"

"No, no of course not. But..."

"But you knew where she was all the time and kept it
a secret?"

Again of course not, but...

"No, Hannah, but if I hadn't been taking so many
drugs..."

"Pain killers for your extremely damaged neck."

"...I would have been more, more receptive to your
mom's...messages." There, I'd said it.

"Her messages," Hannah repeated, using one of my
own investigative techniques on me.

"If my head had been clearer I would have...dreamed

sooner," I mumbled.

It was crazy sounding and I knew it.

"Rachel, this is all the past. It's done. Now we are here." Zen.

And it does no good to review our mistakes when the here and now is so needy, unless that review might help in present.

Were those my own mother's words? Or Hannah's mother's words? Ruth.

I was still waiting for Hannah to respond to my reference to what everyone thought of as Ruth's psychic abilities. I wasn't alone in this thought about Ruth.

Hannah did avoidance. Changed the topic.

"Did I tell you we know where Eddie is?"

"What!"

"Calm down. He's far away."

My eyes must have bugged out of my head because she saw them all the way from Vista. Eddie and I had history.

I should explain Eddie Stowall here. In fact I should explain the whole Stowall family.

Victoria Stowall is the head of the Quilted Secrets sewing group that I first met at the beginning of the month. This group meets the first Saturday night of every month from September to June to assist each other with their quilts. She and her late husband Jake (who died last month) had seven children; three boys and four girls. The boys are named Mark, Luke and John, and the girls are Martha, Anne, Mary and Sarah.

It's not clear which of the first two Stowall boys actually sired Eddie, Mark or Luke, but Luke was the man who raised him along with Eddie's mother Ada.

Mark died in a drunken brawl with his younger brother Luke--over Ada. Apparently both Mark and Luke were having sex with Ada during the time Eddie was conceived. Luke did time in prison over Mark's death. Immediately upon his release from prison, Luke married Ada, thus he ended up raising the boy.

It had taken me two weeks to discover these normally public facts, but the influence of the Stowall family had kept them hidden from all but those who were alive back when the events happened.

Again, Ada was the woman whose death I was investigating at the beginning of October. During that perilous investigation I uncovered much of the mystery of the Jake Stowall family.

Eddie Stowall is the only grandchild of Victoria for reasons I won't get into here. More importantly he's the guy I had a serious run in with last month that resulted in our both being shot. Latisha Harper made earlier reference to the bad business between us and the resultant shootout.

Last time I saw him Eddie was bathed in shadows so I really couldn't tell you just what color he was. But the issue of his color was important enough for his mother to have sewn a representation of him onto the final square of her final quilt as a multi-ethnic character of questionable gender.

Mary and her two older sisters have been actively assisting their nephew Eddie, both financially and logistically. They spirited the wounded Eddie out of the Cleveland County hospital and sent him off to relatives in New York State, effectively evading possible consequences for the shooting business. I should be angry at them. But I'm not. I'm frankly relieved. I felt very conflicted about my part in the shooting.

Because I know Eddie Stowall is deeply damaged by a lifetime of abuse, and may not be able to tell who is friend or foe in his world. Perhaps that's why he shot at me. Perhaps.

As I've said, Ruth McMichaels is Victoria Stowall's sister and Hannah Lilly's mother.

It is a decidedly inbred quilting group, so to speak. Way past nepotistic.

"Where is he?" I said.

"I realize this is upsetting, but you need to know. Eddie is in upstate New York, Fort Alden to be exact. Mary told me. That in itself is astounding. The sisters and I have rarely communicated, like almost never. She also wanted to ask after my mom, of course.

"But then she told me Eddie is living with a Stowall cousin in New York and that he's become quite the cause célèbre. Apparently, and this is the strange part, the cousin thinks Eddie is white."

"He is white. Part." And black, and yellow, and possibly red.

"Which cousin?"

"A guy named Samuel Stowall. He sounds like he's quite rich, socializes with the aristocracy of New York State politics. They hang out together at a local English Pub with half of the political and business royalty of that part of the state. It's called the Tut Pub, or maybe the Pun Tavern, I can't remember which. One of them is a descendant of Benedict Arnold. Mary mentioned someone named Walter Butler."

"Why do they think he's a cause célèbre?"

"Because to those Easterners he was in a Wild Western style shootout. Anyway, the good citizens of Fort Alden are all riled up over the casino the Seneca Indians want to build in Cherry Valley.

"Some of the Cherry Valley folks are investors in the planned Seneca Casino but quite a few of the local organizations and surrounding communities are doing their best to block it, especially Fort Alden proper.

"Mary says they're described as an uptight bunch of evangelicals who don't believe in gambling and drinking, or even dancing. But when I checked the situation out online it seems there's more of an intergovernmental feud going on—at least behind the scenes."

"Anyway, Eddie seems to have jumped into the deep end with this bunch in New York. Mary says he sent her a cell phone picture of his new duds. He was all dressed up in a tux."

"To go to a pub?"

"No, of course not. The Samuel Stowalls entertain on a grand scale. They wanted him to feel comfortable at their estate events, thus the tux. I find this all fascinating. Did I mention I've enrolled for PI classes at the school you went to down in San Diego?"

She snuck this last comment in on a stealth Predator

drone. So stealth I almost missed it. She heard me inhale sharply.

"I'll still have time to work with you guys. Okay?"

"Hannah! You've got tons on your plate."

Home school three children and run a small farm, take care of your sick mom twenty-four seven, clean house, and now attend classes. Yeah, that sounds like a typical American woman.

I had a feeling she was working her way up to asking if she could formally apprentice with us. The State of California requires private investigators to do a lot of time apprenticing with a licensed investigations firm, and usually this activity is encouraged to begin after only a few classes.

"When do your classes begin?"

"First one is Tuesday. I'm really excited. Pete...well, he's supportive."

"Uh-huh. So he's worried."

"Yeah. But I promised him I'd avoid violent situations."

"Uh-ha." So did I. Remembering I had a purpose for the phone call, I moved us on.

Chapter 19

"And the kids? How are they?"

"Great. They're great. Deborah and I just finished reading Pride and Prejudice together. Samuel is working on an improved chicken coop with his dad. Value is mastering crocheting. We now have fifty percent coverage of all head and arm rests on our farm. Be sure to compliment them when you come to visit."

I smiled. I thought I remembered their ages were ten, eight and four, respectively. I could just imagine what a four-year-old's crocheting looked like. But I still didn't know the gender of Value. Val could as easily be a female name as a male. But maybe crocheting was a clue, this usually being a female activity.

"I'm glad they're doing well, Abigail isn't." Okay, that was way too abrupt. Speaking of Predator Drones.

Another pause.

"Abigail...? What's wrong?"

I sighed, unsure of what I should tell her. Or even if I should bother her with all she had on her mind.

"Rachel, you called me, remember. So cut to the chase, I'm prepared."

"I know you've heard about the terrible car accident up on Cleveland County, the one that claimed..."

"Yes, yes. Half the world has. A terrible thing. And?"

"And Abigail snuck off and enrolled herself in classes at Pinto Springs High this past Wednesday."

Another pause as Hannah digested the news about the youngest, perhaps brightest member of the quilting circle. For Hannah, as a homeschooling parent, the prospect of homeschooled Abigail enrolling herself into high school must have carried even more freight.

"Uh, oh. Not good. Gloria must be having a conniption. But...now the school's involved. And...Gloria called you."

See what I mean? Hannah is very sensitive and intuitive.

"Gloria has asked us to help her. She sent us in to retrieve Abigail from school yesterday. I don't have to tell you that did not go well. Anyway, Abigail just called and we ended up making plans to do a little shopping together, go to lunch. So I'm looking for guidance Hannah, maybe some approaches I might take so I don't make matters worse."

"What specifically do you see happening at this meeting-slash-shopping trip?" Hannah said.

"Great question. Abigail is very angry, and she sounded just now like that anger is morphing into depression. My knowledge of the world says teens get depressed fairly easily. This conflict with her mom over her schooling, coming in the midst of this horrific auto accident, I'm thinking this is a dangerous combination. I was at the school yesterday and they're experiencing an emotional tsunami on campus."

"Right. So you're looking for guidance on how to talk to a potentially suicidal teenager." She wasn't asking.

"Yes. I don't want to add to her inner turmoil, if that isn't to cliché a description."

"Probably the definition of adolescence, inner turmoil. But avoiding adding to any feelings she may have is easy. Say as little as possible. Just listen. Don't take her side. Don't play mom. Don't play any kind of authority. Stay neutral. Listen. How is Gloria?"

Listen. Don't talk.

"Pressing her back to the wall."

"Right." She inhaled deeply. "She'll lose this one, even if only temporarily. And the reason she'll lose is because it sounds like no one knows why Abigail went to school in the first place yet. But the thing to keep in mind is the authorities will probably be on her doorstep Monday. And not just the school."

Find out what drove her to enter public school in the first place.

"I already met a real nice gal from Social Services."

"So have you recommended the HSLDA to Gloria? They can offer her legal advice if she decides to go there."

"Right. HSLDA, is that Home School Law...?"

"Home School Legal Defense Association, and there's a branch in California. I haven't heard any religious statements from Abigail at our bees, so I don't think the CHEA is appropriate for them. But if you have, that's the Christian Home Educators Association. They might help out too."

Legal assistance? Does Gloria want to go there?

"Anyway, one analogy which might help you is that you are holding up a mirror between them, but the mirror is two-way in both directions. So they can see their reflection superimposed on the image of the other's reaction. It's a difficult concept."

Zen again.

"Abigail sees herself on one side of the issue and Gloria sees herself on the other--some how you have to get them to stand on the same side of the mirror and look at their dual image as they communicate with one another. Not easy.

"But I can't stress this too much, Rachel, the school is going to come out swinging on Monday. Your job is first to help Gloria duck. Get her to step back, disengage. Then to seek help through other avenues. And maybe remind her that most kids do just fine in high school.

"And then maybe, if you can communicate with Abigail straight on, remind her that she is brilliant—which she is, Rachel. Trust me on this, Abby will get real bored in no time. And then you and Gloria will need to be on her side to help her get back out of public school when the time comes. She could easily skip high school and go straight to college even now, except for the age differences."

Ah-ha. Legal assistance to get Abigail back out of the system.

But then Hannah added, "Unless...there's a boy."

Chapter 20

The mystery grandma at the top of the stairs came out of the shadows and let me fully see her. I'd arrived to pick up Abigail around noon for our shopping adventure. This time Nana escorted her granddaughter to the door.

She was careful. She was also a short, round oldster standing in a dark floral dress, and could have been any of a thousand Eastern Block women I remembered seeing in photographs after the fall of the Wall. I wondered where her babushka was.

She didn't speak. English was beyond her ken according to what I'd heard. But Nana waved goodbye as we drove off, with a smile on her face.

Abigail looked a little better than yesterday. I couldn't say her mood had brightened, but she seemed more focused, less frightened. She was wearing a tee with a Go-Chargers logo on the back, and jeans. I was wearing my L.L.Bean car coat with the removable lining. It was chilly up on the mountain again.

By now you've probably figured out that my accident of fifteen-days-ago and-counting had destroyed my previous vehicle. My beloved ten-year-old Ford Taurus station wagon had been totally demolished in that freeway bullet-ride. It took me ten days to make up my mind what car to replace it with because I really wanted another station wagon. But with the cost of gas skyrocketing, I'd decided on a Prius.

"So how does Mountain Springs sound? There are dozens of stores there to roam."

"Whatever."

"Are you shopping for anything in particular?"

"I can't afford anything. My mom isn't rich. Nurses never are. And my dad's living off his disability check." She stopped and looked at me.

"Can I share something with you that you won't tell

my mom?"

Important question of the day.

"Yes. If you tell me not to share something with her, I won't."

"Okay. Nana gave me a little money just now, so I could find some more...fashionable clothes."

I smiled. "I like your Nana better and better."

We parked close to the west entrance to the mall and began walking. She wasn't warming up yet but I had hopes.

"So tell me the truth Abigail, you and your grandma really can communicate, right?"

She grinned. "Yeah. I learned enough Ukrainian and she learned enough English, so we sort of meet in the middle. But Nana and I pretend we can't, just to spark Gloria's firecracker."

"Nana like's to tease your mom?"

"We both do. I told you, Gloria's a communist dictator. Except she isn't, because she's really anti-communist, but she can't let go of the style of thinking, you know what I mean? Dictatorial. Frankly I think Nana is more comfortable with capitalism than my mother. She actually grew up in a free country, back in the thirties.

"She talks about how different things were in the Ukraine all the time. I think that's why she gave me a little money."

"Great. Let's find something to spend it on."

We approached and entered the magical world of all things new and pretty.

"Oh, no!" Abigail whispered.

"What..?" I followed her gaze.

Along the huge entry hallway were the usual newspaper vending machines, the ones with the top front page displayed in the windows. The headlines were very similar and they fairly screamed out at us.

Bloodcurdling headlines and one grainy photograph repeated over and over. It was one I hadn't seen before. It was a close up that must have been taken as rescuers were attempting to remove the bodies from the bloody I-13 accident three days ago.

Abigail floated toward them and stood reading. I joined her, my heart sinking.

"Pinto Springs Five Die in Night of Drugs/Sex," she read aloud.

"Five Dead, One Barely Clinging," she read another.

"Abby..." She pushed my hand off her arm.

"Mexican Drugs KILL Five American Sons," screamed a third. "They can't get enough of it can they. They're vultures. They're bloodthirsty. Look at this picture!"

There was nothing I could do or say, so I just stepped back and waited for her to move on. Finally she turned and rejoined me on our walk into the mall. The gaiety had evaporated. I saw an opportunity.

"Why do I think it all started with this, Abby?"

I wanted to test the waters, see if we were going to talk about what really mattered today.

"Maybe it did," the tall, thin girl said mysteriously. It was a start.

Have you any special store you want to visit?"

"Well Neiman's would be nice, but I'll settle for Old Navy."

Interesting, her being aware of the difference. We headed toward that section of the mall where other teen stores were also available.

We shopped for about an hour, not attempting to focus on serious conversation. Abigail bought three gauzy shirts and a pair of hip riders. Then she bought some pretty underwear, tiny panties and even smaller bras. She blushed at me twice, so to make her feel better I bought a couple of bikini style for myself.

Then she found some humorous socks and again we both bought a pair, hers aqua and lavender, mine orange sherbet and raspberry red. I made a private plan to wear them to bed with Matt tonight, with the blueberry bikini panties.

Finally by mutual agreement we headed for the Grub Gallery to grab a bite of lunch. We went for the SaladBarSoup. As we munched and slurped, I waited for Abigail to begin to talk to me about why we were really here. Something had moved her to call me, and it wasn't just new clothes.

Finally she went there. "You think my mom will accept my decision?"

I had no idea. I sat back, thinking.

"Tell me, Abigail, had you been trying to involve your mother in this process before?"

"For months. I told you....okay, it was only twice over a period of two months. But both times she just exploded."

"Just exploded...."

She sighed. "I'm a nurse's child, Rachel. I know about interviewing techniques. She just blew up, angry and yelling and telling me she couldn't think about it then."

"When was 'then'?"

She put down her spoon. "Okay, fair enough. I first let her know I wanted to try public school out about a week ago. *Before* the accident. Frankly I'd been wanted to bring it up before that, but I was afraid. She was so adamant, and so negative about public education."

"Uh-huh. So when was the second time?"

"Wednesday morning."

"Before or after you both learned about the car accident?"

She fussed with her soup.

"After."

"And her reaction the second time?"

"More angry. More reactive. She actually said she thought the accident was demonstrative of how public schools can destroy a young person's life."

"What was your reaction to that comment."

She probably knew where I was trying to go.

"Worse than hers. She made me positively furious."

"Were you positively furious the first time she refused to consider your wishes?"

She sipped some diet coke.

"No."

"Why?"

"Okay, fine, because...because I wanted more than ever to go to Pinto Springs after the accident. But it isn't what you think?"

I waited.

She waited, ate a little soup. Wouldn't make eye contact.

I said, "Did you know any of the boys in the accident?"

Finally she looked at me again.

"No. But I know about one of them."

That was when the simmering kitchen fire in the Barbie-Q Delight decided to kick it up a notch and set off the fire alarms. One of the Grub Gallery's cooks needed to return to chef school.

We were hustled out the side doors and our shopping trip came to an abrupt end.

Chapter 21

I was out in the yard seriously kicking some weed butt and fantasizing about beating up tabloid editors when the phone rang. I dashed inside, pulled my dirty garden gloves off, and answered on the fourth ring.

I listened, waiting silently.

"Hello, is anyone there?" Uh-oh. Latisha Harper's voice.

"Hi, Latisha, what's up?" I asked the Social Services woman cheerily. But I wasn't feeling cheery. Harper's call could only mean trouble.

"Hi Rachel. I'm sorry but I've talked myself blue in the face with this principal and he's determined to keep your student on campus."

They've been working on a Saturday?

"A meeting has been set up for early Monday morning with a pretty tenacious guy I know named William Gould. He's from the ACLU. It'll take place in Forsythe's office and he won't accept you as a stand in for Abigail's parent. In fact I hear they are looking for the girl's father big time."

I wasn't surprised. She'd already warned me about the ACLU, and frankly I knew this was the normal course of action with these kinds of conflicts. I'd just hoped Gloria and Abigail could have enough time to work this out.

I wasn't looking forward to standing shoulder to shoulder with the Communist Dictator.

"Wonderful. I'll call Gloria Pustovoytenko as soon as possible. She's working a double shift again today. I'll see what her schedule is on Monday, Latisha. Let's hope she's off."

I knew Gloria's weekend schedule because Abigail had told me her mom was working a double shift this weekend so she could take next Saturday off. Next

Saturday was the November Quilted Secrets bee, and this time it was to be Abigail's quilt we would sew, at her house.

She told me the time of the meeting and apologized again. We said our goodbyes. The warmth was necessarily gone.

At three thirty I called Gloria hoping to catch her during a break. She answered on the third ring. Unfortunately she was still in CCICU.

"Hi Gloria, it's..."

"I know, Rachel, I have your number on my phone." At least I thought that was what she said.

"I'm sorry to bother you at work, Gloria, but I know you will need time to think about how to proceed. I just got a call from the Social Services gal, Latisha Harper. The school principal has set up a meeting for early Monday to talk about Abigail's attendance at the school."

"There will be no attendance. Abigail is in complete agreement with me."

I paused. Took a breath.

"Actually, I don't hear that from Abigail...yet...Gloria. Maybe in time..."

"No time! *Now*. She cannot go to that school without my permission. I am her mother. I say where she goes."

I dropped one of the bombs. "The ACLU will have a representative at the meeting."

"You can handle it."

I dropped another bomb. "The principal won't accept me as a substitute, but of course if you want me to accompany you I'll be glad to..."

"Fine! I *be* there!" She stopped. I heard her breathing rapidly, trying to control herself. "Do I...should I get a lawyer?"

"Not yet."

"I'm right, right Rachel? I am the legal guardian. I am the mother. They must do as I say. Abigail must not attend that school—she will go to the home school because I say so!"

I dropped a third bomb. "Except for Monday. I'm afraid on Monday Abigail must come with us."

I didn't add that she would be ushered off to class as soon as we arrived.

"Why? She has no say. I am her guardian..."

My turn to interrupt with yet another bomb.

"Was that agreed to by the courts Gloria? I mean when you and your husband separated...."

"Divorced. Yes."

"Because, well, they're looking for him. And they might find him. If they do, he'll still agree that you are the only legal guardian, correct?"

I heard a sudden cry in the background, and realized it was Gloria, choking back her emotions and holding the phone away from her hoping I wouldn't hear.

"This is not right! This is not fair, Rachel."

"I know, Gloria."

"I know the public schools. I tell you Abigail will be hurt."

I tried to mollify. "I don't think American schools are as bad as your high schools may have..."

"I'm talking about American schools! Who do you think I see in here in ICU? Just old people waiting for their hearts to stop? I see children! I see high school children mangled and bloodied from campus fights...and, and overdosing on drugs. These schools are *worse* than the Communist schools."

I began to worry that her voice might be heard by a few of those waiting-to-die seniors.

"Gloria, maybe we should talk more later."

"Right now, Rachel! Right now outside my office door is a boy who is a product of the American schools, clinging by a thread to his earthly existence. I don't want my daughter destroyed by this public education like he has been."

Shit!

She was shouting about Jimmy Winters. I shouldn't have called during her double shift. I decided to end the call.

"My other phone line is ringing, Gloria. I'm going to

have to call you back. What would be a good time?"

This hadn't worked out the way I wanted at all. I was hoping to give her time to quietly think over what was coming her way before meeting with her rebellious daughter, while she was busy working and had to control her emotions--but she wasn't quietly thinking anything over.

Now I was afraid she would get fired if I didn't get her off the phone.

"What? I am not being loud, no... Tomorrow, Rachel. We talk more tomorrow."

And she hung up suddenly, leaving me wondering who she had been talking to.

Good grief, Gloria was a cyclone of anger and fear— one that I'd just ramped up.

My stomach churned at the thoughts of Monday's meeting. I needed to talk to someone who might give me more help with how to handle this.

Hannah was busy right now, and besides she didn't have children in the schools. Then it came to me who I could call next.

Chapter 22

I called Geraldine Patrone because her brother was Detective Tom Beardsley. He worked with the Cleveland County Sheriff's, and was an invaluable contact for our private investigation business. And, as I've said, Gerry was like Hannah in that I'd hired her on as a consultant to help me with the investigation into Ada's death.

But more pertinent to the moment, Gerry had been a school teacher before she'd begun her family.

"Hi Rachel."

This actually unnerved me a little, that people knew who I was when I called, I mean even before I'd spoken. It was in some way a sinister reminder of just how little privacy we had anymore, thanks to modern technology.

Then again I could make it a private call, an *unknown*. But nobody ever answered those.

"How's your neck? Will you make it to the bee next week?"

"Oh sure, I'm almost healed," I lied. "Really feeling just fine."

"So, you're able to make it to the bank?"

"What? Sure, why?"

"Because you haven't cashed my check, Rachel. I need you to do that so I can balance my accounts."

Gerry was referring to the check she'd given me to cover our expenses as we investigated Ada Stowall's death. I was reluctant to do so, as I had come to think of myself as their friend, but after what Matt and I went through during our research, maybe Gerry was right.

"You and Matt earned that money, Rachel."

"Okay, Gerry. I'll deposit it today. Sorry about the delay. Now to what I'm calling about, it's Abigail. Have you heard that she's enrolled herself at Pinto Springs High School?"

She hadn't, so I took a few minutes to bring her up

to date. Then she began analyzing as I hoped she would.

"Gloria seems a toughie but she's really very frightened, Rachel. She has a lot on her plate, not the least of which is that she really isn't all that comfortable with America's rules, how slippery they can be. People from former communist block countries may have left because they hated the restrictions, but they often come to feel like they're adrift in this anything goes world of America."

"You saw this when you worked? How difficult it is for immigrants?"

"Of course, but in my case we're talking about Mexican immigrants mostly. Because I taught Spanish I had a lot of kids in my classes who saw taking high school Spanish as an easy way to get a good grade. And I did a kind of case work with many of them.

"But through those cases I saw the children of an immigrant group and how difficult it was for them to communicate with their parents. Imagine, Rachel, having two very different nationalities within your family. Because that's what it is for first generation kids-- especially when the parents have basically fled their native lands.

"Mexicans flee their country as a way to get away from poverty. But in Gloria's case, fleeing from a changing Communist country and all its repression and conflict, it could only be harder."

"Right. So did you ever have experience communicating with those parents and their children, as in mediation?"

"Oh yes. But I can't say I was a neutral person in those mediations. I sided with the kids, maybe a little too much. That was my job, to act as an advocate for my students even with their parents.

"Still, I wasn't unmindful of the fact that foreign born parents have terrible trouble adjusting to our way of life. They're so fearful that at times they regress back to the thinking in their old country and the way things were done there. I understand how they could have second thoughts, you know? But if the kids are born and raised here, well, there is no going back. You see?"

I thought I did. But how would this help me with Gloria?

"Can you give me an example?"

"Well, yes. I remember a Muslim family I became very involved with. The boy was my second student from the family. The girl had already graduated high school, and the boy was apparently the straw that broke the camel's back, no pun intended.

"The parents were from Turkey, a Muslim state you might think of as more modern. A country that you might think people who emigrated from would have an easier time of adjusting. They are a democracy. They have essentially a capitalist economy. But they are also very religious, and their religion supports a very rigid view of the father's role in the family. The simple summary is that both children were completely Americanized, and the son was a rebel and a failing student, which is why I became involved.

"All the boy could think about day and night was surfing. It was his escape from his own failure—and his dictatorial father. Finally he announced he was dropping out.

"His father was adamant that he stay in school. This is an opposite situation from the one with Abigail on the surface, but the difficulties would probably be the same. In my case the father wanted the school to call the police and round him up and bring him back into the classroom. Of course that's not our job in schools. We are not police—not any more. He was almost seventeen."

"What happened?"

"Well, the boy and his father drifted further apart. The older daughter became the boy's excuse to stray even more. She had her own apartment, her own job. Finally, in a fit of rage the father took his wife--against her wishes I think—and reversed their decision of almost twenty years before. They flew back to Turkey, abandoning their children to this evil country. A terrible experience when you think about it. There were no winners in this."

"What happened to them?"

"I don't know. I lost contact with them once the family disintegrated. The boy never returned to school, at least not to mine."

"So you think what--that I should side with Abigail?"

"Well, I can't say that, Rachel. No. You can't go there. Remember, Abigail has the school on her side now—and God help them, the ACLU. It's Gloria that is feeling alone and threatened. I mean, she hired you to be on her side.

"So maybe that's mostly what you need to do. Sit next to her; explain her thinking to the others when she loses her composure. And use your more moderate voice to help Gloria turn her thinking around a little. Maybe that will slow down the train wreck, because that's what she's heading straight into, you know. A train wreck.

"The school will win, Rachel. Gloria needs to get on board that bullet train, not stand directly in front of it. You need to turn her around and help her run fast so she can catch up to it. I think you can do it."

In the end, I asked after her hubby and four boys, and how her ALS charity ball had gone.

"Oh, wonderful, Rachel. We raised half a million dollars for them. But even more importantly we have all on board to help spread the good word about ALS research."

Finally we said our goodbyes and I poured a glass of red and meandered out to peer at the final rays of sunlight glowing in the west. Wisdom was already there, waiting for me, listening to his wild friends.

Chapter 23

Six pm and I was completely frazzled. Wisdom was listening for the hyenas. I needed to hear some wild beast talk too, something with answers as how I should proceed. The glass of wine helped.

My neck was hurting again, and I absently tried to rub it through the Styrofoam collar. It wasn't actually Styrofoam, it was softer. But after a full day it felt like a thick coffee container was twisted around my neck. Worse, the fool brace was wrapped in a soft plastic that held in moisture which itched after awhile.

I reached back and ripped away the Velcro connectors and pulled the damn thing off. I was suddenly bathed by cooling air. Maybe a salty sea wind.

Or, inside a breezy refrigerator.

"Why do you have your collar off?"

"Oh, you startled me, Matt." He'd snuck up behind me again, one of his favorite tricks. In response my neck muscles clinched.

Perfect.

Matt pressed up against me from behind and whispered in my naked neck.

"Does this mean you're healed? Does this mean we can have rough sex again?"

His hands were exploring the front of me as if for the first time--*my favorite of his many tricks.*

"What did you have in mind?"

"Well, if you're ready I was thinking we could use this new position I heard about in court this week."

'One of your divorce cases again?"

He ignored my hidden warning.

"It's called the belly-bottom, but it requires enormous flexibility."

"Who's enormous flexibility?"

"For both of us."

Wisdom groaned and slunk through the open sliding door and into the living room where he dramatically threw himself on the rug. It was his signature disapproving act. I called it moan, drop and roll.

Meanwhile, Matt and I moved as one grasping organism down the deck to the bedroom sliding doors. We wriggled inside. The phone rang.

Shoot.

With a sigh almost as noisy as Wisdom's groan, Matt reached for it and pressed it against my ear. I guess he was all talked out for the day. He disappeared into the bathroom.

I listened.

"Is that you Rachel or am I listening to the air?"

"Hi Luis, how're things?"

(Marvin) Luis Lewis, LIRI apprentice number two.

"Not so good."

"Oh." I waited.

"It's Sandra. We just had another, uh, discussion, about me being a private investigator. I don't know, Rachel. She's really frightened about my work."

"You're the IT guy." I was feeling my wine, demonstrating my exceptional wit.

"Not all the time."

Matt snuck up behind me again. I was thinking the increase in temperature was an indicator he'd taken his clothes off. Yup. Now he was taking mine off.

"Maybe if she learned a little more about your work she'd feel better."

A sense of guilt stole over me. I dismissed it, but it snuck back.

"Yeah, but..."

I needed to end the call. Quickly.

"As in, why don't you bring her over for a cookout tomorrow? We'll barbecue some Yak, drink some wild boar milk, discuss the best ways to take down a charging bull elephant."

"Uh...well...did I get you at a bad time Rachel?"

I ignored the question. He really needed to let me go.

"How about around four?"

"Yeah. Sure. But just hamburgers would be fine."

"Yak hamburgers it is," I teased. Luis Lewis was young and I guess I scared him a little. He hung up without another word. Maybe it was the throaty growl under my voice.

Or he was mocking my silent hellos.

Chapter 24

It was eleven ten, Saturday night, and Matt was still off chaperoning a father at his daughter's wedding with Wild Willie.

Wild Willie is William Townsend, and he is LIRI's apprentice number one. Number one apprentice has two computer IDs, Wild Willie and Towns' End.

We call him Will.

A big bruiser of a guy, in his forties, with a narrow beard, Will had come to us from the famed Deacon Harks agency in Los Angeles somewhere around a year ago, about halfway through his apprenticeship program with Harks.

It wasn't unusual for an apprenticing PI to switch mentors midstream, in fact it was encouraged. The more agencies you worked at during your three years of required on-the-job training the broader your knowledge of all things PI would be.

But that was also when Will had earned the scar the beard covers.

He'd just begun the beard when he joined us and we could see the angry looking red line through the thin stubble. Will had been in an LA knife fight with some gangbanger out of his head on crystal meth.

He never told us the details. Will was a private sort of guy.

In fact, Will was so private that I suspect he has a deep dark secret hidden behind that beard as well.

I have no proof, yet.

I stroked Wisdom's ear-fur as I sat contemplating, a unread book open in my robed lap. Wisdom changed positions so I could rub *his* favorite spot—his rump. I obliged.

A night chill was diffusing its way through the glass of the closed sliding door to my left reminding me that fall was here early this year, and winter might arrive even earlier. But at least it wasn't raining tonight.

The front door slammed open scaring the beeswax out of me.

"Matt! Do you always have to be so dramatic?"

"You won't believe," he said, completely ignoring my remark and throwing his jacket over the chair by the door. He stomped toward the kitchen.

I climbed out of my comfortable seat to find out what I wouldn't believe.

Wisdom was already checking out his master for possible snacks when I caught up with him. Matt ignored him too, so I reached in the "bone closet" as we call it, and pulled out a chicken strip for him. The dog collapsed on the rug with a satisfied harrumph. They were both dramatic.

Matt was behind the bar. He retrieved a beer from the beer fridge, took a long drink, and sat on his stool to begin his tale.

"She called the cops."

"No."

But I wasn't really surprised. Phyllis Schwartz was an 'Angry Bitch'. And Earl Schwartz was her favorite victim.

"Tell me from the beginning."

He put his beer down on the bar, freeing up both hands so he could speak in Italian. Matt wished he'd been born Italian--they cooked way better than the Irish (his father) and Polish (his mother).

"His disguise was masterful. Will did a perfect job. Earl (the father of the bride) wore a blond wig so convincing even I thought it was his own hair, and a slightly grayed blond mustache. I don't know where Will gets his stuff, but he's missed his true calling. He should have been a makeup guy for one of the studios."

"Maybe he was. Maybe that's his deep dark secret."

"What? What are you talking about?"

"Nothing, nothing." I waved my hand over my teacup dismissing the interruption. "Go on with your story."

"Okay. So...where was I."

"Disguises."

"Right. *Jesus,* I'm tired. Anyway, we got to the wedding reception a little after eight. It was beautiful. Phyllis had rented half the La Jolla Grande Especial hotel overlooking the Pacific from a cliff. I mean, waves were crashing on the rocks a few feet away from the cake table. I have to take you to this hotel. It has a great restaurant."

"When?"

He grinned. "So we get there and Earl and I stroll through the front door, all dolled up of course, looking very much like we belonged. Will stayed in the car so we didn't have to use their valet service. Besides, he didn't have a tux."

"So you could make a quick get away."

"Right. So Will is parked..."

"I think we should start calling him William."

"What?"

"Never mind. Go on."

"Are you sure you want to hear this?"

"Yes, yes. Ignore me, I'm tired too."

"Okay. So we enter with a small crowd of other guests and no one checks IDs, no one even wonders who we are. But then the wedding was in the center of a public hotel...which by the way Earl paid a fortune for...so there were plenty of gawkers, and Earl was so well disguised, I didn't think his daughter would even recognize him."

"Who took her down the aisle?"

"Earl calls him 'Shit-Head'. I think his real name is Shyller. Dean Shyller. Anyway, the poor bastard has to stand on a balcony overlooking his daughter's wedding ceremony and watch his ex wife's live-in boyfriend walk their daughter down the isle. I mean, I almost cried for him."

"No you didn't. Earl's a jerk."

Matt ignored me this time, maybe because I mostly whispered my editorial comment.

"After the wedding itself, Earl and I just sort of wandered around the reception trying to look invisible. That was when his daughter Amy spotted him. So at least he got a smile from her."

"Earl won't pay child support."

Matt stopped and frowned at me. "No. Earl won't pay alimony. The children are all well into their twenties and thirties...

"All five of them."

"...and Phyllis has been living with Shit-Head for about ten years."

"Because if she married Shit...*Dean,* she'd lose much of the money Earl should pay to support his wife and five kids. And to make up for boffing a blond wannabee starlet with big boobs. Who he has since married."

"You want to fight or you want to listen?"

"Will we have sex after we fight?"

He didn't grin. He was into telling his story. Besides, we'd just had sex and we weren't that young anymore.

"Okay, okay. Go on." Matt reached for his beer and took a sip.

This taking both sides thing that Matt and I do, him taking the side of the man and me taking the side of the woman, is one reason why we get involved in so many divorce cases. Matt represents the guy's side. I represent the gal's. Of course, we don't always meet most of these warring couples. We work for their lawyers.

"Okay. So, it's like ten fifteen, and the party is going strong, and Phyllis spots Earl. I mean, you would have thought she'd spotted a bomb-wrapped terrorist. She starts screaming and pointing, and finally swearing at the top of her screech owl voice..."

I giggled. "She sounds like a screech owl?"

"Yeah, like a nine months pregnant screech owl in the final throes of hard labor. That is how ballistic she went."

I snorted and said, "Owls lay eggs."

Matt was grinning from ear to ear. His audience loved him.

"Earl froze. Like a deer in a truck's headlights. I guess the poor sucker thought since he paid for the wedding she was gonna' cut him some slack. But then she whips out her cell and one finger dials and talks. *She has the cops on auto dial!"*

I was laughing so hard I almost wet my pants.

"So I grab him by the elbow and yank him away. We made it to the front door, I've got Will on my cell, and I'm thinking I hear sirens off to the north. The cop station must be a block away. Will pulls up, but Earl is protesting. He's enraged now, yelling about how it's *his* wedding. He *paid* for it. He couldn't even bring his wife! And he breaks free from my grip and races back inside. I have to run in after him. I picked up the wig and fake mustache on my way in. Earl had decided to expose himself."

Matt was yelling, and now I was guffawing. I was sure we'd probably woken the giraffes.

Wisdom put his head in my lap and whimpered. He was worried.

"Then...then, well this part is sad. It's all sad, of course. But anyway, when I catch back up to Earl he's standing once again at the top of the balcony above where the wedding had taken place, staring down.

"I didn't say, but the hotel is built into a hill, and the wedding was actually one story down from the entrance level. Anyway, I looked over the railing and saw screech owl Phyllis was now yelling at their daughter Amy, who was yelling back. *'It's over. I'm leaving. You've ruined my wedding mom. You and dad, the two of you.'* She then turned and pointed an accusing finger up at the poor sap. Right in front of the whole wedding party."

"No."

We weren't laughing anymore. That was a painful image.

"Yes. Amy finally lost it. Mrs. Amy whatever-her-name-is-now lost it all over her battling parents. And then she ran off toward the elevators crying.

"I realized the sirens had arrived and were shutting down, and I whispered in Earl's ear, *'So you want to go to jail? Is that what you're telling me?'* That woke him up, and I finally got him out a side exit and into the truck. (That would be our fire engine red pickup truck I refuse to drive to the grocery store, it's so garish.)

Barbara Sullivan

"We pulled off just as the cops arrived. Five cars full of them. I don't know what she said into the phone, but the cops were there in record time."

"Maybe she told them there was a bomb-wrapped terrorist at the wedding."

Matt looked at me appraisingly. *Whoa.*

That was illegal, right? Falsely claiming there were terrorists around?

We started laughing again. And then we moved to the bedroom.

Chapter 25

Sunday morning around eleven I was back outside slaughtering weeds by the bucketfuls.

A cold wind drew my attention to the sky. Clouds were once again threatening us. I really couldn't believe the amount of rain we were getting lately. Here it was only October twenty-sixth and we'd already suffered through a three week long drenching. And now it was building for another.

Usually California was dealing with Santa Ana winds and the threat of fires this time of year, a seasonal phenomenon that had moved itself to September.

Must be some kind of El Niño thing.

Pretty soon we'd be on the lookout for mud slippage ordinarily experienced after Christmas. We were definitely not in Southern California anymore, Toto.

Yes, two weeds at once.

"It's useless."

He was talking about weeding.

"It isn't."

"It's worse than house work."

I two-armed a particularly offensive specimen.

"How would you know?"

He sighed.

"Listen, I'm thinking, now that Abigail Pustovoytenko is going back to school maybe I should ask Townsend to do some surveillance over at the high school."

I stopped my green labors and looked up at him. "Why?"

"Just some stuff I'm hearing."

"Like...?"

"Stuff."

"Okay. Then why not Luis?"

"Because of Sandy. I don't want to aggravate a

complicated situation."

"But Luis makes more sense. He looks like a high school kid. Will looks like a middle-aged wrestler. He'd be noticed."

"Yeah, maybe. We'll see how Sandy is this afternoon. What time are they coming over?"

"They're due around four. Why?"

"I thought I'd go hit a few."

Golf again.

"Okay, just be back by three to help with dinner."

He left and I bent to my endless project, pondering the mysterious 'stuff' he was refusing to tell me about. The phone rang or I might have chased him down and beaten the answer out of him.

My cell said it was Abigail.

"Hey Abby, how are you doing today?"

I took off my garden gloves, weeding was over for the day.

"Fine, but...I have a request. My mom and I need to talk. She said maybe at lunchtime, if you could take me over to the hospital. She's working again, of course."

On a Sunday morning. This poor woman never stopped working, it seemed.

My immediate reaction was to doubt what she was telling me. But in the background I could hear a friendly chatter in what I assumed was Ukrainian.

"Your mom is expecting you?"

I heard her say, "I'll be back on time for your dinner, grandma. Don't worry."

She returned her attention to me.

"So will you take me?"

I felt Grandma's silence was indirectly confirming that Abigail indeed had a meeting planned with her mom, but decided to be certain I would deliver her in person to Gloria.

Better to be sure and not risk Abigail taking a detour to visit with her new school friends, whoever they were-- the ones that were keeping her out until after five after school.

Besides, I was happy to facilitate a conversation

between her and her mother. Maybe we could avoid the ugly meeting on Monday after all.

She told me she was expected at twelve and I glanced at my watch. I needed to get moving.

I hustled back inside, but before I could select a casual but business-like outfit for my outing the phone rang again.

This time it was Hannah, catching me up on the latest about Eddie. Apparently the Cherry Valley Gang, as someone was now calling Eddie and his group of anti-casino agitators, were not just highly political. Last night they'd included a couple of mercenaries at their meetings in the form of motorcycle gang members with criminal records. I reminded myself I needed to get on line and research this group and the events taking place out there in New York State. Then Hannah told me Eddie'd been given a firearm.

Great.

Just what the world needed, an armed probable psycho.

Chapter 26

I tried to reach Gloria for the third time but she was always busy. I left messages, on her cell, with hospital staff. But she never called back.

I was flying blind here, and I knew it. I hoped at least I could connect with Nana in some way to be certain I really had Gloria's permission to take her daughter out of the house. I still wasn't certain Gloria even knew I had taken her daughter to the mall.

But Nana didn't make an appearance this time.

I picked up Abigail around one and we drove mostly in silence toward Cleveland Central Hospital. I parked on the third floor of the hospital's multi story car park--just like the last time I'd been here.

That had been when Gerry, Hannah and I had driven up the mountain to meet with Gloria P. so she could show us Ada Stowall's medical records. We'd met her outside ICU number one which held her offices.

A chill played piano on my spine as I remembered this, and my mood stepped down a sad octave as we walked. That visit more than two weeks ago had made me aware of the terror that had ridden Ada Stowall's life like a beast from hell.

No one should suffer that kind of physical abuse, let alone from her husband—the person she should feel the safest with. The knowledge of the horrors she suffered was the reason I had such mixed emotions about Eddie. How could anyone raised in that environment be normal?

I tried to make cheerful small talk as we moved through the dull hospital corridors but Abigail wasn't participating. So instead I concentrated on the cadence of our footsteps reverberating off the walls.

Abigail was anxious, and the closer we got the more her young face showed this.

Perhaps she wasn't planning on having a happy talk

with her mom. Maybe she was bringing ultimatums. My mood music stepped down another eighth. I tried to fight the negativity.

My plan was to deliver Abigail safely to her mother and then disappear for a while. Gloria's lunch was only an hour. With time walking to and from the cafeteria, they'd have maybe thirty minutes to actually get into trouble with each other.

This could work.

That is if they didn't get food poisoning, the cafeteria food was *bleck.*

I knew from my own experience that our fears about having serious talks with important people in our lives could often be overblown. If you remained calm and focused, things usually went better than you expected.

I attempted to convey this thought to Abigail as we neared our destination. *Her destination.* I was just a passenger, now. Just a listener to an increasingly scary music—perhaps Stravinsky's Firebird Suite, Infernal Dance.

At last we were on the corridor where the ICUs were located. Before us was the long, greenish-gray hall I so clearly remembered from my first visit earlier this month.

Again I thought—*I hate hospitals.*

On the right of this hall were the two large critical care units themselves. On the left were small groupings of chairs, tables and lamps—mini-waiting areas for family members and close friends. I couldn't remember noticing them before.

We stopped at the check-in station. Abigail flashed a smile and offered a cute wave to someone she knew behind the desk, and we were ushered on without further ado.

She must regularly visit with her mother.

My heels continued to throw echoes against the tile walls as we made our way. But the other footsteps had changed tempo: Abigail was moving faster, changing our duet into a jarring disharmony.

In sharp contrast to the dull corridor, I knew the

units themselves to be brightly lit areas, with somewhat incongruously yellow painted walls. The first, the only ICU I'd seen, held three beds. Behind each bed was an array of monitors keeping tabs of the patients.

I also remembered that Gloria's office would be on the right as I faced the unit itself while the patients were on the left inside these large rooms. All this was clearly visible through two huge viewing windows.

Visitors to the most critical of patients were not encouraged to directly interact with them. They could watch, and quietly wait, as the cluster of folks in front of us now were doing. Their private misery was palpable even from a distance.

Two butterflies danced in my stomach trying to catch the beat, but bouncing off each other rudely. My own pace hastened.

Abigail suddenly broke into a sprint calling someone's name. Involuntarily I slowed to a stop. Something was trying to force itself into my brain.

The knot of grief just outside this first window—a small family heretofore in solemn repose--turned as one to face her rushing approach. A man and his wife and two teen children, a girl and boy.

And then it hit me, *the last survivor of the horrible crash on I-13 was in ICU One!*

My slow wits realized this was the family of the surviving boy. They were waiting for God's verdict on their son.

And Abigail knew them!
What had I done?

For the moment I couldn't remember the college freshman's name. Instead I was recalling a handful of bizarre details, mostly the ones in the online messages of John Shaw.

I finally got my legs moving again, wondering what I would say when I caught up to this distressful situation.

Jimmy, that was his name, Jimmy Winters.

As I approached, my eyes were pulled to the right into the gay yellow room. Three bodies were lined up with their feet facing the nurses' station.

A metronome began keeping beat in my head. Click-*click.*

I searched for a soon-to-be enraged Gloria. She wasn't there.

My eyes returned to the parents of this family. But a week of agony seemed to have numbed their senses. They were just staring at Abigail.

Except the boy, who had put his arm around her shoulder.

I began composing words that would extricate Abigail and me from their very private experience as gently as possible.

Time was moving like molasses as this scene played out. I remember it all as a cadenced series of events, perhaps because we had clicked together down the long corridors of the hospital and the echoed sounds of our walk were still repeating in my head.

How was it that Abigail knew this family so well?

The unidentified girl began drifting toward the viewing window, her eyes and mouth widening in horror.

A click. The mother's face closed as the woman retreated from us. From the viewing window.

Another click. The father slowly stood and crossed his arms in front of his body as if to brace himself for a blow. Or to hold himself together.

Click. Back to the older sister halting her drift toward the glass, her face crumbling.

"Judi...," the boy said.

Her name was Judi.

I followed her focus into the ICU room at Judi's unspoken command.

To the occupant of the closest bed.

What?

Click. I nervously stepped closer.

Click. Mother and father began to keen behind me.

There was something wrong with the picture before me. Another step toward the window.

Tubes and wires were everywhere. His head was bandaged but his face was exposed and massively bruised. His eyes were at a swollen half mast, but they were seeing.

Click. Jimmy Winters had raised his head.

He studied his body.

Click. My eyes traveled with his and I finally saw that his body was way too short.

At the edge of my sight, Abigail began to collapse in the boy's arms, giving herself over to the agony we were all standing before.

Oh no!

Click. I took an involuntary half step back from the glass. It was worse.

One arm was suspended in a sling, but the closest arm, the one not in a sling, *wasn't there either.*

Three! He had lost three of his limbs.

Click. Jimmy released his head back onto the pillows. He closed his blood-filled eyes, and entered his final sleep.

The music stopped.

The girl Judi began blubbering and shaking her head next to me. An alarm was sounding, then another.

"But they just finished taking his arm. He's supposed to be okay, now. He's supposed to be okay...." the girl screamed.

"He didn't know," the father moaned from behind me. "All this time and he didn't know."

My mind reeled. The poor boy had been hacked into pieces by surgeons desperate to save his young life.

But Jimmy Winters was having none of it.

His face emptied and his life went away. Jimmy had made his last decision.

An irrationally calm message filled the hallways of Cleveland County General calling the Urgent Response unit to ICU One. It could have been computerized.

It was then that Head Nurse Gloria Pustovoytenko stepped out of her office to rush to Jimmy's bed--*what had taken her so long?*

Another nurse followed from another room to the rear.

Gloria didn't see us. Not at first.

But then she did.

Her daughter Abigail was on the floor out of her view. Jimmy's brother was at her side. But she saw me.

Gloria's questioning face turned toward the closed door to ICU and I watched as she debated walking toward it--my heart pounding.

These are the details I remember of the rest of this awful event.

A white coated doctor whipped by me and slammed open the door Gloria was contemplating, and two more staff members followed him. As if flood gates had opened, doctors and other staff members swarmed around her and Jimmy's bed.

But, Gloria could now hear her hysterical child on the floor at our feet. She stepped away, letting the others have room to get to Jimmy, and rounded the doorway.

She stopped, her face reflecting no emotion. For a moment I thought she had surely expected her daughter to come. But then she shouted.

"What hef you done!?"

The worst thing, I answered her subconsciously.

I turned and stepped aside. There was nothing I could do now but wait for this God-forsaken mistake to play itself out.

But my so-called *connection* with Abigail had run its course. I was in over my head with this teenage girl. I'd raised boys. They weren't nearly as cunning as girls.

Chapter 27

The whole situation at the hospital devolved into chaos as doctors and nurses flew around the hysterical family and into ICU. For a few terrible minutes we stood watching as they worked feverishly to save the boy.

But he was gone, and given that they were still contemplating having to take the only limb he had left, it was a blessing.

Then I'd turned my attention to my charge.

Gloria had more than enough to deal with inside ICU. She was no longer staring me down. One crisis in that threshold room often triggered other crises, and now the old man in the middle bed was in cardiac arrest.

I forced Abigail to follow me back to the car. Unfortunately I had to shame her into coming with me, reminding her that she was not even a family member. She'd tried to protest, something to the effect that she wasn't the only non-family member, but I forged on. I had to get her moving out of the building. She held out until I resorted to reminding her she'd lied and now her mother was probably never going to speak to me again.

Or some such thing. I can't remember my exact words. But they weren't lovely.

I knew tomorrow morning when Gloria and I met at Pinto Springs High School this would still be sitting between us like a dead toad.

I told the nurse at the check in station, or whatever it was, to make sure Abigail's mom knew I'd taken her home and we were gone.

I drove Abigail back home to her grandmother in morgue silence. Fortunately it only took ten minutes. Nana was standing at the door again. No wave this time. No winks.

Maybe misgivings. Had Gloria called her?

I would never know.

The drive up the mountain from Escondido took only thirty minutes, but my return home took twice that due to a dead deer in the road. Deer gawking slowed us to a crawl. Must be a mountain sport.

So I spent an hour flipping switches between fuming at my stupidity and grousing about Abigail's lie.

My whole afternoon had been gobbled up by her little deception. I was feeling no sympathy for her, thinking she had no business interjecting herself into the Winters' grief--even if she was friends with one of Jimmy's siblings.

As I neared our home, I tried to turn my mind back to the rest of my plans for the day, but lurking in the back of my mind—and causing belly angst--was the fact that Gloria and I would be meeting the ACLU in Principal Forsyth's office early the next morning.

Fifty-seven minutes later I raced into the kitchen. I was late preparing dinner for Sandra and Luis and I began pulling things out of the refrigerator, constantly glancing at my watch. And then the silence hit me.

Where was Wisdom? He always greeted me at the door wagging his aging body as if he was one big tail.

Matt returned home a little after four. If I weren't otherwise occupied I'd have been pissed.

I heard him rummaging around in the kitchen where he expected to find me.

He called my name and passed through the dining room and into the living room. He muttered something I couldn't make out, then called my name.

"Rache! Where are you, hon?"

Hon. He always used "hon" when he knew he was guilty of something.

Like being an hour late. Like not being available to help in the preparations for our dinner guests due to arrive in the next half hour.

His voice traveled to the back of the house into the bedrooms. I didn't hear him for several minutes. Finally he returned to the living room and stepped out on to our back deck.

"Where the hell are you Rache?"

I knew I'd lose it as soon as he neared. A sob rose from my traitorous throat. I wanted to be brave. I wanted to keep things to myself. I didn't want to *share.*

 Shit.

Another sob.

"Rache, what...oh fuck. What's happened?"

I was sitting on the tiles holding Wisdom still with the last of my strength.

"Where were you!" bubbled out of my mouth through my streaming tears.

Matt knelt down beside us and put his hand on Wisdom. "Is he bleeding again?"

He hadn't done his husbandly duties, namely blowing the detritus off the back deck and cleaning up the grill. He didn't understand!

"Rache, I don't see any blood, what happened?"

I lost it.

"I can't Matt. I can't entertain Luis and Sandra. I can't deal with anything more today."

I was bawling like a baby. Then Wisdom moved, or tried to. I held tight.

"Is he hurting? I mean, what's wrong with him?" Matt said.

"He was out here sneezing his head off, trying to get the damned lump out of his nose, *that's what's wrong.* The growth has broken through the nasal wall again."

"I don't see any blood..."

"Not yet! But it's coming. That'll be next."

I watched Matt check himself--pausing long enough to get his emotions under control. I hated him for it.

I hated that he could do that and I couldn't.

"Okay, Rache. We both knew it was just a matter of time. Here, let me hold him while you go get yourself cleaned up. Luis and Sandra are probably pulling up to the house as we speak."

"I can't..." I hiccupped. And now a spike of fear that I would be found in this condition by impending house guests stabbed into my heart. *He didn't understand!*

"Hon." Then I could see it hit him. "How did things go at the hospital?"

"Abigail *tricked* me." Okay, I was close to screaming now. Thankfully we lived a fair distance from our closest neighbor. I continued my rant ten decibels lower.

"She wasn't going to meet her mom, to have a nice chat with her. She went there because that Winters boy was failing and she wanted to be there when he died! What's wrong with her? Gloria was in charge of his case. When we got there..."

I paused to wipe my tickling face. Matt grabbed the chance to take Wisdom out of my arms. He set the poor animal free and we both watched him with bated breaths.

He moved away from us and shook his thick coat, reclaiming his dignity. Then he took up his constant vigil on the deck, sitting, facing the distant sounds of wildlife off beyond the hills.

But he wasn't sneezing anymore.

"I think it's stopped," Matt offered cautiously.

"Maybe it has. But..." He also meant I was calming down.

"I know, but not yet. Come on, let's get ready for our guests. You can tell me what happened in the shower."

"He *died*, is what happened. His family was there, and about twenty doctors and nurses, and Abigail. She collapsed on the floor outside ICU. I don't think Gloria will ever trust me again."

At that moment I could read my husband's mind. He was thinking, *oh fuck*.

Chapter 28

I was racing around the kitchen like a maniac preparing the meal. Matt was on the porch cleaning things up. Wisdom had refused to leave his post on the porch, so Matt carried his dinner out to him. I went out to see if I could help him.

"What are you doing?" He was standing over the dog.

"Nothing." Matt.

Then I noticed. "He isn't eating, again."

"No. Go back to the kitchen and finish making dinner before you start crying all over."

"I'm okay, just finished the salad."

Moments later we heard the front screen door slam and Luis and Sandra entered the living room. Luis was used to letting himself in.

"Hey you guys! Don't start eating without us," Luis called.

"Sorry we're late," Sandra sang from behind him. She was gorgeous. I hadn't expected gorgeous.

"You're not the only ones late. I haven't even charged up the grill yet," Matt answered.

I placed the dish of pretzels and guacamole I'd been holding on the table, and turned to greet Sandra.

"Hi, it's nice to finally...." I began.

"Oh darn. I'm starving," Sandra moaned. "Oh, sorry. Nice to meet you, too. I guess I feel like I know you two already, since he talks about you incessantly."

Oops. Luis' surprised expression spoke volumes. I guessed he had no idea he talked about us incessantly. But I know how to make friends, I reminded myself.

"Give me a hand in the kitchen, Sandra. We're running late, too. You can sneak some salad while we're working."

As we entered the kitchen I heard Luis ask, "Hey Matt, what's with Rachel's eyes? She have allergies?"

"Nothing. Wisdom had a bad time for a bit but he's okay now."

Sandy said, "Who's Wisdom...and what's wrong with him?"

The question reminded me that although we saw Luis on a regular basis, Sandy had pretty much remained a mystery to us. She'd been his live-in girlfriend for close to a year now. But we didn't really socialize with the folks who worked for us; we felt it kept things more professional.

I explained Wisdom's situation. She sympathized and began shelling the boiled eggs for the potato salad. At least she was comfortable in a kitchen. Eventually we moved past the small talk, and in a lull, I asked, "How's it going Sandy?"

"Tense."

I was thinking potato salad. But Sandy was thinking of something else. Was she speaking about her relationship with Luis or talking about her current state of mind? Maybe all her earlier abruptness had to do with being anxious about meeting us.

"Want a beer?"

"Sure."

"That's a pretty shirt. Where'd you get it?"

"You like it? I think it clashes with my hair, but Luis loves it, so..." She let the comment linger and returned to the potatoes.

I took in her outfit more closely. She was wearing a red and orange print shirt that was so tight and revealing it could have been an elaborate tattoo. Her strawberry blond hair was pinned up in curls on top of her head. Her shorts were short. Way short.

Oh to be young again, I mused.

I was looking for a way to broach the subject of Luis going undercover on campus when Sandra went just where I wanted to go.

"I really hate that Luis is thinking of risking his life for a living, Rachel."

I took a sip of my beer.

"Okay."

I waited.

"I mean, it's dangerous being a PI, right? Just look what happened to you."

"I guess it can be, Sandy, but usually it's downright boring. I wouldn't say that what just happened to me, being shot and having to shoot someone else, is the norm for a private investigator at all. And there probably are dangers associated with most work people choose to do."

A stock answer to hide my discomfort that she would use my experience with Eddie Stowall to try to get her boyfriend to stop his apprenticeship with us.

We didn't need someone on campus yet, but the situation with Abigail was escalating, and Luis really was the best choice. Maybe we could get Will Townsend in as a repairman, or a volunteer. But it was a long shot.

Luis looked young enough to pass for a high school student and his good looks—dark brown hair on the longish side, square jaw, sea blue eyes in a smooth complexion—and geek tall, would help him connect with the thirteen year old Abigail.

I changed the subject.

"The reason I asked about your blouse is that I've noticed you and Luis manage to dress like superstars. It makes me wonder about my own choice of clothes."

Sandy stopped peeling the boiled potatoes and eyed me.

"Well...you could use some younger looking duds. But I frankly just shop at the usual outlet chains. Maybe if you picked up some teen magazines you could get a feel for their styles."

Teen magazines? It was all I could do to suppress a laugh. She was trying so hard not to embarrass the middle aged woman in the room. Sweet.

I picked up a couple more appetizers and carried them out to the deck. Luis was sprawled on the rattan couch, his long legs spread out before him. A cleaned-up cowboy relaxing after a long day of work on the ranch.

I'd walked in on the same conversation we were dancing around in the kitchen.

"So, are you okay with taking assignments for now, Luis?"

"Oh sure. She's...don't worry about it, Matt. Sandy will cope. She's just a little teary right now. Probably PMS. What do you think about those Chargers?"

Teary? I hadn't noticed. I decided not to raise the subject of his work with her again. As I left, the conversation lightened as the two men launched into a spirited football discussion.

Chapter 29

While I was gone, Sandra had brooded, and she dropped a small bomb on me.

"You know, Rachel I'd have left this guy long ago but he's the best thing I've had between my legs. Ever. By a mile. I just can't get enough of him."

I picked up my jaw and pulled the garlic bread from the oven, briefly wondering how long it had been since I'd heard that kind of girl talk. Not since I was in my twenties and early thirties, I mused. Of course, I asked the stupid question.

"So are you famously jealous of him?"

Sandra's turn to drop jaw. She one-eyed me, wondering if I were competition or not. She decided not.

"Uh, no. I mean, he's mine.... Oh, crap...sure I am. Every female who looks at him makes me want to commit murder. And believe me, girls know. They can read him like a book. A very sexy book. They can smell him from a mile away."

"Pheromones," I muttered.

"Yeah. But he's such a big idiot with this private investigator thing. And he hasn't a clue he's so sexy. Which makes me wonder, if he's so dumb about that how will he survive out in the streets? He needs to get on with his life and decide for real what he wants to do. He's almost twenty-eight. And I'm zeroing in on thirty. We don't have time to waste."

Hasn't a clue? Maybe she was the one who was clueless. Luis was our resident geek, and he was masterful at computer snooping. Of course, we have no idea how or where he finds the information he occasionally supplies us with. It isn't at any of the professional websites I use with my end of the research.

"Well, I guess that remains to be seen, Sandy. Lots of training makes them smarter. Come on, let's join the studs." We were in dangerous territory if she was doing PMS; I was taking a side path out. So call me a coward.

We picked up the remaining dishes and walked out toward the setting sun. Wisdom had finally been lured away from his listening post by the smell of steaks being delivered to the table.

We sat, and I bowed my head silently as the thought that this might be one of the last times our dog joined us for dinner briefly threatened my emotional equilibrium. *Thank you for today.*

When I looked up, Matt and I shared a smile. We rarely prayed aloud, but were comfortable with each other's silent offerings.

I have to admit at this point that I spent much of the rest of our party sneaking peeks at Luis. He was looking more and more gorgeous every minute. Sandra should have kept her juicy gossip to herself. But after our second round of red was poured Matt had to go and ruin everything.

"So, as I was saying Luis, you need to clear the decks during the next few days to help keep an eye on Abigail. Frankly the sooner you're on the high school campus the better."

He was testing Sandy. I was watching Luis as he resumed his slouched down, legs splayed position on the deck couch. I slapped my eyeballs, scolding them for glancing at his crotch. Luis was my two favorite kinds of men, Irish and Italian all rolled up in one.

And young enough to be my son. *Sigh.*

Whoa! I put my glass of wine down and didn't pick it up again. I was getting stupid.

"Campus? What campus? Abigail who?" Sandy blurted.

"Abigail Pustovoytenko...and don't even *try* to say her name until you've practiced it at least six times alone." I said, trying for casual humor.

Matt proceeded to bring Sandra up to speed. I thought she was following, but Sandra was stuck back on high school.

Chapter 30

"That school where those boys were from? The five that were killed?"

"Six. The last one just died today," Matt said. Our eyes met. He was being too rough with her.

"Jesus. No kidding. I thought they were going to pull him through," Luis said, and shook his head sadly.

"All those pretty young girls...." Sandra's voice trailed off.

I thought she'd meant to say boys, but suddenly a vision of sexy Luis watching Abigail on campus with *all those pretty young girls*...while Sandra watched Luis, maybe with a gun under her skin-tight skirt, blossomed in my head.

I stood and carried some of the plates into the kitchen, hoping Sandra would follow me. But she stayed behind, and as I rounded the corner back out to join them a few minutes later I could hear the voices rising.

"No way! The Chargers were totally blanking the Chiefs last month. They haven't got a chance this Sunday!" Thank goodness they were back to sports.

"Commonnn. You and your Chargers," Luis moaned.

I plopped a chocolate on chocolate cake piled an inch high with frosting down in front of them. This is a really mean trick I play.

"Rachel! What are you thinking? I'm trying to diet."

I smiled innocently and cut three pieces, placing a plate before each of them.

"Where's yours, girlfriend?"

"Oh, I can't eat chocolate, Sandra. Makes my tongue swell up. But I enjoy watching others..."

"Oh, that is low, really low."

"Give it to me, Sandy." Matt the hero.

"No way, I'll eat it darlin'. Give it over." Luis the sex god.

Sandra smiled at them teasingly, then took the *eenciest* piece off the end. Then another, then another.

Okay, were we doing Tom Jones here?

This time I slapped my brain, and turned to give Wisdom a hug. His was pressed up against me, still hoping I'd give him some leftover steak.

"Cooked beef is no good for you boy. It gives you the runs, remember?" I muttered to him.

He knew. Like I knew my tongue would swell when I sampled a little of the frosting from the side of the cake later on. When no one was watching.

"By the way, Luis, did you get a chance to observe the homeschooling group yet?" Matt.

"You've already begun?" Sandra said.

"I did better than that. I have a date with two of the teen girls next Monday, a two-fer. Boy, are they hot."

Sandy slapped his leg hard enough to make mine hurt. Luis laughed a little too loudly.

He sounded like my boys when their voices were changing, deep most of the time, but still giggly like a girl's. He was feeling his wine, too.

"Just kidding, sweetie'. Actually, they aren't bad looking once you get past the baby fat and pimples. They're a typical group of adolescents, really. Although there does seem to be some upper age limit. The oldest in the group—a real skinny guy—looked to be about fourteen, the rest were maybe eleven or twelve. Maybe Abigail is just doing what all homeschool kids end up doing. Moving on.

"Anyway, I caught them at the skating rink. I didn't see anything unusual going on. Looked like a nice bunch of kids. Same with the handful of parents with them."

Matt nodded, took another bite. He was thinking Sandy was okay with this. But then she straightened him out.

"Luis isn't ready to do undercover work."

"I'll give him all the training he needs, Sandy. It's really not a dangerous assignment," Matt said. "We're working out the details of how we're going to get him on campus now." He was using his Marine management style to just steamroll over any objections and keep moving forward.

Made me nuts sometimes, but when it worked, it was okay. Tonight it didn't work because Sandy wasn't used to Marines.

"Hey, I'll be okay Sandy. How dangerous can a high school be, anyway?" Luis said.

"Right. He'll be fine, Sandy." Matt.

"You haven't been in school for quite a long time, Colonel. This isn't like sending one of your men off..."

"Sandy, take it easy..."

"It's okay, Luis. That's why we're here, to talk through this." Matt said.

But Sandy was shaking her head dramatically.

"High school *campuses,* as you so quaintly call them, are war zones. Didn't you notice the ten foot tall chain link barriers go up last year? Those fences aren't about terrorists from the Middle East, they're about terrorists from just south of the border. And maybe to keep the little oversexed monsters inside."

"Come on, Sandy. That's really over the top..."

I caught Matt's eye and did a little head shake. He didn't interfere between them again.

"*You don't know.* Even ten years ago when I was attending it was a sick, dangerous place. High schools are...full of drugs...and hormone crazed kids being fed every kind of designer pill the marketplace can produce."

I put a gentle hand on her arm, thinking if she kept letting these emotions build I might have to hold her in my arms to quiet her down like I'd just done with Wisdom. She stopped.

Was there more going on here than fear for Luis' safety?

But Sandra pulled away and turned to confront Luis again, her eyes filling with tears.

"They...I was...." And she stopped again, waving her hands in front of her face as if batting at invisible bugs. She inhaled deeply then began again.

"Luis, it's not the same for guys as for girls. It's just not the same."

She shook head again and stopped herself for good. She wiped away the tears on her cheeks and settled back in her seat.

"Sorry. Too much wine, I guess."

"It's okay Sandy." Luis said.

Luis wasn't seeing the pain she was holding back. He was too young and the moment of truth had passed.

And I was shamed by my relief. I didn't want to think about what must have happened to her as a teenager—and she really didn't want us to know, either.

Wisdom turned sharply toward his listening station, large ears at attention, and suddenly I heard them too. *Braying and stomping their hoofs.* The zebras were chasing a giraffe again. A cruel game the giraffe was defenseless against.

Then I remembered that the zebras were in different section now. Too many silly giraffe tails had been bobbed without benefit of anesthesia.

Sandy slowly stood, and I said, "Do you hear them?"

"Yes! That's amazing."

"What?" Luis asked.

Maybe you had to have women's ears. Sandy and I joined Wisdom and listened while another brief breeze carried us into the wilderness inside the San Diego wild park.

They left about an hour later, all calmed down, Sandy seemingly accepting the possibility that Luis might start doing undercover assignments.

But that night, after cleaning the kitchen and retreating to our bedroom to join my husband, I was suddenly filled with an urgent need. I took him like a she-wolf in heat.

He didn't seem to mind.

And I never realized that I was a she-wolf going through a change from young to old.

Chapter 31

Late Sunday night, I dragged my brain up from sleep thinking to answer a ringing phone before Matt was disturbed.

It was a good thing I caught the call; Matt was growing increasingly perturbed by my unpaid services to the bee women and it was Abigail Pustovoytenko's mom, Gloria. I tripped on the bed linens, steadied, surged forward again, stumbled again, and finally barked my right shin on the edge of a piece of furniture I've yet to identify.

Hopping a crazy path down the hall while alternately clutching my now screaming leg, I stirred the family pictures on the walls to life. Aunt Mable reached out and hit me. In the living room a kamikaze table took out my other knee.

For a brief moment I attempted to hold both shins and keep moving. Doesn't work. The phone blared for the third time, still twenty feet away in the kitchen.

Then I finally woke up. I picked up the receiver a half second into the fourth ring.

Surely Matt was awake.

"Hello." It was practically a scream.

After a pause Gloria said, "What are you doing?"

At least that's what I think she said.

"Trying to get to the phone before it wakes Matt. He has a big day tomorrow."

"You're in bed?"

"Not any more."

"Good, because I can't rest either! You have so messed up my child...."

The rest of it I won't bother to interpret. She was practically crying, also in sotto voce.

"Gloria, where are you?"

She continued. I think she said she was still at the hospital and I wondered how many hours she worked in one day. Surely now that the last boy was dead she could resume a normal eight-hour day.

"...hat you for brrringing her halfway to the ospital..."

"Gloria, slow down."

I was hoping she hadn't just said she hates me. She stopped, then resumed.

"I did not tell er to bring er to the ose pital! She made that up. Now she is liar. Now she is vot every other brain-damaged child at public school is. *Brain-damaged.* There is no teaching there. It is factory for sitting on children!"

"I understand your feelings about this, Gloria, and on some levels I agree but...."

"And just to make you feel as bad as I do it isn't tomorrow your husband has to vake, it is today! *So there!*"

With that she slammed the phone down. Called me back a minute later.

"Rachel! Oh no Rachel, it's that girl, Judi. The girlfriend of the last survivor, Jimmy Vinters, they've just brought her in. She has taken pills. Vot will I tell my child?"

So Judi was Jimmy Winter's girlfriend, not his sister.

Chapter 32

Monday, October 27, predawn

Gloria called me again in the early morning hours while I was out on the deck with Wisdom, listening to the elephants trumpet the approaching sun rise. She spoiled my coffee by telling me Judi Zimmer had died. She was sixteen.

My heart stilled, and I rose from the lounge chair with my cell phone pressed to my ear, pulling my thick terry robe tight around me, and retreated to warmth. The dog continued worshiping the sunrise, blessedly sneeze free, and blessedly unaware of the approach of death or anything at all about death. I hoped.

Then Gloria returned to her favorite topic, *Abigail's Big Mistake.*

"If she survive her second week I be surprised. She's too quiet. I think something wrong." She was calmer this time, so her diction improved.

But again I must caution that I only think I know what Gloria is saying. Slavic accents are bedeviling--must be the Cyrillic alphabet.

"Where are you, Gloria?"

"On way home. I think she vill give it up today. I think she vill return to her friends in the homeschooling group. She vill see that she's too different now to join this main stream."

Or you vill give up trying to direct her entire life, mom. A hard thing for moms to do.

Interesting pictures formed in my mind featuring all those teenagers floating on a river of hormones. I couldn't support her hopes, so I just mumbled a few words so she'd know I was at least listening. Sometimes listening is the best. Sometimes listening is the only.

"But I pray she vill be safe. Not upsetting like first day. Not like Friday."

"Has she talked about friends she's met?" I ventured.

I was thinking about Judi's suicide a handful of hours ago and worried how this might affect Abigail. Teen depression was contagious.

"No. She says nothing. Goes to room and studies. I worry, Rachel. I know this sounds like not much but she stopped painting. This is extraordinary for her. She has spent ten of her first thirteen years drawing and painting every day, usually for several hours. Now nothing. She is brilliant artist. This change is so sudden. You will see when you come to the bee, Saturday."

Oh lord. Only six more days and I'd have to endure another long night of sewing. I reached back and rubbed my neck. Sitting up half the night does nothing for healing.

How in hell was I going to stoop over the quilting rack for eight to ten hours? I definitely needed to work on changing their schedule. Maybe sew the quilt for two half-nights instead of one entire night.

I thought about Abigail's comments at the previous (my first) bee--the one held at Victoria Stowall's home, also up on the Cleveland plateau--and how they'd presaged Abigail's rebellion. There was nothing sudden about it.

Abigail was troubled and now she'd stepped into a river of trouble, Pinto Springs High. I bumped into Matt in the kitchen. He looked like I felt.

Chapter 33

Tonight we would eat homemade beef stew and pear salad (my turn to cook). I'd make the beef stew from a huge can of really delicious Brazilian meat I'd bought a couple of months ago. Add onions, small white potatoes, carrots and mushrooms, a few mild spices. Fresh bread for Matt. Fresh fruit for dessert. *Yum.*

It was still Monday morning and I was trying to get my mind into a better place. I looked over at Matt. We were sipping coffee at our twin computers in our home office--LIRI headquarters. And I was still thinking about dead teenagers. They were piling up a mountain of them way up there on Cleveland mountain.

I sighed and glanced around, and thought this had to be the day I cleaned up our messy work space. I needed to take care of my end of the paperwork. And I was overdue on a research project for Llamb and Stern on the effects of *Lamotoral* on the human personality—a nifty new over-the-counter sleep aid and a name I thought sounded like some new French motor oil. One of their clients was probably attempting to blame the sedatives for making them kill their spouse.

The phone rang and gave me a start. Matt answered. Suddenly I remembered this was the morning I was to meet with the principal of Pinto Springs.

"It's for you. Are you ready for another call?"

I nodded and took the call.

It was Latisha Harper, the social worker assigned to Abigail's case. After polite hellos, she told me she was hearing noises from her gang contacts.

"Abigail may be in trouble, Rachel. Sounds like she shot her mouth off at one of the homies while he was harassing an Indian girl on Friday."

"As in Native American?"

"Yes. The Mexican-American gangs are pretty strong at Pinto Springs High. The school system has been good at keeping a lid on their activities, but frankly they are loath to mess with this or any political hot potato. Hispanic students feel harassed already with their second language issues and the related difficulties with the new testing requirements. Some outspoken families have hired lawyers to represent them."

She took a deep breath, and continued.

"The gang calls themselves the Pintos, from the name of the city--and the fact that one initiation rite is to guzzle a pint of tequila and then take a beating from the other members. The tequila numbs the pain. These are very rough hombres. Most of them are second and third generation members, so their fathers are very involved."

They don't always get the painkiller, as Abigail and I witnessed in the dog park. Gangs were not lovely.

"What about the Indian girl?"

Her turn to sigh. "Yes, I know. It's a balancing act between all these minority groups and their needs. Unfortunately the old rule still applies: the squeaky wheel gets greased."

Latisha finished the call with one bit of good news for me; Gloria had put her challenge to her daughter's attendance at PSHS on hold--at least for now. The ACLU meeting was off. This probably had as much to do with Gloria going two days with minimal sleep over this past weekend as with a change of heart.

Matt and I turned our attention to what to do about Abigail. We had begun the discussion last night after hearing and seeing Sandy's visceral objection to Luis doing undercover work.

"Are you sure we can't just place a bodyguard on campus with her, Matt?" I said after hanging up and bringing him up to speed.

"Aside from the fact that she'd probably object to the intrusion, we can't move forward without school officials approving. That process takes more time than we may have. And from what you've told me about this asshole running the high school and the first meeting you had with him, I don't picture him agreeing to anything that might lend itself to supporting her remaining a home-schooled child. I think he'll deny there's any danger from the get-go."

He was right.

"Yes, but I'm worried about her, Matt. She doesn't seem to have the necessary emotional brakes to keep out of trouble. Her reaction to the gang attack we witnessed was my first warning. And now to hear she's already had a run in with one of the local gangs..."

"Let me call John Clancy and get some guidance from him."

John Clancy was a Captain in the Escondido Police Department, but more importantly he was Famine's brother-in-law. I'd never met him, but I presumed he was African American since Detective Leslie Mosby (AKA Famine) of the Pinto Springs Police Department was. Mosby was also frighteningly thin.

Matt made his call as I half-listened and pondered how the day's workload would be spread. We had a request for papers to be served on a sex offender who'd skipped check in with his probation officer two months running, and I had that research request I was overdue on. And then Matt was to be in court the second half of the day. So even without the meeting with Dr. Forsythe, our plates were full.

I was contemplating unplugging our phones. But that doesn't work with cell phones.

While Matt made a series of grunts and uh-huh noises I Yahooed "bullying and student bodyguards" on my computer and came up with dozens of pages of websites. Some of them had to do with the movie "My Bodyguard".

One of them was about a twelve year old girl living in Seoul who regularly had two bodyguards escort her from class to class after she was bullied by gang members.

A Sunday Herald Sun article was posted regarding bullying claims by a young teen boy. School officials are quoted as denying any proof of bullying, stating, "We've thoroughly investigated his claims of bullying and they are unsubstantiated...the student suffers from learning difficulties and was merely assigned a volunteer tutor to assist him with his lessons."

Apparently the "tutor" shared lunchtime with him.

A California Representative initiated legislation after the tragic death of a local student which she called Safe Schools Improvement Act.

And several articles were written about Phoebe Prince's suicide after intense and unrelenting bullying by many students at her high school, much of which took the form of cyber-bullying.

Bullying was definitely in the headlines. But in the short time it took Matt to finish his call I had found nothing about the legality of placing a bodyguard on a California campus. In fact I was beginning to think it couldn't be achieved, at least not quickly, without using some ruse.

Matt finally hung up and said, "Will was supposed to serve for lawyer Denlop again today. But I'll take that. It's on the way to the Municipal Courthouse where I'm due later. We're serving some cretin in Vista who skipped bail on a child molestation charge. He lives down the street from Hannah and Pete Lilly, by the way, you might want to warn her."

"Oh great, just what the Southern California homeschooling family needs. But why doesn't Will serve the papers?"

"You mean aside from the fact that the last time he served papers on a child molester he broke down the cretin's back door, cornered him in the can and slammed the papers onto his chest so hard he cracked a rib?"

I grinned and said, "Yeah, that wasn't so good." Actually it'd been the high point of our week. "So what are we doing about Abigail?"

"We're sending Will in undercover for the moment. John is calling a friend of his to have him issued a work pass to assist one of the janitors on campus. I don't think she needs classroom coverage at this point, just during class breaks and lunch."

Good. I felt better already. Except for second thoughts.

"Are you sure about using Will?"

He gave me that look again, the one that wonders openly if I'm losing my mind. I hated that.

"What do you mean?" Matt.

"Well, now that we're actually sending someone in, I'm worried about Will being the one. He's so...so..."

Huge and scary.

"He's all we've got, Rache. Anyway, after our little discussion last night about being careful using Luis with Sandra's concerns for his safety, I called Will and asked him to be the point man on campus if it became necessary. It just became necessary, thanks to Latisha Harper."

"Okay. You're right. I'm just worried."

"You want to write that down somewhere so I don't have to hear you keep repeating it?"

Okay, he was getting rude. I rose to go take my shower and wake my brain up completely. Matt called after me.

"Remember, after court I have to meet with realtor Rodriguez, the one who has been scamming all those Mexican-American seniors in upside down homes. I may put Luis on a computer chase with this one too."

As it turned out, I was right to worry. While I was dressing our phone rang again. I hustled into the office to listen in.

It was William Townsend calling only fifteen minutes after stepping foot on campus. Matt had the call on speaker.

"They made me." Will.

"The authorities?" Matt.

"Yep. I was escorted off the campus a few minutes ago. Principal actually walked me to the gate. They're pissed."

"Uh-oh." Me.

"Did you know the big fences around most Southern California school campuses usually aren't locked? Another waste of tax dollars."

"They're probably just there in case Homeland tells them to button up," Matt interjected.

But Will was upset.

"And their so-called guards consist of janitors and grounds keepers doing double duty. I asked the guy I was supposed to be helping. He said he didn't even get a raise for taking on this new assignment. They aren't armed or anything. I call it hazardous duty."

"You're probably right, Will, but budgets are tight right now." Matt.

That was not where Will's head was. I saw my chance to change Matt's overly busy schedule and quickly asked, "Does this mean you can serve the papers in Vista today?"

"Yeah, sure. I'll be there in an hour."

Matt turned to stare at me. He was not pleased.

I was thinking how great it would be for Will to crack some more pervert ribs.

My cell phone rang. I answered it while Matt said goodbye to Will. Then he turned to watch me as my over caffeinated blood made a fast retreat from my head.

I could actually feel the tide going down toward my legs, which made me wonder why nature didn't think I needed my brain while running away.

Which was what my brain wanted me to do right now.

"What is it?" he whispered.

I raised a hand and kept listening, then thought to press the speaker button. The angry voice filled the room.

"*...and if we catch you sending another of your thugs onto our campus I'll report you to the superintendent's office where I fully expect they will begin legal action.*"

Finally I interrupted with a clarifying question.

"Excuse me, but who am I speaking with?"

"This is the *Principal* of Pinto Springs High, and you damn well know that." And then in an aside he asked "What..?" He was listening to a female voice in the background—Chrissie Prichard.

"Oh, well my secretary tells me she didn't have a chance to introduce me, but you should certainly have been expecting my call after I caught your body-guard on my campus. Just what the hell do you and your husband think you are doing? You can't send armed men on campus. Don't you know we are under tight security restraints?" I mouthed to Matt, *was Will armed?*

Matt snatched the phone from my hand and said, "Just what has our man done wrong..." I quickly scribbled his name and handed him a note. He finished, "...Mr. Forsythe?"

"It's *doctor* Forsythe, *Mr.* Lyons...."

"I prefer Colonel Lyons, actually, Dr. Forsythe." I arched my brows and cocked my head at him. His tone was neutral but we didn't need to make things worse by pointing out the man was a fool. He ignored me.

After a brief pause, Principal Forsythe continued. "As I've just learned, *Colonel* Lyons. You are a man of considerable influence for someone who has just arrived in our neck of the woods."

"And how did you learn that, Mr. Forsythe?"

"When I called the police to have your man arrested for trespassing I was handed up the line to some detective who took your side of things, *that's how!*"

"What side would that be, Mr. Forsythe?"

Forsythe sputtered and I pictured him wiping the consternation off his flushed face.

"Never mind, that isn't the point. The police may not want to get involved with campus affairs—as they so coyly put it--but I'm sure the superintendent's office will. Just you keep your goons out of my school!"

Matt called Will back and clarified that he hadn't been wearing a gun.

But now we were back to plan one, Luis Lewis. *Louie-Louiee.* Sandra wasn't going to be happy.

Chapter 34

Unfortunately, not an hour after Will Townsend was sent off the high school campus for impersonating a gangster, and we learned that Luis wasn't available today, Abigail ran smack into trouble.

She called my cell phone half hysterical, and I jumped in my car and took off to meet her at the mountain high dog park where we'd gone last week. I asked her if the school knew where she was. Her answer lit a fire under me. No one knew where she was.

It only took me twenty-five minutes to get there. I was probably speeding. But the whole way I was worrying that she was in danger. The call had ended abruptly. Turned out her battery had quit.

It was a shame there wasn't someone local who could help her out. Of course her mother was sleeping and she wouldn't have called her if her life depended on it.

Victoria Stowall, the Quilted Secrets bee matriarch and distant cousin of mine, was too old and ill to help her, but surely one of Victoria's daughters could have helped. But of course they all worked at their Apple *Fix*ation store-slash-restaurant in Julian.

I certainly understood why she didn't want to turn to her homeschool teachers. This would only give them more ammunition to get her to return to their fold.

Finally, I arrived at the park in the middle of the second lunch break where I found several high school kids meandering amidst the dog owners. I couldn't see Abigail among them.

Unlike some dog parks, the Las Pulgas Preserve (The Preserve of the Fleas, in Spanish, a bit of Mexican humor I suspected) wasn't dedicated exclusively to dogs and their owners. Since the high school was literally just around the corner from the park, it was a favorite hangout for some teens after school.

Of course, they weren't supposed to leave campus during the school day, but some managed to sneak out anyway—like Abigail just did.

After our last visit, when the Pintos gang had conducted a nasty initiation rite here, I was thinking maybe they shouldn't even come here after school.

I finally located her hunched over on a half hidden bench, pretending she was reading a school book. When she looked up I gasped.

"What's that! What happened to your face?" There was a clearly defined red hand print on the side of her face. She didn't answer.

"Who slapped you?"

I was thinking, *call the police, visit the principal and show him why we needed to protect her*, but then she burst into tears and raced for my car. Poor girl was thoroughly humiliated, no doubt. Or was she afraid? I followed her, glancing around, but gang members were noticeably absent.

She scrambled into my car and I joined her. She burst right out with it as I closed my door.

"Oh Rachel, it was awful. I was in the girl's room— they're disgusting places, full of week old used tampons and obscene graffiti—when a group of freshman came in. At first I thought they were seniors, the way they were talking, but then I recognized one of their voices. *She's in my math class.*

"There were three of them, and they were talking and laughing, using really crude language, and then I smelled the cigarettes. Right in school! They lit up as if it was no problem. And they were standing right under one of the smoke detectors."

"Slow down, honey. First of all, are you in pain? Do you think any bones were broken?" The tears had dried up, indignation taking their place.

"What? Oh, no. It stings, but...well that's not the real problem, Rachel. The problem is that these three girls weren't smoking cigarettes at all. They were smoking *pot!* And the things they were talking about. They were giggling and bragging about...about..."

She stopped and looked at me.

"Well, about really disgusting stuff they had done...at the last party they'd gone to. I think it was over this past weekend. I really didn't hear any names, I was just so shocked, and...and I was afraid to leave the stall. I just stood there wondering what to do. Then one of them said she had...I don't know how to tell you this."

"It's okay Abigail. Just tell me what they said. You can trust me."

I have no idea why I said that. If she was about to tell me a crime had been committed she couldn't trust me to be silent.

"Rachel they were bragging about sucking...well, you know?"

"Sucking?

"You know, boys. Their...penises."

She buried her face in her hands and sat that way for several minutes, breathing heavily. But she wasn't crying. I watched while the rest of her face turned as red as the hand mark.

My own emotions vacillated wildly from shock to hilarity, to disbelief. Surely freshman girls weren't really talking about *fellatio*. Seniors, maybe. But not freshmen...only two months into the school year? Good grief, what were they learning in middle school?

And then through her hands she continued.

"Then...I heard another stall door open. Someone else was in the bathroom with us. I bent down to peer under the door to see who it was. I don't know why I did, except maybe because I heard her shoes on the tile floor. She was wearing heels. And then she spoke. Rachel it was the *Vice Principal,* Mrs. White. She was laughing with them.

"She never said a thing about the pot, or their behavior or what they were talking about. She just tossed some inanity out and left...like it was no big deal at all!

"I kept thinking surely she was going to come back with reinforcements and take the whole bunch of them to detention. But nothing. I was just trapped in the stall with these filthy minded girls, all still giggling like they hadn't a care in the world. Then the bell rang. And one of the girls, I don't know her, told me I should come out now so I wouldn't be late.

"Of course, I knew they knew I was there. But the audacity! Well, I just didn't know how to deal. Finally I was so worried about being late back to class that I opened the door and one of them grabbed me and slammed me up against the stall and threatened me. She was in my face with her stinky breath whispering that she would hunt me down like a dog if I told on them.

"*For crying out loud,* the Vice Principal had just walked out and she knew everything! What could I do to them? I started to say that, but then she slapped me, and told me it was a small sample of what would happen to me if I ratted.

"I don't know, Rachel, I just grew so angry. I was just furious, so I yelled at them that they were sluts and that I not only would tell on them, I'd make sure they were expelled."

Oh no.

"Abigail, maybe...." I began, But she rushed right on.

"Then I ran out into the hall. There were still some kids, mostly boys actually, some of the Hispanic boys, you know the ones that wear their clothes falling off their butts. The Pintos. But the girls in the bathroom where white. They weren't Hispanic. So I was confused. And I really didn't know what to do, so I just started walking toward my classroom, stopped running, you know. So I didn't look afraid, even if I was. And those guys started taunting me, calling me Rubia and *Puta*. Right in the hallway, Rachel. Calling me a whore in Spanish.

"Some of the classroom doors were still open. I know the teachers in those rooms heard. Why didn't they do something?"

She stopped and looked up at me with red rimmed eyes, her face now flaming from anger. She was gauging my reaction. I smiled weakly.

"Well...then...I turned on them, too. I know I shouldn't have. But you have to defend yourself. You can't let people think you are weak. I know this. I don't even remember what I said, but I do know I shouldn't have said it. It was in their eyes. They're evil looking to begin with, those gang members. But now they were just dripping hatred.

"And then one of the white girls leapt at me. I didn't even see her coming, and she grabbed my blouse...and...."

She stopped speaking. Now she was shaking.

Abigail pulled down the shoulder of her sweater and showed me that the sleeve of her blouse had been torn. There were red marks on her upper arm.

I tried to talk her out of returning to school. But all she wanted me to do was drive her home so she could change, then I was to take her right back to school.

This time I didn't sit in my car. I marched right up to her front door with her, hoping Gloria was up. Or at the very least, Nana would help me.

But I don't know where her grandmother Nana was. I just stood in the small foyer as Abigail raced up the stairs and grabbed another shirt. A few seconds later she flew back down—her slap mark miraculously covered with makeup—and back out we went.

I didn't call Gloria as I probably should have. I didn't do anything, because I'd told her to trust me. But now I was having trouble trusting my own judgment in this matter and guilt was overtaking me.

I did take the time to talk to her a little, give her some advice to keep her head down and not speak up so much. I told her I'd wait in the parking lot for a while, in case she wanted to change her mind.

I was beginning to wonder if Abigail was in serious danger—mostly because she was unschooled in the ways of school interaction. I know as well as the next fool how to piss people off, have been doing it all my life and quite often when I didn't even mean to. But until now Abigail's human interactions have been very select. She didn't seem to have the common sense a girl her age should have. Picking a fight with three female toughies like the ones she'd described to me wasn't smart. It was downright dumb.

Abigail was lacking in street smarts.

At least the school day was about to end. But then what? Would she be safe walking home?

Matt was in court, Will was serving papers, and Luis was too far away. I sat in my car for a half-hour, but she never came back out.

An hour after that, when I'd returned home my neck was aching so badly, I fell asleep on the bed, comforted by my neck brace. When Matt woke me up hours later, and told me Luis was on for tomorrow I decided not to tell him about my trip, or any of what had happened to Abigail. I should have. But I found excuses not to.

Matt was feeling too negative about my new friends as it was.

I was beginning to hate the sound of the phones in our home, but there it went again. Holding back a burp and the consternation at being disturbed, I climbed out of the *death-grip* recliner chair and fast-walked to the kitchen.

I snatched up the phone and said hello, completely forgetting my anti-telemarketers rule.

"Have you seen slap mark?"

I loved the way this Ukrainian woman started her conversations. She didn't waste her breath on little niceties, she went right to the heart of things. Always caught me off guard, always elicited the first words that came into my head.

"Yes."

Not really a big word, 'yes', but it can result in a big world of hurt.

"What? When?"

Poop! Abigail had *not* told her mother that I'd picked her up at school in the middle of the day and driven her all around Pinto Springs and then delivered her back to 'that evil campus.'

Manure!

"She...told me about it, is what I meant."

I'm usually pretty good at lying--it's actually a PI job requirement--but not right after I've stepped in it, and not right after being woken up.

"You saw her today. *Ven*?"

I paused, collected my thoughts and finally found a path out of the doggie dodo.

"I'm beginning to think we aren't talking about the same thing, Gloria. Why don't we start at the beginning again?"

Okay, that was lame, but it worked.

But my neck started hurting again. I reached for the blasted neck brace and tried attaching it while holding the phone to my ear.

"Rachel, I svare, my daughter Abigail is in dire danger. She is my only child. I cannot let this evil happen to her."

She was practically crying. *Shit.*

"I understand Gloria. Really, I do. Tell me from the beginning what's happened."

She told me she'd discovered the torn blouse and finally forced her child to take off her bathrobe and show her the bruises—"*all over her body*".

This would turn out to be a prescient comment, but at this point I believed there were only three "bruises" on her, a slap mark on her face and two hand prints on her upper arms from where the ugly fellatio expert had grabbed her. At least, that was what Abigail had assured me.

Of course, I hadn't actually seen Abigail's body, but I was also thinking Gloria hadn't either. I remember being thirteen and I wasn't getting nude in front of anyone at that age, even my own mother.

So either Gloria was exaggerating, extrapolating, or emoting. Or Abigail had been brutalized in the bathroom and had lied to me about it.

Gloria's yelling at her daughter brought me out of my contemplations. She was practically screaming at Abigail about wearing makeup to school.

"This is vy the other girls attack you! They don't like *hussies*!"

Maybe that's what she said. She might have said the other girls don't like huskies.

"Gloria! Talk to me or yell at your daughter, but not both."

"What's going on?" Matt said. He was standing behind me listening to my kitchen conversation. At least half of it. He finished reattaching my neck collar for me.

I turned around to look at him, and shook my head. Neck pain shot into my head during which I made several faces, first *don't disturb me*, then *ouch that hurts,* and then, *uh-oh, I didn't tell him*. Must have been a sight to see.

"Rachel, she has clothes in her closet I did not buy her! Where did she get the money to buy clothes? Did you shop for clothes with her Saturday?" Gloria said.

"Make excuses, hang up and tell me what's going on," Matt growled. He was controlling his voice, but his emotions were coming through loud and clear.

I turned sideways to him and closed my eyes. I was in a mess.

Matt whispered in my empty ear, "Do you want me to talk to Gloria?"

It was probably time. I handed the phone to him with a sigh and stood by listening.

He said, "Uh-huh. Yes. Uh-huh." Then several more uh-huh's.

Only hearing one side of a phone conversation can be extremely frustrating.

Finally he said, "We'll have a young man on campus tomorrow morning keeping an eye on her whenever she's in the halls. His name is Luis Lewis. Tell her to take a friend to the bathroom with her. And not to go anywhere without a friend. "

Gloria said something else.

"No that's his real name. And yes, we've thought about that. Rachel has talked with the librarian, Stephen Norton, and he's agreed to keep Luis in the library looking like a busy volunteer during classes so he doesn't look out of place. But whenever Abigail is out and about in the halls or in the cafeteria, Luis will be watching."

Gloria said something else.

"No problem, Gloria. We're happy to help." He hung up and turned to confront me.

"Were you going to tell me about Abigail being attacked at school this afternoon?" Matt said. We were standing. I hated when he did stand up chats with me. They're so *One-Minute Manager*.

"You're already nagging me about going back to the bees, Matt. I didn't want to add to your negativity about the group. And...you were tired when you got back. I thought I could handle it."

"One, I'll try to stop nagging you about going back to the bees. Two, I'm always tired at the end of the day, but you still need to keep me in the loop. And three, no one can handle serious problems alone. No one."

"Really? Then why don't you share all your serious problems, like what went down today?" I was fishing. I knew something had been bothering him since he'd got back.

He sighed and deflated, and looked down at the kitchen floor, which reminded me I had to mop.

"Fair enough. When I contacted Luis today about going in tomorrow I heard Sandy yelling in the background. She's definitely not on board about this." Double poop.

Chapter 35

Tuesday, October 28, 11 am

Things seemed to go better for Abigail today, something close to normal I hoped.

Luis had yet to report in, but I was taking that to mean there were no problems. Meantime I was making plans to attend this evening's memorial service for Jimmy and Judi. This smaller event would be held at a Lutheran Church in the heart of Pinto Springs, unlike the one for the other five boys, which had been at the school gymnasium—and frankly had been a fiasco according to Abigail.

The kids at the school lost it completely in an orgy or grief. Two of them ended up at the emergency room downstairs from Gloria.

I was about to make a call about this evening's event when my phone rang. It was Gerry Patrone calling again—the billionaire's wife.

"Are you ready to sew your hands off again?"

"Hi Gerry, I think so. My neck is much better. How's your family?"

"Up to no good, of course. The boys, that is. I get older by the second chasing them from one after-school event to another."

"They play sports?"

"Well, of course the youngest two don't, but Mack and Jack are always into whatever the seasonal sport is. Football is about to wind down. Then it'll be basketball."

"Mack and Jack. How cute." It was out before I could catch it.

"Thanks. Yeah, Marshall thought it would be fun to name them something we could rhyme. Their four nicknames are Mack, Jack, Zack and Pack. Pack is our own made up 'ack' nickname, he's really Patrick."

"Oh." I hoped that didn't sound critical.

I quickly moved on.

"So what's up?"

"The reason I'm calling is to ask if you've heard anything about Ruth? Well, and of course, Hannah. How's Hannah doing? I can't imagine losing my father in a violent act and then having to watch my mother slowly slip away...."

"She may not be slipping away," I said.

"Oh?"

"No, I...I didn't mean there's anything concrete, just a feeling I have that maybe Ruth will pull through, even though she got the worst of the experience."

"Her heart is stronger. It was a heart attack Paul suffered, wasn't it?"

"Yes." I was feeling foolish, like I was speaking out of turn.

Gerry said, "I mean, I know she's still semi-comatose, but I'm wondering how bad off she really is. Martha Stowall just called me to say her sister Anne would be sewing in Ruth's place Saturday night..." Martha and Anne were two of Victoria's daughters. "...and Martha said she'd heard Ruth was actually slipping."

That took my breath away. I made a mental note to visit Hannah ASAP.

"I don't really know, Gerry. I talked with Hannah Saturday and she didn't say much then. Actually we were conferring about Abigail at the time. I'll try to get over to Hannah's house this week and see how they're doing."

"Okay. Please let me know what's up Rachel. You know, Marsh and I could help. I mean, it's hard to take care of an invalid in your home and Hannah and Peter are living on a shoe string. Peter's only employed halftime, and I hear Hannah's massage business is falling off too. It's the California economy."

"Yes. Things are tough everywhere right now." I was really feeling uncomfortable. Like a gossip.

There was a pause in the conversation, as if Gerry expected me to continue. I waited her out.

"The other reason I called, Rachel, is that Andrea tells me Abigail has started going to school. And she says Gloria is just about nuts over it. Says she called you guys to come pick Abigail up on Friday. How'd that go?"

Not good. Abigail and I had a bad day—including witnessing a gang initiation.

No, I wouldn't tell her that.

I pondered how I should answer. On the one hand, this was a business matter, and client confidentiality was all-important. On the other hand, these bee women have known each other for far longer than I've known them. And on the third hand, I was wishing to become one of them.

But if this was common knowledge among them why was she asking me?

Stalling, I quipped, "Like a hyena hunt in the middle of stampeding wildebeest."

"Huh?"

Okay, that made no sense. But then Gerry's attention went elsewhere as I heard quarreling voices of kids rising in the background. Maybe that was what made me think of wild beasts. When she returned her attention to me again I'd finally decided what to share.

"Actually Gerry, Gloria has formally hired LIRI to help her so I'm not at liberty to discuss details, but...well, let me just say that Abigail isn't transitioning as well as you might hope."

"I wouldn't hope at all, Rachel. She's a genius. She doesn't belong in our dumbed-downed public schools."

"Oh. You, too." Maybe the bee ladies were all in agreement that Abigail shouldn't attend school. But Gerry was a school teacher. I was surprised at her words.

Gerry said, "Yes, me too. I'm afraid I agree with Gloria on this. So, with all due respect to your privacy issues, Rachel, let me again ask you to keep me informed in case there's some way I can help out. Just to put it bluntly, sister, I know private schools are expensive, and I also have avenues through which I can donate assistance to folks in need that don't make it personal. You know, like scholarships and 'volunteer nursing agencies' that show up out of the blue. It's one of the ways we give back to society, Rachel. So let me know what you find out about both Hannah and Abigail, okay?"

Sister. I liked the sounds of that.

"Definitely. But the situation with Abigail is tied up in a legal dispute now, and we're helping her work through it."

"I know. I found out through some of our other contacts that Gloria caved to the ACLU. But she shouldn't have. She has a legal complaint against that school, Rachel. Abigail was legally registered at another school and Pinto Springs has no business fighting her mother over the registration issue."

The toy tussle continued in the background. And I was getting her message. She had contacts. She had opinions.

And I have a contrarian mind, so at that moment I found myself mostly musing on the rights dof kids to have a say in their own childhoods. Furthermore, this was an interesting side trip I had no time for now.

"Let me check with Matt on this, Gerry. But that is not to say I won't share with you to the degree of letting you know it's time to get involved with Hannah and Ruth's situation. Right now I think we have a handle on Abigail's problems."

Those were words I would eat and they would almost poison me.

"Okay." She wasn't happy. This was a *sister* who wasn't used to being told to wait. She continued.

"I also heard from Martha that Eddie Stowall has gotten himself into a pickle back east. Have you heard he's in New York State?"

"Hannah told me he was staying somewhere near Fort Alden. Why, what's happened?"

I turned to stare at the darkened television screen and spotted Wisdom out on the deck, looking toward his wilder cousins again.

"It's all over the news. It sounds like some local union is up in arms over plans to build an Indian casino just a few miles away in a small community called Cherry Valley. They want to call it the Cherry Valley Casino."

I mumbled a response. Wisdom was standing strangely—head way down.

Gerry said, "Eddie's right in the middle of this issue. Apparently a Stowall cousin he's staying with out there on the east coast is heavily into local politics. The union supported the cousin for a councilman's seat in the last election. He didn't win. But now some union thug, a Walter somebody, or somebody Walter, has brought in some bikers to discourage the Indians. At least I think that's what's happening. It's a big mess. Martha is very worried about Eddie. And now it's on the national news."

I tried to remember what Hannah had told me. It didn't sound like it was the same story I'd gotten from her. Then I briefly wondered if Gerry and her billionaire husband were in some way involved in Eddie's business, too.

Whatever the story was, unions, politicians, bikers, investor groups, gangs, maybe they were all the same thing in the end. And I was thinking Eddie could probably take care of himself. Might teach the bikers a few tricks when it came right down to it. I really didn't have warm feelings toward that strange man.

And I was looking at Wisdom with his snout screwed up tight. He was pawing at his nose. He was going to sneeze.

"Listen Gerry, I've got to go. It was good to hear from you."

"What? Oh sure. Can't wait to see you soon. And let me know if Matt needs Tom's...."

But I'd placed the phone down and didn't hear the rest of what she said, as I dashed to wrap my great beast of a dog in my arms and rub his nose gently with the salve the vet had given us. The smell of it reminded me of old fashioned camphor but it took Wisdom's attention away from the pain in his nose. At least for now.

Chapter 36

Tuesday, October 28, Evening

Matt dropped me off at the Pinto Springs Lutheran Church of Promise for the memorial service for accident victim Jimmy and his distraught girlfriend Judi.

I was surprised at the size of the church, and then equally surprised to find the building jammed with hundreds of folks. I began searching the crowds near the entrance where Gloria and Abigail had said they'd meet me. I was eager to confirm that all had gone well her fifth day at high school.

Finally I made out a familiar face. *Uh-oh*. It was the Alphabet Bomber herself, Andrea Kelly, she of the tri-colored red hair and raised body art. Andrea is one of the Secret Quilters members.

In her early twenties, she is the second youngest in our group of eight quilters, so naturally Andrea and Abigail are friends.

The last time I'd spoken with Andrea she dropped every epitaph I knew because she wasn't pleased with my (*unpaid*) work on Ada's investigation. At the time, Andrea was defending Eddie to me. In her mind I was attacking him.

There was no way then that I could reason with her that an exploration of Ada's life must necessarily include her family members—and Eddie was Ada's son.

At any rate, I wasn't sure where I stood with her now, and two large death moths did a loop de loop in my stomach.

It was a *memorial service* after all.

And then I remembered a second reason why Andrea would be here. She wasn't just Abigail's friend; she was a graduate of Pinto Springs high school.

Andrea had been taken in by Victoria in her early teens when her parents rejected her for her sexual orientation. No wonder Andrea has such anger.

Still, this elfish twenty-something had a hard edge.

But my trepidation was unnecessary. When our eyes met she smiled broadly--as if nothing untoward had gone down between us. Ah youth, brief knowledge and briefer memories.

I smiled back and we moved through the noisy crowd toward each other. We attempted to make small talk, until I realized the noise level in the church vestibule was way too high.

Why was I expecting this event to be somber? These folks--I grant you some of them teens--were yukking it up, acting like they were about to see a rock band.

Abigail and Gloria emerged from the crowd a few seconds later. After another brief attempt to communicate, we left the raucous vestibule. Inside the church proper we found room on the same pew. I sat on the outside, next to Gloria.

The tone was more appropriate for the occasion in here, definitely less jovial. Photographs and flowers on the low altar were a reminder of our purpose. And behind them were two closed caskets in dark wood.

"I don't believe the way Californians dress for church," Gloria groused.

I had to agree. Few people wore black, but that change had occurred years ago. Even fewer dressed up for the event. Parents and kids alike looked more like they were attending a school basketball game.

"It's a good thing we came inside. The place is really jammed." Me.

"I hate sitting down front." Gloria.

I looked at her questioningly then followed her pointing finger. We'd landed ourselves just two rows back from one of the grieving families.

Grief was contagious, at least to me, and I was glad I'd thought to carry tissues.

A heavy set boy turned to look back at Abigail with red rimmed eyes. Come to think of it, I'd seen him in the corridor of the hospital Sunday, just before Jimmy died. At the time, I'd thought he was a relative of Jimmy's since he was with Jimmy's parents.

Then I remembered, I'd thought Judi was their daughter and she turned out to have been Jimmy's *girlfriend*.

So who was this boy waving to Abigail?

Across the aisle, Jimmy's parents sat disconsolate— with pictures of Jimmy directly in front of them on the altar and his casket behind them. On our side of the aisle, were Judi's parents, photos of Judi and her casket. And this boy was with them.

So was he Judi's brother?

I couldn't see Abigail's response to his tearful wave. Across the whole setting on the altar was a huge sign, "Jimmy and Judi Together in Heaven."

There was no opportunity for talk during the hour long service of course, unless it was to say kind words about Judi or Jimmy, but afterwards we stood around in the vestibule again, sipping a sweet punch and munching tasteless cookies. It was then I found out how threatened Abigail felt.

"I don't *know* how to calm them down." Abigail was whispering to Andrea as I returned from the ladies.

"Just keep your mouth shut!" Andrea whispered back fiercely. "I just hope it's not too late."

Abigail looked like a frightened deer, her eyes reflecting her fear.

Andrea's eyes had turned to slits as she scanned around them. Stealthy. Suspicious.

So Abigail was still having problems at school.

Gloria returned from somewhere to reclaim her daughter and escort her from the church, taking her by the elbow with a firm hand.

"I'm not ready to leave!"

"I have to get to work, Abigail. We're leaving now."

Gloria's hard stare at Andrea was a clear warning not to interfere by offering to drive Abigail home.

"I have to get back to Victoria," Andrea said quickly.

Was she staying with Victoria Stowall? At the first bee I'd learned she lived in San Diego, in the Hillcrest area.

"Mom! We can't go outside yet."

I looked out the huge glass windows toward the sweeping front lawn where additional groups of people were lingering. Three gang members of Hispanic descent were brazenly glaring back in at us—not twenty feet from the windows. My heart sped up a beat.

"Actually now is the best time for us to leave, Abigail," I said. While there were lots of people still milling around.

Then I spotted our saviors.

Right behind the three Pintos, Matt and Wild Willie Townsend approached like two knuckle-walking silverbacks emerging from a dark forest.

Will was one imposing dude, all two-hundred and fifty pounds of him, with dark looks in more ways than one that went darker when he was angry.

Matt, with his six-foot-two muscular frame and years of practicing intimidation as only a Marine can do, was shoulder to shoulder with the big black man.

The three Hispanic boys must have followed my gaze and they turned to see what I was seeing.

The silverbacks took their menace up six notches toward *peril.*

Timing is everything. Gloria, Abigail, Andrea and I marched shoulder-to-shoulder out the front of the church. I was hoping the boys were getting an important message.

In retrospect, I was badly underestimating both the reach of these gang members and the level of violence in their world.

Chapter 37

Wednesday, October 29, 8:12 am

I have to admit I'm worried by these new fangled communications tools, so seemingly intimate yet so blatantly public. They were foreign and comfortable all at once. *Social networking* meant putting your every casual thought out for the world to see--as if there were no such thing as danger. No such thing as perversion. No such thing as lurking evil.

Having instantaneous ubiquitous communications with the electronic world you would normally reserve for people you know well--an unrestricted chronicling of your daily habits shared universally--was a little like traipsing down Dante's rings, chatting it up with the tortured souls of the underworld. How do you know one of the condemned and trapped might not get loose from their hell-bound state to reach out a claw?

Youngsters don't know this, may never know this fully, but the world turned sharply in the nineteen-nineties. Now we can deceive each other, in terms of presenting false personas of ourselves, with such clever aplomb that it's almost painless. Except for the occasional teen suicide—sometimes caused by online bullying, and sometimes caused by adults posing as teens.

Still we persist in regurgitating the sludge inside our darkest fears and flaunting our most base desires, as if an anodyne to our psychic pains. There are some truly sick people out there in the electronic never-never-land.

Whatever, our first message of the day from aka Louie-Louiee (our second apprentice PI) appeared on my computer screen in the form of an email explaining how to follow him on twitter.com.

Matt watched over my shoulder as we stumbled through the instructions and bumped into subject matter formerly reserved for bedrooms, bathrooms and after hour bars.

By the time we found our way to his page, he'd written several lines.

The "sub" was of course, Abigail. And Luis used a partially abbreviated language reminiscent of some Eastern European country that needs an airlift of vowels for their language. Maybe Bosnia.

Louie_*Louiee* kds half dressd, waitng outsd in cld
7:38 am Oct 29
Louie_*Louiee* sub wlking 2 hmroom. hals jammd.
7:40 am Oct 29
Louie_*Louiee* am stll wtching.
7:41 am Oct 29
Louie_*Louiee* sub wlkng 2 sci, hals jammd again, sme jostlng, no gngs.
7:50 am Oct 29

Matt and I locked eyes.

"Okay, what'd he say?" Matt.

Right. I translated for him.

"Kids half dressed, waiting outside in cold.

"Subject walking to homeroom. Halls jammed.

"I am still watching.

"Subject walking to science, halls jammed again. Some jostling..."

"Okay, okay. I get it. But should we be doing this on a public web page?" Matt.

I shrugged. "That jostling could be those girls who are harassing her."

Luis continued.

Louie_*Louiee* wlkng 2 lib, hals mstly mt. no eyes.
7:53 am Oct 29

"What's he mean 'no eyes'?" Me.

"No one has spotted him. But he should move while the halls are full." Matt.

This time Marine talk. I was getting dizzy.

"Let's see if we can tweet him back."

We looked for a place to write on his page. There wasn't any.

"Is this just a one way conversation?" Matt.

This was definitely not going to work. What if other students stumble upon his page, even if it's new? But then a question came to me.

"How did he get on campus?"

Matt explained that Will had made friends with the school janitor-guards and grounds keepers. Especially a pair named Dell Harper and Evita Wilson.

Another message appeared.

"I think you're right Matt. We should have him text us."

The phone rang and I snatched it up expecting it to be Luis. It was Sandra, his significant. I could feel the young hormones through the phone.

"He dressed like a geek. Even wore a weird vest and pens in his breast pocket. I thought he was supposed to pass as a volunteer?"

"How old did he look?"

"Scary. Like a fifteen year old. Changed his hair, shaved real clean, made me horny as hell. He almost missed the school bus."

I grinned. I loved this girl. I glanced at Matt and his eyebrows danced on his forehead. Kind of like Wisdom's brows when I say "bone?"

Then I wondered how Luis got on the bus. Maybe the bus driver was female.

Chapter 38

Another tweet arrived.

Louie_*Louiee* im shlvng. bleck!
8:38 am Oct 29
Louie_*Louiee* ok, clss of half dressd kids arriving 4 lib-ed. cud be dicey.
8:40 am Oct 29
Louie_*Louiee* im gud, 1 calld me dweek, pushd me over as i squattd. still shlvng. need nee pads. need iPod.
8:49 am Oct 29
Louie_*Louiee* bll ring. odd times. find-follow, ff
9:31 am Oct 29

"Bleck?" Matt.

"Super Mario." He needed to spend more time with his grandchildren. "I don't know how we're going to translate this into our log."

"Exactly as it's written," he said. "It's in code. That could come in handy somewhere down the road. Great denial defense."

I stared at him. "We're going to be sued?"

He shrugged. "Could happen."

I didn't want to think about it.

Again the bell tolled, It was Matt's cell phone buried somewhere else in the house. He went searching. I listened from a distance to his half of the conversation. It was another lawyer looking for divorce spies.

I continued to acquaint myself with Twitter-dom. There were some incredible looking (gay?) men posing in provocative poses as the backgrounds of their pages. At least, I assumed the photos were the actual people who were tweeting. Anyway, I was fascinated. It's a girl thing.

I returned to Luis' page.

Louie_*Louiee* hals hectic, evn explosive. wy wrse than 10 yrs ago.
9:32 am Oct 29
Louie_*Louiee* weird: 3 pintos hssl am. ind. while othr kids wlk away. teachrs ddab.
9:33 am Oct 29

"What's that mean?" Matt was leaning over my shoulder again.

I interpreted. "Halls hectic, even explosive, way worse than 10 years ago. Weird: 3 Pintos hassle American Indian while other kids walk away. Teachers ddab...I'm not sure what ddab means."

Matt put his pondering face on. "*Ddab*. Deaf...deaf, dumb and blind?"

"That fits."

"What are Pintos?" Matt asked.

"The high school Chicano gang. They're everywhere. But where's Abigail in all this?"

Luis answered our question.

Louie_*Louiee* ok, sub is lokng. shodn't lok.
9:34 am Oct 29
Louie_*Louiee* sub def. not gud. own worst enemy?
9:35 am Oct 29

Matt began typing on his cell phone. This was a painful thing to watch. He's literally all thumbs. Ten of them.

I stood and looked at his email message to Luis. "Intercept her."

"How do you know he'll get this? He's on Twitter, not reading his mail. And what about his cover?"

The whole internet realm was making me crazy. Who could keep up with it?

"But it's on his phone.... Okay, maybe you're right. I'll call, to be sure"

But another tweet arrived. And we both knew we couldn't call him.

Louie_*Louiee* phew. bll rng as I severd her i contst. Bck to lib and bleck.
9:36 am Oct 29

"Bell rung as I severed her eye contest. Back to library and bleck." Me.
"Fuck. Stupid girl isn't minding her own business." Matt.
"No, seems not. Maybe Gloria's right." Me.
"What?"
"Gloria doesn't think Abigail can deal with the rest of us mere mortals. She's a perfectionist. She's hypercritical."
Matt sighed and slipped an arm into his jacket.
"Listen Rache, I've got to meet with a guy from the City of Escondido about a job. I'll keep my phone on so I can monitor what's going on. But you'll have to cover this for us. Just keep your cool."
"Aye-aye, sir." He handed me a work order slip which listed the details of his trip to the city so I could make the necessary entries in our log. I kissed him good-bye and returned to my vigil.
Luis' next entries weren't for another hour. I was thinking it was going to be a long day of babysitting the computer. But then more tweets appeared. My anxiety rose with each one.

Louie_*Louiee* bll rng, TG. im suferng i-strain. no offns, R: bossmn is tyrnt. bll saves me. Only break from mnotny when 3 pints mxitup in lib. boss just watchd. What givs?
10:28 am Oct 29

I *was* a little offended at his remark that the librarian was a tyrant, but shelving books is monotonous.
I wanted to text him that school rules don't encourage teacher involvement anymore. I wanted to, but couldn't. Luis had yet to respond to the text email Matt had written. Another message arrived.

Louie_*Louiee* sub talkng 2 sad chub guy. Pintos watch.

10:29 am Oct 29

Chub guy. I wondered if that was the heavy set boy at the memorial.

Louie_*Louiee* ind grl and sub have neighbor lockers. pints again, intrcept this time chub not me. pints r like cockroaches.

10:30 am Oct 29

Louie_*Louiee* bell. back 2 lib 2 wait lunch and bleck.

10:33 am Oct 29

From wherever he was, Matt wrote Luis he'd send in Will. I know this because Luis wrote back on Twitter not to. He'd handle it. Matt wrote: Spoken like a Marine.

At least Luis was checking his emails.

"But he's not a Marine," I whispered miles away in our office.

He was a big kid. I continued to monitor Luis' messages with growing apprehension, knowing we had to get him on the phone and knowing we couldn't or we'd blow his cover.

Chapter 39

She was tiny, as if her height had been badly affected by her diet when she was a child. Or maybe Indians were usually tiny. Her name was Betty Wolftooth, which Abigail thought was *sooo* cool. They were talking about high school and whether or not they liked it. It was hard since they were both freshmen and took a lot of flak from the upper classmen.

Of course, Abigail had made her decision and the devil himself couldn't deter her from staying in school. Betty had moved to a sore topic for her—her older sister.

"She got pregnant two years ago...when she was only fifteen. Never did know who the father was. And now all the boys think I'm going to put out for them, too. Believe me that is the last thing I want. I think I'll have to wait until college to find a nice guy who likes me for who..."

"What happened to your sister?" Abigail said.

"What do you mean?"

"Like, why doesn't she know who the father of her child is?"

The conversation stalled as Betty Wolftooth thought about Abby's question.

"I'm sorry, Betty. That was way too..." Abby began.

"No. It's okay. I was just deciding whether to tell you or not, given what's going on. But maybe a little truth wouldn't hurt with all this mass hysteria around us.

"You know, Jimmy Winters wasn't such a nice boy as they're making him out. Well, maybe he was in some ways, but...he's the one who ruined my sister. They were in the same class, and she had a big crush on him. Well, one day he noticed, and asked her out."

Betty Wolftooth shook her head disapprovingly and looked around. Abigail did too, looking for those nasty girls. But there were dozens of kids hanging out in the quad, as they called it, eating lunch and gossiping. Betty continued.

"Jimmy and Judi had always been an item, maybe since they were babies. So my sister...her name is Karen...she was stunned when Jimmy asked her out. Any way they, like, *dated* for a while. And then all of a sudden he quit her.

"Karen spent the rest of that summer crying her eyes out. And then the phone began ringing. All of Jimmy's friends were asking her out.

"My dad thought it was cool, having a popular daughter, but my mom, well, she just kept quiet. Mom never even got to high school. She's worked in the fields from the time she was eleven, and she'd been pregnant with our oldest brother by the time she was fourteen. That's what she told us anyway, after...after Karen turned up pregnant."

Working the fields as a child? Where did this happen, Abigail wondered. Surely not in America.

And why did Betty's dad want her to date? Abigail thought if she had a dad anymore, he'd be against her dating.

"Not long ago my sis told me Jimmy had only dated her so he could lose his virginity. She swears they never did it, though. And she said she didn't do it with those fast-handed friends of his either. At least not at first. In the end, one of them got to her. I won't tell you which one. It doesn't matter now anyway. He's dead. And afterwards my sis ran away. My mom is taking care of the baby."

Abigail could feel her mouth was catching flies and she consciously closed it. Wow. Double wow.

"And, like those boys are after you now?"

"No, not those boys. Those boys were all in that car accident, or they've graduated or something. The ones chasing after me now are their younger brothers. You know how it is."

They needed to change tracks, Abigail knew. This was too painful for Betty. And too weird for her.

"Sure, I know. So you plan to go to college?"

"Of course."

She was insulted and Abby quickly added, "I don't want to. Maybe an art school somewhere. But even that would be stultifying. All they do at college is brain wash you into thinking just like them...most of them are a bunch of dried up old hippies still trying to justify their misspent youths. Really, I'd rather travel, visit places I can paint, visit other artist colonies."

"Misspent youths?"

Betty looked askance at Abigail. Abigail grinned foolishly.

"My mother's phrase. My mom is an immigrant, from Ukraine. She ran away and came to America in her late teens. She's old-fashioned."

"Does she work?"

"Yeah. She's a nurse, actually the head nurse, at the local hospital. In the ICU."

"*Really*. Wow. I was thinking I might want to be a nurse someday."

"You'd be good. You should pursue that." Abigail said. She tried to hide the sense of pride she was feeling in her mother's career after Betty had shared her own mom's abbreviated education. But secretly, she didn't see how anyone so short could be a nurse. How could she reach the patients up on those elevated beds?

"Anyway, I don't think we can afford a college education for me now anyway...now that my dad, well..." She didn't want to tell Betty that her dad was still alive and a complete *coward.* She didn't want to tell her anything about her dad.

Truth? Her lame father would never pay for her education anyway, even though he could probably get her something from the government because he was permanently disabled.

More truth? Her mother *desperately* wanted her to get a four-year college degree.

Betty said, "Your dad died huh? Sorry. My dad is still alive and he's still working in the fields, except when he can get an odd job helping someone with their gardening business. Where do you think you want to go to art school...or, find an art colony?"

Abigail didn't bother to correct Betty's misunderstanding about her father.

"Artists' Colony. Well, Paris of course, that would be my first choice, near the Sorbonne. You can find them near any major art school really, but just not *in* the art schools. They sort of hang around the fringes doing the real experimental stuff. That's what I want to explore. But the new center of art is really in South East Asia. There's a real revival going on there. The people of that region are so smart and they've been so repressed and stultified. Maybe Cambodia."

Abigail watched Betty raise her eyebrows. Surprise? Reproach? Was she sounding too...out-of-time...*geekish*. Like she'd been living in a time-capsule?

"Who's repressing them?"

Was she kidding? Was she being ironic?

"Oh, you know, just old practices and poverty, and of course some pretty stultifying dictatorships. My mother fled a Communist country, you know? She hated it."

Abby had just learned this new word, stultifying and realized suddenly she was over using it.

"*Why?* I think we need a dictatorship. I think democracy is a dumb idea that clearly isn't working. We'd be way better off if we had some benign leader. We need a movement for the little people."

Abigail stared at her in disbelief. Under this tiny girl's head of beautiful black hair was a radical's brain? Or was she a rebel...?

Or was Betty toying with her. That thought came just after she blurted out, *"You want us to live under a dictator's thumb?"*

She glanced around, realizing she'd spoken too loudly. My god, she was sounding dumb.

But then Betty went off on a tangent that almost had Abigail believing her.

"What's the difference? We're under the thumbs of a handful of billionaire capitalists now. And some of them are as stupid as those college professors you just talked about. My mother says the fat cat rich guys left America behind in the nineties. Just up and left the country, taking all their wealth with them. They all just moved their companies to poor countries where they could pay slave wages. And now look where we are."

Abigail was flabbergasted. What she'd really wanted was to head the conversation to something not so controversial or so personal.

Then the bell rang, saving her ass.

"Cripes, I really hate the sound of that bell. Rattles my nerves. Come on, Betty, we better get inside."

Truth. The bell made her feel they were like cattle being herded down a chute to their deaths. And then short little Betty took the lead!

"Get moving Abigail, your mind numbing education awaits you. It's worse here than in any college you'll never attend," the Native American quipped as she marched them back inside.

Way too late Abigail realized she should have argued that the country hadn't begun as a democracy, it had begun as a republic, where the people got one carefully controlled vote for their representative in government and then they were supposed to step back and let the chosen leaders make the decisions.

Democracy was an aberration only recently evolved, mostly in California with the excessive use of propositions.

What she really should have said was...but then the door to her classroom closed behind her.

Abigail had no idea who this girl was. One thing was for sure, this was no meek, ignorant farmer's daughter. And maybe Abigail had just learned the most important cultural lesson of the day, from the mouth of a radicalized Native American—she was a babe in the woods and the wolves were everywhere and everyone.

Chapter 40

Abigail's mind drifted in the boring English class. She spent most of the hour thinking about her conversation with Betty Wolftooth--until she bumped into a painful memory of her own.

Not that Abigail had a sister but she had a close— *really close*—girlfriend once. And that girlfriend was the reason she'd run off to Pinto Springs High.

Without meaning to, her close girlfriend had betrayed their lifelong friendship.

Her name was Gracie, and Abby and Gracie had been closest friends since...well, since before she could remember. Back when they were five Gracie had saved her life by pulling her back from a bad fall. But when they were both thirteen—just this past summer in fact— Gracie betrayed her.

She'd come over for a sleepover at Abigail's house and while they were both sitting at her kitchen counter in the very wee hours of the morning Gracie shared something terrible with her.

"Abby?"

"Yeah." Abby's mouth was full of a chocolate filled donut. She was hoping the chocolate would help keep her up. It was already past one and Gracie seemed to have an endless supply of energy.

"I was wondering if...if maybe you could tell me something."

"Sure. What?" She swallowed hard trying to force the lump of moist dough stubbornly refusing to go down her gullet into her stomach. Next bite would be smaller. Then she turned a serious eye toward her friend.

"What's on your mind?"

Gracie was nervously pulling the outer crust off her plain donut bit by bit.

Abby looked around as if maybe her mom or Nana might suddenly be seen lurking in the dark shadows of the living room, waiting to hear Gracie's secret.

It was a secret, wasn't it?

"Well, I've never told you this, but...."

She stalled again.

"Go ahead Gracie. You can tell me anything remember? We're best of friends."

"Right. But, well, I've never told anyone this before, so...."

"Goes without saying, blood-sisters never rat on each other."

They'd become blood-sisters when they were eight or nine. It was a childish act of bonding that they'd seen done in some long ago movie where you sliced your palms and then grasped each other's hands as if in a handshake and pressed your blood into each other's veins.

Gracie offered her a meager smile then lowered her head and peeled more donut skin.

"What is it Gracie?"

Without looking up, her lifetime friend said, "I was raped."

Abigail about fell off her stool. She quickly glanced at Nana's door. It was closed, but she knew the old woman to have dogs' ears, so she grabbed Gracie's hand and pulled her off onto the porch where they could huddle on the couch.

"When!"

"Oh, a long time ago now. Almost a year. It was last summer, actually."

"And you never told me?"

"I...couldn't. I was...." Gracie began picking at the skin around her thumbnail now that she had no donut to worry. Abigail grabbed her hands in hers to still them.

"How? What happened? Who..?"

Gracie sighed deeply, as if a great burden was leaving her chest.

"I was out wandering near our Lake Hope house. My parents were entertaining, and well, you know how I've told you it's so lonely up there, all adults all drunk all of the time."

"So you went for a walk what time?"

"It was late, after dark. Maybe after ten. This guy, I suddenly realized he was following me."

"Oh God, Gracie. Who?"

"I don't know. I've never seen him before. But he was wearing a trench coat, like really weird, you know, because it was hot and all, the middle of summer. Even up at the lake. And...suddenly he threw it open and he was naked!"

"Jesus! What did you do?"

She looked up with her big brown sheep eyes now filling with tears. "Nothing."

Abigail grew animated with the urgency to hear what had happened and was waving her arms around now, and said, "So you screamed...and you ran? Right?"

Gracie just shook her head no, then looked back down at her hands in her lap as if wondering what new part to peel.

"Didn't you tell your folks?"

She shook her head no.

"Gracie! The cops, didn't you call the cops?"

She shook her head no. Then her whole body shook. She was sobbing.

Abigail wrapped her friend in her arms and held her still, whispering, 'Oh God, oh God' over and over in her ear. What else could she say?

Finally they both calmed, and sat holding hands again, knee to knee, head to head, in the dark shadows out on Abigail's sun porch.

"The thing is, Abby, well, I'm just so afraid...."

"What?"

"Well, I thought with all your experience you'd know...."

Abigail could feel herself stiffen but she wasn't sure why.

"What..?"

"You know, I was wondering--could I still have a baby?"

"What?!"

"Well, I just am afraid I'm still going to turn out to be pregnant, you know...."

"Gracie! It takes nine months. I thought you said it was a year ago."

"It was. Almost. So you think...you're sure? I couldn't...."

"Wait a minute, what experience? What do you mean with all my..." But she never finished her question.

Abigail was thinking she must surely mean her experience through her mother the nurse. And it was true that Abigail knew a lot about medicine, but no, Gracie meant something entirely different.

"You know, you and Barry...."

"Barry?"

Well wasn't this the night of surprises,

"B.O. Barry? Jesus, Gracie, we're just geek friends! You know, World of Warcraft friends. We talk on Skype, help each other. What are you thinking?"

It might have all been forgiven and forgotten except the look on Gracie's face said it all.

And then Gracie added, "Everyone knows about you and Barry, Abby. And, what I need to know is with your experience and all...."

Abigail shut down the memory. It was too painful to review further. They had gone to bed quickly after that, but from that point on her friendship with Gracie was caput. And so was her friendship with the rest of the homeschool group.

Nasty gossips.

B.O. Barry, for crying out loud!

Then she'd met Buddy at the art classes and as the saying goes, the rest was history.

Chapter 41

At twelve thirty-six the doodoo hit the fan. For ease and efficiency, Luis went on Twitter.

Louie_*Louiee* lookng 4 sub at locker.
12:36 am Oct 29
Louie_*Louiee* still looking. Noise round bend.
12:37 am Oct 29
Louie_Louiee kids chantng. fight! am movng. no sign of indian.
12:38 am Oct 29
Louie_*Louiee* tchers runnng away. not gud.
12:38 am Oct 29
Louie_*Louiee* in nxt hall. am movng. crwds thck.
12:38 am Oct 29
Louie_*Louiee* sum1 on the grnd. gang boys fists n screams.
12:39 am Oct 29
Louie_*Louiee* krst its her! they have her dwn, im movng in, send will.
12:42 am Oct 29

They have her down!
I let Matt call Will, and raced to the garage. As I drove up the driveway there was one last message.

Louie_*Louiee* gang leadr sez how come u no learn lil 1? nice kds hlped. sub up but hrt. gang leadr oldr. sum1 calld hm Manada.
10:43 am Oct 29

I took off from the house in Escondido like a Peregrine falcon in a hunting dive. Twenty-three minutes later I was in Pinto Springs. I was setting new records on the winding back road. More than once I came close to running off the road into oblivion.

Almost as bad was navigating the suddenly protective high school campus. I had to pass through three layers of security before gaining access to the administration area. Fortunately, people knew who I was and quickly accepted that I was there in lieu of Abigail's mom. I hoped it wasn't Luis who'd smoothed my path. I wanted him to stay under cover as long as he could.

For all I knew, his cover was already blown.

When I met up with Abigail she was in worse shape than I feared. Sitting on the little bed at the back of nurse Kaplan's office, Abigail was bloodied and still blubbering. Her blouse had been torn so badly she had to hold it together with both hands. One knee was bandaged with the pant leg rolled up. One eye was swelling. A trickle of blood still oozed from one nostril.

She was alternately sobbing about how the other kids had seen her breast and growing agitated that the Indian girl was still missing.

She burst off the bed and into my arms. This time she would let me take her home to her grandmother for the rest of the day. The vice principal was nodding his head as I led her away.

I'd searched for the infamous Learner and Mosby, aka Pestilence and Famine, on my way in and again now as we scurried down the empty halls. Unfortunately, I distrusted the two Pinto Springs detectives as much as I did Eddie Stowall, and I was afraid they'd take her from me.

This was all way over the top and I knew it. But after the scene at the hospital with Abigail when Jimmy died I may have needed to redeem myself to Gloria.

I wasn't surprised the detectives weren't here. This case hadn't risen to a level where they would've been brought in anyway. But I wasn't relieved at their absence. Their appearance on the scene would have meant the invisible wall that universally separates municipal jurisdictions had been breached. And that would be good because the school officials were clearly overwhelmed by their gang troubles.

School systems are leery of police involvement in their affairs, because as recipients of vast amounts of property tax dollars they are very invested in maintaining the story (fiction?) that schools are doing a fine job of educating and keeping our kids safe.

When I got to my car Luis was standing by it, thankfully unscathed. I put Abigail in the car, and closed the door so we could talk.

He then told me what I already knew.

"The Pinto Springs cops are here. They're in the office with Forsythe discussing the missing Indian girl. One of them is a captain, maybe now we'll get some real protection on campus. The principal has a lawyer standing behind the desk with him." He shook his head and made a disgusted face. "What's the damn world coming to?"

I couldn't tell him. He seemed relieved but I couldn't support his reaction either.

"That Indian girl is still missing. I'm going out after her as soon as Will gets here."

"Matt approved that?"

He wouldn't make eye contact.

"That's not our job, Luis."

I couldn't believe I was even saying this, but I had to. Luis could run into things he was in no way prepared for, and Sandy was figuratively lurking at the back of my brain--looking over my shoulder to make certain I didn't imperil her man.

"So you be certain to wait until Matt arrives too. Okay?"

"Yeah. It's just, every minute counts in kidnapping cases."

I glanced at Abigail. She was half sleeping, her head against the car window, unaware of Luis comment.

"We don't know she's been kidnapped, Luis. Maybe she just ran off embarrassed. Maybe she's back home with her parents as we speak."

But she wasn't.

Chapter 42

8 pm, Wednesday

Matt arrived home long after I'd eaten. He looked at me, still sitting at the dining table, and silently went away down the hall. Fifteen minutes later he came back with a change of clothes and his hair wet.

His absence at my table had brought back lonely memories of the years we'd been separated during our marriage. He'd been sent away on Med cruises, a second tour in Vietnam and finally Iraq, all of which had accumulated to about five years of our marriage.

I couldn't imagine how young military people were coping today. Iraq and Afghanistan were pulling families apart at least fifty percent of their lives.

I reheated Matt's meal and placed it before him. He poured himself a large glass of red. I was doing hot tea tonight. I still had a few calls to make.

"They can't find her. She's obviously been kidnapped. Her parents don't know where she is and they insist she isn't a runaway. But the goddamned authorities won't call in an Amber Alert. Some bullshit about waiting twenty-four hours. The school is holding them back." Matt took a bigger sip of wine.

"I wondered why I didn't see it on the news. Are you going around them?"

Wrong question. He was already seething. He choked down some chicken. I waited. Finally he shook his head.

"Too costly. I need them right now for Abigail. Besides, I don't think it'll help tonight anyway. Not up in those mountain towns. Will and Luis canvassed the surrounding neighborhoods of the school, did a little door-to-door. But they're white collar. She won't be there if she's still alive. We need to get into the barrio."

"You think..." I couldn't even say the word 'dead' lest I make it true.

"No, no, of course not. I'm just pissed. Damn principal is the worst bureaucrat I've seen in years. His job consists of do nothing and look busy."

He sipped some more wine. Finally I added my two cents worth.

"Abigail told me she knows Betty Wolftooth."

"Yeah? How long has she known her?"

"She met her yesterday and had lunch with her today, just before they were jumped in the hall. She also told me girl gang members were involved in the attack. But it was all Hispanics. The white girls she'd overheard in the bathroom were nowhere to be seen."

"The worst thing is the teachers did nothing. They ran the other way." Matt stuck a couple of fries in his mouth.

"I know. I read Luis' online stuff. Abigail doesn't know any of this—that Betty is missing or that the teachers turned their backs--but maybe she should." My voice trailed off, unable to censor my fears.

"You're thinking she shouldn't be there?"

"I don't know what I'm thinking, Matt. I'm just frightened for her now."

"Yeah. But it isn't all bad. Luis told me three of the school soccer players helped him rescue Abigail--a Hispanic kid, a black and a white. Will's got their names so he can connect with them, maybe tomorrow. They might come in handy later--help us reach into the different neighborhoods.

He finished his meal and retreated to the living room. There was nothing more to say. I went to the kitchen to finish cleaning up.

Around nine my cell phone rang. It was Andrea Kelly and I braced for an onslaught of swear words. But she was calm.

"I tried reaching Abigail. Nana answered, said something in Ukrainian I took to mean Gloria was at the hospital and Abigail was in her room. Then she hung up.

What gives?" The pixie was abrupt when she wasn't being dirty mouthed.

But I was wondering why she'd called me.

"What have you heard?"

"Well, Mary said something. She's heard there was a fight on campus."

Mary was one of the three daughters of Victoria Stowall who owned and operated the Apple FIXation store in Julian, California, to the north of Pinto Springs.

But more importantly, Mary was also aunt to Eddie. Eddie shot me a couple of weeks ago.

"Are you living with Victoria now?"

"What? No. I just visit. She's got Sarah living there now."

Sarah was Victoria's fourth and youngest girl, the one who was brain damaged in early childhood—and therefore did not work with her three older sisters.

I remembered hearing Sarah and the other Stowall daughters making noises out in the hall during the prior bee. Sarah had been upset at the time and her complaints sounded more childlike than adult.

"So are you gonna' tell me?" the Pixie demanded.

"Abigail had a run-in with the Pintos gang at school today. She got hurt. I took her home."

The conversation lagged for a minute. I out-waited her.

Finally Andrea said, "Why don't you try? Nana can cough up a couple of English words when she has to. Try to reach Abigail. She trusts you, Rache. She told me you were a straight shooter and you were good to her. You did what she asked and didn't rat on her."

Matt was the only one who ever called me Rache—at least that I'd noticed. I tried to remember if Andrea had ever even met Matt. I didn't think so. I smiled.

"Okay. I'll give her a try."

"I keep looking for the Amber Alert on that Indian girl. What's up with that?"

So Andrea knew that the Native American girl Betty was missing. Then she must have known about the fight. She was testing me to see if I'd be straight with her, too.

I began to feel manipulated.

I looked over at Matt and took a few steps out onto the back deck. It was chilly but not cold down here near sea level. Wisdom accompanied me. It was his job to protect me from the wild donkeys, baboons and opossums that hang out in our neck of the woods.

I stroked the silk behind his large ears as I talked.

"Cops won't call it in."

"Shit!"

Okay, I knew sooner or later she'd start talking like a Marine. Just cover your ears.

"Can Matt..?"

I cut her off.

"I already went there. He says it'd damage his relationship with the cops and Abigail needs all the connections she can get."

"*Fuck.* What if I call Gerry and she calls her son Tom?"

"Still might backfire. Matt thinks we wait until morning and then act. I want you to trust his judgment, Andrea. But if you can figure out why the cops won't act on these cases, let me know."

"Me? Figure out cops? Well, of course there is the ever virulent Stowall clan influence in and outside of the cops and sheriffs. But that wouldn't be it."

"No. Maybe the school is dragging their feet to keep the truth out of national newspapers. This one is sure to go there eventually."

"Oh yeah. Bad press."

My dinner was turning in my belly, a sure sign I wasn't making the right moves. But I hadn't a clue what the right moves were right now.

Matt blew me off the deck with a quiet voice that stirred my hair and sent chills down my spine.

"Hang up."

I said a quick good-bye to Andrea and turned to face him.

You might think I find it frightening when he acts real tough like that. I don't. I find it sexy. I controlled the inner grin overlaying my anxiety at getting caught sharing our business with Andrea.

But Matt's mind was elsewhere.

"You've got to convince Abigail to stay home tomorrow. I'm going around them in the morning. That girl deserves an Amber Alert."

"You're going to confront the cops?" He didn't answer me.

"I'm going to bed. I'm beat. Come in from the cold." My libido limped back into its hidey-hole somewhere in my brain.

I sighed and stepped back into the kitchen. I really didn't believe I could talk Abigail into anything. And I was beginning to fear that she had arrived on campus at the beginning of a serious sociological change in the Pintos Gang.

Social Worker Latisha—who'd been cooling her heels in the Prince's outer office--made a point of telling me she'd never seen the gang so brutal, adding that there were no other missing children. She hoped we could nip the problem in the bud.

I was thinking we had a full grown Venus Flytrap on our hands.

Chapter 43

I called Abigail to see if she was okay. Nana handed her the phone immediately. Guard dog Nana. Good for her. But then the dog in Peter Pan came to mind and all sense of security evaporated.

The timidity in Abigail's voice told me the extent of her trauma. The vivacious, outgoing Abigail was submerged, held down by emotions I needed to help her understand. So I probed her for facts.

"Tell me what happened, Abigail. Tell me everything you remember because we need to solve this puzzle."

She paused then haltingly answered.

"They whispered to me. They kept whispering to me as they tore my blouse off, disgusting things...." Her voice melted away like a pale fog.

"What did they say, hon?"

"Awful things. What they wanted to do. What they would do soon...."

"Go on, hon. Tell me specifically. They may have let something slip, something we can use."

The silence extended to minutes, then hours. I thought she'd hung up. But finally she went on.

"I won't repeat it, it was disgusting *crap*!"

Anger. Good.

"But, all the while I heard their sister group, a gang of Hispanic girls, beating on Betty. I...I turned...they beat her face...." She started sobbing again.

My heart was in my throat. I thought to stop but knew if I let Abigail go on she'd better avoid a deeper slide into depression later. She needed to talk it out and I might be the only one she could do that with right now.

"Did they say anything about who they were? Did they mention gang names? Try to remember their exact words, Abigail."

"The one...the one on top...."

"The one on top of you...." I repeated her words slowly.

"He was older. He wasn't a boy."

This was what Luis had implied in his urgent message to us. He'd also given Matt a brief description of the guy as they began searching for the girl--a Hispanic male, medium height, medium weight, black hair, no facial hair, no visible scars.

It could have been any Hispanic male on earth.

"How much older?"

"He was a man. An adult. Maybe in his late twenties or thirties. And he smelled bad. Like his insides were rotting. And...there was something else...."

She stopped again. I didn't think in the middle of this trauma she would have noticed much more. She continued without my bidding.

"I can't remember. I think...I don't know, maybe I saw a tattoo, because the letter H keeps popping into my mind. I remember! He'd rolled down his eye lid, pulled down like he was trying to remove a particle of dirt, but then he held it there so I could see...I think...I think it held tattooed letters, M and H—really close together. Is that possible?"

MH.Luis had said his name was Manolo. So now maybe we knew his last name started with H.

From my many hours of research I knew tattoos could be done anywhere on your body if you could endure the pain. But I didn't need to share that with her.

"I don't know, Abby."

And finally the dam broke and the timidity was washed away.

"I hate him! I'll always hate him. I'll never let him have power over me, or any part of me!"

"Good girl. You keep saying that to yourself, Abigail. Say it aloud, so you can hear the affirmation in your own voice. He is nothing more than a piece of evil you bumped into. And that is over."

"Yes. But Betty, have they found her? I'm so terribly afraid for her."

I thought about dodging the question, but trust was vital.

"Not yet."

I hoped Matt was in the other room working his way around the blockage in the PS cop shop, getting the Amber Alert up as I spoke instead of waiting for morning.

"What else did this bad dude say?"

Abigail grew more thoughtful. "I'm not sure if I heard him right, but...when one of the others, one of the high school gang members, reached over and started...started playing with my...*I can't*...my breast. He played with my breast with his filthy fingers."

She stopped.

"More crap," I said. "What did you hear," I encouraged.

"Okay. I get what you're doing. I'm okay. Anyway, the guy on top of me, he barked at the high school kid.

"That's just what it sounded like too, not words, a sharp *bark* sound. Then he sneered at the gang member and told him...he said, 'Never mess with the merchandise, cacahuete.'

"I looked it up, that means peanut. Peanut is what they call a beginner gang member, but the high school guy was the leader of the gang, of the Pintos. It should have been a real insult to him but he just jumped back like he'd been slapped, you know, by a parent taking a swing at him."

A sudden sense of urgency filled my chest. There was definitely something more serious going on here.

"Listen to me Abigail, this is important. Matt's going to push for an Amber Alert for Betty. Don't share this, because he wants to keep his role in this below the radar. He's afraid it might come back to hurt you. And..."

How could I word this so she wouldn't rebel? So she'd believe me.

"I know. He wants me to stay home tomorrow because it will be more dangerous. And I know you have a guy--I think he's your apprentice, *Luis?*--watching out for me. I know he'll be in more trouble too.

"But Rachel, if all we ever do when the bad guys come looking for us is run and hide aren't we encouraging them? Aren't we giving them permission to attack us? No. You tell your Marine husband I'm not a coward. I'm going back to school."

Half of me was disappointed, half of me was elated.

She was constantly amazing me with her maturity. Or was this something else? Was she just clinging to her stubborn side?

Then again maybe that was why we had stubborn sides—so we'd stick to our guns.

And off course somewhere lurking in our chromosomes were the genes of a mule, so....

But I was digressing. Big time. Time to hit the rack.

"What about your mom?"

"I haven't talked to her yet. But it isn't her decision. It's mine."

I spent a few minutes after the call arguing with myself over whether a thirteen year old should be allowed to direct her own life.

I didn't win.

Chapter 44

Thursday, October 30, 7:30 am

Matt rattled the newspaper while changing pages during breakfast. We don't often share a sit-down breakfast, but the weather on our deck was particularly mild this morning, so here we were with Wisdom moving anxiously around our almost empty plates.

His excited snuffling made me worry he might begin sneezing. I put my plate down for him to lick.

"Have you been following this Cherry Valley thing?" Matt asked.

"What? Oh, you mean the gang problems where Eddie is. I don't remember telling you."

"You didn't. I'm reading a newspaper article."

"The article is on Eddie's gang?"

"No."

He was giving me that look again. I was lost, so I just reached for his part of the newspaper and began reading.

"Good grief. There's been a massacre? When did this happen?"

Another look.

"Seventeen seventy-eight. Read it again. Past the first paragraph."

Sarcasm.

I did. My face reddened. The Cherry Valley Massacre had indeed occurred during the American Revolution. The news headline and first paragraph was about the ironic comparison of events over two hundred years ago and today's contentious squabble over the planned Seneca Indian casino in Cherry Valley.

"Oh, here it is. Monday night. Sounds like some local gang joined forces with the Seneca Indians casino group and overran the PTA meeting at Fort Alden Elementary.

They scared a bunch of women and children. It doesn't say Eddie was involved." Me.

Sarcastic stare.

I ignored him and happily continued.

"But the good news is the casino is still going forward. Apparently the Senecas are upset over the local government attempts to block their plans to pilfer seniors' hard earned social security checks, so they brought in some ex-military types on bikes. Eddie's one of them. But *of course* that isn't mentioned here. In fact, none of them are named. Don't you wonder why?"

"PTA meetings aren't high on the list of important topics in Cherry Valley? The newspaper publisher is a part owner of the planned casino? Sloppy reporting?" Dripping sarcasm.

I grinned and continued to paraphrase the article to him.

Then Hannah called, exhibiting her mother's scary capabilities and interrupting my monologue.

Matt was reading the sports section anyway, which I had been reading before he so cleverly distracted me with the News of the Back Side section.

"Mary just called me and said a hysterical Eddie called her a couple of minutes ago..."

"Hysterical?"

Matt arched his eyebrows. I put her on speakerphone.

"...and she said he was caught in the middle of a fight that wounded dozens. And yes, he was hysterical-- Eddie still has a lot of those female drugs he was forced to take in his system. Besides, it wasn't just fisticuffs. A couple of the so-called Indians—more like drunken bikers--tried exacting revenge in the old fashioned way, by scalping an old geezer who fought back. Apparently a lack of hair saved him. Mary says the papers are concealing the truth. They don't want anti-Indian sentiment to spread across the country, possibly causing more pro-and anti-casino riots." That was when she burst into laughter and lost all control.

"Anti-Indian? What...?"

She was laughing too hard to hear me. Finally she came back to the phone.

"It's all over the internet if you know where to look. Try searching under Cherry Valley messacre—with an e. There are two videos circulating of the event already, and it literally happened hours ago."

Matt quipped. "Is it time to buy stock in this casino?"

That sent Hannah off on another round of giggles. Finally she stopped and told me what I really wanted to hear.

"Anyway, you'll be happy to hear they're moving Eddie even farther away. Mary says he's on his way to Boston soon. Stay tuned for another problem to begin brewing there, maybe tomorrow. Oops! *Deborah,* what have I said about using that tone of voice with your brother?"

And she was off to tend to a skirmish of her own, leaving me with a head full of questions I never got to voice. She definitely needed to cut back on the coffee. Zen Hannah was turning into Hyper Hannah.

Chapter 45

I still had questions I wanted to research about Eddie and his gang activities, but Matt and I needed to prepare for a very long day reorganizing our office. We'd scheduled a meeting with Dom Jacob & Sons weeks ago. Dom is the recognized business expert in reorganizing small businesses in our area, and we were lucky enough to have the man himself coming to work with us. We hoped to be done by noon.

I struggled with the decision whether to wear my neck brace or just try to gut it out, but common sense got the best of me and I put the damn thing on. It would be grueling enough lugging around file folders without stabs of pain in my neck.

Dom was of course fully licensed and bonded. Dom, himself, had been in business for over thirty years without a complaint. But to be certain no confidences were jeopardized, I had spent some of yesterday attaching those heavy duty black file clips to every file in our drawers. Dom would only get to see the title of the file.

Unfortunately most of them were the names of our clients. There was little we could do about this aspect of risk. We just had to assume Dom was only here to reorganize our filing system and our office procedures, and yes, even to move furniture around. Not to spy.

Matt was only partially onboard with what he sometimes considered my insane librarian's need to organize things, especially information. But he hadn't said no. I was keeping my fingers crossed that he didn't just halt the process halfway through.

Dom and a helper, a big strapping guy I could halfway hear Matt's brain-wheels churning over—he would be an excellent partner to Will Townsend—

arrived right on schedule at eight a.m.. In other words, helper guy was huge.

Eight a.m. is an ungodly hour to begin work. I believe it's half the reason why some people opt out of working for a living all together. My brain was still back in REM land. At least for now I was calm. The anxiety attack would come later in the morning and it would be over Abigail's safety.

We'd been working hard for several hours, making great progress. Matt had really gotten into the whole thing, and even taken the project over completely from me. I let him. When he did organize, he was really very good at it. Then came a call which stopped us in our tracks. Almost.

The call was from Luis.

We had decided that Luis should use a less public communication than twitter.com this time. So he was text messaging us by cell. The sound of the phone raised the hairs on my arms--but this message was a simple update telling us lunchtime for Abigail and her 'friend' was about to commence.

Interesting thing about this hair-raising activity, if you thought about it in animal terms--like a dog or gorilla--you could see that it was all about making yourself look bigger, more threatening, because you sensed danger nearby. So I suppose the hairs on my back were standing, too. But they're so small I didn't notice. In fact, I couldn't really swear I even have hair on my back. I should probably check.

These are the silly thoughts that sweep through my brain during tense moments.

This would be a second opportunity for trouble to come Abigail's way, the first having been before classes in the morning. And that had gone fine.

Actually after yesterday we knew anytime she was out of class she was in danger.

I was left wondering who her friend was, but asking him questions wasn't a good idea. It could take his mind off his job.

So I turned the phone for Matt to see and concentrated on Dom Jacob's continued stream of directions. I was dutifully taking notes. His helper was shifting files in the background on changes we had already agreed to.

Anyway, I turned the cell phone to vibrate only. The ring was upsetting. Like an alarm.

Seconds later the cell phone vibrated on the wooden desk and I looked down to read, "lunch bell. sub heading out, am right behind her."

My heart beat a little faster. If anything happened, we'd be an hour getting there. I cursed myself for not thinking about this and having Will stand by somewhere in Pinto Springs. It took a handful of seconds for the next text to arrive.

"sub is stalled. watching another indian girl + pintos. friend is encouraging her to move on. am holding back."

Matt moved next to me and began reading the texts with me. Dom's chatter came to a stop. He probably could feel the tension in our home office. Plus we were both staring at the phone.

More vibrations.

"sub has j of a complex. pintos tormenting Indian, teach's closing doors again!"

Abigail did indeed have a Joan of Arc complex. My heart went out to her. I was capable of that same delusion. My guess—it was in our genes. And the teachers needed to be fired for dereliction of duty.

Then again, gangs were hazardous to deal with.

Then the messages stopped. We tried to return out attention to our project. Had just enough time to get our thoughts into organizing again.

Vibrations.

"indian down! send will. forcing sub from hallway. send willi to follow Pintos and indian.>

Sweet Jesus. Follow them! They were taking the Indian girl away?

My heart leapt into my throat, saving me from an unseemly verbal outburst that would have driven Dom

Jacob out the door. My j of a complex was leaping to the fore.

I poked Matt and he read again, pulled out his own phone and sent a message to William Townsend to assist Luis Lewis at Pinto Springs High School. But this was Will's day off and we didn't even know where he was.

My neck tightened another notch and I straightened, telling myself to relax. But my eyes constantly flew to the tiny LED screen on our desk.

It was twelve more minutes of now useless instruction from Dom before Luis texted for his last time this day, during which a troop of miniature silverbacks ran offense against my stomach lining. But when it came it only ratcheted up our concern.

"pintos made me. abby safe."

We still had no idea whether Will had received his text, or what was happening to this second Indian girl, so my heart settled on a fast trot until Dom Jacobs finally left. We needed to get up to Pinto Springs and see what was going on ourselves. The reorganization project would have to be continued another day.

Chapter 46

At noon, we thanked Dom and helper and said our goodbyes.

Not long after, Luis made a live call to calm some of our fears. Abigail was unharmed and Rosalia Fousat, the second Indian girl, had returned to class after briefly disappearing down a hall with two Pintos. Though scared out of her wits, she appeared to be unharmed.

Maybe one of those teachers I'd been thinking bad thoughts about had taken action before the Pintos could spirit her away. Maybe those same Pintos would try ripping her away from campus again later. My sense of urgency was not allayed. We needed to get up the mountain.

Will was still unreachable. We were hoping he was now disguised as a guard/janitor somewhere on campus but Luis hadn't seen him, nor had we heard from him. I was beginning to think he was out of town. Maybe on Mars, where they didn't get text messages.

By the time Matt and I had somewhat straightened our office so we could at least continue to work from it, grabbed a bite of lunch, changed our clothes and driven up the mountainside, it was almost three--long after school had let out in Pinto Springs High.

We still didn't know what went down at the end of the school day, as we'd been traversing mountain turns in and out of cell phone dead spots when the final bell rang. But even after we'd arrived, calls to Luis' phone went unanswered. So we were thinking it would be best to stay in the area in case Luis asked for help again.

We were thinking worse things as well, but trying to stay positive.

All of this is how we came to be walking down Main Street, Pinto Springs in an effort to control our anxieties. I spent a lot of the time stealing peeks at the sky, wondering when the clouds' dark swollen bellies would open.

Still possessing a certain village charm about it, Pinto Springs was especially interesting this late afternoon because there were young artists about everywhere. They were decorating the shop windows with Halloween scenes.

These were high school artists, of course. Abigail had told me somewhere in all of this that it was a Pinto Springs tradition for the junior and senior year art students to compete for the honor of decorating a shop window, both on Halloween and on Christmas.

Each window had two artists working on it, so another lesson of this crafty contest was cooperation.

A chill wind reminded me how close to winter Cleveland County was. Down the mountain, off of the mile-high plateau, it was barely fall. But the regular rains up here would soon be turning to snow, and this Southern California village would don a fur-lined parka and morph into a winter playground.

The threat of rain must make these students wonder why they were bothering, I mused. They were working with poster paint which would streak and run with the first drops of rain.

I held hot tea, Matt held hot chocolate, and we were silent in our strolling observations, listening as we went to the conversations, which were largely about every day teen things.

They spoke nothing about the recent deaths of the six local boys and nothing about the weather that was making me think I was in Maine. And more importantly, nothing about another kidnapped girl.

But then a few words caught our ears. "...she doesn't stop making trouble with those gang boys we'll all be in for it..."

We stopped in our tracks, pretending to look at a nearby Halloween effort. But they must have noticed us because the two girls who'd spoken those words said nothing more.

Then I truly took note of the window at which we'd paused.

"Look at this one Matt."

I had to prompt him, I think because his mind was still back at the office reorganization. No. Of course his mind was with Luis, and our inability to connect with either of our apprentices. Or on to the next assignment for our small private investigations firm.

"Umm. Not bad." He stopped and turned to take it all in. "Actually, pretty good. Grandma Moses."

It *was* Grandma Moses in Halloween dress. Dozens of scary little scenes spread across a blanket of yellow-green grass.

Every symbol of Halloween seemed hidden somewhere among the leaves and gravestones. Spooky mansions, demons with pitchforks, even a Freddy Krueger mask. More enchanting than scary, and very well painted.

I turned to who I took to be the best of the two artists, a lithe teen with auburn hair down to the middle of her back, thinking it was her project and that the other girl was a second place winner just there to help complete the complicated mural.

"This is wonderfully imaginative. Have you a list of the items people should look for? You know, like an I-spy puzzle they can solve?"

Auburn Girl froze, tensing up as if I'd growled at her. The other painter, a rather homely little thing with oversized facial features turned and answered.

"Yes, I made one up and ran it off at the school yesterday."

And she pointed to a piece of paper hanging on the wall next to her, and a small supply of identical sheets anyone could take.

I was thinking she had more paint on herself than on the window, but her enthusiasm made me smile. I still didn't catch that this was her work until Auburn Girl suddenly packed her paints and brushes and huffed away.

Stunned, I watched her go, unsure what to say.

"Willa. Wait, we haven't finished."

I watched a pained expression cross Messy Girl's face. Then saw it slide into a bit of anger, and lastly resolution. She would finish her work of art alone if necessary.

Maybe art didn't lend itself well to committee work, I mused. Matt pulled on my elbow, but I had to make this better somehow.

"Well, you're almost finished. It really is a wonderful painting."

"Thanks."

Then I wondered why I'd assumed the auburn-haired girl had been the lead artist. I decided it was because her work was cleaner, her brush strokes more exacting. So perhaps they'd been paired to learn from each other. Perhaps the teacher saw that one of them was gifted in her painting and execution, while the other had an expansive and multileveled imagination. Perhaps the teacher was thinking that together they would make an excellent artist, but alone they each lacked an important ingredient.

We moved on to another window but the milk in my tea had just curdled.

As I sat on a bench waiting for Matt to return from a head call, my mind wandered toward the effort to protect Abigail that still lay before us.

On the way it bumped into fatigue, and finally Elijah stumbled across my crooked mental path. Elijah was the prophet who challenged the people to choose God over Baal. Then another gently whispered message stole through my brain, ear to ear.

For I hear a mighty rainstorm coming!

I recognized it from Kings. I couldn't tell you chapter and verse. I just knew it was a warning that danger was filling the skies and it was time to get down off the mountain.

I looked up at the blackening clouds. I wouldn't recognize the voice in my head as Ruth's for several days. After I remembered that Elijah wasn't talking about the weather.

Chapter 47

As we drove down the driveway to our Escondido home we spotted Luis sitting on a front step petting Wisdom. The first words out of Matt's mouth expressed our frustrations. The first words out of Luis' raised our fears.

"Why aren't you answering our calls?"

"Pintos stole my phone. Abigail is fine, but that second Indian girl has been kidnapped—as school was letting out. Her name is Rosalia Fousat."

I inhaled sharply then unlocked the door and let us all in.

He continued explaining as we entered the house and Matt retrieved another company cell phone from the first office. He handed it to Luis.

I listened from the kitchen while preparing Wisdom's dinner meal.

"I hope you didn't leave any sensitive information on the phone they took, Lou. Bastards will probably use it against us."

Luis just grunted.

"Like Sandy's phone number, for one. Maybe you want to warn her."

"Shit."

Luis hadn't thought of that.

Matt handed the young man a beer and the two went out on the porch to sit and confer. I joined them.

"So tell me what happened." Matt.

"What a mess. They struck right in the middle of the main hall again, dragging the poor screaming girl out a side door. Fucking teachers…"

He turned a worried face toward me.

"Uh… sorry, Rachel."

I waved his concerns away and he continued.

"Anyway, those useless pieces of shit just turned away. Most of the other kids ignored her screams too. And what could they do anyway?

"All the guards were busy helping direct traffic off campus, manning the security gates out front. Freakin' principal was probably under his desk. They headed for the baseball field and I chased them, but they counter-attacked."

That was when I noticed the bruise on his face, just below his left eye.

"Let's go inside, guys. It's getting cold out here," I said. He could still be in shock.

Wisdom chased us inside. I lit the fireplace and closed the windows. The house was filling with a chill.

The men resettled on the couch.

"I know I shouldn't have, Matt. I'm sorry. I know my concern is with Abigail but she was okay, while this poor girl was being dragged screaming across the back field. Did you know the so-called security fence has a cattle exit? You don't see it until you get right up on it, but the fences actually miss each other at the back of the field, and run parallel to each other for a section. Coyotes are probably laughing as they slip through it at night to eat the rabbits. At least the cattle aren't getting in."

He stopped to take a swig of beer, then continued.

"Anyway that's how they got her off the campus, right out that opening in the back fence. It's unmanned for Christ's sake! That school is run by a merry band of fools."

He took another slug.

"I went inside and gave the principal a piece of my mind afterwards. My cover was blown anyway. They need an armed guard posted there! Hell they need armed guards all over that campus! It's a freakin war. I can't believe I couldn't stop them. They were without fear. They seemed more brazen and violent than any high school gang I've ever heard of."

Matt tried to calm him. "Take it easy. You did what you could, Luis. Don't berate yourself."

"Well, at least I know Abby is safe. I spotted her heading for home on foot with a whole bunch of kids. She was a football field away by then. No way I could catch up."

"On foot?" I asked.

"What? Oh, yeah. She doesn't take the bus. She told me the kids are mean on it so she hoofs it home. It's only a couple of miles, although I argued the point with her at first. But a whole bunch of them walk together so she should be okay. I trailed her the first day. Moms and dads are everywhere watching out after them. It's really a nice town that way. That's why I can't figure this situation at the school out. It's like these guys have suddenly arrived from another planet."

Matt muttered, "Or another country."

I added, "I don't think they expected any of this. Listening to the conversations in the office after the deaths of the boys, the first time I'd come to pick up Abby, they seemed totally unprepared for emergency situations. It was like they were used to their peaceful mountain community, protected by height and distance from the dangers of the rest of the world."

"Yeah, maybe that's it. But they need to get up to speed fast, now. Just being out of their league won't cut it. This violence is escalating so fast they'll need the Marines soon." Luis.

"We're here."

Matt had automatically spoken these last words as well. I didn't think he was even aware of the spontaneous response—then he rose and walked away to answer our ringing doorbell.

I did my own muttering. "Or maybe they're under orders not to get involved. I'll call and make sure our charge arrived safely."

I grabbed my phone and walked into the kitchen and speed dialed Abigail's home. I held the phone to my ear until a foreigner answered in Cyrillic. Nana.

Meantime Matt opened the door and Sandra flew by him and took up station in front of the fireplace and began shouting down at Luis.

I stepped further into the kitchen to ask Nana if Abigail had arrived home okay, but I could hardly hear her—or understand her. And the noise in the living room was escalating so I moved back to the doorway. Sandra was pitching a fit.

At least Nana wasn't upset. Abigail must be home.

"You could have been killed! Look at this! Look at this bruise, and *blood!* What are you thinking Luis? You've got to stop this."

Blood? I hadn't noticed blood.

She turned her female fire on Matt. It was a strange sight for me to see. I couldn't decide how to respond. Finally I decided he could take care of himself.

"You can't send him out into the field again! He's an apprentice, for god's sake. *He's supposed to be working in the background on the computers.*"

Matt let her blow while standing his ground. See? He's a Marine.

I hated it when he did that to me.

So did Sandra. She turned up the volume on her already high-decibel attack.

"Luis, this is it! It's me or him, you hear? I can't take this waiting to find out if you've been killed. You don't even answer your phone! I can't...."

Good grief, she'd been calling his missing phone. Luis lost it.

"I can't leave Abigail. Will can't do this, Sandy. There's a goddamned war going on up there. I have to help those poor kids. And I told you last night, this *is* my job. I'm not a computer tech, Sandy. I'm a private detective...or will be."

His voice went suddenly quiet at the end. He'd made his decision, which only tilted Sandra over the edge.

"I mean it! I mean it!" She raced back to the front door, and stood holding her hands in her curly blond hair as if she thought her head was about to blow.

My thoughts exactly.

I held my position in the kitchen doorway, the now dead phone still at my ear. Nana had stopped making incomprehensible sounds and hung up.

"You can't put me through this every day. *I matter too!*" And she raced out the door as upset as when she'd arrived.

I chased her out onto the lawn, thinking I should try to answer some of her concerns. Wisdom followed me, his tail held high, his ears at full attention. He was wondering where the battle was so he could jump in and help.

Beautiful Sandra climbed into her little red Corvette and sped away up our driveway and out of sight. *A hysterical, blond Santa Claus in a Corvette--taking her gifts home with her.*

I have no idea where these errant thoughts come from. But after that silly thought I contemplated her outfit. It was Corvette red. Maybe I should buy clothes that are the same color as my car?

Then another silly thought: *She had a Corvette?* While Luis drove a beat up ole Chevy Geo?

Of course, she was probably paying for it....

Hmm. Wish I had a Corvette, I was musing as I walked back into the house. Wish I was a twenty-something adorable blond again, come to think of it.

It must be some kind of defense mechanism, thinking stupid things when all hell breaks loose and there's nothing I can do about it. Then I saw the look on Luis' face and I snapped back to reality.

A few minutes later sad guy left, like a hungry polar bear after another day of no seals. He wasn't getting any blubber tonight either.

Matt told me later Luis promised he'd be there at the school in the morning whether his cover was blown or not. Abigail was his kid now, too. He wouldn't abandon her. And he wasn't letting those bastards steal any more Indian girls.

I was certain he'd been a Marine in another life. Probably had died young and that was why the angels sent him back in a beautiful body.

Chapter 48

I have to tell you--from this point on I maintained a level of anxiety that matched the state I'd functioned under during my final years as a librarian. That previous instance of elevated anxiety was due to my having been pushed above my glass ceiling by the bureaucracy train I was on.

Of course I could have let the flood of excellence behind me pass around me, but....

No. I really couldn't. I was excellent, too, if slowing with age. And my boss thought that was an attribute. She called it thoughtful, deliberative, and other hyperbole. But she was even older than me.

Matt began making calls to force the principal to accept Luis' presence on campus Friday. I did too.

Two missing young women from campus meant that no female at that school was safe at the moment.

I started with Geraldine Patrone, blond bombshell with four kids, wife of a billionaire, but much more importantly, sister of sheriff's detective Tom Beardsley.

We may never know which phone calls lit the fire under the Pinto Springs Police and Cleveland County Sheriff's departments, but they were all over the place by the time Luis arrived on Friday morning.

And now the national news was covering the kidnappings. Cleveland County was acquiring a bad rep.

The doorbell rang. I looked at my watch—almost eight. Matt was already at the door, Wisdom at his side, his tail wagging.

It was Will. Matt greeted him with a half-angry query. "Hey, man, where you been?"

"I made a trip up to LA to meet with the Deacon. I think we may need some help down the line with this gang problem at Pinto Springs, and he's Southern California's duty expert on the subject," Will said as he stepped into the house. He was looking a little sheepish. He'd turned of his cell phone—probably to spend time with his woman. I went to get him some coffee so the men could work it out.

Will was referring to Deacon Harks, a well respected expert in gang activities centered in LA County. Will did a stint with the Harks Private Investigations agency in his first year as an apprentice. Then he switched out of that area down to ours and joined our team.

Matt led him out to the porch. Sunrise was magnificent out there on the eastern side of the house. The primates around the corner were chuffing and howler-ing in excitement.

"Good idea. But I'm afraid the whole thing has escalated yet again," I heard Matt say as I returned.

"Yeah, Luis told me."

I took a back seat, letting the men carry the conversation while I thought over what Sandra had said to me Sunday during dinner preparations.

I'd been thinking Will was a secretive guy because he had some dark secret in his past. But Sandra informed me Sunday while we were making dinner in the kitchen that he's so quiet because his main woman, Amanda White, is up in Los Angeles. And worse, she's still upset with Will for moving south to San Diego County. Sandra said she was refusing to join him. But I saw it as she couldn't. A woman's career was as important as a man's.

Amanda White was an LA girl born and bred, specifically from Watts, and she needed to stay there because she has a good paying county job as a social worker in the community. Good paying jobs are hard to come by, especially these days. Knowledge of a community on this level is non-transferable. Moving would be a serious challenge to her career.

And this turns out to be his deep dark secret—not at all what I was thinking.

I was thinking he was either a stone cold killer with murder in his past or maybe that he was afraid of the violent LA streets. Not that he had a girlfriend with whom he was struggling to maintain a relationship.

What really killed my romanticized version of Will's dangerous persona was to discover that he'd left LA because of the smog. Apparently he was born an asthmatic and the dirty air was getting to him, bringing back some of his symptoms.

Not the scar hiding under his beard.

Will had returned to LA to reconnect with Deacon Harks in preparation for a possible escalation in our current situation at Pinto Springs High.

I'd actually read some of Deacon Harks' online writings on the subject of how to work with gangs after Sandra's comment. His business webpage leads to a blog that is quite detailed. In fact his connections are legion. Dozens of web pages point to his essays, and his site points to dozens of others. He's created a veritable web of interconnections.

And his dealings with those gangs were becoming the stuff of legends. Unbelievably, I discovered that gang members themselves have discussion boards now, and they can be pretty aggressive in protecting those boards from imposters--like a retired librarian trying to educate herself with a few innocent questions.

Their rage chased me back to the edges. In time I might learn to imitate their peculiar virtual lingo, but for now all I could do was lurk.

My mind raced back from my musings as I heard Matt suggest that maybe he should travel north with Will on one of his trips to meet with Harks himself.

"No, man, that isn't necessary. I can handle it."

Matt just stared at him, confused. This was where I jumped in.

"Besides, Will, I think it's time we met this lovely lady of yours. What's her name? Amanda White?"

Now both men were staring at me. Aren't secrets wonderful? Especially when you get to spill them?

Will stammered. Matt grinned.

"Yeah, Will. We need to meet your lady Amanda," Matt said.

"Uh, sure. But she could come down here, maybe. Have one of those cookouts with you guys, like Luis and Sandy just did."

Uh-oh. He figured out Sandra told me.

Then the phone rang in our back office, saving me from shoving my foot further down my throat, and I chased its insistent sounds down the hall.

"The shit's gonna hit the fan tomorrow, honey-chile."

"Hi Latisha. That's fine with us as long as they wear flack vests and carry so they can help defend those poor children, and their cowardly teachers."

"Don't pick on the teachers, hon, they never signed on to do no combat in the halls."

I blinked. This was true. She'd tilted my view back toward the middle.

"You're right. So what's up?"

"This call isn't about your young man, if that's what you're thinking. Forsythe still figures that cute thing to be a volunteer who is horrified at the violence...like all the rest now banging down his office door. A parents' group is preparing a suit against the school for not protecting the Native Americans on campus. They've hired two of the county's top guns, McClellan and Jones from the law firm of the same name. Strange thing is the parents' group is made up of mostly whites and blacks."

I began to suspect Latisha was enjoying a glass of wine. I grinned.

"Is that the African American law firm you gave me a card for?"

"Yes. There are no Native American law firms in the area. I've checked. The missing girls' parents have been pretty quiet about the whole thing, so far. The local NA's up on the mountain can be like that, basically they keep to themselves. I'm not sure why they aren't coming forward. I don't know if they're conferring with their tribal councils right now or what."

"Why? Why aren't they fighting mad and making noise, hiring their own lawyers?" I said.

"It's certainly the way I'd be if it was my kids being kidnapped, but they just don't act that way. May have something to do with their self image, as in being a *peaceable people*. Or maybe it goes much deeper. Maybe they had the anger beat out of them one too many times over the centuries.

"There are several tribes living up in the northern part of Cleveland County, on streets with names like 'Seminole Patch', 'Tippecanoe Trail' and 'Walkingfoot Hills, remnants from the various Indian Removal treaties back before the great Dispersal era. They're mixed in with the more local tribes of Southern California, like the Baronas, Cahuillas and Palas. Maybe the fact that they aren't all from the same tribe weakens them, deprives them of a common voice.

"Anyway, consider yourself forewarned. Tomorrow is going to be messy. Let your cute young man know."

I thanked her and walked back into the living room to be confronted by Matt. Will had left for home.

"When were you going to share that juicy tidbit with me?"

"What tidbit?" Of course I knew perfectly well that he meant Amanda, so I switched gears and told him what Latisha said about Luis.

Chapter 49

Buddy was the reason she'd found the courage to escape the homeschool life and foray into on-campus school life. Buddy, as it was turning out, might be the only good reason to stay.

Listening carefully for Buddy's return from the bathroom, Abigail took two steps inside to glance into Judi's closet. And then a third, and a fourth.

The *now-dead* Judi, she reminded herself, and reflexively clasped her hands in front of her in a pose of respect.

Wow. *All* her clothes were colorful. No drab grays and tans for her. She had been about the colors of life! Not the drabness of modesty that her mother the *Former Communist* insisted she wear.

The posters of current pop stars, of course--Miley was there, Hannah, Taylor, Adam, Justin...and some of them had been *signed!*

She must have attended live concerts. How did she get back stage to get autographs?

She even had a Lady GaGa poster.

Then she spied Judi's makeup table. It was just like a movie star's with light bulbs all around the edges and a little padded stool in front. She had almost every color in the rainbow for eye shadow. Probably every color of lipstick available. Wow. Wow. Wow. She picked up one of the golden tubes and held it in her fingers as if it were really made of gold.

"What's up?"

"Oh! Buddy. I was just...I mean, I was seeing..."

"It's okay. My mom is kind of stuck on leaving things the way they are for now. You know, like a memorial, like...she said she can still smell Judi in here. My dad is real worried about my mom. She's like, losing it."

He turned away, rubbing at his eyes, and Abigail followed him into the living room.

"I'm sorry Buddy. The door was open so I just found myself drifting in. Please. I didn't mean any harm." Damn! Their moment might never happen now.

"I said it was fine. Give me a minute."

He stood by the front window staring out at the gloomy afternoon. It was so chilly Abigail was thinking....

"Maybe it will snow. Do you think?"

"Maybe."

"Buddy, if you want me to leave...?"

"No! I want you here. I hate being alone in this house now, and my folks won't be home until after five. Please, Abigail, stay with me."

"Of course, hon."

He smiled. She'd called him 'hon', an endearment her mother called her by...and used to use on her father, if she remembered correctly. She felt her face flame up.

He put his hand on her chin and raised her face to his.

"I like it," was all he said.

They stood in his living room, she was pressed up against his chest breathing like a gazelle after a sprint to safety, their lips inches apart. Would this be the moment? Would he finally kiss her?

She placed her hands lightly on his chest and she could feel his heart beating as hard as hers--unison beats telegraphing their desires across the jungles. He smelled so sweet, so wonderful, a mixture of sweat and chewing gum.

Suddenly she realized why she had her hands tucked between them. She felt funny about her breasts touching him. They were so small. And...and she could *feel* them tingling, she knew they were *pointing* at him.

Their time together would run out if he didn't hurry up and make his move. She leaned closer to him. He leaned toward her a little more.

And *finally* they kissed.

It was soft and warm, a little moist. She wondered if that's the way her lips felt to him. They held their lips together for a full minute, just like Judi had told them to do.

Judi.

Judi had talked to them about kissing two months ago. She'd caught them clinging to each other in the side yard, after returning from one of the art classes, the ones Abigail and Buddy had taken over the summer. That was back when all they could do was stare into each others' eyes.

Abigail pushed herself back and looked at him through a thin layer of tears.

His eyes shined, too, and the magic moment retreated. But it had happened. She wasn't a dumb kissing-virgin any more.

Chapter 50

Friday, mid-morning
"I thought you said you couldn't get involved, that this was Pinto Springs' jurisdiction."

I was addressing Cleveland County Sheriff's Department Detective Tom Beardsley. We were standing outside Principal Forsyth's office.

"Some of the kids live out in the county," Tom muttered.

I was uncomfortable because I'd just added a third cup of coffee to the two I'd had this morning and I was wired enough to scrub down a couple of elephants.

At the moment the Prince was entertaining a contingent of two sent by Homeland Security to investigate the possibility of terrorist involvement in the local kid gang and to evaluate the school's perimeter. I knew this because the secretary had told me. Some how this made her feel important.

This prompted a series of questions in my mind, uppermost of which once again was whether the school was thinking Muslim terrorists would work with home-grown gangs--or was the government thinking this?

Of course, there are known links between the world's drug habit and Al-Qaeda, the Taliban. But... was the American government now thinking that Al-Qaeda et al were infiltrating the South and Central American drug trade, and their extensions into our own country?

A chilling thought indeed.

Waiting in the wings out here with us was a task force of one sent by the FBI to assure the interrogations of the gang kids were done according to international law because some of the kids might be Mexican nationals. And there were a couple of lawyerly types-- dark suits, big bellies—maybe the ACLU here to defend the rights of the two missing Native American girls, or to assure the Pintos boys were read their Miranda rights the moment it became apparent charges would be made. As soon as those thoughts passed through my head, I began wondering how the gang kids' parents could afford lawyers. Maybe they'd been appointed in advance.

I also noticed someone acting as an interpreter for the gang kids' parents, speaking in rapid Spanish.

Oh, and Pestilence. Pestilence was here.

I should explain here the two feared Pinto Springs police detectives Pestilence and Famine. They were all that was left of an original Four Horsemen who had ruled the roost at PSPD DETDIV for nearly two decades until budget cuts had reduced them to two.

Even though Matt insisted they were good cops, their physicalities repulsed me.

Learner—dubbed the White Horseman of Pestilence-- had a grease burn that draped over his nose and spilled onto one cheek. Rumor has it this was the result of a childhood kitchen accident. (More than once I've tried to picture this "accident".)

His pale skin also contained some internal poison physicians dubbed pustular psoriasis. Again, I'd looked it up. Ugly sores was my label.

Mosby on the other hand was one missed meal away from starvation. Basketball-player-tall and weighing less than your average anorexic teeny-bopper, he gave gaunt a new image. And of course, this was the reason for his nom de guerre, the Black Horseman of Famine.

I'd last seen the black walking stick in an autopsy theater and wondered at the time when they would put him up on one of the gurneys.

But my distaste for these two detectives went deeper than their physical characteristics. I'm not that shallow. There was a dance the two did—seemed always to have done—that left me disliking them both. They constantly butted heads as if their individual survivals relied on their mutual antagonism. There was clearly some history I was missing between this black and white pas de deux.

Maybe they were just staying in character—good cop, bad cop. A nonstop rehearsal.

I winced as Learner turned a dead eye on me. His face was literally exploding. I wanted to recommend stage makeup.

In answer to my original question about why he was here, Tom said loud enough for Learner to hear, "I'm heading up a taskforce to work with Pinto Springs because the Indian girls are actually county residents."

Learner slid our way.

I said, "Luis Lewis reports there's increased chatter on the web talking of revenge."

Tom shook his head. "What do you think? We're finally looking at the demise of our bastardized legal system here?"

He was talking to Learner, who didn't answer because it was clearly rhetorical. I wasn't sure if Tom was referring to the people in the room with us or the influence of the internet on our thinking and general character.

"So what brings you here?" Learner asked me from inches away. I almost shrank back.

"We're hoping for a moment with Dr. Forsyth to ask permission for Luis Lewis to remain on campus. He needs to keep an eye on Abigail."

"I'll get him a volunteer tag from Captain Spangler. He knows Matt."

Strange. He was being nice. And then I realized this probably had more to do with my husband's reach than my winning personality. I mused that the excessive official presence in the school's administration offices this morning were no doubt in large part due to Matt's efforts to get an Amber Alert going for the two missing Indian girls.

Which hadn't yet happened. I didn't know why. My blood began to boil just thinking about this.

The two men continued their conversation as if I wasn't there. I hated that. Knowing Learner thought he'd effectively dismissed me, I stayed.

"They're checking IAFIS on some prints taken from these lovely boys, see if there's any way we can hold them for questioning." Learner.

"Okay. You might want to include some of their fathers." Tom.

"Wish we could. Can't prove they're involved yet." Learner.

Three local reporters stepped in behind us, and Learner snapped his fingers at a patrolman holding up the doorsill.

"Tell 'em the presser will be held at ten. Get 'em outside." Learner.

"He's doing a press conference?" I asked.

"No." Learner, with full on dead-eye.

I listened as the two men chatted each other up as if I weren't there. My boiling brain pondered what I assumed was the stalling at the top.

An Amber Alert is put out by the US Department of Justice. There were five basic requirements for an Amber Alert to be enacted.

One, law enforcement has to confirm an abduction has taken place. More specifically, the abduction has to be a "stranger abduction."

Two, the child must be at risk for serious bodily harm or death.

Three and four, sufficient descriptive information on the child must be available, and the child must be seventeen or younger.

And five, then and only then would an NCIC (National Crime Information Center) data entry be made listing the Amber Alert, and would then be flashed throughout the United States. In special instances, other countries could be included in the official advisement to be on the lookout for the missing child.

I'd been wondering who was holding up this process, so of course I asked.

"Detective Learner, who is holding up the Amber Alert?"

"My boss. You wanna' talk to him? I'll give you his number."

Was he serious? I couldn't tell.

"What's the hang up?" Tom, deflecting.

Learner sighed, and said, ticking points off on his fingers, "One, one of the parents claims the two girls have been threatening to run away for weeks, two there's no threat of bodily harm--yet, and three, these girls apparently have never had their pictures taken."

"Even at school?" I asked.

He didn't answer, but he made eye contact with Secretary Chrissie Prichard, who'd been listening. She turned and retrieved a couple of year books from the shelf behind her. Prissy, as I called her, was smarter than I thought. She began rifling through the pages.

"Good suggestion. We think it's a dad who's thrown a wrench in the works. He's angry over his daughter's dress. Neighbors indicate he's been having loud arguments with Betty Wolftooth, the first to go missing.

"In fact, your guys over at Seminole Patch confirm that they've gone in twice in the past month to calm the guy down."

Tom nodded, a look of chagrin on his face.

Great. So poor Betty and even Rosalia were out there in the unknown with no help. Just great.

The patrolman returned from his corralling of the media.

"Did you put some tape up?" Learner barked.

"You want the whole campus surrounded, boss?"

Whoa. Was that insubordination?

I chimed in. "Especially the back opening in the fence. That's how they got the girls off campus."

"There's an op...?" Learner's face went redder, if that was possible, and he sped down the hall toward the back door after snapping more orders at his lazy helper.

I figured he wanted to beat the FBI guys to the discovery. I'd thrown him a life ring without realizing it. Maybe Learner and I would be friends, now.

Tom was smiling at me as we parted.

By the time I got home the school day was almost finished and Luis had received his volunteer name tag.

The overwhelming presence of officials high and low had kept a lid on the problems at the school, and thankfully we were now into the weekend. I only prayed things would remain as quiet during the Halloween celebrations this evening.

Happily, today's parents were very careful with their children when they went trick or treating.

Chapter 51

After leaving the Pinto Springs high school campus, I headed for my monthly DAR luncheon at a San Marcos country club.

I'd only recently learned that membership in the Daughters of the American Revolution had been in our family at least since my great-grandmother Ivy MacIver. In fact, it is from Ivy's first marriage that my lineage flows back to the American Revolution. After discovering this fact buried in my mother's memorabilia late last spring, I'd joined this distinguished organization.

I loved that my great-grandmother's name was Ivy MacIver—loved the alliteration--but I wasn't so much in love with the fact that Ivy had married twice. This I had learned from another source.

It turned out that Ivy's first marriage—one I'd been completely unaware of--connected me to the Stowall Clan. I'd first learned about this at the beginning of the month at the first quilting bee I'd attended with the Quilted Secrets women.

At any rate, I went to my third DAR luncheon and then hopped back in my deliciously new hybrid Prius and started for home. As I came to a road with a familiar name I suddenly remembered why it was familiar, and made an impromptu detour to visit Hannah and Ruth.

Then I worried all the way to Hannah's house that she would think me rude for just popping in.

I'd never been to the Lilly's Vista home, but I thought I remembered it was around thirteen acres.

And sure enough it was, filled with lemon, orange and avocado groves--and occasional meandering grass cutters called goats and llamas. The Lilly farm also had one chestnut and one piebald horse, and a quartet of chickens that serenaded me as I drove closer to the house on a tired asphalt driveway.

I was willing to bet there were more chickens off somewhere else on the property, as one of the visible four was a fancy rooster.

Parking near the two large barns situated on the right, I concentrated on slowing my brain down. Too much tea on top of too much coffee.

Ohmm. Ohmm.

Two really deep breaths.

Okay, I was ready. My tummy butterflies were settling.

I walked by a one-acre organic vegetable garden that dwarfed our backyard Victory patch. Maybe she had relatives coming in to help her?

Hannah's house was quite large, the central part of which went up two stories. A wooden clapboard exterior painted in slate gray was fronted by a broad veranda that ran around the far side out of sight.

Too late I saw that I could have driven all the way up to the front, where the decaying asphalt driveway curved around from right to left and ended in a wider parking area.

Abandoned toys hid in a patch of weeds to the left. Nearby them a wooden sand box was being reclaimed by nature. My mind strayed, or was led down winding reveries.

Was everything on its way to the beach? Would the universe end its days in a puff of sand? Was from *kaboom* to *poof* the real natural order of things?

Was the caffeine overdose turning into a major crash? Or was I slipping into a nap? Oz-like, walking through a field of poppies.

Ahead, a broad stairway invited me up to a veranda and I stepped onto a slate walkway leading there. The sense of fatigue increased.

Or maybe I'd merely entered another realm. Farm-speed.

In sharp contrast, a profusion of orange, yellow and white mums pretended they weren't a garden along the right side of the walk. A fat rosebush with the last of the summer's white glories still clinging to it huddled next to a late season blue sage on the left.

Winter was coming, but it would be mostly mild with occasional nippy nights down here on earth's floor. I was renewing my love for Southern California with every step.

On the steps up, three pumpkins pretended to be the three bears to a straw-man Goldilocks. Spilling down from this grouping were a variety of gourds, some carved and some painted. An artist's skills had arranged them to look as if they weren't arranged.

A hanging swing-couch and three wicker chairs told of lazy evening gatherings on the left side of the porch. None of the furniture was new. The blue-gray paint on the veranda needed a touch up. It was all charming and comfy. I almost veered left onto the swing, but then I spotted another point of interest.

This family was very into Halloween. Someone had even painted a large front window, like the store windows we'd strolled by yesterday. Only this mural was professionally done.

Taking a closer look at the intricate painting on glass I finally realized I was looking in upon Sleeping Ruth.

Surprised, I took a half step back. The ultimate suburban farming family were serving grief in their dining room.

The mural may have been done to cheer Ruth but also to conceal her from prying eyes.

A small tow-headed boy shyly opened the front door and said, "Who are you?"

"I'm one of your mom's sewing mates. Call me Rachel."

Hannah called *"Val"* from somewhere deep within the house--probably in the kitchen canning veggies—and the little boy took my hand and led me inside.

An armory of shot guns, rifles and pistols blanketed a wall in the wide hall. They were mostly antiques.

Observing my observations, four-year-old Value said, "They're up high so I can't mess with them. My dad hid the ammo."

Ammo. I bet he'd looked for it.

Okay, what was wrong with this picture? Hannah's a liberal, right? Probably votes Democrat? Probably hates war and weapons?

"They were my dad's. I moved them here and just mounted them for my mom. She's in there." Hannah's chocolate voice said. She was drying her hands on a dishtowel-morphing-into-rag as she greeted me.

But my eyes weren't ready for a closer inspection. I was tearing up over the memory of what Ruth and her husband, the now deceased Paul McMichaels endured a short while ago—the same event that landed Ruth in this at-home hospital bed.

"I saw. I was admiring the mural...."

"My dad did that!" Value shouted joyously.

"I could have done it!" Another boy, this one older, middle Samuel no doubt.

"Could not!"

"Could *yes!*"

"Nuf." Hannah quelled the word-war. This second boy was less blond than his little brother, and a foot taller.

But capturing my attention finally was Ruth, ensconced in a hospital bed complete with side rails and IV stand. My eyes turned crispy and I wrapped my arms around my body protectively.

Hannah just observed, letting me adjust.

All around the still comatose old woman were more objects that clashed with my perceptions of Hannah. The plum colored floral wallpaper held a dozen tchotchke shelves of various natural and painted woods.

Propped up on the small shelves were vases and dolls and demitasse cups. When I spotted a Nixon for President button on the closest, I knew they weren't Hannah's.

"You've begun moving her here?" I said softly.

We'd drifted a few steps into the room.

Tossing the rag-towel over her shoulder, Hannah hugged me for a long moment, whispering in my ear, "You're the first to dare come visit her. Thank you."

I was instantly relieved of my etiquette concerns. And the tears brimmed.

She pulled back and smiled warmly.

About my height, Hannah is the picture of comfort, with long brown hair, a beautiful natural complexion--as in no makeup and perfect rosy skin--large expressive blue eyes and of course the deep chocolate voice.

I was sure she could smooth talk her way through a field of jelly fish without once getting stung.

"You brought her things here and put them all around her." I repeated the obvious for lack of knowing what else to say.

"You don't have to whisper. Let's go include her in the conversation. I know she's listening."

We moved fully into the dining room.

"My mom and sis even wallpapered for Grandma. It's the same pattern she has at her home on the mountains. Don't you love it?"

"I sure do, Samuel." Val had disappeared into the back of the open house.

It was difficult seeing the hardboiled, tanned little woman I'd instantly connected with only a month ago reduced to this near-death still life. About the only thing I recognized was her white hair still flying about her head like a fog being swirled by ocean breezes. Her eyes had retreated even further into her head. Her once regal nose pointed heavenward from this prone position, a sharp spire. The skin of her face was stretched like rice paper over her bones, distorting the shape of her mouth into a grimace.

I noticed something and leaned closer.

"Grandma's eyes are always moving, like she's watching a dance partner's steps. She's just waiting for the right time to stop dancing and return to us."

Startled, I turned to look at the new voice behind me, this one caramel.

"You must be Deborah."

She of the scolding older sister's voice, I thought but didn't say. I knew her to be ten. I didn't know she had such piercing eyes. Nor that she was almost as tall as her mother and thin as a beanpole.

She was wearing a colorful floral peasant blouse and striped Capri tights and below them, knee socks knitted one-handed by two drunken clowns. None of the colors she wore had anything to do with each other, but they were all happy.

I won't bother to describe how the rest of us were dressed except to say we were wearing boring solid colors in various shades of camouflage.

I was going right home after this and revisiting my wardrobe.

Deborah said authoritatively, "Right, and this is my middle brother Samuel. Value has just done another disappearing act. We've had to banish him because he's into counting now and constantly reciting number combinations. This week he's counting in twos. And you're the lady who saved Eddie."

Samuel piped up, "I can count in *any's*."

"I..." started to correct her, but she waltzed over my words.

"There's no such thing as any's, Sam. My mom says if it weren't for you, Eddie would still be hiding in that horrible house, or maybe worse. You were the only one brave enough to go after him and bring him up from his cellar."

"His aunts actually..."

"Of course, I mean his inner cellar, the one he'd spent most of his life in..."

"Take a breath, Deb." Hannah inserted, and wrapped an arm about her daughter with a smile.

"Okay."

The alert ten-year-old assumed a pose of silent vigilance next to her mother. Her large eyes were forest green in contrast to her mother's Wedgwood. And then she turned to watch her middle brother leave and the light filled her forest eyes with gold.

Looking back at Ruth I suddenly realized I'd taken her hand in mine. I did, didn't I? *Take her hand?*

I frankly couldn't remember doing so. The last thing I remembered was landing next to her hospital height bed and placing my clasped hands on the sheets. Then I'd turned to be swept away by Deborah's river of words.

Hannah interrupted my astonishment, saying, "How'd it go with Abigail today?"

But she was also glancing down at my odd handshake with Ruth, a slight frown on her forehead.

I filled her in on the nonsense the various authorities at Pinto Springs High School were passing off as taking decisive action.

Then Hannah switched gears suddenly.

"Have you seen the news?"

I glanced toward the darkened television in the living room aimed in the direction of Ruth. "No, should I?"

"Turn it on. I'll wait."

She wanted me to let go of her mother's hand. The ten-year-old raced me to it.

It was an old fashioned analog, probably from Ruth's home, and it took a full minute to open its cyclopean eye. For some reason, I wondered as we waited if Ruth might want to return to her own home once she rose from her coma.

It was frankly rather strange that Hannah was going to so much work moving her mother's things to her home while the old woman was unable to express an opinion on the matter.

But then, Ruth's husband Paul was dead now. Maybe grandma would love coming to live with her grandchildren. I found myself studying Hannah, trying to figure out why she was showing no signs of grieving for her dad. She hadn't even mentioned his recent death. But I wasn't necessarily the one she would have expressed her grief with, either.

Then I glanced down at Ruth—still holding my hand--and remembered that it could be quite possible that Ruth didn't yet know that her husband Paul was dead. She'd been buried under a pile of rocks at the time, while he was tied to a tree a few feet away.

Unless they spoke to each other during their long ordeal.

My heart grew so heavy at these thoughts that I was tearing up. Poor Ruth. Poor Hannah, putting on a brave face. Finally, I forced myself to break the connection with Ruth, pulling my hand away.

I did so with difficulty. Ruth's grip on mine had increased while we were connected.

"We don't have cable or dish, so we bought an adapter and now we watch the local channels. But all that's ever on is Oprah and the news. And now *this* is on every channel." Deborah the disapproving.

I smiled in spite of myself.

"It's nonstop." Hannah added as I tried to absorb what I was seeing on the television.

"What is it? Are we at war? With...*China?*"

"Certainly looks like it, doesn't it."

We were watching a mob carrying sticks and rocks and clashing with Boston police on the harbor docks. The shot pulled back to take in a wider view and in the background I could make out two freighters loaded to the gills with goods.

The first of them had Chinese characters on its hull. I really couldn't see the second one, except that it held more of the angry mob on its upper decks.

Another *Boston Tea Party*.

"It's the news du jour."

Her comment reminded me that Hannah once was a newspaper reporter, and now works the farm, and does occasional massages. And of course she was moving toward becoming an official LIRI apprentice.

Her husband Peter still worked for the Chronicle covering the news beat.

"Any shots fired yet?" I asked.

"The *'Shot heard round the world'*--quite literally this time. Started around noon Eastern, and from what I'm reading on the news blogs the world is reacting. The market bounced down four hundred points and then recovered its senses to close about where it started."

She explained what I'd missed while taking care of LIRI business—that around noon a bunch of Bostonians had broken through a police barricade and gained access to the Chinese freighter.

That was when the gun was fired, to draw media's attention to the proclamation.

"They're protesting the delivery of foreign made goods. They want our government to return manufacturing to our shores and to strictly limit imports. It'll never happen. That's an Indian freighter behind the Chinese."

Hannah shook her head in parental disapproval.

"You do know that Eddie is in the middle of this somewhere."

"No." Eddie. The mere mention of his name stopped my breathing.

"Mary called me again this morning about when all this began. She said Eddie's living with another Stowall cousin in the heart of Boston's historical district. The family actually works for the Boston Historical Society.

I thought to ask, "Why is Eddie moving about so? Has Mary or anyone else explained this to you?"

"No. Maybe they think the cops are still after him about his shooting you. Maybe they're happy to have him anywhere but here. I frankly don't know why he isn't just a complete basket case as a result of his lifetime of abuse."

I said, "Well, not his whole lifetime. I mean, maybe the first fifteen years were better...."

"No. The first fifteen years were probably the worst." She stopped and stared at me. We both knew none of his childhood was any good

"Mary'd told me they've had him out practice shooting. With guns, for crying out loud!"

My eyes traveled by themselves to the wall of armament at the Lilly entrance.

Hannah, standing very close to me by then as we peered at the ancient television, whispered in my ear, "They were my dad's." Her voice was an inch away from an avalanche of tears. I looked in her eyes and briefly shared her pain.

That was when colorful Deborah made the crackup statement of the day—which saved us from the rising sadness.

"But someone spilled the Boston beans and warned the cops 'cause they were waiting when the mob arrived." Then she laughed uproariously at her own joke.

Yep. Ten.

We laughed with her. It was all a bit ridiculous, wasn't it? The world was here now, not back there two hundred twenty-plus years ago.

A little while later, as I moved to leave Hannah's house, I glanced once more toward sleeping Ruth. That was when the final shock of the day struck me.

I could swear I saw Ruth's toes wiggling under the sheets and blankets.

I'd been thinking she might not survive--at the very least, never rise from her comatose state. But I came away knowing she would.

That must have been what Deborah meant when she said her grandma was dancing.

Chapter 52

It was after two by the time I arrived home from Hannah's. When I walked in the front door I found my pet, Wisdom, scratching at his nose with his paw. Fighting a surge of fear, I raced to the back for his medicine and managed to get it down his throat before the sneezes began.

He retired to his deck post to listen for the wild things he wished he was.

Then I went to our office and discovered a note attached to my computer monitor reminding me Matt was on a job in Temecula. A solitary blinking light on our message machine caught my attention next. I pressed the replay button.

Cleveland County Sheriff's Detective Tom Beardsley's recorded voice informed me that a body had been found in the woods out behind Pinto Springs High.

Whose body? Another jolt of fear surged in my breast as I listened to Beardsley's less than full explanation and a list of bad choices rambled through my tired brain: one of the Indian girls, one of the Pintos gang members, Abigail..?

Finally his message told me it was another of the Pintos gang members, a boy. Thankfully not Abigail, or another Indian girl.

Then I began wrestling with whether it was any of my concern.

Again, Tom Beardsley was the brother of my part-time apprentice Gerry Patrone, who was another quilter with Victoria Stowall's group. Tom was keeping us in the loop as a friend, not as a deputy.

I thought Matt would surely have wanted to be there if he knew about it, but of course he was in Temecula. My heart sank. The longer I listened, the more I knew I was making another drive up to the mile-high plateau.

I left a message on Matt's phone that I knew he wouldn't hear until way too late; then I changed into warmer clothes and jumped back in my car.

I reached the school shortly after three. Some late stragglers were still filtering away from the campus at the end of a long week. It had been a long two weeks of grief and fear, but for now they would turn their minds toward Halloween trick or treating and act like the kids they really were—an activity that would begin in another couple of hours.

I glanced around for Luis. It had been when Tom had mentioned that Luis was with him that I decided I should make the trip to the campus.

Behind the school, I crossed a large multipurpose sports field—where Beardsley had indicated the boy's body was located. The crime scene seemed well-organized, complete with a small contingent of reporters being held at bay by a couple of cops and a strip of yellow plastic. I could see a knot of officers inside the perimeter a few feet away.

Nearby them, Beardsley was talking with Luis Lewis. Beardsley spotted me and came over to hold up the tape. I scooted under. Luis waved as I approached. I was still wondering why he was here. For that matter, why was I?

"Where's Matt?" Beardsley asked.

"He's on another job. I tried calling you but your phone went straight to message."

"Yeah, crime scene procedure."

"What's up? I mean, you seemed eager to have Matt here, so I came." I was staring at Luis, who was looking kind of sheepish. Was Luis overstepping his job here, again?

"Yeah, well...."

He didn't finish his sentence, I thought at that time because some of the other cops had moved closer to us. I looked around, trying to look casual, trying to dispel a rising sense that Luis had ensnared me in something I didn't belong in. I was wishing I could reach Matt for clarification.

The east side of the high school grounds was bordered by a narrow wooded area that follows a brook, mostly live oak trees and evergreens. About a hundred feet wide, the woods ran half a mile or more from the road at the front of the school down into the neighborhoods to the southwest. The river the woods surrounded stretched for miles from south to north, due to the slant of the land up here on the plateau.

On the other side of this bit of nature was the wealthy neighborhood the authorities had had difficulty gaining access to during the recent searches for the missing Indian girls, because it was securely gated.

"Kid's been tortured, mutilated just like El Hidalgo does," Luis said by way of a greeting. I stared at him. So, did this make it our business in his mind?

"We don't know that for sure..." Beardsley.

Great. So was Luis fantasizing?

"Yeah, well I've been researching Southern California gangs, and what those ME photographers were describing as they left was just like the stuff I read about the Tijuana gang that's threatening...."

"Uh, maybe it would be best if we kept speculation to a minimum for now." Me. I was losing my calm. So was Tom.

Our young apprentice finally noticed the frown on the detective's face and shut up.

But now I was thinking, *Tijuana? A Mexican gang is active up here?*

I had heard about El Hid somewhere recently. So was this the same as the El Hidalgo Luis just mentioned? I wanted more info on them, like were they rivals of the Pinto Springs gang? But this was not the time or place. The ME's people were coming and going. Which gave me an idea. I began fingering my camera, already hanging around my neck. I had my backpack full of PI tools, as well.

"Where's the body?" Me.

"Back a ways, over there," Beardsley answered, indicating the direction with another nod of his head. "ME's with him now."

"Do they have an ID on him yet?" Me.

"His wallet says he's Angel Jesus Escudero. The kid was a Pintos. His parents are over to the left, talking with Learner." Beardsley.

I could hear them. They were grieving. I glanced quickly and saw that Detective Learner was with them. And I could do without another look at Learner's erupting face. Beardsley continued.

"Learner has the lead, of course. But he told me it would be okay for you guys to go in if you want."

I was stunned. We were just PI's. Cops were usually pretty defensive about involving civilians in their business. But, maybe it was time to let Luis know what he was meddling in.

"Who's the ME?" I said as I turned to face the woods I knew contained the crime scene.

"Doc Marana. The weird guy. You saw him...." Beardsley began.

"Right, at the Stowall autopsies."

So he would know me on sight. I'd have to be discrete; even better, hidden behind the shrubs. My relationship with Marana was...strained.

"The body is about twenty feet in, near the river. ME's been there about thirty minutes so far. May be wrapping it up soon." Beardsley.

So we should move in now if we're going to.

"Okay, I'm going in. What about it Luis?" Me.

Luis looked like I'd asked if he'd like to jump in a snake pit with me. I stifled a grin. Our apprentice needed some training in crime scene etiquette and how to keep his nose where it belonged. This seemed as good a time as any.

"You don't have to follow me, Luis. I'm just going in for some pictures."

"No, no, I can take some notes." He was stammering, but at least he was game.

"Good idea."

As we moved away from Beardsley I cautioned Luis to be discrete. We moved through the thicket toward the body and the sound of Marana's droning voice. He was recording his observations. I pulled back some branches and found myself within twenty feet of the victim. I let my eyes and ears take the lead, signaling Luis to stop before we broke Marana's concentration. He was bent over the body with his back to us.

His assistant was aware of out presence, however, and he anxiously eyed us as he took orders from Marana.

Engrossed, Marana was moving like he was half his six foot five or so frame. In the outdoor light the medical examiner didn't look half Persian and half Indian as I'd told Sandra the other night. He looked half Indian...and maybe half Chinese, and half...whatever. He was still mostly Will Smith. Which was hard for me to take. Why would anyone who looked like Will Smith want to work with corpses? Then again, here I was....

Marana's position had been blocking our view of the boy's head and upper torso as I quietly snapped a few pictures of the surrounding area. Suddenly he moved and exposed the horrific sight of the victim.

I heard Luis inhale sharply. I felt an overwhelming sense of sadness.

The damage done to the young gang member's face and chest would make it impossible for his own mother to recognize him. His hands were pulled underneath him, probably tied so he couldn't struggle. The body was in full rigor mortis—right down to his toes. Flies were everywhere.

Marana dictated into his recorder as he circled, unaware of us.

"PMI indicates it's been more than twenty-four hours. Rigidity has passed. Insect inclusions will tell us more. Added note: the parents state their son has been missing for only a few hours."

I wondered why the parents didn't report his absence immediately, and why they were fudging on the time. But then, they were a gang family. The boys probably came and went as they pleased after the age of twelve. Maybe ten. Whenever the gang demanded it.

Luis made a gagging noise, which reminded me this was a teachable moment.

"PMI stands for post mortem interval," I whispered for Luis' benefit.

"How come nobody heard this going on?" Luis *almost* whispered back. Oops.

Marana's head snapped around and he growled, "What the hell are you two doing here?"

But he wasn't looking for answers. Marana called the nearest cop to task, demanding who had authorized our presence. The young man squirmed.

Then Luis said, "The family hired us...to investigate the killing."

Uh-oh. But I moved quickly forward and snapped close-ups of the body.

"The *Escudero* family? *Really?* We've only just told them. What are you, ambulance chasers?"

Double oops.

I continued taking pictures as we retreated. Suddenly I stopped and slipped sideways, toward the brook.

"Are those drag marks on the ground, Dr. Marana?" Me.

The look on his face told me he hadn't noticed them yet, and suddenly he was barking orders left and right for a larger perimeter to be formed and for the photographers to return.

When Learner raced past us in response to Marana's loud commands, I couldn't help but say, "There's no sign of blood splatter at that scene, either."

Chapter 53

Abigail waved to Luis as she left school and walked home with her new group of friends. Only she wasn't really going home, was she?

Luis was cute. And nice. And there'd been no trouble today. She was sorry to think this would probably be the last day she'd have his protection.

Luis was *really* cute.

But he was also old, and probably had a ton of girlfriends. And her guy was cute too in his own way.

Where she was really going wasn't home. Where she was really going made her thrill deep down inside. Maybe with fear, but also with excitement and this new warm feeling she got whenever she touched him, like now, pressing up against his warm shoulder.

The other girls were giving her some respect now, because she had a boyfriend.

The next thing Abigail had to do was find a way to buy some more in clothes. She felt like she was wearing old lady clothes now. Her communist mother never let her go shopping alone, never let her out of her sight, period.

She was almost fourteen, for crying out loud.

She'd become so desperate to meet some kids more aware of pop culture--kids *not* homeschooled—that she'd even been thinking maybe she should go live with her father for awhile.

He didn't agree with her staying home all the time. But he was another kind of problem altogether, and frankly didn't support her art much either.

Her father was a mess. Cripes, she hadn't seen him in forever anyway. He never kept his court-appointed days with her, was always too sick.

So she'd found another solution to her mother's possessive nature and everything was working out just fine.

Mom was working—*all night again.*

Nana thought she was going to a Halloween party.

And what neither of them knew wouldn't hurt them. She'd be sure to get home by ten like Nana had more or less said.

"I be sleep by ten, little one."

Nana was turning out to be pretty cool about this all. They were like co-conspirators now.

Buddy jostled her shoulder sending another shiver down her spine.

Chapter 54

I got home from my second trip up the mountain just after five. It was dark and a group of small children were just beginning to make their trick or treat rounds on our street. I was thinking about getting the candy together for them when I drove down our driveway. But that thought was erased by the sight of my man on our front porch.

Matt was waiting with his arms crossed over his manly man chest.

I loved that pose.

I ignored the pose and marched past him.

"Is dinner ready, I'm starved?"

Then the house phone rang.

"I'll get it," he barked, still very angry.

Matt had called me on my cell on the way home and told me he'd found the message from Tom B. and wanted to know what I was up to.

I told him what I'd been up to.

He blew his top, called up Tom Beardsley. *Fucking Tom Beardsley.* Like it was his fault. I defended Tom, but Matt was too angry to hear me.

I ended the call by telling him I was driving and couldn't legally talk. Then I hung up.

My hubby needed a time-out to get control. By the time I got home he was close, but not all the way there yet. I decided to pretend there was nothing wrong. Sometimes that worked.

"Who was it?" I called as he returned to the living room. I hadn't looked at his face yet.

"Tom Beardsley. Says he's got a text from Luis that indicates he's in trouble. We should check our cell phones."

Oh, no. The last time I'd seen Luis Lewis he was still out in the field behind the school.

"He hasn't checked in with me. Check yours Rache." Matt.

I did. He peered over my shoulder as we both tried to make sense of what we were reading.

The first bunch of Luis' text messages indicated another girl had been taken by the gang members, another Indian girl.

"Sounds like it was just after you left. Where were the cops when you left? What time did you leave?" Matt.

"The police were still back with the crime scene for Jesus Escudero. I left well after four. Why would a student still be on campus?" Me.

"Wait, here he says the girl was out front of the school, waiting for a ride home. He says he was told to look for her out front." Matt.

"Told, who told him?" Me.

"...he's following the river in front of the school, south toward the Chicano neighborhood. Damn. I hate his abbreviations." Matt.

"Is he chasing the gang members? Do they have the girl?" Me.

There were pages of his text messages that I hadn't seen. Then they started coming in real-time.

"Oh, Matt!"

Another text arrived.

"Fuck! He's in trouble." Matt.

It sounded like the Pintos had him surrounded. Then came his last text.

"No girl. Just me."

"Call Will and tell him to meet me up on the mountain at the school," Matt shouted at me as he ran down the lawn to his truck.

"Watch out for the kids!" I called after him.

Alone, I waited for more text messages but none came. Then I worried that it might be the same gang that killed the young boy found behind Pinto Springs high school. What if they got hold of Luis?

But the second body found that long day and night wouldn't be Luis Lewis'.

PART TWO

woof and waft

Chapter 55

Saturday, November, early morning

Matt and Will were going door-to-door through the Chicano neighborhood in south Pinto Springs in search of Luis. I was at home, waiting.

When Matt first called me around nine, he'd said that about fifty local Chicano and Native American parents had joined the police in the search. They were growing desperate to find their missing children—the two Indian girls, and another Pinto gang member who'd apparently been missing for about as long as Jesus Escudero.

The second time Matt called it was after midnight, right after dealing with a guy whose front door looked like it was accustomed to battering rams. Matt began by saying he decided not to ram the door but to knock politely--even though by then his frustration level was so high he wanted to bang heads, not doors.

"A fucking scrub jay answered the door."

His words surprised me. I'm the one that thinks in animal kingdom, not Matt.

I asked him what he meant.

"The guy was eyeing us sideways, head up and cocked, and flapping his wings around like he expected menacing would chase us away." He tried to chuckle, it came out sounding raspy and sere.

Jay didn't know my Matt. Jay didn't know Matt was a Marine, I thought, but did not say. I was just waking up from a brief nap. My brain was only half on, so I mostly listened.

"*'What-chew you want bitch?'*" Matt.

I assumed that was the Jay's line.

"Will wasn't happy with the man's *'tude*, so he stepped right into the guy, pushed his bulk up against him and forced him back inside his own nest."

I have been there when Will got upset. It wasn't pretty. Matt stopped and I listened to distant voices in the background wondering whose they were.

"We are deep inside the Pinto Springs barrio, Rache. We're embedded with the cops. But I figured it was time for a break before Will started World War III."

It wasn't a barrio, just a poor neighborhood to the south of Pinto Springs. Then the bomb dropped.

"They found the second boy, a half hour ago."

"And?"

"Dead. Gorge Castillo, age fifteen. Forever. They slit his throat, let him bleed out in a drainage ditch about two miles from the kid you saw this afternoon. Sounds like he was also tortured. That's what got Will so uptight."

My stomach flip-flopped. I pushed myself off the couch and paced to control a sudden surge of emotions. *Oh, God.*

"Where's...Luis?" Me.

"Yes. That is the question." Matt.

His tone said so much more. We were both thinking the same ugly thoughts. There was little else to say. After a few minutes, we drifted into closure.

I hoped I'd soothed his mind a bit, telling him I loved him. But now I was wide awake. So I got a cup of warm tea and sat back down to ponder and stare sightlessly at the television. I turned it off, suddenly afraid I'd learn about Luis through some uncaring reporter's story.

The phone rang around quarter to one as I was beginning to snooze. Matt jarred me again with his brief intro.

"Go to bed, Rache. It's over."

I held my breath. *What's over?*

"I'll be on the way home soon. They found Luis. He's alive."

"How..?" He interrupted me, thought I wanted to know how Luis was found.

"The scrub jay caved after our second visit. Will is very persuasive when he wants to be. He suggested maybe they were in over their heads and maybe they should help us get these bad guys."

He paused to answer a question from someone off to the side."

"Matt, *how is Luis?*"

He sighed. "Not good. He's hurt. They...roughed him up a bit. I'll tell you more when I get home. Sandy's on the way to the hospital. You better get some sleep. Luis is in the good hands of Gloria P. now." *Intensive care!*

"How badly was he hurt? Will he be all right..?"

I was talking to the air. Matt had hung up.

I knew I'd never be able to sleep, so I just settled back down on the couch to await him.

Of course I did sleep, at least for a few hours. At some point Matt slipped in the front door noiselessly and went to our bedroom, leaving me to my meager rest. And now I sat staring out our deck window again, this time at the sun rise. Wisdom was out there listening for the sounds from the newly renamed San Diego *Safari Park*.

Tonight was the all-night quilting bee. My neck hurt just thinking about it. And there was still no sign of the two missing Indian girls.

Chapter 56

Sometime around noon I fell back to sleep, capturing a few more hours of rest before Abigail's bee. I woke from my nap to sounds of Wisdom sneezing on the back porch.

Matt and I calmed him as well as we could but he was tearing himself up, poor baby. And now his nose was bleeding again.

We gave him another tranquilizer and shared a look that said we'd have to do something more on Monday when the vet's office opened again.

We weren't discussing what that something was, but we both knew we were running out of options. The vet had told us after the last procedure—a removal of the first tumor below his eye—that short of chemotherapy or radiation therapy which would leave him blind in one eye, there was nothing else to do but make him comfortable.

We weren't that rich. We also would not feel right about spending money on sophisticated medical treatments many people on earth had no access to.

I flipped channels on the television and discovered that the Saturday afternoon news was giving Gorge Castillo credit for trying to stop Luis' beating. Matt was inclined to agree based on his experience with the boy's parents, who were now preparing to bury this good son next to his little sister, who had died at the age of eight of bone cancer. I glanced at Wisdom again. Was he experiencing this terrible death so he could someday welcome little children into heaven with a knowing heart?

My vision clouded over as I fought to keep from crying. So then I turned my emotions on the television, when for their own perverse reasons the producers on the news channel segued into a report of another killing on the Arizona border.

Both Matt and I thought the media did a terrible disservice to Mexican-Americans and those still trying to escape the poverty in their native country by depicting them as a pack of rabid drug lords invading our country.

Mostly, they are hard workers willing to take a low-paying job. But unfortunately, like the people of Afghanistan, if you have no other way to make a living than to cater to the Western hunger for illegal drugs, then that's the route you take. And unfortunately, some small percentage of those crossing the border did.

In the late afternoon, Matt and I drove up the mountain road again to Cleveland County's plateau.

The first thing we did was visit a sleeping Luis in the hopes he'd regained consciousness. We found that Sandra had gone home and the nurses now in charge of ICU weren't telling us much. Of course Gloria was at home preparing for tonight's bee.

If it weren't for the bandages and bruises, you'd think he was asleep, I mused. It gave me shivers to find him in the same bed that poor Jimmy Winters had occupied.

As we left, another connection came to me--other than the obvious age differences he looked a lot like Ruth. Behind bruised and swollen lids, his eyes were chasing ghosts too.

And then we headed for Abigail's house just a few miles from the hospital. My protective Irish lad was taking no chances on me driving home tired in the wee hours after this bee, by dropping me off there with a promise to pick me up at dawn.

It was not until three days after the bee that I found a LIRI journal that Matt maintained during the long night ahead. It contained a full accounting of the events leading up to the capture of the bad guys from his perspective.

Chapter 57

Saturday, November 1, 6 pm

He drove away in an angry silence as I trudged up the cement sidewalk leading to Abigail's front door. Matt was still upset that I'd decided to go ahead with the bee despite all that was happening.

Or maybe he was displacing his guilt over Luis. *Our* guilt.

Because, maybe Sandra had been right, Luis wasn't ready for dangerous assignments. He shouldn't have single-handedly chased after the gang as they swept away yet another innocent Native American girl.

But then I wondered if I wouldn't have done the same.

Three days ago on Wednesday afternoon, when Betty Wolfgang had gone missing, we should have noted Luis' reaction. He had been hot to chase after Wolfgang then. At that point we should have cautioned him about intervening during a violent act. The better idea was to follow at a safe distance and wait until the situation had subsided. And call for backup. Maybe even a posse.

But, we'd had no idea what gang we were really dealing with three days ago. We'd thought it was just the Pintos, just a homegrown gang--with violent tendencies, yes, but usually only during specific activities such as initiation rites and after nights of drinking.

Now we suspected we were dealing with international terrorism. I shoved my ricocheting anger-guilt aside and prepared my face for the sewing ladies.

Inside I expected to find seven quilters, plus Gloria and Nana. Our oldest quilter was Victoria Stowall, the matriarch of the Secret Quilters group. I wondered if this octogenarian would make it to the bee this month. She was quite ill.

Age-wise, mine would be the next name on my mental list. Then there were homeschooler Hannah and fashionable Gerry, my two part-time apprentices, a couple of moms in their forties. I related strongly to these two women, and you might think of the three of us as the center of the Secret Quilts—at least chronologically.

After tonight's events, some would think of us as the Three Musketeers.

A counterweight to our middle-aged center was the group of three youngest quilters, Elixchel, Andrea and Abigail. Elixchel was a six-foot-tall, raven-haired, Mayan goddess and Andrea was a five-foot-two undernourished, edgy, pixie lesbian. Abigail was the baby of our group, and it was her quilt that we would be completing tonight.

I'd worn my LL Bean all-weather coat and matching brown Crocs, but in the large canvas bag I was carrying I had jogging shoes and other things I liked to carry—just in case. *Just in case what?*

A curtain moved in the window to the right of the front door. Then the door opened. I finished climbing the steps.

"Hi, Gloria…"

My happy greeting died in my throat. Gloria had her angry face on.

"What's up?" I said, not sure I was being welcomed in. She just stared, looking grim, her mouth a thin line. She was fighting tears.

Oh God, don't tell me Luis has….

Finally she stepped aside, so I could enter the small foyer. My heart was suddenly beating faster.

Ahead were the stairs up to the bedrooms. To my left was the small room I knew to be Nana's—the door slightly ajar and a light within.

On the right was a small kitchen-dining room space, and beyond it was a larger living room. An arched doorway lead to something I couldn't see from my vantage. Whatever it was, it sat even further to the right, off the living room. I spotted Hannah talking with Elixchel. They looked grim.

Finally I turned back toward Gloria, tuning my ears to receive Ukrainian-English. I was hoping I'd given her enough time to compose herself.

"Okay, out with it. What's wrong?"

"Abigail isn't here, that's vot's wrong." She scowled, and her lips shut tight again. There was a wail trying to get though those lips. Now I was frowning.

Actually I think I always frown when listening to Gloria. Maybe tensing my forehead muscles helps with the translation process by pulling my ears forward—like a dog listening hard.

Probably not. Probably I was frowning because I'd received an emotional blow to the chest. It was well after dark. It was her quilt we would sew. No way Abigail would go missing deliberately tonight.

"Where is she?" It came out a whisper. It was a stupid question.

"I hef no idea. She hasn't called. She didn't tell her Nana anything. She just slip out the door sometime round noon and never return." Her voice hitched.

"Have you called her friends?"

"The ones I know—her homeschool friends. They haven't heard one peep from her since she went to public school!"

Gloria walked away into the kitchen, now very close to losing it. She began angrily pulling things out of the refrigerator and otherwise busying herself, mumbling as she did. I listened, noting she was listing the reasons why she could do nothing more than worry at this juncture. And then her worry turned to anger, and she sputtered about how Abigail had been late and missing on and off for the past two weeks.

Chapter 58

Hannah came up behind me, slipped my coat off my shoulders and took the large satchel I'd brought. I was so tense I almost didn't let got of it.

"What do you think?" I said in an aside to Hannah.

She shrugged and said, "Andrea doesn't know where Abigail might be either. Elixchel hasn't heard from her in a couple of weeks. I'm sure she'll show up. She's very rebellious right now."

But what if..? Storm trooper butterflies assaulted my stomach. I said a silent prayer that Abigail would be okay, that she'd walk in the front door any minute to join us.

I glanced toward the small group of women standing around in the living room. This time Andrea's jagged-cut garnet hair was tipped in army-green and black. Elixchel was wearing tawny sweats with a long-sleeved turtleneck in pearl gray--cougar colors that emphasized her onyx hair and bronze skin magnificently.

I didn't see Gerry or Victoria. But there was a new female to meet. I locked eyes with her briefly.

Gloria continued to set out refreshments, banging cups and saucers, putting on a kettle of water for the tea. I thought I could see the new gray sprouting in her brown hair under the overhead kitchen light. Was she aging before our eyes?

A hungry shark punched his way into my stomach to join the storm troopers. I would spend most of the night feeding the beast to keep it from eating away the lining of my stomach.

"I'll let Matt know she's missing." I opened my phone and typed him a short text message.

Of course Matt turned off all electronics when driving. It's against the law to use phones while en coche in California, a law I had mixed emotions about.

Anyway, he wouldn't get the message that Abigail was missing for at least another thirty minutes. *If he checked.*

"Maybe when Gerry gets here...."

I was thinking but not saying--*she should contact her brother, Tom Beardsley.* Hannah nodded agreement, as if she'd heard my thoughts.

The shark swam, the butterflies cheering him on. *Bite, bite, bite!*

I bit the corner of my lower lip and nodded to Andrea and Elixchel. I was suddenly feeling totally inadequate. What should I do? What could I do until Matt checked in? I knew the police wouldn't act until Abigail's absence sounded more suspicious. I glanced at my watch again, still before seven. Not that late for a thirteen-year-old.

"Let me introduce you to my mom's replacement quilter," Hannah was saying, while guiding me deeper into the living room.

We approached a graying, late middle-aged woman—maybe in her early sixties--wearing a light blue sweater over jeans. On her feet were some snuggly-looking blue slippers. She wore metal rimmed eyeglasses.

"Anne, this is Rachel Lyons, our other new quilter."

Of course. Gerry had told me this way back. She was Anne Stowall, one of Victoria's damaged daughters—the ones that had been sterilized at the insistence of their crazed father Jake, who wanted to end the spread of hemophilia in his branch of the Stowall clan. It was another era for medical ethics, apparently. Or yet another example of the frightening extent of Stowall connections and influence, that a Jake Stowall could force sterilization on his children.

Except now we all knew that Eddie, Jake's grandson, was alive and fertile and out there roaming around freely.

The last time I looked at him he was a cross between male and female, overweight, and dressed like a hip-hop version of an American cowboy. I doubted he was making babies, yet.

My anxiety increased as we shook hands and Anne started making small talk. I wasn't sure I could concentrate on small talk right now. She was telling me how much she appreciated what I'd done for Eddie. *Huh? I'd shot him*. What was she thinking?

I prayed my face didn't betray my inner turmoil. With all that had happened in the past twenty-four hours, it was a wonder I could remember my name, as my mother used to say.

My brain was tracking big fish, butterflies, handshakes with messed-up women, terrified Gloria as she banged around her little kitchen...and how many more minutes it would be before Matt finally landed in Escondido and I could give him another problem to deal with.

Of course, I say the Stowall girls are messed-up— *how could they be anything else with what was done to them?*—but I really h ad no idea who they were.

In an effort to slow my thinking down, I took the measure of Anne. She looked like a shy duiker, diving into bushes in search of crumbs left by the other animals. Her nose was elongated and her blond hair stuck up around her head in dozens of little ringlets that also made me think of Little Women. Or little baby birds flying around their birdhouse. Her body was bottom heavy with foreshortened arms forever poised as if to sew or forage. Definitely a duiker—with bird attributes.

But her diminutive voice made you think pigeon or owl as she seemed to end every other sentence with a purposeless 'who-who' sound.

"I've seen you before Rachel, although I don't think you noticed me. It was in the hospital, when you were down a room from my nephew Eddie, *who-who.*"

She was referring to the shooting event that landed both Eddie and I in the hospital; him with my bullet in the fatty tissues of his hip and me with the top of my left ear being trimmed a tad by his bullet. The Gunfight at the not-so-O. K. Corral—Ada Stowall's front porch.

The *who-who* was some sort of nervous tic.

It was Saturday night and thirteen year old Abigail was out and about in the dark—the day *after* Halloween. Anne finally stopped yammering so I could actually greet her.

"I'm glad to meet you too, Anne."

Really? At least one of them enabled Eddie to shoot me last month—by giving him a gun. And maybe another tried to drive me off a road. And now it seemed everyone wanted to arm Eddie.

But probably not Anne...Anne was the middle child of seven. Middle children were usually fairly subdued.

"Same here. You did a good thing for Eddie, although Mary has mixed emotions about it, and Martha is...well, she's Martha, *who-who*."

She was referring to her functional sisters. The fourth Stowall daughter, Sarah, was outright brain damaged—or so I'd heard. Despite my misgivings about Anne and her whole clan, this unpretentious looking woman was coming across as someone you could trust. For now.

I shouldn't generalize about them, I reminded myself. Before Anne, I'd only met the very elderly Victoria--and Jake and Luke, both of whom had been corpses at the time.

But Luke had worn his oddness like a coat of many colors.

So, I should not judge them unkindly, I repeated to my brain. It helped that she was shorter than me. Anyone you can look down upon is perceived as less of a threat--part of that whole stand-or-sit psychology of the animal kingdom.

Unless it was a little dog. Little dogs bite. Another of my unreasonable prejudices.

Hello brain. Earth to brain. Settle down!

Dear God, where the hell was Abigail? My watch still said it was before seven. Had it stopped?

"I didn't think you girls quilted," I managed to say in a normal tone. I think.

"Well, we don't like to. We had an overdose of quilting when we were young, as you can probably imagine, with my mother's obsession I mean. But...."

She stopped and looked toward the still unidentified room off the living room, and I knew suddenly that Victoria Stowall was probably out there. Victoria, had been recently diagnosed with ALS, more commonly known as Lou Gehrig's disease. I was frankly marveling that she was here at all.

"Well, you catch my drift. We all feel we need to spend more time with mom now, *who-who.*"

Maybe it was a form of asthma, she sounded like she was clearing her throat.

"Will!" I blurted.

"What?" Sweet Anne was now frowning, big time.

Even Hannah jumped.

"Excuse me. I have to make a phone call...."

My adrenaline-racing brain had finally landed on Will Townsend, who might be able to help us immediately.

Chapter 59

I raced into the bathroom.

It was a reflex. We aren't supposed to use modern-day devices like electronics at the quilting bees. A minute later I came out. Will wasn't answering either. My brain continued to simmer just below boil. But at least the visit to the bathroom had slowed down my breathing.

Back to the introductions, and more about the women I quilt with.

As I've said before, Elixchel (pronounced Elish-shell) is model beautiful, over six feet tall, with long black hair with bangs that circle about her face, enhancing her Egyptian features. Her patrician nose spoke to Rome. Caught in the right light her dark brown eyes could seem to be all pupil. And her cinnamon-bronze skin called up her Mayan roots.

Elixchel moved with the grace of a jaguar which may be why she renamed herself.

Born Elizabeth Chavez thirty or so years ago, she decided to rename herself recently to celebrate her Mayan heritage. So she combined the name Ixchel--the Mayan jaguar goddess of midwifery--with Elizabeth and came up with Elixchel.

We have all agreed to use that name now, although Andrea spent much of the last bee teasing her about it.

Andrea is the exact opposite of Elixchel.

Petite, mostly red-haired, as I've said, she tips her hair in varying colors--Andrea Kelly is in her twenties and Victoria accurately describes her as the punk quilter in the Quilted Secrets group. Complete with tattoos, nose-ear-lip-brow rings, and army boots.

Well, not tonight; tonight she was wearing hiking boots. But she was in another pair of baggy fatigues as I've stated—the ones with a half dozen pockets all over

them—and an Army green t-shirt emblazed with Che
Guevara's face in black.

She was currently wearing a camouflage jacket over
all of this so her tattoos were mostly covered.

Last month her dark red hair was tipped in various
shades of hot pink and purple. This month the tips were
green and yellow. So maybe she was using some
washable dye that she could rinse off and change to suit
her mood. Or match her outfits.

Both Elixchel and Andrea were taken into Victoria's
home at some time in their lives, but I'm not clear if they
were actually adopted. Their reasons for leaving their
birth families were very dissimilar. Elixchel's mom and
dad died as the result of a terrible car crash on a trip to
Mexico and Andrea's Christian parents simply couldn't
accept her lesbian status.

"We all miss Ruth so much, Hannah. Especially her
dry humor," Elixchel was saying.

But maybe not her right-wing religious and political
views, I thought but did not say. And then another
thought hit me.

"Who'll take Abigail's place if she doesn't turn up?"

Okay that was my second stupid remark of the
evening. There would no doubt be others.

If she didn't turn up we'd all be out on the streets of
Pinto Springs searching for her.

In fact, maybe we should be out there right now.
Except part of me was thinking Abigail had ditched her
very own bee to spend time with her new friends.

"I will," Gloria said from behind the kitchen bar.

"You quilt?" I said.

"Have for years. That's why Abigail got into it."

A pained expression passed across Gloria's face and
she quickly turned her back to us and shifted plates
around in the sink.

My eyes caught Hannah's and we shared a moment
of concern.

"Don't worry, she'll show up. She's just asserting
her newfound adulthood," Andrea quipped.

Surprising me, the second thing the caustic pixie said was, "How's Luis?"

I gave them what little information I had, and asked how she knew him.

"We were watching his tweets when he was over at the school, until he announced he was going private." Andrea shrugged.

Elixchel said, "It's just as well. I was loading my gun and putting my shoulder holster on when I read the part about the attack on the first Luiseño girl. I'd have jumped in my car and gotten myself killed with the second for sure, if I'd known about it."

There was a pause in the conversation while we took in her comment. I was guessing she was kidding.

Andrea was too. She said, "You don't own a gun."

"Yes I do."

"Because of--" Andrea began.

"Don't go there." Elixchel snapped.

Elixchel was warning her away from something. I was still relatively new to this group and I looked toward Hannah. But Hannah and Anne seemed as clueless as me.

I looked at my watch. Five more minutes and I'd try Matt again. On every phone in our house, if necessary. Then I'd try the neighbors.

I stepped away to join Gloria in the kitchen—actually an open space with a low counter defining it on a third side that acted as a bar or breakfast table. So there was no real privacy, but I needed to ask her what I should have thought to ask initially.

"Gloria, have you contacted the police about Abigail's absence?"

"Yes. Called dem ven I got home—had to do a couple a hours at verk to cover lunches and breaks, so I vasn't back until after four. And den I tought she was upstairs. My mother never even told me...."

She put her hand up to cover her face, then quickly turned to the fridge and opened the door to pretend she was busy retrieving something. I waited a moment for her to calm.

"Did they send anyone over to take a report?"

"Yeah, some young guy, told me not to verry. Here's his card. Told me to call dem if she don't show up before ten. Smartass started telling me kids her age are out all hours of the day and night now. I lost it. I tink I'm doing more harm dan good. Maybe you and Matt...."

Her voice trailed off again, and this time she used a dishtowel to blot her eyes.

"Dis is not like her, Rachel."

"I know. We'll press our case again, Gloria, as soon as Matt calls. But you'll have to deal with the authorities. They'll expect it. We can help you though."

I left her then and returned to the others, feeling less panicked. At least Gloria had started the ball rolling. But now I was thinking we had to contact Learner. He at least knew the seriousness of what was going on at the high school. He'd understand that there could be connections here.

I could see Andrea's brain mulling over whether to continue her customary harassment of Elixchel or not. But Gloria saved us by saying, "Come on out to the sunroom and take a look at my daughter's art."

She was talking to me.

It was then that I noticed the two paintings adorning the living room wall behind the couch. They were huge renditions of lilies, one done all in white and green tones and the other almost a mirror picture with the lilies in shades of lavender and purple. Her painting was exceptionally good, just as I'd been told it was.

"She's in her floral period now," Gloria said as she led me to the mystery room I'd wondered about. "Before the flowers she mostly painted horses and dogs."

Anne followed us along.

The sunroom--actually a closed in porch that led down from the living by two steps--was enormous, running the full depth of the condo and twenty feet wide, it also seemed to have the night sky as its ceiling it was so tall. The two solid walls—the front wall and the shared wall with the rest of the condo--were covered with Abigail's wonderful recreations. Not just lilies, but daffodils, tulips, sunflowers, roses and even a humble dandelion—in mauve on midnight blue.

The other two walls of this room were broken up by large windows, but even there Abigail or Gloria had hung some of her smaller paintings.

"Does she use oils or acrylic?"

"Mostly acrylic, it's easier to work with than oil. A couple are done in chalk; a few in watercolor."

And then I spotted Victoria in a recliner chair in the far corner of the room. She moved, and the light next to her switched on.

Chapter 60

This was the exact way I'd first met Victoria at her house last month. I was frightened by the sight of her then and was reminded of that fright again now.

Victoria looks like Stephen King's grandma. Fat, wrinkly, dressed like someone's nightmare, she wore what could only be called a "house dress". It was colorless in the near dark. Over that was a baggy white sweater with stains around the wrists. Sprouting from black leather walking shoes was a pair of dark brown knee high stockings reaching for her thick knees.

I retrieved my satchel from the living room and opened it as Hannah and Victoria quietly chatted, but not about Abigail, I noted. Maybe Hannah was thinking Victoria needed to be protected, because of her illness.

Returning, I solemnly held out Ada's quilt, now draped across my forearms. It was an intricately decorated album quilt covered with biblical scenes—and full of painful memories.

The hand quilting group had given it to me last month, hoping my research skills could be used to crack the mystery of Ada's death. It had indeed contained family secrets that were part of the answer they sought.

"I assume this quilt goes to you, Victoria, since she was your daughter-in-law."

"No! It goes to Eddie." Andrea shouted. She was watching us from the doorway, and she swooped into the room like a red headed hawk and tore the quilt from my arms. It almost weighed as much as her, and she swayed as she tried to adjust it in her arms.

Joining us, Anne shook her head and her short curly hair wriggled around her head like peevish yellow and white budgerigars.

BARBARA SULLIVAN

"No, I can't agree, Andrea. Eddie has no home at this point. I'm sure his grandma will give it to him when he's ready."

"What are you talking about? His home..." But she didn't finish. Instead her beady eyes grew as the implications of what Anne was saying sunk in. Eddie had lived all of his life with his parents' Luke and Ada until a couple of weeks ago, when his encounter with me had set him free to roam.

"What are you up to?"

"Calm down, Andrea. The County has made the decision to have the old Stowall house torn down, along with several other vacant homes in that run down neighborhood. They feel it would be a wonderful place to establish a county park, complete with a small zoo," Anne said.

Wahoo! I wanted to cheer. Not just for a new zoo, but because the neighborhood Eddie had lived in looked to me like it was suffering from a sixteenth century curse.

"What the..." Andrea glanced at Victoria, and swallowed the F word waiting at the back of her throat. "When did this happen? Don't they have to have public meetings on this kind of thing?"

Anne remained calm in the face of Andrea's storm. And my storm-trooper butterflies were still coaxing the shark.

"No. They're taking the land under eminent domain laws which have recently been expanded by the Supreme Court. And frankly we're in agreement. There really was no hope of selling the house, given its current condition and its history. And the entire neighborhood is either upside down in debt or occupied by very old people who are slowly dying off, *who-who*," Anne said.

I excused myself in order to try Matt's cell phone again. Again it went directly to voicemail. Where the hell was he?

The argument in the other room continued. I half-listened, my arms folded protectively across my body. I

- 254 -

began reviewing the steps to take in the case of a missing child. Abigail was a child, not a teen. A child.

"Where will Eddie live?" Gloria asked, her suddenly small voice sounding much like her daughter's. Fear was sapping her strength.

Inaction was sapping both our strengths.

"The house contains only bad memories for him, Gloria. This is for the best, really." Anne said with finality.

But Hannah persisted. "What about the Stowall family cemetery?"

"It will be moved to the County Cemetery on High Street. For the time being if Eddie returns to this area he'll live with his grandma or he can stay with me. I have a very nice three bedroom home about halfway between Julian and Iguana."

Julian is the town north of Cleveland County where the three Stowall sisters own and operate the Apple FIXation restaurant and store.

Iguana, twenty-five miles south of Julian and inside Cleveland County, is where Victoria Stowall lives, and Ada's home is--soon to be was—a couple of miles away from Victoria's.

And where we were standing and making this idiot small talk was in Pinto Springs, the largest city in Cleveland County and still further south and east of Iguana, by maybe twenty miles.

So large a city it had a wonderful police department, one with an excellent detective's division, one we should be calling right now.

"Why the..." (A quick eye check to Victoria.) *"...don't you think he'll return?"* Andrea was growing more agitated by the moment and for some reason I worried that she'd lose it entirely.

"He probably will, Andrea. If you'd like to keep his quilt for him until then, that will be fine," Victoria said in her ancient voice, now not just deeply hoarse, but also quavering. "I have more quilts than I know what to do with."

"Or I could keep it for him, Andrea," Anne said.

"No way! Your house is full of cats. They'll tear it apart."

Victoria stopped things from escalating by lifting the quilt for Andrea to take.

Andrea retreated into the living room temporarily mollified, holding the quilt tightly in her arms.

I didn't care who had it as long as it wasn't me. And now I was wondering how many cats Anne had.

I checked my watch. Matt should have reached home by now. I would try our house phone next.

I finally thought to ask Gloria if her daughter had called or otherwise contacted her or Nana at anytime during the afternoon--which is when Nana emerged from her little downstairs bedroom by the stairs.

"Oh, gud, she's awake finally," Gloria muttered as she spotted her mother and moved towards her. The two began gabbing in Cyrillic

A few moments later Nana returned to her room and we all stood staring at Gloria expectantly.

Gloria noticed at last and said, "My mother says Abigail called around two to say she was with friends, but she didn't say who they were or where she was." Gloria's shoulders drooped. Now she just looked dispirited.

I was still thinking it was wrong that Abby wasn't here for her bee, but a little more of the pressure went out of my emotions.

Then the doorbell rang and Gloria raced to answer it. But it wasn't news of Abigail, it was Geraldine Patrone finally arriving. She would be the last quilter to arrive this evening.

Gerry was even taller than Elixchel, thanks to an outrageous pair of backless heels, outrageous because each big toe was adorned with a pink pompom. They looked like 1930's Hollywood bedroom slippers.

Come to think of it, she looked like a thirties Hollywood starlet. Maybe this was her Halloween costume, and she just loved it so much she was wearing it again tonight.

Gerry was the mother of four boys and a smart business woman, but to look at her you'd think she was a complete airhead.

Wearing her signature animal skin prints--this time an orange-and-white, tiger-striped big-shirt over black-and-white leopard-print tights--her floppy mop of blond curls added to the illusion that she looked down upon us from dizzying heights.

She and Elixchel approached six feet from opposite sides.

Over her left arm she carried a new hot-pink and silver pocketbook with the capital letter C all over it that probably cost a thousand dollars. It was big enough to carry her SUV. As she threw a light, gold-lamé jacket on the living room couch, the label flashed *Oscar de* something. The fold in the metallic fabric hid the rest.

Gerry was glamorous. I would be too if I'd married a billionaire. After dumping her things on the couch she joined us on the porch.

"Hey! It's the stitching sisters, back together again! How are you all doing?"

Geraldine Patrone may be the somewhere-around-forty wife of a billionaire, but she was also the mother of four boys. I mothered three boys and they drove me into the ground with their constant activity. Gerry was thriving...and may even be tapping into their energy source.

Of course that would be cookies and ice cream. She'd definitely put on weight since last month. Maybe she was pregnant, I viciously thought.

Don't ask, I told my brain as my mouth prepared to make a fool of me again. Besides I'm not that shallow, I reminded myself.

"Okay, what's wrong? Is it my outfit? You don't like flamingo pink and orange sherbet? You can't handle the switch from faux cheetah to faux leopard? You abhor the extra eight pounds I've put on and we haven't even passed Thanksgiving yet?"

I forgot to mention, Gerry's watch--*yet again? Tsh, tsh*--was her familiar pink Gucci with blinding diamonds.

Also, her fingers ended in ten different elaborately painted designs all inspired by Halloween, and she was still wearing Elizabeth Taylor's diamond on her wedding finger.

I would have to be careful not to watch her sew tonight, it might make me mad. With this thought I knew Gerry had lightened the mood—appropriate or not. At least my brain was tracking better and the butterflies had quit teasing the shark.

Suddenly I realized there was no rack in the room. Then I looked up.

Chapter 61

There are basically two types of hand quilting racks for group sewing. One is a free-standing structure that is designed to allow gradual expansion as the topstitching is completed. Some of these are fairly light-weight and can be transported as necessary, but they are almost always left out as display racks when not actually in use.

We'd sewn on the free-standing version at Victoria's bee the first Saturday in October--a heavy wooden structure that her late husband Jake had made for her years before.

(Jake, whose body I'd found seven weeks ago, burnt almost beyond recognition, a victim of the sort of familial foul play for which the Stowall family seemed to be infamous, had finally had his death ruled a homicide, partly due to my insistence. Of course it was irrelevant since the killer was dead, but it's the little victories in life that matter.)

So when I'd first wondered where the rack with Abigail's quilt was, I'd thought Gerry might be bringing it with her—perhaps swinging by Victoria's house to retrieve it and stuff it into her huge SUV. (More on Gerry's huge SUV later. Suffice it to say I'm both green with envy and disturbed at her unabashed and wasteful display of wealth with this vehicle.) However, after getting over Gerry's new outfit I returned to the question of where the rack was and finally thought to look up.

The second type of group quilting rack—a suspended structure--is stored on the ceiling.

Of course, if I'd thought it through in the first place I'd have remembered that Abigail and Gloria had been quilting together for years, so clearly they had to have a large quilt rack somewhere in the house.

I was curious what this experience would be like. I had misgivings as to the stability of a hanging quilt rack, especially if its support derived entirely from the wires attached to the ceiling—and you had eight women quilting on it at once.

Unless....

Again I looked around, and lo and behold found four support structures tucked away behind a small pile of un-hung canvases. They looked a little like saw horses and I assumed it was on these that the rack would rest once it was lowered.

It seemed as if Abigail's quilt was already loaded on the rack, but of course I couldn't see well in the dim lighting on the tall room. Besides, all that was visible was the bottom layer of the quilt.

The doorbell rang yet again and this time Gloria almost ran to the front door. My heart ached for her.

"Abigail..?" Gerry said. Then I heard Matt's deep voice, and relief washed over me. He stepped inside.

"Wow. Is that your husband? How do you rate?" Elixchel said. She was drooling.

It was true. Matt was drop-dead gorgeous. The gray at his temples was added spice. The six foot two muscular frame was more spice. And the Irish attitude made him just so flamingly spicy I should have my head examined for letting him leave the house alone. And I haven't even mentioned the crystal blue eyes.

"Rachel isn't chopped liver either, Lix." I heard Andrea say.

"*Lix?*" Elixchel said testily. "It would be Lish, if it were a proper diminutive..."

Uh-oh.

"Okay, what's going on? Where's Abigail?" Gerry complained as I walked toward Matt.

Behind me Anne said, "She's not here. She went out at noon. Gloria is frantic."

Chapter 62

Matt led me outside by the elbow and we sat in his car to discuss my two messages. He'd never gotten back to Escondido. After the second voice message from me, he'd stopped the car, listened to them, turned around, and made a couple of calls.

"Okay, what does Gloria know?"

"She's missing, is what she knows, has been since noon. The young cop they sent over to answer her cry for help tried to convince her it was normal for thirteen-year-old girls to be out until ten pm."

"Fuck."

Okay, I told you he was a retired Marine. They tend to swear a lot, especially during combat. Relieves tension.

"Matt, her accent, it gets in the way, especially when she's upset. The young cop probably couldn't even understand what she was saying, half the time. And then there's her personality."

He nodded.

"At least she's reported. We'll pick it up from there. Here's what we're going to do. Pay attention. One: Will is on the way. We're going to connect with Harks. Unfortunately I didn't get to meet Harks as planned, but Will knows him well and he's the link."

As I've said, Harks is the PI in Los Angeles Will Townsend had begun his apprenticeship with. He was an expert in gangs.

"Two: we'll connect with Tom Beardsley to get the county folks involved immediately and Detective Learner..."

"Pestilence. I...."

"I know he's hard to like but he's good. And he's necessary. He'll bring the PS cops along. And I've been cultivating them through Captain John Clancy in Escondido PD. He's Mosby's brother-in-law. We're down."

"Down. Fine. I didn't mean you shouldn't contact Learner. I agree completely with that move. And if the cops agree, maybe Tom B. could be the point of contact for Gloria. Gerry can help interpret between them, and she'd be another calming influence on Gloria. Frankly Matt, Gloria is terrified. I've never seen her like this, not even when those boys were dying all over her ICU. God only knows what her experience with criminals and cops in communist Ukraine was. And then there's Gloria and Abigail's recent history over schooling. But you should keep reminding them about her run-ins with the Pintos. Or maybe not, I'm not sure."

I was rattling on, a behavior that made him nuts. But I'd been holding back a steady stream of ideas for too long.

He was looking at me with that dead one-eyed stare only Marines and cops can do so well. And sometimes husbands.

I stared him down. If we were home this could lead to other things.

"You are going to sew tonight. Do you understand? I'll handle this."

"Door-to-door?"

"Yes. And phone canvassing. Harks has the names now. We'll find her, Rache. Stay calm. Trust me."

I did, of course. Always have. As much as I can trust anyone. But....

"Okay, fine. You'll keep me informed, or you know what will happen." I was still imitating his dead-eye.

"Step-by-step and blow-by-blow. I promise. Which reminds me, has Gloria called Abigail's cell?" I had to admit I didn't know if Abigail had a cell phone. I'd never seen her with one. I told him I'd ask.

She didn't, turns out. Gloria thought they were a toy, but I thought Gloria couldn't afford it.

"Be careful Matt...."

We kissed, and I could have sworn I heard several females swoon in the house.

When I got back inside the rack was down, the overhead lights were on, and the quilt was spread wide.

Stunning.

Simply stunning.

I joined the group of admirers looking in awe at Abigail's completed part of the quilt. The lighting for our sewing was now exposed above us and turned on, as it had been hidden behind the quilt. Before us, illuminated as if by heavenly light was Abigail's top sheet. The oohs and ahs lasted for several moments. A butterfly flitted into my belly asking me, *Is your quilt top good enough for this group of experts?*

We were each expected to complete a top sheet with its dramatic stitched-together design before our particular bee—an event that occurred once every eight months, of course, because there were eight of us.

At least, there were supposed to be eight of us, but now they seemed to be dropping like flies.

Bad thought. I erased it immediately. Abigail was fine, probably just tardy.

This was the part we were all expected to do on our own then present at our particular bee so we could all do the quilting. The "quilting" is the act of sewing the top sheet to the middle padding and the bottom sheet into one comforter.

Abigail's top sheet was a mosaic pattern. I've seen pictures of mosaics online, and even in a museums, but never like this, up close, where I could touch it. Three thousand or more tiny squares of fabric combined like the tiles of a floor mosaic to create a dramatic picture.

I looked for the smallest of errors in lining up the many corners and didn't see a single one. The alignment was perfect.

For a design, Abigail had recreated one of her lilies on an undulating navy blue background. This lily was done in purples and aquamarines and touches of flaming red and flamingo pink at its center. It must have taken her hundreds of hours, I mused.

"Okay ladies, we're ready to begin sewing now that Gerry is here," Victoria said.

It was traditional for Victoria to signal our beginning. It was traditional for her to tease the mother of four for being late, her wrinkled old face grinning slyly as she did.

Gerry moaned, but it was all part of the act.

Suddenly Gloria collapsed on the porch rattan couch in tears. The sight of her brilliant daughter's quilt had brought her terrors to the surface again.

It took ten minutes of talking and soothing to get her calm again. I told her what Matt was going to do. I told her to trust him, just as he'd said to me.

She listened and agreed just as I had with him. As much as she could. Inside I knew she was containing a raging need to rush screaming into the night in search of her child.

Then we returned our attention to the quilt. Our next task was to roll up the three layers of the quilt to a more manageable size.

The width of about ten feet would remain open. The length of the quilt, top to bottom--again about ten feet-- would be shortened so that we could reach the center of the quilt comfortably to create a starting line of stitches. To begin with, the quilters would sit four women at the top and four at the bottom.

One of four small sewing supply tables that would be arranged around us later was moved closer to the hanging quilt.

The first step was to assure that the three layers had been smoothed properly when being attached to the top and bottom dowels of the rack, something that Abigail and Gloria had done alone a few days before the bee. Victoria was a perfectionist and demanded perfection from each of us.

Victoria directed us to check the smoothness of all three layers before removing the two ten-foot side dowels, which were not actually attached to the quilt. They were used only to stretch the top and bottom dowels apart.

With four of us on the top and four of us on the bottom, we tugged and re-pinned the quilt as necessary until Victoria was content with the alignment of the three layers.

Next, I listened as Victoria instructed us to remove the two parallel sides of the floating rack. The excess length of the quilt would now be carefully rolled up onto the top and bottom dowels.

That done, we next turned our attention to the shorter dowels needed for this first stage of the quilting, which had been stashed near the wooden support horses. Then, the two shorter side dowels were secured. There were notches in the wood of these side dowels that the ends of the ten foot padded dowels would rest in. Four of us supported the corners, and three of us held the other dowels while Victoria placed one short dowel for maximum stretch along the left side.

She reached for a well-used strip of material from the supply table earlier positioned for easy access and quickly wrapped and secured her corner. She then moved to each of the other corners and repeated this process.

Now that the quilt was secured in its frame, with a four-foot-by-ten-foot field of material visible, the side stretchers were attached. These stretchers were plastic, paddle-shaped grippers that first were wrapped around the side dowels by thick rubber bands, and then were tightly clamped down on the three layers of material. I'd seen these plastic grippers used to secure the sides of deck awnings and figured we were good for up to fifty knots of wind.

Then Victoria told us to place the side horses under the side dowels to steady the rack. The gentle swaying stopped. We were finally ready to sew. I glanced at my watch; it was well after eight and full dark out with occasional gusts of chill mist. But inside we were toasty, and loading up on tea and sweets designed to keep us awake.

Victoria sat in her central position on the side facing the windows, and then instructed me to sit opposite but offset by one diagonally to her, just like the first quilt. My back would be to the cold glass for the rest of the night. At least there was a couch between me and those large windows.

Elixchel sat to Victoria's left. Gloria was told to sit on Victoria's right, where Abigail would normally have sat. To the right of Gloria was Andrea the pixie vixen.

On my left and directly across from Andrea was Hannah, and on my right sat Gerry, who was exactly opposite Victoria. The remaining seat Anne took. A wave of sadness swept over me as I contemplated that this was where Ruth would have been--to the right of Gerry and across from Elixchel.

All of this was so familiar to me from the first bee I half expected a fireplace to appear at one end of the room to help cheer us. But the room was warm enough without it, and fortunately there was no infernal Regulator clock to tick and chime away the endless hours as there had been in Victoria's sewing room.

I don't know whether Victoria was stalling the process in the hopes that Abigail would appear, but that was what she did. We would take two breaks during the layering and stretching--breaks in which we mostly stood around and stared at each other anxiously.

I began worrying that we would never finish this quilt. We had been ready to sew at that first bee by seven, but this one was starting much later.

At long last, we approached the readied quilt. We sat. Again we endured more stalling as Victoria prayed, or whatever she did, with her head bowed. We respectfully waited for Victoria's ritualistic behaviors to take us where we needed to go.

With one last great sigh, Victoria led us into the long night of stitching. She lifted her ancient and gnarled hands to the quilt, one on top, one hidden beneath, and placed the first stitch.

A muted sound of rain began tatting the roof above us.

Under the special lights hung from the ceiling to illuminate our careful stitches, the space around us slowly melted away as we watched her focus on this most important part of the quilting, the beginning stitches that would bring the three parts together into one. I mused that for hand quilters this was akin to the Father, the Son and the Holy Ghost joining as one Comforter.

Like a drum roll of expectation that didn't know how to quit, the sound above us intensified.

In my now seated position, hands clasped in my lap and tingling in anticipation--I said my own prayer, that Matt not be caught in the frigid rain suspended above Pinto Springs. And then it fell in earnest.

Chapter 63

Matthew Lyon's LIRI Journal
Saturday, Nov. 1, 8:15 pm, dictated outside
Rosemary's Café

Met Will outside Cleveland County Hospital in hopes Luis was awake and coherent. Turns out he wasn't. But Will had good news.

His connection with gang expert Deacon Harks could be the break we need. We've got 43 square miles of mostly undeveloped forest to search for Abigail Pustovoytenko and we need a goddamn lead or two.

Will reported Harks is arranging to come down from LA tonight with a couple of his people. He's been hearing rumors up his way that Hidalgo, the Tijuana-based cartel, is infiltrating SoCal. Hidalgo, ironically enough, was an honorific for Spanish nobility—fijo dalgo means son of something—SOB is more like it.

Will confirmed the Hidalgos' tag sign is MH with the M blended with the H. That's what Luis thought he saw carved into the chest of the Pinto found dead behind the school.

Will and I entered the hospital, dodged the reception desk and made our way up to the private room Luis has been moved to from ICU. Will ran interference with a security guard that was trying to run us down, probably ordered to prevent any further gang retaliation. Like we look like 'bangers. Jesus.

Luis was out and looked like death warmed over, covered in bandages, tubes and monitoring wires. Sandy must have left to catch some shuteye—a lucky break. She'll be tearing me a new one next time she sees me, I'm sure.

The nurse indicated he hadn't woken yet and might not for several days. I asked her to get a doctor on the horn, that we had a kidnap victim that Luis might be able to help find before it was too late. She wasn't happy but she went off to find one.

I snapped a capsule open under Luis' nose, but couldn't rouse him. That's when the doctor—Carnes was his name—came in and started lecturing me about cerebral edemas and messing in police business.

Cerebral edema. Goddamn 'bangers.

Called Beardsley on the way out of the hospital; he told me what I didn't want to hear. The Amber Alert for Abigail was going nowhere—not enough evidence she was "in peril." I told him to try Famine and Pestilence over at PSPD, to keep pressing.

Will followed me to a coffee shop downtown and we had grinders and talked about Harks' posse. Will said he'd be bringing Chicanos, which is good, as my Spanish isn't gonna cut it.

I told Will to take a few of Harks' men and work the condos on La Suenga, two to a door, bottom to top, with guys at the exits so no one sneaks out. Will said he thought the gang leaders will be in SFRs, overpopulated houses, not condos, and that the first floor guy will just call upstairs and warn off the others. He could be right. But we aren't getting jack out of the gang leaders anyway. Need to find some vato who might be willing to talk.

Will thinks Harks might be able to sweet talk 'em. I'll work with him. We'll see.

Chapter 64

By tradition, Victoria was the one who began the sewing. The rest of us would then join her, slowly, so that a good smooth base was formed. The stretchers made it unnecessary for us to wait for Victoria to complete a full foot of her section this time, but we still had to wait for her to establish an inch or two of all her lines. Then each of us in turn could lay down our set of rows, working outwards from her good beginning.

She bent to her briefly solitary task. I watched in admiration as ancient hands placed each stitch without a tremor and with no sign of weakness. I wondered if it was sheer will that made this possible. But I also mused that her steady hands were a testament to the ALS medications I knew her to be taking. I sent a thanks to God that I was blessed with living in this modern era when so much was made possible because of our medical knowledge.

My turn arrived. My hands positioned themselves as if by their own will and I was transported back to a month ago, to the first time I'd sewn with Victoria. And then from there, I traveled back in time by hundreds of years to Colonial America. We were doing what the women of those times had done. They had come together to quilt, and eventually to share their cares and concerns as the sewing progressed.

More than fabric was being stitched together as a whole in this room.

We sat on wooden chairs--chairs I knew would become a torture by the time the long night was over. Again, I wondered why. Victoria reportedly had said that it was to keep us awake. But I was convinced I could stay awake on a cushion as well. Maybe I'd lobby for comfort next time.

Surely Colonial women had used cushions.

Gerry's cell phone interrupted my silent grousing. She dug deep in her fabulously expensive bag and pulled it out. Since she was sitting right next to me I half listened. It was Tom, her very junior detective brother, but I really couldn't tell what he was saying. Gerry made a series of neutral noises in response to his masculine words.

But finally she broke into Tom's monologue to say, "She's right here, Tom. I'll just give her my phone."

She handed it across to Gloria and thus the long night of painful waiting took another step toward its eventual end, whatever that might be. And with this act Gerry had moved her nervous brother into direct communication with Gloria.

We all listened as Gloria made similar innocuous noises of understanding and acceptance, and then she hung up. At least she didn't cry.

Gerry pulled out her charger cord and handed that across to Gloria as well, suggesting she plug the phone in behind her and keep it nearby for her to use during the night.

Finally, Gloria said, "He has no news of my Abigail. He just calling to connect." She kept her head bowed, I believed to hide her emotions.

Topstitching on a quilt is the sewing that connects the three layers: the top sheet, the stuffing, and the bottom sheet or backing. Topstitching is the quilting stage.

Of course, on any quilt the top sheet of the quilt holds the key design element.

It can consist of many pieces of fabric sewn together to form the design or be one solid cut of material which is then embroidered or stitched upon decoratively to create a design in that manner.

But however it is done, the top sheet contains the design, while the *topstitching* holds the three separate layers of the quilt together.

I mention this, because topstitching can *also* be decorative, as is most obvious in single color quilts where the only design element is the topstitching.

Therefore with a solid color comforter—usually white or cream--the emphasis is on the elaborate design of the topstitching, not the sewing together of multicolored pieces of fabrics. There are many two- and three-hundred-year-old examples of solid color quilts in museums across America.

Pieced quilts evolved as an expedient way to produce a "new" blanket out of used pieces of material—clothing, even food storage sacks--when no large piece of fabric was available.

But Grandma's old nightshirt wasn't very interesting after fifty or more washings. And Grandpa's one suit might have survived several threadbare elbows before the lapels finally gave out. So bringing together interesting patterns and colors in large enough quantities of fabric to create an eye appealing quilt had always been difficult before the advent of machine-made fabrics.

Once machine-made fabrics became commonplace at the local general stores of America, this new folk art took off. American women had found a new way to express themselves, and the popularity of quilting blankets out of many scraps of material increased dramatically.

A very elaborate quilt uses several design elements at once in the process of its creation. In those cases the quilt was usually completed entirely by one person. Ada's masterpiece had been such a quilt, the one that I'd been handed at the end of the last bee.

However, what we were confronted with at this point was what topstitching design to use on Abigail's quilt. Unfortunately she was not here to tell us her preference, so we agonized over what was best--which at least distracted us from agonizing over where she was.

Since most quilts today contain at least two design elements on one quilt--the top sheet design and the topstitching design--the topstitching becomes very important.

Selecting the best topstitching pattern for your particular quilt involves not letting one design overwhelm the other.

So we sat for a few minutes debating whether to do a subtle topstitch or a more active one. The subtle topstitch of choice is called stitch-in-the-ditch.

Stitch-in-the-ditch is exactly what it sounds like. The stitches are laid down in the "ditch" formed between two pieces of fabric, or *in the seams* themselves. Done properly, they're not even visible on the quilt from the top side.

This was my personal choice. This method of topstitching would allow her picture to dominate the quilt.

Gloria had thought a cross hatch design, one that evoked the pattern on a garden trellis, would make more sense because of the large mosaic flower pattern we saw on her quilt.

Fortunately for us we went with the subtle stitch-in-the-ditch, because as it turned out we were dead wrong about Abigail's quilt.

Chapter 65

Matthew Lyon's LIRI Journal
Saturday, Nov. 1, 8:21-9:30 pm, dictated in Los
Gatos neighborhood of Pinto Springs

We found two gang houses right off the bat, driving down Vista Verde through the middle of Los Gatos, or Little Mexico. They were the ones that looked like a junk yard crossed with a garbage dump. Vatos with their pants falling off eyed us suspiciously from the front yard of one; the second house looked vacant. We noted the locations and drove on, figuring it best to wait for Harks and his team.

Las Pifia Park on the west side of Little Mexico is another hangout that Harks should send a few of his men to.

My attempts to light a fire under the local authorities had stalled. My man in San Diego, fellow ex-marine now in law enforcement, might come through. I told Will that I thought the stonewalling stank of...I don't know what. But two days to issue an AA for the first Indian girl and the second forced by media attention? Something's not right. Beardsley better make Abigail's happen, and soon.

Will asked if I was sure she'd been kidnapped. I don't know. But I'm assuming the worst for now. We'll decide what to tell mom if we find she's shacking up with some guy, though according to Lewis, the only guy he's seen her with is a chubby 13- or 14-year-old who looks like he's got more estrogen than testosterone flowing.

Harks called around nine as we were cruising Los Gatos, noting what gang houses we could ID. He said he was still on the road from LA and gave us a lecture, via speaker phone, on the state of the gang nations.

The Crips came first, in the late 60s in LA, the Bloods formed in reaction to them. Crips may be short for cripple—one of the early members had a bad leg. They're a loose affiliation of some 200 gangs, as often at war with each other as with the Bloods and Chicano gangs. The gangs don't mix ethnicity much, though there are a few Asian Crips gangs.

The binding tie was the 'hood. As with politics, all gangs are local.

By the early '80s, the Crips were big into the drug trade, PCP, amphetamines, pot. Getting into crack was hitting the big time for them. But by the late '90s, they were looking for more turf, and sex-trafficking looked good to them, according to Harks. Forcing vulnerable girls and women into prostitution made good money.

Harks reminded us that gangs were about security, money and status for their members; they act as a slum-government for those with little hope of employment and no interest in the system, who see status as fancy cars, beautiful women and money to spend.

"We see the gangsta going down. They see the gangsta living it up—if only for a while," he said. Gangs also become a government of the caught—prison gangs, where the guards let the bad guys do what they want to each other, sometimes because they have to, sometimes because they think it's a just reward. Prison's a breeding ground for domestic and international terrorists, Harks said.

He meant the Mexican Mafia. La Eme. Founded in '57 in the state prison in Tracy. Their prime symbol is 13 in its various forms—Roman numeral, number, a blend of the two, three dots. M is the 13th letter of the alphabet.

La Eme brought in weapons gang members only dreamt about before. Drugs were the income stream, murder was the means of enforcement and kidnapping women for sex was both reward and income stream. Women are even lower on the gang totem pole than the wannabes, according to Harks.

He hopes we're dealing with a local gang that's gone really bad. He's afraid we're dealing with international terrorism in the form of the Mexican Mafia, Los Hidalgos, aka MH for Miguel Hidalgo, leader of the Mexican War of Independence.

Los Hidalgos are the main gang running female slaves below the border. They control the Mexican drug and sex slave traffic in many border towns, especially Tijuana. A veritable stone's throw from Pinto Springs.

Harks said he figures there's too many users, too many suppliers, too much money and too easy communication to stem the gang tide, then signed off.

In the middle of all this, Will had gotten a phone call from Beardsley so we pulled over and he stepped out of the truck to take it. Beardsley had crapped out. It was 9:30, Abigail had been missing since noon. She could be anywhere in the hemisphere by now and nobody was officially looking of her.

Chapter 66

Gloria's mangled approximation of English led us off. We'd expanded and now conversation could begin. Gloria's need was greatest.

Between interpreting her Cyrillic and anxiously awaiting Andrea's pejorative outbreak—an alphabet bomb would be dropped, I was sure of it, before the night was over—my brain was itching.

Add in the nerve-jangling call of the identity crisis bird Anne, *Who-who, am I?* Well, you get the picture—I was gunning for a king-sized headache.

Suddenly little Andrea proclaimed she was boiling and dramatically stood and whipped off her mannish jacket.

Boiling? You could ice skate on my back, but then, the windows were behind me.

Of course, it was a ruse, so she could show off her raised tats. Last month I'd been introduced to Andrea's latest artistic work: four raised tattoos of religious symbols. At least Christianity was on her front, her chest to be exact. The other three were one on each shoulder and one centered high on her back. It made my spine itch. I wasn't sure whether to bless myself or fall to my knees and go prostrate facing Mecca. At least they had mostly healed. No more oozing, raw meat look.

"What? No new embroidery this month," Elixchel quipped.

"Embroidery?" My third stupid utterance of the night. *Just wait for Pete's sake, explanations are bound to come.* Elixchel enlightened me.

"That's what she calls this deliberately tortured art, Embroidered Tats. You do know she works part time in a parlor, don't you?"

"No, I didn't."

Andrea sat down, done with her modeling and educated us.

"I like the raised art. It accents certain areas of the tat. So I have my artist hammer me—use a heavy hand when applying the dye—so I'll keloid.

"I keloid naturally anyway, so when I want a flat tat they have to use a very tiny needle with no hooking at the end—it'll get bent if it's been used before or handled badly. Can even happen in the packaging."

"So you deliberately scar your body?" Anne.

Andrea said, "Well, a tattoo *is* a scar, isn't it? The trick is to apply the tat so just enough scar tissue forms to hold the pigment forever. *These* are 3D or raised tattoos." She pointed at her chest with a delicate finger. I was reminded what a contrast Andrea was; so small and feminine on the outside, so masculine on the inside. "Some people call them hammered, because the tat artist uses his hand like a hammer. But I like to call them embroidered. Catchy, no?"

"Black people also keloid easily; that's where African tribal body art comes from. Of course you can get keloid scarring from picking at your scabs or going out in the sun too soon, too."

Elixchel said, "But my favorite of her body art projects is her hair, of course. You should have seen the Mohawk...."

My phone rang and I quickly rose from the quilt to answer it. No one stopped me, not even Victoria with her belief that we need to recreate the exact experience of Colonial quilting bees.

Under these circumstances, we would definitely take phone calls.

I stayed Gloria with a raised finger as she started to follow me. I needed to take the call alone. I should have gone into the bathroom.

Once in the living room my nose discovered that someone had cut into one of the pies--peach.

Whoa. I was in trouble now. Peach was one of my favorites, along with blueberry and of course apple and, and...*cherry.*

Oh, God, they were all out on the counter. As long as they'd been uncut I was safe, but now that someone had broken into the peach pie, I was doomed. Swallowing a sea of drool, I flipped my insistent cell phone open and quickly said hello.

I don't get ads on my cell.

It was Matt. I listened as he hurriedly brought me up to speed. Then he hung up. It was all so fast I didn't get a word in edgewise. How did I know if he hadn't left something out?

Maybe he was in danger.

No, Matt would naturally want to get back to what he was doing. But now I had a thousand questions rushing around my head like a forest full of Capuchin mothers searching for a missing baby.

I placed my hands on the kitchen counter trying to think what to do. That was when I cut a piece of pie. Which led to picking up a fork and....

"Who was it?" Gloria demanded, inches away from me.

My mouth was full. I half-choked it down and mumbled, "Matt."

"And? Come on now, Rachel, don't hold out on me."

At least I think that's what she said. So I turned toward her, thinking, *where the hell is Tom?*

But maybe they weren't together. Maybe Tom doesn't know what Matt knows. I stalled, pretending I was still choking down the pie, trying to decide what to tell her.

I decided to go with the truth. She'd know if I was lying, she was a trained nurse—symptoms were her specialty.

"Matt says there's been another killing. They've found a third Pintos gang member out behind the school grounds. It's recent. And they're going door to door now with the help of some folks from LA."

Her face fell into a flat mask. Another child had died at the hands of these violent people. *Would Abigail be next?*

Gerry's phone finally rang. Gloria ran to grab it and began speaking in Cyrillic. She caught herself and switched to English. We all listened to her listen to Tom, probably telling her pretty much what Matt had just told me.

Tom was nervous. His voice was so loud I could even make out some of it from ten feet away, and he concluded that he would have to keep it short because he was busy at a new crime scene.

"How did he die? He didn't' tell me." Gloria said, looking at me. Elixchel and Andrea had turned to face us, both of them chirruping "Who? Who died?"

And now they were all standing. Except Victoria. She sewed.

"Matt didn't say either, Gloria. He was rushed. He's in the middle of a neighborhood..."

"Don't hold out on me!" She was close to screaming.

"I'm not Gloria, really," I lied. Then I added, "But if I do, it will be because it's necessary. I might not tell you something Gloria because it's best if you don't know. It's like watching Congress make sausages. Who doesn't come away with indigestion? Some of us even get sick. Do you understand?"

I thought of another analogy. Chalk it up to too much pie.

"You don't let relatives into the operating rooms of your hospital and Matt and Tom won't tell you hurtful, useless information. He will even keep things from me sometimes, for the same reason."

Like I was doing right now.

I wasn't about to tell her the gang member's head had been sawed off and was now missing, and that the enraged and grieving family had identified the boy only by his clothing. And that now there was talk of gang warfare racing around the Pinto Springs barrio. Someone had pointed their collective fingers at the Scrub Valley High School across I-13.

Football rivals, for cripes sake.

But the ploy to redirect the rage had worked. Scrub Valley High contained another large ethnic group—

Asians of all types. And there was a Vietnamese gang presence there comparable to the Pintos.

I thought this was evidence of just how clever the Hidalgo gang was. Matt and the rest of the authorities knew it was the gang from Mexico killing the Pintos boys. Hidalgo was warning the Chicano parents in the barrio not to cross them.

I tried to see this misdirection toward the other high school as good news, that maybe it meant Hidalgo was growing afraid.

But I really was seeing these monsters as just hopped up sadistic nuts.

Gloria slumped down in her chair, her hands temporarily stalled. Next to her Victoria continued sewing as if she were deaf.

"I need more." Gloria whispered.

"I know." I would too.

I thought about it again and still came to the conclusion I wouldn't give her more. Our new quilter Anne saved me.

"Where did the word kidnapping come from, anyway, *who-who*."

All hands stopped sewing.

I was studying her who-who's by now. It didn't always happen. And it didn't seem to matter if her sentence was ending in a vowel sound or consonant. But it almost always happened when she was at the end of her thoughts on something.

Hannah saved us all by launching into one of her homeschooling lessons.

Chapter 67

"In Federal criminal law kidnapping is the removal of a person against their will, usually to hold that person imprisoned without legal authority.

"However, all our laws are handed down to us through English common law. In other words, kidnapping and murder are what's called common law offenses as opposed to statutory offenses. Statutory laws are court decisions that have happened since the establishment of the United States.

"I know this because Deborah wants to learn more about Medieval times. We're into Renaissance Fairs now. And I'm studying California laws to get my PI license. So it's kind of an overlap."

"Really! You're going to be a private investigator?" Elixchel-the-incredulous.

"Yes. I'm actually hoping to apprentice with Rachel once I've gotten a few classes under my belt."

I was picturing her farm. Her chickens and her children and her mother, and her one-acre garden...and I figured it would be a while before she formally asked us.

"But where'd the word kidnapping come from, *who-who*?" Anne whined.

(Had I just met her seven year old self? Miss-misunderstood? Must've been awful being the sandwich child in a seven-decker. You'd never taste her among all the other ingredients.)

Everyone started sewing again. We returned to the familiar behavior associated with our bees. But the terror of not knowing was just below the surface.

"I'm getting to it. You have to remember that common law was originally set down in the Middle Ages-- after the fall of Rome.

"In those dark days when common law was evolving, judges' decisions were addressing the properties of men. The kings owned the land and all the people who lived and worked on it. This system was called feudalism.

"To make their men-folk feel better about being surfs—being owned by a king--the kings declared them all kings of their own houses. So the prevailing attitude of the courts—actually the king's court, quite literally—in the middle ages was that any man in the village could own a wife, children, goats, sheep, and chickens. But they 'rented' their homes and farm lands, which all belonged to the capital K king. The good kings accepted rent in the form of goats, sheep and chickens."

"Soooo, what did the bad kings take in payment?" Andrea.

"They owned their wives?" Elixchel.

Hannah stared at her. I couldn't read her face. She continued.

"The most common profession in the early middle ages was keeping goat herds. Goats are very hardy. They breed like rabbits and eat anything at all, and of course they produce lots of milk. And they can be left out in the fields over night, which is more pertinent to this story. Because—unlike cows and horses--they're small enough when they're young that you can pick one up and slip off into the dark, with the poor thing quietly bleating under your arm and without the goatherd noticing until full-on morning. By then you could be six villages away.

"Big goats could be quite aggressive, so they were mostly left alone.

"A young goat is called a kid. In those days it was spelled, kide, with an e. It was Old Norse. At any rate, when it was discovered that a kid had been napped the penalty was quite severe, because you weren't just napping the little king's kide, you were also napping the big King's kide."

"So napping means stealing, like stealing a few minutes of sleep." Andrea, the co-teacher.

"Huh. That makes sense." Anne said.

"Exactly. So my best guess is that kidnapping as a legal term came about to cover the offense of stealing a young goat, and was later applied to child stealing. In much the same way, child labor laws were changed in the early twentieth century so that making children work for more than fourteen hours a day in a factory was declared unlawful under existent animal cruelty laws."

"Whoa. Fourteen hours a day was considered an *improvement?*" Elixchel.

"Yes, and I share your horror, Elixchel. Anyway, the first usage of kid as slang for a child was recorded in 1599. I know this because Deborah asked the same question you did Anne. And the word kid was established as informal usage for a child by the 1840's in most English dictionaries.

"It makes sense to me. I have two goats and they are aggressively inquisitive, almost human in their need to learn," Hannah finished.

I wondered why she never seemed to get lost in the grand halls of her knowledge. But the capacity to put together a mini-lecture on the fly probably came from that same genius.

"And we eat them?" Andrea-the-vegetarian.

"Unfortunately, we are omnivores, Andrea." Me.

Stunning me, Victoria said in a quavering voice, "The real importance of the development of common law during the Middle Ages stems from the fact that our Constitution was written based on English common law, which is also a Christian-based law."

She was changing the entire direction of our conversation—toward a history lesson about the beginning of the United States. I found myself drifting in and out of this discussion by the women as my mind returned to wondering what Matt was doing and where Abigail was.

Finally, I returned from my internal thoughts.

"Of course, these gentlemen sitting down and declaring themselves to be independent of England was one thing. Fighting the war was quite another."

She looked around at us to be certain we were clear on some point I'd missed entirely. Or was she lost, confused? It was hard to tell what her emotions where, her ancient face was sagging so profoundly.

"We finally defeated the British in October of 1781." Hannah said with finality.

"Yes." Victoria said, her voice full of tremors and doubt. "They were finally defeated. But it wasn't until the Treaty of Paris in 1783 that the British formally abandoned their claims on the Colonies.

"Why I tell you all of this is because for the British, the Americans had kidnapped their colonies. The grievance was theirs to their way of thinking. We were attempting to steal their lands from them, not free them."

And so we were back on topic. My phone rang again. I stood and moved the call into the bathroom this time.

"It's definitely a Mexican gang Rache. We're all in accord on this now."

He meant from Mexico. So it was true, no longer just our supposition.

"How do they know?"

"They found the poor kid's head. It's been mutilated with the trademark cutting the Hidalgo Gang in Mexico uses."

I didn't want to hear. *Hidalgo.* They were vicious. They were cruel beyond sanity. I shuddered and leaned against the wall. *Abigail. Oh, no.*

"We have to find her, Matt! We *have* to."

"We're looking. Others are joining the search. We have about two hundred now, mostly parents, some cops. It's growing. They can't ignore the situation any longer."

"What do you mean? Do you mean there's no Amber Alert?" I said bitterly.

"Calm. You and I need to remain calm," Matt said. It was his favorite line when neither of us felt calm and hell was breaking loose.

I was trying, but the wildness I'd seen in Gloria's eyes earlier worried me. She had to be kept safely in this house. And yes, calm.

And I kept telling myself I was helping her by continuing to quilt with her. Then suddenly Matt's voice changed, down an octave, and to a mixture of coffee grinds and honey, with some street-wise jalapeño tossed in.

"Mrs. Lyons, your man is right. You need to keep your mind calm. We will find your young friend and we will find her alive."

Then Matt returned.

"That was Harks, he's just arrived. I've got to go."

When I returned to the quilt I overheard Elixchel asking, "Do you think maybe they're going to take the three girls to Mexico? You know, to sell them?"

The terrifying question was left unanswered by my sudden return, or maybe she'd struck us all dumb by going there.

Chapter 68

No one asked me questions this time. I had pie flakes on my face, hopefully covering up my emotional turmoil. After ten minutes of silent sewing, the bravest woman in the room began to speak, although she had several stops and restarts.

"As my daughter's representative, I tink ve should tell stories from our teen years. She vas so excited to share her story dis morning. I didn't know vat it vas about, but...but...it vas trilling her no end dat she would share a virtual teen experience vith all you old people...as she put it. Anyway, I'll begin vith mine."

I fought the tears, swallowed hard, and blinked repeatedly trying to fan my tears dry, all with my head bowed sharply toward her quilt, praying I wouldn't start a tidal wave of emotions by showing my own. *Breathe. Breathe.*

Andrea stood and walked toward the living room. A few minutes later she returned with some music flowing behind her like...well, it was indescribable.

At least I thought it was until Elixchel said, "How lovely. A cross between an eighties rock band and a Pakistani funerary dirge performed under-veil by three shrouded slave women after a night of sex with their main-mullah."

Yep. That was what it sounded like.

"Glad you like it, Shel! But it's actually a modern Ukrainian rock band. Found it on the 'net."

"Turn it off."

We all looked up. I smiled. The queen had just spoken and Andrea stood with her imp smile fixed firmly on her adorable butch face and turned off the music.

Adorable butch face. Was I beginning to find something sexy about Andrea? I reassessed.

"Ukrainian teenage years. I thought the music would be perfect," Andrea tossed over her shoulder on the way to the stereo. "But...I thought Abigail would be telling her tale, something sappy, something second-gen 'krainian."

Krainian sounded like cranial.

"Okay, varning heeded. I keep it light, little sister. Actually dis story is," Gloria said, and began.

For the next thirty minutes I strained to understand Gloria's tale of the dating practices of Communist Ukraine blended with memories of the natural wonder and beauty of her homeland.

She softened the story, but it was sad nevertheless. Ukrainian women often left their homes in an effort to find a more modern world to live in, but sometimes they got lost in the underworld bars of Europe, and their fatherless babies were sent to state orphanages.

Gloria was lucky. Her parents and her superior school work saved her from any of the bad endings that Ukraine had to offer young women of her generation. Gloria added that in Communist Ukraine, school was almost free, even nursing school.

Near the end of the story my phone rang again. Sighing deeply, I rose and moved toward the bathroom again.

"The parents of the Indian girls have gone to the FBI to claim that one of them heard their daughter saying they thought the gang was out to get Abigail. We have an Amber Alert now."

That was most of what he said. I had a celebratory piece of blueberry pie to choke down the bitter news and tears. Even knowing it was coming, I felt gut-punched. Abigail was being declared an official missing person. I waited for Gerry's phone to ring so Tom could tell Gloria for me. I wasn't going to be able to without bursting into tears.

Chapter 69

11:45 pm

We opened the quilt another three feet and took a second break from the sewing. Hannah did her first round of neck massages, working the tension out of our upper bodies slowly with her magic hands. For a few minutes I was calmer. The anxiety that had taken up residence in my belly in the form of butterflies and a shark, briefly slept.

We stood around the kitchen and living room preparing for the next two to three hours, stretching our bodies, soothing our fingers on hot cups of tea. There wasn't much talk, just a lot of eye contact, mainly toward me. They expected me to do something. They expected me to enlighten them about the phone calls. But it was all unconfirmed bad news.

Gloria was more than agitated. I did the best I could to convince her Abigail was better off knowing her mom was home waiting for her. Tom had apparently found some good words, too, because between the two of us, Gloria stayed put.

Finally we returned to the quilt.

Anne would tell the next teen story.

But before she began Gerry said, "Look at the little figures. There are embroidered figures on the quilt. Do the rest of you have any?" Gerry had come in late.

I searched my part but all I could see was hundreds of small squares of fabric.

"What is it?" Elixchel.

"I'm not sure. Can you see from your side, Anne? I think it's positioned facing you."

"Sure. It's a boy and girl holding hands in between the scales."

Scales?

"Right, and there are a couple over here, too. Only here they're reading a book together," Andrea said. "That's so sweet."

I couldn't tell if she was being sarcastic.

"Maybe we'll find others when the quilt is opened even more," Gerry said.

Anne cleverly steered the conversation.

"Speaking of boys and girls together, Martha set me up with a date for my senior prom. She didn't want me to graduate from high school without experiencing one. Martha had gone to hers with one of our cousins, but she said it was worth it just to see the gymnasium all decked out and all the other girls in their beautiful dresses.

"This was in 1968 and lots of girls were still dressing up in those days. I can't imagine what they're wearing now--our whole culture has changed so. I was seventeen and still pretty sweet, but the dance was bittersweet at best.

"Martha made my dress, *who-who*. She bought yards and yards of red velvet material. The skirt went to the floor. It had a scooped neck, and long Arthurian sleeves—you know, the ones that end in a point over the back of the hand? And even though crinolines weren't very in that year, I wore two to lift the heavy shirt away from my body.

"The fellow she told me to ask to take me was a year older than me, so he'd graduated already and was making a living working at his dad's garage. Martha knew him. He wore a nice dark suit, and everything was just fine, the dinner, dancing and conversations, all of it was fine. Except at the end of the evening I realized he was putting something in our punch. He didn't give me very much but he sure drank a lot of it himself.

"I think that's when I first realized how unhappy he was, being back at a high school dance and all, *who-who*.

"From the prom, we went to the home of a friend of his. I didn't know any of them. And there was more drinking there. Finally we left."

"He drove toward our house but parked a short ways away on a side street and I knew I was in trouble.

"He started kissing me. He smelled awful, and his beard was very rough. He rubbed my chin raw. I realized he was struggling with the back of my dress, looking for the zipper. His hands were all over me.

"I kept pushing him away. He kept telling me I 'owed him'. He grew angrier and angrier as he tried to get at me under the tight bodice of the velvet dress, but Martha had hidden the zipper under my arm. He kept pulling up my skirt...but then got all caught up in my crinolines.

"Finally he quit and lit up a cigarette. He rested his head in my lap as I sat in silence wishing he would take me home, too afraid to say anything.

"When he finally did, he just dumped me out at the main road and as I ran up the long driveway to our house my crinolines fell off. My hair was all torn out of its lovely do. That was when I started crying.

"When Martha found the burn hole in the front of the red velvet dress she'd made she was furious. I'm not sure what about, me getting nearly raped or her lovely dress being ruined."

"Jesus, Anne. That's really shitty. What'd you do about it?"

Victoria was so surprised at Anne's story she didn't even reprimand Andrea for the bad language.

"What could I do about it? The damage was done. Martha and I tried to figure out a way to save the dress, but it was right in the middle of the front panel. And frankly I hated the dress by then. I knew I'd never want to wear it again."

"The dress didn't matter, Anne. You mattered," Gerry said quietly.

"Yes," Hannah intoned. "You were damaged by this event, not the dress. I hope you find a way to deal with this long dormant pain."

"I would have snuck into his dad's garage and slashed every tire on their shelves! I would have broken the windows of his car in the middle of the night. I would have...."

"We get it Andrea," Elixchel said. "You'd have fire bombed his house. But revenge is...."

"Damn right I would have! The son of a..."

"Enough swearing!" Victoria said.

Me being who I am, I said, "Shit, Victoria, why not let a little venom loose? Maybe it would be damn therapeutic for her."

"Hell yes! The son of a bitch should have been punished." Elixchel. Victoria turned to stare at her as if she'd been struck across the face. Then she turned to look at Anne.

"Of course. You are all right. I'm sorry, I don't remember this event at all."

"I never told you mom. I was ashamed."

"Again, I'm sorry Anne. You were always the sweetest. You seemed to be okay with...things. You deserved better." Victoria bowed her head and returned to her sewing.

I looked over at Gloria, suddenly wondering how she was taking this mother-daughter conversation. She was blinking rapidly, trying to hold back the tears.

Maybe anxious over the pain she was causing her mother, Anne launched into a debate about the latest women's college basketball teams, which she took to uproarious extremes. I watched her grow so energized, her budgerigar-hair bounced about her head like startled yellow miniature parrots. I thought Andrea and Hannah would wake the neighbors—or at least Nana--with their rowdy description of the last University of Connecticut game against Tennessee. They had us all grinning by the end of it.

Finally we sobered and returned our thoughts to the darkness surrounding this little home. That was when Hannah gently steered the conversation toward Eddie.

"Have any of you heard anything more from Eddie?"

And we listened and sewed as Anne recounted Eddie's latest trials and tribulations on the East Coast, she talked of the attack in Boston Harbor and the massacre the week before.

When she wound down Gerry asked her, 'Is he still in Boston?"

"No, he's left there. I think he's out in Kentucky right now visiting with some other family folks. He certainly is getting an education though. Learning all sorts of new things after all those years...well, you know," she said, referring to his hellacious childhood of abuse and neglect that had surfaced after the events surrounding last month's bee.

We did.

Chapter 70

Matthew Lyon's LIRI Journal
Sunday, November 2, 12:15 pm, dictated in Los Gatos

Los Gatos was a closed door to us and it's clear that the Hidalgos had slammed it. Didn't help that I looked and sounded like a cop to the Pintos we were trying to get leads from. At house after house we were told to get the fuck away before we got them in trouble. They wouldn't say with whom, but we knew.

Half an hour ago, learner had signaled me from the shadows behind a small store to tell me that wheels were turning behind the scene. The FBI and Homeland Security were finally working angles and using their contacts to learn what they could. I was glad to hear other agencies were finally getting involved. But it all came down to these people. Any real help had to come from these Pintos and their families and they were scared shitless of the Hidalgos.

Three of their boys had died brutally. What did they care about somebody else's girls?

It was time for another visit to Luis Lewis.

Chapter 71

It was after midnight. The rain was thickening, the wind changing from whispers to howls. And the exhaustion of sewing for hours on end was once again reducing my body to painful fatigue. At least my neck was holding up, thanks to extra massages from Hannah.

Gloria broke my sewing concentration saying, "Abby was studying Phillis Wheatley's poetry when she decided to run away."

"She hasn't run away. She's just missing," Andrea snarled.

Gloria waved a weary hand. "The whole homeschool group was studying the African slave who was allowed a pen and paper to write down her poetic thoughts. It was right after that Abby decided to return to school, so I reread some of Wheatley's Poems in Various Subjects, thinking maybe I'd find a clue in them as to why...."

Surprising us all, Gerry interrupted with a spontaneous recitation. Later she explained she'd memorized this passage for one of her high school Spanish classes and then she had the class translate it into Spanish.

"'Twas mercy brought me from my Pagan land,
Taught my benighted soul to understand,
That there's a God, that there's a Saviour too,
Once I redemption neither fought now knew,
Some view our sable race with scornful eye,
'Their colour is a diabolic die.'
Remember Christians Negroes black as Cain,
May be refin'd, and join th' angelic brain.'"

Andrea spoiled the mood by saying, "Sure. That's the reason Abigail ran away to school. Because Phillis Wheatley corrupted her mind and made her rebel."

"Wheatley was a British supporter," Gerry said simply.

I pondered that comment. Did Gerry think Wheatley should have been a Rebel supporter, perhaps in hopes that one day she too would be liberated? Or did she think Wheatley supported the British because the poor frequently aspire to be rich, dream of it nightly, and therefore fervently follow the lead of the rich in any given society? The British of those times reeked of Kings and nobility.

Or was Wheatley's locale the reason for her British support? I scratched my brain for a few seconds trying to remember which of the colonies Wheatley had lived in.

Hannah said, "Massachusetts. She was born in West Africa in 1753. At the age of eight, she was carried to Boston as a slave girl and sold to John Wheatley. They named her Phillis after the slave boat."

"You've read...." Elixchel began.

"I teach," Hannah answered simply. "I homeschool our children," she added, and glanced at Anne.

"I know, hoo-hoo."

Gerry. "By the age of twelve Wheatley was reading Greek and Latin. She loved the poets of the times the most...."

"Pope, Milton, Homer," Andrea said.

I took the measure of the pixie again. We collectively smiled at her.

"I read the works of slaves, the few there are. I'm lacking in basic civil rights in my country, too."

We collectively stopped smiling. I checked . Was she comparing her shtatus as a lesbian in the United States to that of a slave? Apparently. Andrea was beginning to open my eyes to things I hadn't realized they might be closed to.

"Her first poem was published December 21, 1767." Hannah.

"Wow, you really studied her." Gerry.

"That's my mother's birth date."

Her mother Ruth.

Gerry. "John Wheatley and his wife were enlightened. They allowed Phillis the life of a white person, and her brilliance was sometimes recognized and sometimes disdained."

"Depending on whether you thought slaves should be given full rights or not." Hannah.

"When did she die?" Elixchel.

"John Wheatley, her protector and mentor, died in 1778 and she was freed as per his will. She married a John Peters. Little is known about him, except that he was an African American, and that they had three children and lived in abject poverty in Boston. She died alone after the deaths of her three children in 1784. She was not yet thirty-nine." Gerry.

"She died of slavery. The whole family died of slavery." Andrea.

"But she was freed," Elixchel.

"Yeah. But the world around her wasn't happy with that. They couldn't find decent work. They lived in a slum. Her whole family died way too young."

Hannah said, "You should wander the old graveyards of New England. It wasn't uncommon for babies to die young in those days. It wasn't uncommon for people to have short, hard lives."

"True." Gerry.

"Before modern medicine and indoor plumbing," Anne said.

"True." Gerry.

"But the rich white people lived longer by far than their slaves." Andrea.

"True. All true. Aren't we wonderfully educated ladies?" Gerry.

We collectively smiled again and bowed our heads in concentration once more, and stitch after stitch was laid down on Abigail's quilt.

Chapter 72

The next two teen stories came from Gerry the wife of a billionaire and former high school Spanish teacher, and Andrea, the disgruntled pixie with civil rights issues.

Gerry's was a sweet tale of innocence. Apparently she spent her high school years bouncing from one crush to another without connecting with a boy. My thinking on this, beautiful girls can be too threatening for young men to approach, especially if they were at all shy. That seemed to be Gerry's saving grace.

Finally she lapsed into another discussion of the early history of American quilts and quilting which got everyone involved. Gerry had found a website making the claim that Betsy Ross' flags were actually quilts. No one at the bee disputed this assertion.

I made another run for the bathroom, and as I returned I overheard Andrea's strident pixie voice.

"...Luke should never have been allowed out of Donovan...."

The now deceased Luke was Victoria's second born son. In his early days he killed his older brother Mark in a drunken bar fight over Ada. In the end, he was responsible for more familial crimes.

"Andrea! For heaven's sake, what earthly purpose could such a statement have?" Gerry was red-faced livid under her fountain of blond curls.

Victoria rose painfully from her chair at the quilt and lumbered toward me as I was arriving back in on the porch. I thought perhaps she was headed for the now vacant toilet, but she turned toward a comfy chair in a dark corner of the living room and lowered her heavy body into it.

Elixchel scooted an ottoman under her feet. And I watched as Victoria's face retreated into the shadows. She slept for a while.

Returning to the rack Elixchel made brief eye contact with me and shook her head ruefully.

"When Victoria returns Andrea, you will formally apologize to her, do you hear me?"

"Yes." A contrite pixie.

Then out of the blue Elixchel asserts that Mexicans feet the same way today as the British did about their former Colonies, that their property was stolen from them—only for Mexicans it's the thirteen contested southwestern states. Like they've been kidnapped.

Huh? Contested what? My mind had drifted.

"Thirteen contested states..?"

Elixchel glared at me, and snapped, "You want to talk slavery, talk Chicano."

Then she returned her glare to Andrea.

Victoria, mostly silent--and I thought pretty depressed given her illness and her family troubles--was no longer a barrier between her two foster children. I wondered if they'd go at it again.

But they held their animosity in and the room fell silent for another half hour--until Andrea started telling her tale, a few minutes after Victoria's return.

"Just change the pronouns and you'll know what my teenage experience was. Except it wasn't with another teen. My first sexual encounter was with my gym teacher, Ms. Oakley. I spent every gym class mooning at her and she noticed.

"Catherine Oakley is beautiful, her curves are all muscle. Her hair is curly like a guys, she was so like a guy I got confused when we finally got together at her apartment..."

"When was this?' Victoria suddenly demanded.

"Years ago, forget about it, Grandma."

"I'm not..."

They stared at each other, realizing something had changed. Andrea's grin widened into a real smile. Victoria matched her grin and raised her one.

"Yep. You're a grandma!"

The last time I heard Andrea call her Grandma Victoria had shouted that she was no one's grandma. But now we all knew about Eddie and he was her grandson.

Another thought flitted through my mind like an exhausted butterfly--Grandma Victoria and strange Eddie Stowall were connected.

This was when Andrea went where I thought no one should go. Story telling was supposed to be voluntary.

"But Gerry, billionaire friend of mine, what was that mushy story you told all about? Are we to believe you are a real air-head? A dumb bunny blond? A brainless fool? Surely something weird must have happened to you in your teen years."

Gerry looked up, a sudden look of...guilt? fear? anger? flashing across her face, and then she willed her face into a smooth mask.

"So how about you tell us a teen story that reveals who you really were at that age.

Gerry inhaled slowly, brought her blond flop of curls up as high above us all as she could, and said, "Okay." She turned a Godfather's smile on Andrea.

"Okay. But you have to promise not to...."

The room resounded in a simultaneous and unanimous agreement to non-disclose. Hannah even crossed her heart and put her right hand up, although she never said, "Hope to die."

"Okay."

That was her third okay. This was going to be good.

"When I was seventeen, in my second month on campus...."

"UC Santa Barbara." Hannah.

Gerry looked at her. Then she returned to her story.

"It was October fourth, the Sunday night after a long weekend away celebrating little bro's birthday, which is October third, so I'm certain about the date. And I was sitting on my miserable college bed, alone in our room, slamming out a quick paper on the American Revolution, something to do with taxation without representation, my typewriter wedged between my thighs...."

"Oh." Andrea.

"...when my right hand, all of its own, slid off the typewriter and discovered my—pleasure point."

She looked around at us, checking our willingness to go further. We were willing.

"Okay. Well, the next part is unbelievable but true. I was such a virgin. I was such an innocent." She closed her eyes tight and breathed three times.

"I didn't finish the paper, I hardly slept all night, I kept staring at the girls in my dorm, wondering— wondering who had brought this...this...lesbian behavior out of me."

Andrea burst into screaming laughter and fell over backwards off her wooden chair on the floor. She was ROFL-ing. She was still laughing when Elixchel picked her up. I was wondering if her laughter was overdone.

"Okay, you're right. I was one dumb bunny...."

Again, she was interrupted when Andrea shouted, "Sexually retarded!"

"...but I couldn't figure out why else such a strange and probably immoral thing was happening to me, so I walked around campus trying to look busy all day, even climbed the stairs to the top of the psych department and waited outside the office wondering if this was where to get an appointment to see a shrink. At long last I finally called my mom."

"What did she say?" Hannah. Her laughter was more peaceful--more a low chuckle.

"Well, of course she told me it was normal. Told me she'd been masturbating since she was thirteen—what took me so long? God, what an ugly word that is." Gerry put her red face in her hands and stayed that way for a few moments.

It took us another ten minutes to resume sewing and stop giggling. Of course, as I look back on it now I realize this was a turning point for us this night. A point at which the stark terror of a missing Abigail turned into something we could manage, something we needed to work hard to rectify. And then a final thought occurred to me which I spoke.

"Gerry, why did you give me an incomplete genealogy last month?"

"What? What do you mean?"

"I mean, the one you gave me was a smaller version from the one I found at the library. Yours didn't show my connection to the Stowall family tree. The one in John's book does."

Looks passed between Gerry and Victoria, and I suddenly knew that Gerry had been given the genealogy by Victoria, so my brain began analyzing.

"My mother gave me that copy, Rachel. It was the only copy I'd ever seen." Okay, so I was wrong. Gerry seemed disappointed.

"So you're related to us then?" Hannah said.

"Great! We're all in the same family." Andrea quipped. *Sarcasm?*

"Everyone is, ladies. Everyone has always been in the same family." Elixchel.

Of course she meant biblically, as in all of us are derived from Adam and Eve, according to the bible, I reasoned.

"Even if you discount dis Judeo-Christian account of our beginnings, even if you belief in Darwinism, you must ultimately see us as all connected now dat we've identified so much of the DNA common to humans." Gloria. Very analytical.

"And fish. And plants, for that matter." Andrea.

"*Who-who.*" Anne. Then I wondered what Anne meant by that.

Chapter 73

From Matthew's LIRI Journal
Sunday, Nov. 2, 12:45 pm

I slipped by the nurses' station while they were in the back office setting up patient meds. Found Lewis alone and apparently asleep. He opened his eyes when I touched his hand, tried to speak and had a coughing fit. I gave him some water but reminded him he was on IV liquids and to take it easy.

I was tired and distracted and told him Abigail was missing too abruptly. His heart rate sped up and threatened to trip the monitor alarms. I told him to breathe deeply and stay calm and asked him if he knew where she might be. He indicated she had a boyfriend named Buddy and seemed head-over-heels about him. Just as I asked him for a last name, a nurse stuck her head in and started a ruckus. Luis shook his head and I ducked out before I could get thrown out.

Called Rachel from the emergency exit stairwell to tell her but she cut me off saying she "couldn't talk in the pie room," whatever the hell that means. Just as well. Didn't want her trying to find Buddy herself. Glad she doesn't have a car there. Hope she doesn't try to borrow one.

Chapter 74

I drifted away from the quilting rack around one, and suddenly found myself climbing the stairs toward Abigail's bedroom. I needed to search for clues. I'd thought about this earlier, but Gloria had said she already searched. It was time for me to give it a try.

Standing on the threshold of her very messy, little girl's room, I was driven to the brink of tears. She was so young. Just a baby, really, with stuffed animals on her unmade bed and a closet full of pastel clothes. Feminine. Much more feminine and child-like than her art. I wondered if Gloria had a hand in decorating the room.

"I've searched." It was Gloria. She'd followed me. "You said."

"Tvice. That's vy it's such a mess. The second time I vas...hysterical. No, I vas angry. I just threw stuff."

I nodded. So probably looking for clues in here was now pointless. But I spent ten minutes searching places she hadn't, including taking apart a framed photograph I found tucked way in the back of the closet shelf.

"Dat's her father," Gloria whispered. "I didn't know vat she'd done with that picture."

There was nothing hidden between the cardboard backing and the picture. Maybe the jewelry box had a false bottom. But she didn't have a jewelry box that I could see. I stooped to look under her bed. A lone sock. Some dust. Crumpled paper. The rug was much thicker and healthier under there.

"How long have you lived here, Gloria?"

"Ve built the add-on for Joe. Abigail was three when ve move in."

Ten years. But her secret life was new, so I decided she hadn't turned to cutting holes in the walls to hide things yet. I didn't move the furniture. There were eight or ten of her paintings on the walls. I decided not to take them down for further examination. This was all too recent, Abigail's rebellion. That sort of stealthy behavior would come later.

"Okay, let's get back downstairs with the others."

But it was too late. Gloria was quietly weeping, actually more like seeping, the tears gently rolling down her cheeks, her mouth aquiver--but making no sound. She seemed practiced at this silent crying, maybe she'd learned the technique in Ukraine, where privacy was hard to come by. Maybe she'd practiced it here in America, with her new husband who didn't seem able to cope, who refused a kidney transplant even though her status as a nurse made him quickly eligible for one. It was an odd thing to see, a silent cry.

My mother had learned to do this in her eight years of dying. The doctor had called it depression crying.

By the time we returned to the rack I was really down and I knew another shot of sugar wouldn't help. Then my phone sent a shot of adrenaline through me.

I raced into the bathroom like I had the runs and pressed my phone to my ear.

"Matt?"

"Who else? Can you talk *now?*" He was referring to our last call.

"Okay, don't get edgy. Tell me what you know."

But I wasn't angry, I was cheered. His voice did that, and now his words. He gave me hope, as he told me Luis was awake, and what he'd learned from him. My tired brain got stuck on Luis.

"He's awake? He's going to be okay?" Me.

"Yes and yes, I'm waiting." Matt.

Right. Buddy's last name. "I'll call back."

I raced back into the quilting room—as I was now coming to think of it. They looked the same—heads bowed, concentrating on their sewing--until I heard Elixchel's words.

They stopped me in my tracks. Her voice held a barely contained sob.

"Heavenly Father we beseech you, send us your comfort. Send us an answer that saves our little sister,

Abigail. Bring her back to us now. Tell us where she is so we can bring her home safe and sound. In the name of Jesus Christ our Lord and Savior, amen."

I raised my own head, unclasped my hands and spoke from the elevated living room stair. I had something I simply had to ask them immediately, prayer giving or no.

"Who knows Buddy's last name? Buddy is a name, not another word for friend. Luis thinks that might be where she is."

"Luis is awake?" Gerry said. But her words were instantly eclipsed.

Gloria shot up out of her chair and turned to face me. She looked like the weight of the world had just been lifted from her shoulders. She was beaming a hopeful smile under a brow heavy with fear. She looked borderline insane.

Oh no. We couldn't afford to get our hopes up that high.

"Wait. Buddy Zinzer? Do you mean Judi Zinzer's younger brother?" Andrea said.

Zinzer. The family at the hospital looking in on Jimmy Winters as he lay dying. "He's a chubby guy?" I said.

"Chubby guys don't haf sex. The fat makes estrogen," she told herself.

Definitely edging toward madness. Gloria had suddenly gone from worrying if her child was alive to worrying if she was having sex.

"Well, yeah. I mean he's thirteen or fourteen. He's still got his baby fat. So I guess you could call him chubby." Andrea.

"Where do they live?"

"I don't know. I just know them from art classes. Judi was a so-so artist who took instruction from the same guy I did, a Frank Rizzo. He was a babe...according to Judi. And of course Abigail was in class. I guess...."

Andrea was still talking but from the looks on their faces I could tell no one knew where the Zinzers lived, so I stepped away and began dialing Matt, praying he was still near his phone. I busied myself as I waited for him to answer, searching Gloria's kitchen.

"Vat are you looking for?" Gloria said.

"Your phonebook. I want to look up the Zinzer's address."

"I'll do it." She was eager to do something, *anything*, to help.

"He's probably on the road…" I muttered.

"*Here it is*, one twelve Avenida Riada." Desperation laced her words.

I drummed my fingers on the counter as the call slid to voice mail. I left a quick message then redialed.

I redialed again, and another time, getting more frustrated by the minute, worrying that maybe his phone had gone dead and he wouldn't receive my messages.

"Maybe I should get in my car and…*shoot*. I don't have my car."

"I'll drive you." Hannah and Gerry both said, and we were preparing to leave the house when my phone rang again.

"Matt!"

I listened as he told me he got the message and they were on their way. He added I was not to call him again. He would call me when he had some news. Then abruptly hung up before I could say another word.

"Weird."

"What?"

I looked up. "Oh nothing, Gloria. He was really rushed, is all. They're going over to the Zinzers' now." And he'd told me not to call him again. Huh?

I have to tell you that was when my thoughts turned from dutiful wife-partner to…. But not yet. First I returned to sewing, to think.

We slowly regrouped around the quilt and finally sat down to sew again. I kept my phone on the table right next to me, and next to the cups of tea and plates of crumbs. My eyes kept flying to the wall clock about thirty feet away in the living room. Everyone else seemed to be glancing at Gerry's phone.

But neither Matt or Tom called. Not for ages, and our collective hearts sank as reasons why they didn't floated from one to the other of us without ever being spoken.

Chapter 75

Victoria had suffered so much within the last month-
-so many deaths, so many losses. I wondered if she'd
still been in shock when I'd first met her last month and
that was why she seemed not to be feeling the pain. Or
was it the ALS and the attendant meds muting her
emotions?

But now one of her charges—she thought of the
young girl as one of her foster kids—was in deep
trouble. After our initial joy at contemplating that Abigail
was just hanging with her boyfriend, reality crept back
in. It was way after midnight. Thirteen-year-olds didn't
stay out that late unless....

A solitary tear made its way down Victoria's face
over the cracks and crevices of age. A gnarled and
spotted right hand darted up and quickly wiped it away
then returned to its work, a knuckle now glistening.

Her hand had been wiping away tears for several
minutes, hadn't it?

I spoke one of my rambling thoughts, "...unless they
fell asleep."

I was barely holding it together. I knew they all felt
the same. I pondered more pie, and grease came to mind
instead. My tongue felt coated with lard.

Hannah decided to tell her teenage story around
one-thirty. Actually, Hannah's story was much like
Gerry's, one of crushing innocence and unrequited loves.
She repeated Gerry's statement that she didn't feel she
fit in. That she was an outsider skirting the fringes of
high school life in homemade and hand-me-down
clothes. Maybe most teenagers felt this way. Maybe that
was adolescence in a nutshell—a perpetual bad fit.

And then she startled us by changing direction.

"I thought in honor of my mom and dad I'd share a
little about Ruth's high school romance with Paul

McMichaels. You know, she would have done the same if she could have been here. Maybe you can help me along, Victoria."

Victoria nodded without looking up.

"They met when they were kids, grew up in the same small town, Pinto Springs of course. But they *really* didn't notice each other until the hormones kicked in.

"My dad, Paul, was a football player, and mom was a cheerleader. She used to tell us stories about how the other kids teased them, calling them the Mutt and Jeff of Cleveland County High School. That was what Pinto Springs High was called back in her day, when there was only one secondary school in the whole county instead of the four there are now."

I listened as she explained to the younger women at the quilt that Mutt and Jeff were two cartoon characters in the Sunday comics sections of most major newspapers back then—in which one was very tall and one was very short, like Paul and Ruth. Which made me wonder how long it would be before the "younger" members would have to be told what a newspaper was.

In short, I drifted in and out of Hannah's gentle story, brought back to the present constantly by the growing pains in my hands and neck, and my fears for Abigail. The sewing was taking its toll, and I worried that I might need my hands to save myself in the coming hours...to hold the gun I'd brought in my large bag.

My stomach clenched at the thought. And I would forever wonder what made me bring it.

Chapter 76

Matthew Lyon's LIRI Journal
Sunday, November 2, 1:45

We found the Zinzer house empty; scrawled across the living room wall, written in blood, was HIDALGO. The we consisted of Detective Learner, Beardsley, an assortment of cops, Will and me. LIRI was here at the behest of Learner. I think he was testing us.

There was blood everywhere. Sprayed on, splashed on, and left in smears. Will and I moved slowly through the house, trying not to react.

The house looked like the aftermath of a Hidalgo signature mutilation and murder scene, only there were no bodies yet. Maybe there was still hope.

Forensics arrived and went directly to work, trying to identify how many had been cut. Next step was to find out Buddy and Abigail's blood types.

Learner took one look at the back bedroom and said, "Someone bled out here. Maybe two."

Last thing I wanted to hear.

Marana arrived, angry as usual and taking it out on his assistant, though he was happy to target me instead as soon as he spotted me. Made a crack about Rachel and I needing to be on the payroll soon. To head off a confrontation, I said we were just leaving.

Learner, to my surprise, turned on him and snarled something about the fact that Rachel and I had unearthed Abigail's last known location and that maybe Marana could make himself useful by helping search the woods for the bodies.

The news that there were no bodies yet set Marana back on his heels. I knew he was thinking he could have stayed in bed until we had something for him to examine.

"We thought they were here," Learner said coldly. "The sheets were bunched and bloodied to make it look like there was a body wrapped in them. My guess is whoever was cut here hasn't been taken far."

"Your *guess*. My day is made, Detective." What a big shit. He finally moved his bulk out of the doorway and into the bedroom. Learner, Will and I headed back down the hall.

One of Learner's guys, Stone, approached, saying that Buddy's parents were on their way back from an out-of-town memorial service for his sister Judi. Christ, this poor family.

They'd be arriving in about an hour and so far they didn't know anything beyond what their neighbor told them when he called them an hour ago to say that some out-of-control party was going on at their house. Said neighbor is now in tears over not calling the cops sooner.

Learner told Stone to cordon the block off and keep the press out.

"Send Wilson and Sharkey out to I-13 to catch them as they come off the ramp. Take them downtown. No, take them to Mountain Rise. Let the hotel manager know we'll be using a back door to put them in a top floor room. Warn him to keep quiet. Don't need the press sniffing them out."

By this time we're in the kitchen, next to the table. I noticed something wasn't right—chairs were pulled way out from one side. I asked Will to get in touch with Harks and have him meet us ASAP. The Feds would be taking over very shortly, and I didn't want that to hamper our search for Abigail. I wasn't particularly confident the Feds would be any more effective than the locals had been. The whole thing would probably just become more *political*. Christ.

I noticed something down low on the kitchen wall, behind the table. More red marks. I gestured to Will.

"Blood?" he said. I pulled out my flashlight and we crouched down. We were alone in the kitchen. I leaned in and smelled the marks on the wall. "I think this is lipstick. Take a look, Will. Do these markings look familiar to you?"

I snapped a couple of pictures.

Will drew a blank at first, then said, "It kind of looks like Russian writing."

Or maybe Ukrainian, which uses a variation of the Cyrillic alphabet. Rachel's always complaining about Gloria's accent.

"Maybe Gloria taught her daughter Ukrainian."

"So, you think Abigail wrote this?"

I nodded. Maybe they left her in the kitchen at some point. "Learner and Marana need to see this."

"I need to see what?" Marana loomed in the doorway, a crime scene photog a pace behind him. He'd been watching to see what we'd do.

I stepped back for the ME to get a closer look at the markings on the wall and watched as his expression changed.

He ordered the photog to take some shots and stared at me for a moment. I waited him out.

"So, you know someone who understands the Cyrillic alphabet."

I nodded. "Abigail's mother..." I began. Marana interrupted to say that he knew.

So he could call her but he wanted me to but he didn't want to ask.

"We'll need this translated." He was getting impatient. I knew, and Marana probably did too, that with his low EQ he'd fuck up any contact with Gloria. We needed her to translate this. I decided a working relationship with Marana would be more valuable than the satisfaction of making him grovel.

"Rachel is at Gloria Pustovoytenko's house now."

Marana nodded then seemed to decide an olive branch was in order. "We've been through three nights of little or no sleep," he said brusquely.

A limp-dick apology.

"We're all wiped, doc." I let that thought marinate.

I thought about how to proceed. I could forward the picture to Rachel but she'd run right out and start looking for Abigail herself. No, I needed to drive over and do this in person.

I told Marana I'd get Gloria to translate the writing and headed to the living room.

My cell rang. It was Harks.

Will and I headed out to the Chicano neighborhood that was the heart of the Pintos gang's turf and parked on a side street. Harks was waiting. He'd brought along his Mexican gang counterpart, a guy named Rodriguez. Harks' strength was his knowledge of black gangs but he knew how to tap other resources. The four of us huddled together in the Deacon's SUV and I made my first big mistake of the night by shoving the Ukrainian message to the back of my brain. I was too focused on what Harks had learned. Or not.

Rodriguez whined that the Pintos were stonewalling and I was instantly annoyed by his tone. I wondered if he could be trusted.

I was expecting some kind of progress. I glanced at Harks. Unreadable.

Rodriguez said they were working on one gang banger and were close to getting him to spill.

Harks remained silent. So I filled them in on what we found at the Zinzer house. Briefly. Harks and Rodriguez grimaced.

Rodriguez said they had gotten this much out of some Pintos—that the Hidalgos had taken over the local gang and now Pintos were turning on Pintos, families were confused and scared, and the Hidalgos weren't just trafficking in drugs. Sex slavery. Good Christ.

"If we can get this Garcia guy off by himself..." Rodriguez trailed away.

I said that was an excellent idea, silently cursing that they hadn't managed to do that already.

Chapter 77

"When I was fifteen I met Jake Stowall. My maiden name was Driscoll, but I knew a distant relative in direct line of descent was another Stowall. I was reassured by an old country doctor from those days there was no genetic danger to marrying someone in the same 'clan' as it were.

"He was wrong. But back when I was fifteen, there was nothing wrong with Jake Stowall. He was handsome...looked a little like Ronald Coleman, a romantic heart throb in many of the movies of my day. Oh, and I should tell you, this was nineteen forty-one," Victoria said.

Andrea gasped. "What? You mean you're not fifty-nine?"

Everyone chuckled, especially Victoria—which was a lovely thing to see. We needed a laugh right about then. The tension in the room was as high as I'd ever seen it. Frankly all I could think of was *why hasn't Matt called me to tell me Abigail is safe?*

But it had only been fifteen minutes. They were probably still going through the bureaucratic chains of command before they could act.

So I tried to concentrate and smile and laugh appropriately as Victoria told her story of their sweet romance sixty-seven years ago. Her distant memories were perfect, although no doubt modified by the passage of so many years.

It was when she told us how gentle he was as a lover that Anne rose and left the room and an uncomfortable silence followed her departure.

Finally, Gerry said, "I'm bushed. Why don't we take another break?"

As we streamed toward the kitchen to see what new caloric fancy would be unveiled this time, I could hear the cell phones snap open around me. I resisted the urge. He would call me when there was news. Andrea beat me to the bathroom.

After devouring a *FIX*ation Apple Crumblesmash--*don't ask*, you'll gain weight just hearing the explanation--I took note of who was on the phone.

Anne was chatting up someone I thought was Mary but it turned out to be Martha. Elixchel was having a difficult conversation with someone who'd actually called her. She found a distant corner to converse in, and finally stepped out onto the back porch where she could tell that someone to pipe down, or whatever. It was cold and wet out. It didn't take long.

Hannah actually woke her husband Peter to talk with him, telling him they were still looking for Abigail. She too moved away from us so she could whisper things.

Andrea was still in the bathroom.

Gloria was alone on the couch, her head hanging low. Gerry and I stood facing each other, making small talk.

The eruption came after twelve minutes of this electronic divide.

"See how we become!" the other side of Victoria roared. "See how you have left each other to stand and sit alone. *This* is your brave new world order. This is your idea of togetherness!" And she climbed back on her steed and rode magisterially back to the quilt rack.

Actually she was using a cane. Elixchel raced to her side just on time to keep her from toppling over. I heard phones snapping shut as we all joined her contritely at the cloth.

All except Andrea that is. She had taken the bathroom as if by force and wasn't giving it up. I was wondering where the next bathroom was.

"Do you think she's okay?" Gerry asked, next to me. I shrugged.

And then, as the room sat in silence, a loud growling, gurgling, gagging noise emitted from the bathroom giving us the answer.

"It wasn't the Apple Crumblesmash. She didn't even eat any, I don't think, *who-who*."

I almost burst out laughing.

Now I was thinking Anne was as decisive as an Okapi in the same manner Andrea was as discrete as a rainbow lorikeet in heat--even vomiting. Andrea finally emerged from the bathroom another ten minutes later. She was so pale even her camouflaged jacket looked faded.

Maybe it was. And now I was wondering if the fear we were all experiencing over Abigail's wellbeing was more than she could handle. I was praying it wasn't the flu. But at least the toilet was available, and we all took our turns. Coward that I am, I chose to use it last.

Anne started up the conversation again. "Martha just told me Eddie's met some fascinating people on his travels. It seems he called Mary. Anyway, he's been out hunting with the relatives."

Hunting? Uh-oh, that meant he was becoming more proficient with guns. I truly didn't trust this man, hard as I might try.

Pushing back from the quilt to stretch my back, I glanced at my watch and wondered for the fourth time why there was no word from Matt. The frustration I felt was slowly turning to dread.

My eyes strayed to the black box staring back at me from the living room—the television.

Chapter 78

A message popped into my brain—almost like a phone text, almost like a memo from...Ruth!

Speak to Nana.

I fairly jumped out of my skin. What the hell?

I resisted the urge to go to Gloria's mother's bedroom door. Surely at almost half past two in the morning she was sound asleep.

Okay, so I was losing it. Too much caffeinated tea and sugar. Too much fear and worry. I'm excused for going mad.

That was when Nana appeared before us, wearing only a floral nightgown and walking barefoot, with a piece of paper in her hand.

"Mat*u*sia?" Gloria said as she turned and slowly rose from her seat.

Mat*u*sia—Mom--began reading from the paper *in English*.

"Avay they've flown,
The road leads down,
To down of van free son,
Where pigs are prone
To hear men groan.

Avay they've gone
To vait for dawn,
And rend their sweet reason,
And hearts turn stone
Says Sleeping Crone."

Hannah stood so fast her chair almost pushed over backwards behind her.

The first look on her wonderful Zen face was one of shock. Her second was of soft anger. Her third was the pout of a two year old. The two year old spoke.

"Oh great! Why doesn't she ever send *me* messages?"

Oh great? I watched Hannah's face retrieve reality as she surveyed our faces.

"My mom, Ruth, she loves poetry."

Gerry beat me to Nana to retrieve the note. We studied it together.

It was written in Ukrainian. And Cyrillic letters. And without poetic form. It was all one big paragraph of gibberish-sideways letters, upside down scribbles, italics everywhere.

"Can you write this in English for us, Nana?"

She shook her head and returned to her room. But the secret was out, or so Gloria thought.

"So, you speak English efter all, old woman."

And Nana's English had been clear, while Gloria's was unintelligible at times. Especially when she was upset, like now. So I must again say I only *think* that's what she said.

Maybe Nana had been sleep walking and sleep talking.

Channeling.

"Okay, Gloria we need this written in English complete with punctuation and poetic form so we can study it." I handed her the note.

Gloria began translating. It took her a while. In the end we managed to get the exact words down that Nana had originally said. When she finished, she turned to hand it back to me, saying, "It's called Mass Psychogenic Illness, and sometimes collective obsessional behavior."

This was said in perfect English. Maybe when she was speaking in medical terminology she could do this. And she was referring to our collective belief that Ruth was in some way a psychic messenger.

Andrea said, "And mass hysteria, as in *female* mass hysteria. Shame on you, Gloria."

"I'm sorry. I'm not insulting you. But you need to know Nana and my Abby hef been dueling poetry, competing in writing poems to each other in their separate languages. I tink they vere each trying to teach the other their specific tongues. Any vay, Abigail became obsessed with details revealed last month about Luke and Mark."

The warring brothers. The oldest two sons of Victoria and Jake, both of whom had loved Ada.

I wouldn't realize the importance of this information until much later, after we had finally deciphered the poem. Or maybe just before.

The sewing had stopped. We were sure to a woman that this message contained the location of Abigail--and none of us had even blinked at our complete and immediate acceptance of Ruth's paranormal capabilities.

I wasn't surprised. They had hinted of Ruth's magic abilities at last month's bee. Last month Andrea had called these messages *Ruthmonitions*. I had personally received messages from her as I lay nearly comatose after my terrible car accident—the one that left me with a yanked neck.

And Abigail obviously wasn't where Matt had expected her to be—at Buddy's house. What was he doing? By now he would have called to tell us she was dead.

But before we solved the poem, we formed our Sisterhood of Ruth the Prophetess.

"I told you Ruth has magic in her brain." The angry pixie.

For a moment I'd thought the multicolored tips of her red hair had flashed florescent, but her words were said in a mumble, as if she still didn't quite believe. Then Elixchel piped up.

"We've always known. We just haven't known the extent of her abilities. I mean, think of it, she spoke to Nana in Ukrainian."

"Or Nana heard her thought-messages in Ukrainian," Gerry said.

So they all thought Ruth sent messages.

There was more. It was like they were all suddenly finding the courage to bring their belief in the unbelievable out of the closet.

"I didn't know, whew-hoo."

Anne of course, with a sudden accent in her tic. Anne who had not sewn with her mother's group before. I looked back at her mother Victoria, expecting some reaction, but she was bowed to her work, busily sewing.

Ruth was her sister. Surely Victoria knew what Ruth was.

A brief worry flitted through my tired brain...*Victoria's getting way ahead of us.* I almost picked up my needle again to catch up. But more important things lay before us. We needed to solve the puzzle sent from Ruth. And we needed to....

The final psychic message--I think it came from my own brain--was, *turn on the TV.* So I did. It was all downhill from there.

Chapter 79

I looked at my watch, two forty-five. It seemed like an hour since I pressed the on button of the ancient analog television. It was *still* warming up. I wondered if the digital converter box on top of the set was even working.

Finally, a picture emerged and I flew through local channels looking for news. But the west coast was still asleep.

Then Anne's cell phone rang. She answered and we watched her pale complexion blanch to that of a ghost. She abruptly sat down on a corner chair.

"Mary." She closed her phone. "They're missing, but they found...blood all over the Zinzer house."

I finally landed on CNN news and found a live report.

"...this is gruesome, folks, we aren't going to show pictures of this, and we only have a few details on this exclusive report yet, but there's been another brutal attack in otherwise peaceful Pinto Springs, California. Our sources indicate police and others are scouring the Hispanic neighborhood in south Pinto Springs. Apparently they're looking for the brother of a young woman who recently committed suicide...."

I flipped channels to MSNBC, then FOX. They were all covering it. I returned to CNN and heard, "I think it's a shame that the authorities in Cleveland County are pointing fingers at the Hispanic community there. Do you think these are racially motivated killings, William?"

"There's no evidence to suggest that, Conway, but given the strain between...."

I changed the channel back to the local news. The cable channels were all about ratings and inflammatory opinions helped raise them. But there still wasn't anything on the local channels. It was way too early.

"Try NBC, Rachel." It was Gerry. I handed her the controls and stepped away. My stomach was churning.

Where the hell was Matt?

She lowered the volume and except for the muffled, barely controlled, crying of Gloria--standing outside staring off into the wet darkness--the house was in shocked silence.

Eventually CNN broke its promise and went live.

They were near the crime scene set up around the little house. The gathering reporters were hoping for the arrival of the parents. In the meantime they were trying to get some of the outer rim cops to spill the beans.

But they would wait for a very long time. Mr. and Mrs. Zinzer wouldn't return to their home on the mountain plateau for weeks, and only then to move.

Finally, we heard a uniform say, "The kid's been tortured. They think he's been taken somewhere else."

Buddy, not Abigail.

I stepped further away, back into the quilting room. Victoria was still sewing. One by one we retreated from the painful news coverage. All except Gerry, who listened for the rest of us. A few minutes later a shivering Gloria returned to her place at the rack. She cold had calmed her emotions, but it took several minutes for her hands to stop shaking so she could sew again.

I marveled that she wasn't in a wailing pile of fear and grief on her bed, by now. She was redefining the word stoic.

What did it mean that there was no mention of Abigail? Had the reporters just not caught onto the fact that there had been a young girl at the house as well? Or was she somewhere else entirely?

We were powerless; all we could do was wait. I was seething at Matt for keeping me in the dark, even though on some level more professional I understood why.

Weird thoughts filled my brain as the minutes dragged on and my body froze up from the painful ritual of sewing for hours. At some point I realized my mind was just trailing along, totally unfocused.

Andrea broke the spell I was under, saying, "It's your turn Elixchel. Tell us your teen story."

"No."

I thought it was a simple answer. Understandable. Forgivable in light of the circumstances. But Andrea was neither understanding nor forgiving. She persisted. Elixchel resisted. I wished Victoria would bellow at her again--seemed to be the only thing that tamed the little pixie-shrew.

"You *have* to...Abigail would have wanted this!" Andrea finally cried.

She caught the meaning in her sentence and glanced around embarrassed.

"I mean she *wants* us to do this! She's not dead. She's not going to be dead. She's a strong girl and she can fend for herself when necessary. She'll find a way to escape, or...or she'll be found, alive, and not even damaged like Ruth."

I've cleaned this up. Andrea was actually chanting derivatives of the F-word and its various synonyms throughout her mini-soliloquy. I thought you could do without them.

"Why don't you quit while you're behind, Andrea," Gerry said darkly. The mad lorikeet ran out of steam.

But I wasn't surprised by the change in tenor from Gerry. I'd seen Gerry take charge before. Underneath the Gucci and fake animal skins and mile-high mound of blond curls was a strong-headed, intelligent woman to match her billionaire husband.

"Okay. My turn to bare my soul before this haughty crowd," I said.

I almost looked around behind me to see who'd spoken. But someone had to bring us back under control, so I went with it. I told my teen story.

It was as boring as I could make it, full of first kiss stuff, stolen around corners with a young boy, how we entered high school together the next year and suddenly went our separate ways.

And I told them about my first Pearl S. Buck book, the one where the Japanese raped all the Chinese women. It scared me off of kissing for a full year. Probably just as well.

And I told them about my childhood dog dying when I was eleven. And the replacement dog my dad bought, just for me. He'd said *this dog will be yours to raise and train, Rachel.*

I smiled at the memories. Duke had been my first shepherd, and from that day forward all I ever wanted for a pet was a shepherd--which made me think of Wisdom. How was he doing, all alone at home? My lovely Wisdom.

At last we returned to the ferreting the meaning hidden in Ruth/Nana's cryptic message-poem.

It wasn't until much later that I learned that Ruth had kept small black, leather books full of her prophecies—most of which were in verse. All of them described what actually happened in the extended Stowall clan.

Chapter 80

Gerry said, "What does the third line mean? 'To down of van free son?'" We discussed and argued and sewed for several minutes but couldn't come to any conclusions.

Until Elixchel said, "What if Nana meant to say town of van free son? Maybe we just need to think of a town that sounds like van-free-son."

But we couldn't think of a town that sounded like that, and frankly the whole thing didn't sound right. The meter was right, but it just didn't make sense.

"Okay, how about if you compare the lines, 'away they've flown' in the first stanza and 'away they've gone' in the second stanza, don't they go together?" Hannah said.

"Okay, and if you compare 'the road leads down' in the first stanza with 'to wait for dawn' in the second stanza, they match." Anne.

"Right. Same with the last two lines of each of the two stanzas, they match meter and they rhyme too." Gerry.

"But the middle lines in each stanza, the two odd metered lines, 'To down of van free son,' and 'to rend their sweet reason,' they use the same meter and they rhyme and all, but, well, I just don't get it." Andrea.

"Why don't we read it like, all in one paragraph? The way it was written down. Maybe it was never meant to be a poem." Gloria.

So we did. It still made no sense.

"We're chasing our tails, ladies. Let's give it a break and see what comes to us." Me, thinking maybe Ruth would clarify if we opened our minds--and our mouths, and ate some more delicious pie, in the kitchen. My fingers hurt. My neck and back hurt. My butt hurt.

But we didn't go into the kitchen like I was wishing we would. Instead we sewed and I chased my thoughts round and round in my head like a puppy after her tail, until I heard Elixchel's voice filtered by my jumbled thoughts.

"...got my degree in accounting at the local community college. Bookkeeping actually, I'm still working on the accounting degree."

She was telling her teen story after all. The least I could do was listen.

Andrea said, "So that's where you met Javier?"

Elixchel stopped, as if frozen in time. Her head hung low, her long black hair trailing by her face, her fingers poised to start another stitch. Stalled. We waited.

Finally she said, "Yes."

It was like a sigh, really, from somewhere deep inside her, or maybe back in time, but from a long ways away. We watched her set her needle in the quilt and wipe at her cheeks with her hands. The Panther Queen raised her head and looked at us through reddened eyes shinning with some awful truth.

"Yes, that's where I met Javier Escobar."

She spoke his name as a native, enunciating each perfect vowel, the v as a vibrating b, trilling the final r's. His name pushed her pronunciation toward Spanish so completely that her next few sentences were spoken as if not in her native tongue, but as if she'd just ventured over our southern border to visit a while. I briefly wondered if she had some hidden Indian language inside her soul as well.

"I had to take a science class that spring. I selected geology. He did too. That's where we met.

"He was...magical. He was beautiful and magical. He was even taller than me and carved looking, as if from...a tiger's eye gemstone."

She paused and looked off to the side, seeing things we could only imagine. She wore a Mona Lisa smile under her glistening eyes.

"We studied gemstones in the class. Did you know that tiger's eye is a chatoyant gemstone? The word chatoyant comes from the French phrase *l'oeil de chat*, which literally means cat's eye. Chatoyancy arises from within the fibrous structure of the material, from fibrous inclusions or cavities within a quartz stone."

Her fingers briefly toyed with the anchored needle as if they wished they could begin the rhythm of the stitches once more.

"Tiger's eye is also described as pseudomorphous and that word is used to describe a mineral compound that appears in an untypical form."

Her Lisa smile wavered briefly. She looked down at the quilt again.

"As in metamorphosed, changed, usually under great pressure and heat."

Elixchel's voice had turned to melted silk, her words sticky fibers moving languidly in the air. We were mesmerized. *Something terrible was this way coming.*

She looked straight at us again, at least I thought she did but her eyes were still not seeing us. They'd settled on something that sat between Gerry and me. *A ghost perhaps.* I fought the urge to confront the intruder.

"He was the tiger's Eye, and I was mere sand. I was very young and he thought he was very powerful. Not just a gemstone, but a jewel with no limitations. A diamond with no flaws. I learned that hot summer that his skin tasted like his root beer color."

Her eyes floated down toward the beautiful quilt. She whispered the rest, as if the words were dangerous.

"And in the fall I learned he was married." A solitary tear slid from her eye. And finally the dam was broke.

Absolute silence greeted her announcement. There was no judgment. As one, we understood her emotional war. Finally, as if she were still wrestling with the decision, she spoke again.

"I told him I never wanted to see him again."

Suddenly she looked like Charlie Brown, her eyes wide and lost and full of the unfairness of life. I couldn't remember ever seeing such emotional pain in a woman's eyes before. The proud panther was no where to be seen.

She bowed her head and tried to return to her sewing. Andrea wasn't letting up, but Elixchel had left her story and all of us knew it, even the feisty pixie. Nevertheless, the pixie gave us a hint at what wasn't being said.

"Okay, we'll accept this for now. But next month you're going to tell everyone what's going on with your beautiful tiger's eye now—how he mistreated you."

Mistreated you. When? How, as in rape? As in beatings? I searched Elixchel's down-turned face, listened harder to her silence, but there would be no answer to these and other questions tonight.

I marveled at the odd relationship between these two "adopted" children of Victoria. They seemed ever ready to war. But why now, why after this powerful confession would Andrea make painful demands. Premonitions crept into my head—this time my own.

Javier was back. He'd come back to claim her again as old lovers sometimes did, hadn't he? This would explain the freshness of her pain.

But it was Alphabet Bomber Andrea who spoke to our collective growing concerns.

"Javier should be in Donovan Prison. He's not just a stalker anymore. He's dangerous, and he should be put away like the murderer Luke--who should have spent his entire life in prison. We need to help you stop him, Elixchel."

Good God.

She said all of this in battlefield dialect, as in F bombs and B bombs and a few S bombs. I marveled that Victoria didn't chase her out of the room as she had last month, only this time brandishing a sword of righteousness as she chased.

Perhaps the cutting words about Victoria's son Luke had effectively stripped Victoria of her moral imperative. My immediate reaction was one of embarrassment for Victoria. As bad as he'd been, Luke had been her son.

But then it hit me.

"Donovan Prison! *To down of van free son.*"

They stared at me; then I watched them agree with me that this must be the meaning of that confusing line in Nana's poem. Nana had heard "Donovan Prison" but her Ukrainian mind could only come up with down under free son!

Donovan Prison in south San Diego County was only a few miles away from Mexico.

I tried to reach Matt again, but again he wasn't answering.

Chapter 81

Around three Hannah got up and took my place at the rack. If part of a quilt was to be left unfinished it had to be an end piece. And I couldn't sit still long enough to sew more than ten stitches at a time. They knew I had to have time to think through the problem with or without Matt.

"Abigail can finish this one section when she gets back." Hannah gently said. "It will help her feel ownership of her quilt."

They had all murmured their agreement, and I silently prayed Hannah's optimism would play out. I personally had a belly full of fear that Abigail might never see her quilt again.

The issue with quilting was that you had to sew from the center out to the edges.

Every quilt has variations in the tightness of the stitching used in forming and connecting the many blocks that eventually comprise the top-sheet—even when only one person is doing the work. Wrinkles can appear and must be carefully smoothed out or eased in the overall quilt as the final layer of sewing is done. Thus the constant stretching and pinning done throughout the long night.

Of course you could also sew in daylight, I mused angrily.

I was at the windows again, staring out at the darkness again, wondering where Matt was again. Thinking another piece of pie wouldn't be so bad after all. I was just short of the DT's with the amount of caffeine and sugar flowing in my bloodstream now. Why not go for broke?

At least I wasn't overwhelmed with fatigue as I'd been last month.

Dread and fatigue had crept over the rest of them however, like a malevolent Stephen King fog.

I spent a lot of time in the bathroom, too, peeing and appreciating the cleverness of their wallpaper. The room was covered with decoupaged old newspaper articles, some from Boston and some from New York, even a tiny local paper from somewhereville, Connecticut. It was brilliant really, in case you forgot to bring reading materials.

I bumped into Nana at least twice on my trips around the house and we shared our grim thoughts nonverbally. I let the spirit of this old woman comfort me. She was this month's Ruth.

Somehow I needed an older woman as a mentor in my life...like my mother had been until--before she developed dementia. Come to think of it, she even mentored me through her demise, as well as she could, as well as her slowly dying brain allowed.

I would come home from long days at the library in North Carolina and find her sitting staring--I know now, blindly—at the small television set in her bedroom.

Pretending for me that she was okay. Pretending she wasn't terrified...for as long as she could. My eyes welled up and I shook my grief away and returned to stare at the stitching I was no longer doing.

I pondered the question, what if Abigail was dead? From there my thoughts drifted morbidly from one dark thought to another until my leg tingled and I looked down at my phone.

Finally!

It was Matt. I flew to the living room to keep the call as private as I could in our little space and angrily flipped open the phone.

"Tell me," I barked.

He fumbled an explanation why he hadn't called me, ending up telling me they feared Buddy was dead, judging from the amount of blood. The ME had indicated it was all from one person, presumably Buddy.

"We finally turned on the TV. It's all out there, on the national cable channels Matt! Including all the gory details. Nice way to find out, dear." I was pissed.

"I'm sorry Rache. I've been incredibly busy. And the press is everywhere now. It isn't helping."

"Where are you?"

"Back in the barrio, although the locals don't like to think of their neighborhoods that way. So I should lose the..."

I cut him off.

"So what are you getting from the local gang members?"

"Zip, mostly. They were frightened clams until Will finally connected with one family. We're outside their house now, trying not to bring future gang wrath down on them, pretending we still have nothing, and beating off the press as well as we can."

"But you have something now...you said 'mostly'."

I heard Matt sigh.

"Well, we have willing talkers. But don't go getting anyone's hopes up. None of it is useful information so far."

"The last thing we have is high hopes," I muttered. He heard me, and grunted.

I'd been wondering how to tell him about the cryptic poem-message. I decided to tell him it was from Nana. I certainly couldn't say it was from Ruth. If I said it was from Nana he could believe maybe she'd been holding back on us and knew where Abigail was all along.

Maybe.

Except...how could Nana know where she'd been taken now? Oh darn. I'd just have to talk my way past his objections.

"Rache?"

"Yeah, I'm just thinking."

"We need Gloria to take a look at some symbols written on the wall in Buddy's kitchen."

"What?"

"With lipstick. I'll send you a picture of them then you need to have Gloria look at them."

It took a moment for the picture to transfer. I stood staring at what were clearly Cyrillic letters. But how should I show these...maybe last words from Abigail...how can I show the grieving, terrified Gloria..?

Nana solved my problem.

"Vot are doze?"

I nearly jumped a mile. Nana had snuck up behind me, and was peering over my shoulder at the image on my phone.

"Oh," she said. "Main, den a line, den road. Must be a dress." She drifted away, back to her small downstairs bedroom by the front hall. I watched her glance up the stairs to the darkened bedrooms above as she went. Her face was an older version of Gloria's, also filled with fear.

A dress? What did she mean "a dress"? My brain was trying to shut down; I was way past my bedtime. Wait! Address. She meant address. Main...line! Mainline, or Main Line Road.

I wondered if Matt had heard her comment and put the phone to my ear again.

"Matt? Are you still there?"

"Yeah. Did you get the symbols?"

He hadn't heard. He sounded as exhausted as me. He needed to hear about Nana's poem first. Main Line could be anywhere.

"Matt, just listen to me for a minute, okay? Nana has some information. She's given it to us...you know she only speaks Ukrainian...but she told us in broken English, as if...as if it was said to her in English and she wanted us to understand it correctly. So she...okay, okay, never mind. Here's what we have." My turn to sigh.

"Rache..?"

"They've gone south. We think Nana said 'Where pigs are prone to hear men groan, down under.' Elixchel thinks Nana means *Donovan*--the prison. And just now, well, Nana saw the letters on my phone and she said it was the word for main and then a line and then the word for road. It makes sense, you know, so close to the border. Maybe if you faked it, told the Pintos you already know about their...hideout, or whatever it's called, near

Donovan prison, at Main Line Road—you could get one of them to tell you more. Matt? Are you still there?"

He wasn't of course. He was going into action, without me!

Now I was really lit. My pacing always increases when I'm furious. So I made the rounds of the first floor of the condo several thousand times until even I knew I was being a pain.

I came to light staring once again out the side windows of the sun porch. It was still dark. But at least it wasn't raining. *Enough with the crazy rain.* This was Southern California where it almost never rains.

My hands were so tensed from holding them in fists that I held under my armpits--as if I were afraid I might swing at the next human who crossed my path--that I couldn't have sewn if I wanted to.

I was shouting in my head, barely able to control my anger, and I knew my face reflected that. Tended to make me look crazy. Fortunately I was faced away from the others, all dutifully sewing on the quilt--where I should be right now.

Matt was probably right. I was better off sewing.

But even with my sporadic sewing, my fingers ached. I pressed them against the cold glass, hoping to ease the swelling and thus the pain. A chill leapt from its surface and skittered up my arms into my brain like a grave beetle going for the sweet breads.

But this chill wasn't from the glass, it was from my stalled heart.

It was from the set of demon eyes staring back at me through the pane...only a few feet away...the whites lit by the bright quilting lights...his gray iris's challenging my memory.

Eddie! I snatched my hands back as if from dry ice.

He was here! He was in town again. This odd, this terrifying man.

I took a half step back.

But he wasn't so odd looking any more, was he? He almost looked normal...except for the shades of gray.

Not his hair, his whole body. Why did I always see him in grays?

Another half step.

"No."

I didn't realize I'd spoken until I bumped into Hannah's chair...the chair I'd begun the night sitting in, but now was Hannah's.

I was losing my mind. It was the caffeine. The sugar. And the image was gone. Poof. So no one else would see him. Even if I was insane enough to tell them.

"Rachel?" Hannah.

They were wondering what was going on.

I turned around and sat down slowly in my new seat--breathing like a race horse before, during and after the race. I was staring at the bit of quilting I needed to finish and never would. My hands fiddled with the surface of the quilt, tried to return to the task at hand, but my mind was a million miles away.

I had to tell Matt. Eddie was back!

I flipped my phone open and looked at it. It was perilously close to dead.

Chapter 82

Abigail felt her mind slipping as she listened to the terrible noises coming from the next room. *Poor Betty and Rosalia.* Those filthy beasts were raping them again. Making their terrible animal sounds, screeching and cheering each other on. All night long Abigail had listened to the screams and moans, and other noises she tried to block out.

The tears began to flow again as she thought of the terror of the past eight hours. And Buddy, and how they'd killed him.

Surely he was dead by now, after what they'd done to him. They...*cut him.* Cut him everywhere. And all because of me. It was me they'd been after, he just got in their way, fought their attempt to steal me.

Because I got in the gang's way at school. Because I couldn't keep my mouth shut. Because I wanted to protect Betty and her friends.

She stifled a cry that kept trying to crawl up her throat.

The Indian girls would be dead soon, too. They couldn't survive the violence much longer. Their protests were weaker and weaker with each renewed attack.

Her heart sped up in her chest as if she were running away, and she pretended she was.

She pretended she was fleeing across a clover-filled field and halfway across as the sun was just breaking over the horizon, a beautiful fire-breathing dragon swooped down from the night and carried her off into the dawn.

A sob forced its way up her throat and her eyes flew to the door. *They might hear you! Be quiet or they'll come hurt you too!*

The assault had abated and the dirty little house settled back into a dread-filled silence.

Abigail's shoulders ached as if she were stretched on a rack. Her wrists were tied to the bed posts so tightly she couldn't feel her hands any more. Her ankles were tied together—which made her hope she wouldn't be raped, like the others. At least not yet.

She squirmed and almost cried out again. She had to pee so badly she didn't know if she could hold it much longer. Yet her mouth felt like the inside of a pottery kiln. She could barely produce saliva any more.

The smell of the filthy mattress filled her with renewed nausea as her eyes began to float in her head-- as if they were coming loose, as if they were eager to leave so they couldn't see death as it approached...or the hell she was about to be delivered into as it came to claim her like a hungry wolf.

He was taking her to Mexico. He called himself ContraCristo, and he claimed to be the eldest son of some drug lord in Tijuana. His papa, Antipapa he called him, was going to "savor her first juices" and then she would be taken who-knew-where. The worst part was he was actually beautiful to look at.

But that shouldn't surprise her she realized; evil usually was beautiful, so it could hide itself among the flowers and pretty birds, and humans would smell deeply of its fragrance and long for its song.

She drifted away again in the stinking cold, almost sleeping, almost free, halfway to hell.

PART THREE

remnants

Chapter 83

If I used my phone again it would be dead.

The quilt was almost done, except for the last section of one corner, the part I couldn't complete because of my crazy thoughts. What should I do? What was Matt doing?

Where was Abigail right now?

I stood and took in Abigail's quilt in its entirety again. When we'd first begun so many hours ago the quilt had been laid out between the boards for all to see, but I really hadn't focused on it clearly, I could see that now.

Back then in the beginning I'd thought the subject of the quilt was another of Abigail's beautiful lilies. But no, it was something all together different. The aquamarine and purple image I'd seen swooping across the navy to light blue background was a...

"It's a dragon, isn't it? Those reds and pinks are the flames." My throat was croaking, my voice sounded as deep as a man's.

Gloria looked up at me with exhausted eyes and said, "Why, yes. Didn't I explain?" She looked around at the others and saw that she hadn't.

"Abigail is into dragons now. She calls this her Dawn Dragon. See, how it flies from the dark navy colors toward the very light blues. She has a poem she's written...I should get it for you all and read it..." Tears were puddling at the corners of her eyes. She sighed, shook her head, changing her mind. "It describes the dawn dragon and how it flies out of the night carrying the sun in its mouth to start the new day."

Gloria's choking words faded away into her third or maybe fourth flood of tears of the night. I had to do something, anything, to keep it together.

The sleeping television set called me to it. I moved into the living room and turned it on once more. In the background I heard Anne's peculiar ring tone—the Flight of the Bumblebee, fitting for a woman who made her living off of apples and all their delicious manifestations: pies, dumplings, strudels, fritters. Can't have apples without bees.

She flipped her phone and began speaking in hushed tones with occasional who-who's as I waited for the analog to warm up.

Fatigue and sugar waged war for control over my mind. Finally a picture emerged, and slowly sounds. I flipped through the channels. It was almost four in the morning. Surely San Diegans were waking up. But no, not yet.

Giving up I returned to FOX. But they were following another stupid car chase. Wait. It wasn't a chase...those were aerial shots of a small home somewhere out in the boonies, with all sorts of black vehicles racing along the approach roads in the dark.

Anne stopped talking and just gawked at the screen. I turned up the volume. Victoria sighed noisily behind me, still sitting at the quilt rack.

"...authorities have been gathering for the past half hour, centering their attention on this rural Chula Vista home. You can see, Greta, they've got some people trapped now. Road blocks are being set up to the north and south on the only public road in. And...yes, I think we have the location now of those poor girls who have been kidnapped. And maybe the boy."

I was thinking it was an on-the-scene Geraldo Rivera type reporter—standing by the roadside as official vehicles sped by--even looked like him. *Maybe Geraldo's been cloned*, my sleepy-hyper brain whispered to me.

"Our sources are saying the boy has probably died, Geraldo. And aren't they also thinking the two Indian girls...Betty and Rosalia have been killed and dumped by now?" Greta. Greta from Fox. Wait.

Ohmygod, it *was* Geraldo! I marveled that he was seemingly able to be everywhere.

"I don't think any of them are dead! They better not be, Greta. The whole world is watching this now, and the rotten bastards who have them will be hunted down like dogs if they hurt a hair on their heads...."

Okay, I have to admit to you now that I have fantasies about Geraldo. He's such a strong, sensitive man.

The camera finally pulled back and there it was! Donovan Prison in all its blasphemy. I really hated prisons. Why hadn't the human race figured out a better way to deal with our misbehaving and broken people yet? Even microchips inserted directly into the brain would be better than keeping people in cages unfit for zoos.

I turned for the kitchen--I needed sustenance to listen to any more—and almost tripped over Gloria who was standing staring at the news with two fists pressed against her mouth.

Suddenly I spotted something chocolate and gooey on the groaning counter, and someone yelled, "Who for cripes sake brought fudge? I can't resist *fudge*."

Uh-oh. It was me.

I had to get out of here before I went stark raving bonkers, and I had to be down there where the action was. I barked, "Gerry! Get your car keys, we're going south!"

"I'll come too, I can do research on Gerry's new iPad while she drives." Hannah, springing into action.

Gerry had her coat on before I could find my jogging shoes in the big bag I'd brought. They were underneath my Rossi .38.

At the last moment I turned to acknowledge Gloria's needs a last time. We shared a look that fed me for the rest of this frightening morning, one that I knew well from my own life--the pain of being the person who must wait and wonder. Flashing across her face I also saw fear, courage and determination. Nana's door slid open and she joined us in this silent communication.

And then I turned to perform the duties that females of the wilder mammals on our planet most often do.

Chapter 84

I only thought of Eddie seventeen times on the drive down. There were even moments when I thought I saw him following us in that infernal white truck with the ram bumper.

Who was he? I still didn't know if his horrific, abuse-filled childhood had broken him, created a sociopathic monster, or done something far more complex. I only knew he scared me.

We were heading for Main Line Road.

In the end it was Hannah who drove Gerry's XLX970 (the third wonderful car I'd seen her drive since I met her last month.) Gerry chose to sit in the back and plug in her newest iPad with video mirroring installed and pointed at her home television connection.

But back to the SUV: the XLX has a base price of seventy-six thousand dollars. Gerry's XLX 970 (she called it her Grand Junction, because 970 is the area code for that city—but I was thinking it was a lowercase grand junction of some kind she was referring to) had tech upgrades I was betting put the monster over a hundred thou. The average house in America costs around a hundred and eighty thousand. The average American condo is about the same cost as the XLX970. It would fill me with guilt to drive one of them. But Gerry wore it well, like one of her trademark faux-animal coats.

And besides, she has four boys to deliver around town.

For those of you in the know, even the iPad doesn't guarantee WiFi connectivity everywhere. But of course Gerry had the upgraded iPad WiFi+3G. And she'd spooled on and on about having easy Free WiFi Radar, so with all the extras and frees, we were tuning into to live television just about most of the time. But then, this was Southern California.

Only once did I try to call Matt, but I hung up quickly when I thought about what he would say when he discovered we were on the way. I didn't want to hear his objections. They were undoubtedly correct.

I was going in anyway.

It's the fifth gene on my motivation chromosome. I see a problem. I get involved. I take charge. I don't sit and watch others do anything and nothing. I do!

Funny how I was just discovering this gene...after a lifetime of taking orders and being a (mostly) passive librarian-type. Funny how I turned out to be a heroine, at least in my own mind.

Dark rivulets began running down the windshield about halfway to our destination, and Hannah's racing drive turned to a creep. Another of Southern California's road-kill fogs was settling in.

Gerry said, gazing out the western side window into the darkness of pre-dawn, "You know, more people are slaves today than ever before and the numbers are increasing. And worse, children and women are the most often targeted. That's because even though slavery exists as forced labor and indentured servitude, most of the victims of this vile crime are used for sex and pornography. These girls we are going to save are children. Maybe not very young children, but they are all freshman in high school, and they are still children. I know."

Gerry was referring to her teaching experience, on the high school level. She was also thinking about the kind of individuals we would be encountering when we finally reached our destination. My belly shark leapt for joy, and I now knew the names of two of my stupid butterflies, Svetlana and Igor. They were doing Le Corsaire, most of it en pointe, on my stomach walls.

She continued, as if speaking to herself, "I think I need to do a fundraiser for this issue. Maybe connect with Demi and Ashton. They're doing great work in this area."

I woke up. *Demi Moore and Ashton Kutcher? The cougar and her cub?*

Matt and I definitely have to get on the Patrone's guest list.

"You better hurry." Hannah.

As in, the marriage won't last? But she wouldn't expand on the statement, even if I was dumb enough to ask. Hannah was too much of a lady for that.

The fog rivulets turned into rain streaks. I was praying we'd reach our target before the sun came up, because using the iPad, we'd watched the television coverage and there were police cars, black FBI SUV's, green Homeland Security vans, and giant white buses I knew to be SWAT Team transports--and maybe even ME vans--multiplying like maggots all around the area to the east of the little house.

It was lit up like a football stadium—like an early sunrise. Surely the kidnappers knew they were about to be attacked.

And just down the road to the south a media convention was setting up with enough satellite dishes to cover the Olympics. How did they get them there so fast?

The iPad grabbed my attention again.

"...Hidalgo, the horrific Mexican drug gang that controls most of the illegal trade in Tijuana now, is run by someone who calls himself Antipapa. The locals are terrified of him. His first born son is his emissary to the United States.

"His son is nicknamed ContraCristo. Nice family, huh, Bret? I hope he gets as good as he's given. My version of biblical vengeance."

"Everyone's, Geraldo."

I guessed Greta had gone to bed. I was wishing I could do the same. The heat in the car was so high I was doze-viewing. Gerry's fingers flashed around her iPad in a blur as she changed channels for more info—or was she researching something?

I said, "Maybe we should turn down the heat so you don't fall asleep at the wheel, Hannah."

"I'm fine."

I'm not, I wanted to reply. But she was driving. Then my brain kicked in despite it all. "You know, they've got this place surrounded...."

"That's what I was wondering. How are we going in?" Hannah.

She was hyped on adrenaline--the joy of danger. Her other life was homeschool, kids, homeschool, cleaning, homeschool, farming....

"Except for the south and west sides. It looks like it's all open fields next to the house on those two sides. Let me see if I can find anything more current...." Gerry said. She was working her iPad, changing Google views of the mostly vacant land around the little house.

"But what about your XLX? I don't want the billionaire calling me up in the middle of the night." I said.

"It's a rental. Don't worry. He doesn't behead horses."

Okay, I didn't say that, she did.

So that was why she had so many expensive cars. Probably wrote the rentals off as a business expense.

"You know what I'm wondering..." Hannah said. "...how did these Hidalgo guys know about Abigail and her friend? And why did they go out of their way to attack her? And Buddy. How did they know about Buddy?"

"Good question. But we know that the Hidalgos had infiltrated the Pintos. So they were present when Abigail pissed off the Pintos. Maybe that's when they decided to add to their intended prey, the Indian girls. To escalate things. Maybe they'd been sampling too much of their own drugs to think straight; to remember that stealing a white girl would bring the wrath of the American government down on their heads." Me.

Gerry said, "But why would they go north of the border to kidnap Indian girls when they are more easily available in Mexico? I'm thinking the Hidalgos now messing around in America were under orders to do something very different, something more exploratory, in the area of drug trafficking. And maybe there's something about these particular Indian girls we still don't understand. Something that connects them to Abigail, something that makes these particular girls more valuable in the sex-slave market.

"Brains. Abigail is very intelligent, and an artist. What do we know about Betty and Rosalia?" Me.

"Unfortunately, not much," Hannah.

"*Listen to this.*" Gerry.

It was Geraldo again. We listened.

"Folks, I've just received an email from some people in the Pintos Springs area. They claim to be members of the local high school gang, the Pintos, the one that was infiltrated by these bad dudes across the border. They're saying that they're really sorry about what's happened to these three women...."

"I bet they are, Geraldo, two of their boys have been found murdered so far," Bret said.

"Three, Bret. I know. But the point I'm trying to make here is they are telling me they're getting a posse together to go down to this little house south of Donovan Prison and rescue these girls...."

"Uh-oh. That will complicate things, won't it, Rachel?" Hannah.

But I wasn't listening. I was planning.

"Look up Donovan prison, Gerry," I said.

She did. The mission statement of the Richard J. Donovan Correction Facility listed its primary facilities and functions. The facility is a medium-high level prison.

Gerry. "Look at this. It's got some sort of 'sensitive needs yard.' What do you think that is?"

Hannah. "Maybe for the mentally challenged."

"More likely for the violent-impulses challenged," I offered.

Gerry. "Oh, and look, Donovan prepares non-citizen inmates for release to US INS for return to their native lands. How nice."

Hannah made a humming noise. I was thinking they were being insincere.

Gerry. "Maybe it's a safe house, for the gang."

Then I wondered, "Why would a criminal gang set up a safe house right outside such a big law enforcement program? Aren't safe houses usually for the recently incarcerated, a place where parolees adjust to real life again? "

Gerry. "Exactly. Maybe not a safe house. Maybe a hideout."

Hannah. "Maybe it's just a vacant house that the gang has confiscated. But why? Unless they're planning on breaking someone out later in the day, maybe while that someone is out in one of the low level security areas."

"A vacant house with electricity working...." I mused aloud.

Hannah hummed again. Was she doing something Zen-like?

Gerry. "Okay, then what are all those law enforcement types doing just sitting around near the little house? Why don't they go inside and rescue the girls?"

Exactly what I was thinking. And then Geraldo answered some of our questions.

"Listen to this Bret. It turns out this little house belongs to one of the top guards at the prison. Apparently he and his wife have lived there for thirty years or more. Cue the map, boys."

The view on the iPad switched from Geraldo-by-the-road to a fairly detailed aerial shot of the house in question.

"Good grief. They've got helicopters flying directly over the house. I guess it's not going to be a sneak attack, after all."

Gerry was kidding. The football stadium lighting had already squashed that idea. I was studying the layout of the house.

Hannah. "Can you see the surrounding land?"

"Yes. We're looking at it now," I said.

Hannah. "Maybe the cops are waiting because the house wasn't vacant. Maybe they don't want to do anything to get the guard and his family killed. Or, maybe...because they don't know who it is the Mexican gang is waiting to break out of prison. Maybe it's both situations, and they're waiting for the actual escape attempt so they can identify this big bad boy that is sitting in a medium security facility when he should be in solitary confinement in a high security facility."

So there could be a family caught up in the middle of all this?

Gerry. "Look, is that a dirt road leading up from the south? It's hard to tell in the dark, but maybe it is. Maybe that's how we can at least get close."

Hannah. "And then what?"

Exactly. I had a semi-plan, but I wasn't sharing it with my two apprentices. I didn't want either of them getting hurt.

Then the aerial view swooped around to the east side of the house where the cop convention was being held.

Gerry. "But...God. I can't stand this. It's like they're...they're unable to decide what to do."

Hannah. "They're wasting time! They should rush the bastards."

Gerry. "Probably taking a vote. Probably a bureaucratic work slow-down is in progress. Probably the union wants overtime for everyone before they proceed."

Our collective rage was boiling.

Me. "Okay. Okay, let's keep calm. Let's map this out."

Gerry picked up my thread. "We'll take 805 to 905, and then go east on Otay Mesa. Then find that little dirt road, and....and, hey! Look. Is that a hill to the north of the house?"

For the next eleven minutes we blundered in and out of fog patches searching for turnoffs.

Chapter 85

Matthew Lyon's LIRI Journal
Sunday, Nov. 2, 5:05-5:20 am dictated outside the
Main Line house

I was doing all I could to hold my temper in check.
But we were stuck in one big cluster-fuck.

Nobody was taking charge. There were no generals.
Check that. They were all generals.

Everybody was posing for promotion pictures. I hate
political gamesmanship—screws up the world. Which is
probably why I never made general.

And then we heard that a contingent of Pintos were
on their way down the mountain to add to the chaos.

I remembered the comment one parent had made
during this long night: *"Our boys aren't like that. They're*
like the Marines, man, they suffer and die and go to
prison in defense of their homies, and they protect each
other. We're all about protection...not selling the women
and girls."

Okay, I could buy that they thought of themselves as
like the Marines. But we didn't need them coming down
here to enlist.

Will Townsend pointed out that if we waited much
longer the Hidalgos would figure a way out of their little
mess. I agreed.

He wanted to know why we didn't just go in and I
asked him what plan he had in mind. I was frustrated.
But the truth was, there was nothing we could do now.

Will pointed out that the house was out of view. "We
could just slip around the corner while these morons are
all arguing with each other and take the house by force."

It's not like I hadn't thought of it. I just wasn't eager
to die tonight. "They aren't going anywhere. We have

them surrounded," I told Will. At least I thought we had the little house surrounded.

I spotted a brief splash of light illuminating the hill to the immediate north of the house where the Hidalgos were presumably holding the girls. It was gone just as fast as it arrived.

Probably searchlights from the chopper-soup flying around over our heads. But then another thought crept into my brain and my eyes returned to the now dark ridge.

I asked for the binocs from Will. Night Hawk A-222s. They were damn good, which they should be, at just under three grand a pair. That was why we had only one pair.

I began scanning the scrub covered hilltop.

My first thought was *tell me that isn't Rachel. Tell me she didn't' drive down here to do something stupid.*

My second thought was *maybe she'll do something that will force our hand.*

But I couldn't see any movement. I tried speed dialing my wife's cell again. Again it went straight to voicemail. Maybe it was dead.

Everything was fucked up.

Chapter 86

We'd bounced from crevice to crater for almost three miles across an "open field" to the west of the house, moving from bump to bigger bump, until we rounded behind the house. My teeth were rattling by the time we found our target—a small hill to the north of the hideaway house.

Gerry had discovered on her iPad that the name of this modest mound was *Snakebite Hill*. And I hoped all the snakes were already hibernating.

We skirted Snakebite until we located what looked like a road up. At least it seemed like it was, until we were fifty feet in, when the road disappeared. Then we pushed our way to the top like a snowplow climbing an avalanche.

Hannah protested all the way; Gerry insisted she keep going. She was a billionaire's wife.

By the time we crested to level ground the front bumper and grill of Marshall Patrone's XLX970 rental was holding enough fodder to feed a whole hopping herd of Australian Red Kangaroos.

I was thinking maybe Matt and I would finally get to meet the owner of the local soccer team—and maybe one of his lawyers.

And then we thought to turn off the headlights.

"Do you think they saw us?"

"Don't worry about it, Hannah. They're too preoccupied with their infighting to pay attention to a probable reporter finding his way to the top of the ridge. Have you got the flashlights, Gerry?"

I needed them to remain calm.

But I was worried. After the mess of media we'd passed on the way in, I knew the cops would be chasing us out soon, if they'd seen us, no matter who they thought we were.

Hopefully they hadn't.

I was also hoping it would be the cops chasing us, not the bad guys.

Below us, we knew, was the entire event, the cops, the FBI, unmarked cars, cruisers, crime scene van, SWAT team vehicle, and behind them the television vans and a gaggle of geese I knew were reporters there to protect the rights of the criminals as well as the victims. This whole mess was to the left, or east, of our real target however.

On the way down I'd begun to think the long green vehicle visible on Gerry's iPad wasn't what I thought it was. Who knew what new agency might have joined this circus.

Gerry said, "Let's get the lay of the land. Turn the light switch all the way counter clockwise, Hannah, so the interior lights will be killed. That way we won't light up like a Christmas tree when we step outside."

Hannah did as she was told. Our resident genius was still shaking in her boots from the goat-climb up Snakebite Hill.

Then the three of us piled out of the XLX and let our eyes adjust to the moonlight, which was fairly strong. The fog hadn't reached this far inland. We could easily make out four- and five-foot-high bushes all around us.

We were standing in a bush forest, for cripes sake.

That was when I noticed Gerry still had on high heels. They were gold lame sandals, actually. What was she thinking--we were going to a cop party? At least I knew she wouldn't go far in them. I wanted my apprentices staying up here where it was safe.

Hannah, on the other hand was wearing well-worn professional hiking boots, probably eco-friendly. I was dressed for a night jog, all in L.L.Bean colors. We were a sight.

"There's scrub everywhere up here. What's the plan?" Gerry.

"Find a coyote path?"

"Good idea Hannah." I wondered if I'd missed her sarcasm. She was hard to read sometimes, and I was very nervous. "Now be sure to keep your flashlights aimed at the ground while we observe."

For the next ten minutes we searched for a break in the underbrush while Gerry ouched and eeked with every half barefoot step. Finally we found a small clearing from which we could see the dimly lit safe-house about a quarter mile down, four football fields. I pulled out my binoculars and began studying it. Much later I would learn that Matt was searching for me around the same time.

"You know, I don't understand these guys kidnapping Indian girls. White girls I can see taking out their revenge on, but aren't Mexicans a mixture of Spanish and indigenous?" Hannah.

"Sure, but like any human society there's a pecking order. Besides, the indigenous people have been fighting with the Mexican government on and off for years." Gerry the former Spanish the teacher.

"Well, that's been settled right? I mean the latest war. And those people down by Guatemala are Mayans, aren't they? As opposed to Aztecs, or any of the other indigenous groups sprinkled around Mexico?" Hannah the brilliant student, honing her knowledge.

"In the Yucatan Peninsula, yes, they're modern day Mayans. But the struggle continues—they don't think of it as a war, per se. And the Aztecs are strictly an ancient people. They no longer exist as a separate group. Their genes are floating around, but not so you could claim heritage. Sometime around the twelfth century the Aztecs took to wandering from their mostly central Mexico region...."

I wandered away, only half listening to them. I needed to find a way down this hill.

"But the Mayans continue to exist largely separated from the general Mexican population. They are considered Mexico's Indigenous people. They are mostly centered in Mixe, Oaxaca." Gerry.

"Mixe, as in mixed?" Hannah.

"It's a city. Oaxaca is a city but it's also the name of one of the Mexican states...."

She was teaching. I was searching.

"The indigenous people of Mexico have been treated with a combination of disdain and romantic fascination for years...but the Mayan population numbers more closely resemble our African-American subculture. They number between eleven and thirteen percent of the total population of Mexico. And the last real Mayan *'war'* was the Caste War of the Yucatan...."

Gerry made air quote marks as she spoke. I stepped down a narrow path, first one foot then another, hoping they continued their discussion for several more minutes, until my path down was concealed from them.

"Over a hundred years ago." Hannah.

"And bloody. The Mexican people have always had difficulties with the fact that they are a mixture of races...the Mayans—who are a darker color than most Mexican people...."

Another few steps. Hannah and Gerry's Socratic discussion faded further away, a fact that gave me confidence that no one in the little house below could hear them.

"Anyway, we really don't know what happened to the Aztecs. They took to wandering in the twelfth century...."

I heard a door slam faintly below and pushed further down the narrow path, fighting my way through the thick chaparral where necessary. The female voices faded away behind me. New male voices—in Spanish--were luring me forward. Some of them sounded drunken, angry.

I never stopped wondering where the snakes of Snakebite Hill were as I crept down. Only snatches of the women's conversation reached me now.

A faint light was forming to the east. The sun was preparing its rise. *Dawn Dragon was approaching.*

The small house where I assumed all three girls were being held was a one-story, low-roofed, L-shaped structure. The short bottom of the L faced west. The long side of the L was facing toward me, on the north. The top of this side was facing east and I was assuming this was the front of the house as a gravel driveway led up to it from the cop circus out on the primary road. That circus was surprisingly hidden by a copse of trees between the house and that hard surface road.

Along the short bottom leg of the house were a scattering of vehicles—two or three, it was hard to tell in the dark, the cars were all black. The driveway must run around the south side and end up at the back, probably off the kitchen.

I continued filling in the interior in my mind, as I made my way through the chaparral. The activity at the back of the house was why I decided to enter the house from the front.

The lower I went on the hill the clearer the copse of trees became, actually a row of riparian trees—Arroyo Willows, Black cottonwoods, and California Sycamores. I realized the brush was thinning. I stopped and assessed. I also loaded my gun, a simple six-shooter, and held it in front of me, remembering the last time when the gun had gotten stuck in my coat pocket.

I figured the four windows directly in front of me now were for the living room at the front, and a couple of bedrooms off a hallway leading back toward the kitchen. An odd arrangement; maybe the house had been expanded over the years.

"What about the Incas?"

I was startled by the sudden sounds from Hannah and Gerry. Were they following me, or had the wind shifted.

"...Incas are Peruvian..."

Then an external light flashed on at the back of the house. I waited. No one exited. My heart was pounding.

Switching off my own LED light I searched the house and its surrounds for any sign of movement. A couple of shadows moved occasionally through the dimly lit interior.

Finally my fear subsided to a dull anxiety again and I moved forward.

I could now make out the several vehicles parked at the rear of the structure. One was a large black SUV with the rear door opened, the other two were smaller black sedans. They were definitely positioned for escape.

From behind I heard, "Rachel?"

"Where are you?"

Damn! They were calling out!

I raised my hand hoping to still them when I heard Gerry say they needed to be quiet.

Ya think?

I stumbled on a bit farther—a sense of urgency filling my breast--until suddenly the growth around me disappeared entirely and I found myself fully exposed looking down a grassy hill.

I crouched.

Waves of fresh wet grass and a darker undercurrent flooded my nostrils with earthen delight. Primal messages of the night. My bunny nose had been alerted. And my bunny ears were standing tall for the sounds of coyotes. *Delicious grass, dead ahead. Danger a few feet away. Dawn about to rise.*

I was profoundly aware I was a mere bunny.

I thought I was hearing snatches of conversations from the house, still half a football field away.

I had to act soon, or...

My heart began tripping in my chest as my mind roamed the field of possibilities before me. What a time to wonder what I was going to do.

I thought back to the orange hazard cones we'd run into on our way down Otay Mesa Road. We'd turned back at that point, as all the east bound cars were doing. But unlike the others, we whipped off to the north across the field as soon as a long break in the traffic allowed us to. That dirt road had taken us up Snakebite Hill.

Now looking out across that bumpy plain from this new vantage I could see another dirt road leading across it, directly from the back of the house toward Mexico. It would cross Otay Mesa fifty yards or so from the roadblock.

The cops would never spot them in the chaos of the u-turning vehicles, as they made their run in the half dark.

And then all they had to do was continue to weave and bump—as we had done—across the next couple of fields until they found the road that led to the border crossing.

A matter of meters and yards, not kilometers and miles.

I knew Abigail was in increasing danger as the light grew. Dawn was a perfect time to escape. Dawn was when they'd act, when human eyesight was at its weakest. When colors and shapes and patterns flowed in and out of each other like a two-toned charcoal landscape, gray on slightly grayer.

I had to act.

If we could sneak our way across those fields as we just had, then those killers could. And the Mexican border guards wouldn't dare to stop the son of El Antipapa.

Music started playing.

Chapter 87

My heart jumped into my throat like a monkey fleeing a leaping lion. It was my cell phone.

Nearing hysteria, I fell back into the deeper brush, fumbled with the *gee-dee* device trying to open it and smash down the green on-button to receive the call and stop the stupid jingle.

My eyes skittered back and forth across the windows only a couple of feet away...*or so it felt*. No one looked out them at me. No one stepped out onto the still well-lit back stoop. No one had noticed the idiot tune at the bottom of Snakebite Hill.

It was Matt. The last guy on earth I wanted to speak to right now. I pressed farther back into the snake-filled brush—turned my back to the house. Held the phone to my ear.

"Speak Rache!"

"What!" I finally whisper-snapped.

"Why are you breathing so hard?"

"I'm having sex with a couple of really gorgeous twenty-year-olds, why?"

"They better be females. And that better not be you up on that ridge, because half the cops in Southern California are on their way to you."

He was lying.

"I'm busy Matt...*sewing*."

I was lying--too late. He knew I wasn't sewing. Life is all in the timing.

"Tell me where you are Rachel or I'll..."

"You'll what?"

"I'll wring your neck, is what."

No he wouldn't. *The next time he would see me he'd wildly embrace me in his mannish arms and practically bear hug me to death while whispering in my ear that he loved me and needed me.* But I didn't really know that now.

I said, "Have you got your damned warrant yet?"

"What...?"

Too late again.

"I saw you Matt. Hunkered down a half mile from Abigail, doing nothing. How long do you expect you and all the Homeland Boys are going to wait for permission to go in and save her?"

"Rache..."

"Six miles, Matt. Only six miles between them and the Mexican hell they have planned for those innocents..."

"Rache..."

He was stymied. He couldn't speak above a whisper anymore than I could. We were both stymied, but I was stuck in my little pocket of fear, looking back down on Abigail's prison. Waiting.

For what?

"I'm busy Matt, and unless you want to get me killed, don't call back."

I shut down the call. Then I turned off my cell so he couldn't call back and jammed the *gee-dee* device back in my jeans pocket.

A female scream ripped the air like tiger claws ripping through living flesh. The scream went on from ripped flesh to torn flesh to shredded, bloody dying flesh....

Chapter 88

I could feel the solitary scream that rose from the house more than hear it, as if the pressure of the cry pushed through the growing fog, sending vibrations up to my viewpoint, until it arrived as drops of terror splashing cold against my face.

Fog! The impending sunrise was forming another protective cover for the bad guys' escape.

The ice water facial woke me as if from a stupor and my feet started moving.

I ignored the cries of reason in my head. I was one enraged elephant momma chasing danger from her baby. I was suffering from an extreme sugar rush, on a sugar high, wildly sugared up to the point of sugar insanity.

To my right as I careened down the green carpet, which wasn't nearly as smooth as it pretended to be, I spotted movement coming toward the house. Just a float of clouds at first, caught by the corner of my cornea.

Until it pulled out of the dimness of the near-night and formed itself into a whitish grayish truck with a funny flat nosed front. A funny, bull-nosed...*like a bulbar! A homemade bulbar!*

A *giant* bulbar, like the one that had transformed my beloved red Taurus station wagon into a speeding bullet less than a month ago—while I was driving down a California freeway going sixty-plus miles an hour.

The white...*it was white*...pickup truck with the flat sheet of scarred metal driven by...driven by...*Eddie!*

Eddie was here! Eddie was racing toward the back of the house faster than I was stumble-running down the grassy knoll, and unless he stopped soon he would plow right the blazes into it!

Finally, I spotted one of the men in the nearest window, staring out at me as if he was seeing an angel of hell descending on him.

He was a gangbanger if ever I'd seen one, a Mexican gangbanger, with an eye patch propped above his left eye in the signature headgear of the Hidalgo's.

They thought they were pirates, for cripes sake. They thought they were freakin' Johnny Depp look-alikes!

I raised my pitiful revolver—which wasn't an easy feat while trying to stay on my feet, arms pumping rhythmically in apposition to speeding feet--and the man in the window slid back into the darkness behind him.

I ran straight at the side wall, but turned at the last moment and landed, *slam*, with my back plastered to the stucco.

Ouch. Stucco is rough...especially when you hit it at ninety miles an hour.

My heart was pounding so loudly I was temporarily deaf. So at first I didn't hear the cavalry coming from the east. And then I did.

Matt must have alerted the Homeland Boys to the fact that his flipping-out wife was racing down the north hill toward the Hidalgo's, raised gun in hand, and that gave them the *imminent danger* they needed to finally start their engines and make their assault.

I had forced everybody's hand, as the saying goes.

Chapter 89

My heart was pounding.

The dark was fading like filaments of mist in candle light, microscopically. You more sensed the loss of dark than saw it.

Hysterical voices were darting around within the house; Eddie's truck door slammed; and the mechanized Boys to the Rescue were making their interminable way around the bend through the row of riparian trees. Slowly. Lights off. As if to take us all by surprise.

Idiots. Where were the Marines when we needed them?

Holding my Braztech Rossie revolver .38 special up by the side of my head I calmed my breathing by remembering I'd just practiced at the Escondido range Friday.

I listened. The girls had gone silent. My heart was trying to escape my chest, using a battering-ram to get through my tender flesh. My back was screaming *ouch, that hurt!* to the stucco wall which now felt partially embedded in it. Thank God I'd put on a sweatshirt; it was the only thing between me and the rough cement. And I imagined my hero husband was leading the charge of the good-guys, only a hundred yards away but audible.

I peeled myself off the outside of the house and, bending low to get safely under the side windows, I raced around toward the front of the house, up onto the front stoop. It looked remarkably like the back stoop, except for a sickly potted plant.

I could have sworn I heard Matt shouting behind me, but it was probably just a subconscious voice...*or was he sending me Ruth-messages?*

Or maybe my subconscious was trying to tell me to run the other way.

The front door was open. I could see straight through to the back door.

Believe it or not, Eddie stood in the back doorway in full cowboy regalia. Once again I flashed back on the bizarre encounter when I first laid eyes on him last month, pale and androgynous, wearing cowboy gear in his empty, haunted house, finally discovered by the outside world.

Déjà vu cowboys all over again.

He tipped his ten gallon hat to me, and stepped into the kitchen and moved for the rooms I hadn't identified at the back of the house, way ahead and to my left.

I did the same, stepped inside. My breathing doubled. I wondered if he was as terrified as I was.

I peeked around the corners of the entryway to see who was possibly hiding inside the living room. It was empty.

Where were the bad guys?!

Still super-charged on sugar and adrenaline I moved into the living room and stoop-walked—arm and gun extended—toward the narrow hall leading through the house. I clicked the living room lights off when I came to the wall switch. We needed to escape in this direction and I wanted our departure protected by the dark. Then I clicked off the hall lights, after first identifying where the hall doors were.

One on the left and two more on the right.

I moved to the first bedroom, on the right, rounded the corner in the same way I'd entered the house, arms outstretched, prepared to shoot if necessary. The room was dark. With the hall lights off, I mostly sensed there was someone in the room, prone, on the bed in front of me, so I slid the door closed and switched the room light on.

My breath stopped in my throat as the image inside the room blossomed like some evil flower before me.

Tied flat on her back, naked, beaten and bruised, her legs spread eagled to expose her bloodied genitals, lay Betty Wolftooth. She stared sightlessly at the ceiling above her, mouth open, breathing shallowly. She was missing a front tooth. Her lips were split. There were bite marks on her breasts. That was all I could bear to take in.

My courage departed between my legs toward the floor and I almost fell to my knees. No I didn't wet my pants. The sensation was caused by internal flows, not external. My body was moving toward shock.

But the shouted Spanish behind me and the sound of a bullet passing through flesh and thudding to a stop in some distant wall somewhere behind me woke me from my terror-bound state, and I moved quickly to her bedside, dropped the gun on the bed like some cast-off chore and began tearing at the ropes tying her hands.

Betty Wolftooth was beaten in more ways than one. Her first freed arm fell back on the greasy pillow under her head and lay there nearly lifeless. Her eyes were open, but she wasn't focusing. Her color was gray, maybe because it was still pre-sunrise, but her face was a mask of death-acceptance—the final stage of dying Elizabeth Kübler-Ross had defined decades ago.

Fighting off a rising sense of hopelessness, I finished untying her ankles and her other hand, and picked up my gun. I would have to leave Betty to continue my search.

Where the hell was my cavalry?! Eddie might well be dead by now.

My legs were shaking as I moved down the dark hall into the second closed door, this one on the left. Dark and silent, and again I was forced to turn on the overhead light, and what lay on the bed before me brought home again the urgency of my actions. A couple, not much older than Matt and I, lay side by side, hands tied in front, staring sightlessly at the ceiling. They had clearly been executed.

I took them to be the original occupants of the house. Their ages encouraged me to believe they might have been living in the house alone. Additional younger people would seriously complicate things.

To the sound of more shouts and another gunshot, I approached the third bedroom, on my right.

It was empty, but a puddle of blood at the center of the bed suggested this had been a torture room for another of the girls.

The urgency to find Abigail expanded, so I left and moved into the fourth bedroom, this one on the left but with the entrance around the corner, out of sight. Ahead was the kitchen. To the left I knew was the bottom leg of the L.

I almost didn't make it around this turn. My terror was growing exponentially as I listened to the fighting at this part of the house, Eddie's part.

My breathing slowed. Another loud retort pushed me forward and I rounded the corner and slipped quickly inside this last bedroom. *There she was!*

She had clothes on! She was tied, but apparently not raped, nor bruised.

"Rachel!"

"Shhh." Which is librarian-speak for be quiet.

I rushed to Abigail's side and began undoing the ropes that painfully twisted her wrists above her head.

She was their prize, the one they needed to keep undamaged for optimum resale value.

With that bitter thought, I whispered, "You've got to help me. I can't get Betty Wolftooth to respond."

She swung her legs over the side of the bed and swayed for a moment as she realized her hands were inoperable. She shook them, trying to move blood through them again. I watched, waited. Until I could tell she was with me.

Abigail whispered, "Where...show me." Her voice was scratchy-dry and I wished I had water to give her. But we had to move.

I led her, my arm around her thin back, pushing her forward toward the front of the house and Betty.

"Brace yourself. This is ugly. We need to get her up and outside." Me.

Abigail nodded, and I felt her spine stiffen under my half embrace.

It took a few seconds for Abigail to adjust to the horror that Betty had been reduced to. But finally we pulled her and tugged her into an upright position, and moved her into the living room.

"I can't...she's like dead weight...I need to rest," Abigail half moaned. She seemed to be slipping into depression right before my eyes.

I looked at the still dark freedom waiting just outside the front door, but Abigail was too weak, so reluctantly I moved us toward the couch that was on the eastern wall of the living room under a large window.

My mind was racing, trying to decide how to proceed, and the thought that helped me to move them to the couch was that maybe I would be able to see Matt and friends arriving through the front window. Maybe that sight would stir them forward again. I lowered the two girls down on to the couch, and stood to search the gray dawn.

Instead, I saw the first arc of brilliant yellow as it popped above the dark horizon. It took my breath away and I stood for what seemed like hours mesmerized by the sight I'd seen so many times in my life.

Inexplicably, an image taken by a powerful lens-- made for the purpose of peering into the distant universe, by motes of life on planet Earth that we call astronomers--popped into my mind. This light about to ascend before me reminded me of that image. I'd seen it at Mount Palomar Conservatory, when our boys were young and Matt and I had first lived in California. The memory held me tightly in its grip.

The image was one of several photographs of galactic activity--ancient light's passage through the void to the camera's lens, and thus to our eyes--of surging gas formations, eternally billowing flames, rising and swirling. From our distant vantage, the radiant red and yellow clouds, captured by cameras attached to a Mount Palomar telescope, formed horses' heads out of the blind and deaf energy swarming the universe. As wide as our galaxy and as high as heaven itself, the horses' heads reared majestically against a black backdrop of nothingness sprinkled with blue diamonds.

The pictures have stayed with me for decades, not just because of their intense beauty but because I had seen and would see lesser examples of them in other places and at other times—including times like this one.

The many random configurations pretending to be life had echoed repeatedly in other marvelous sights on my trip across life. They spoke to me of what ultimate purpose that seemingly random, blind and deaf energy could possibly have.

The stunning was everywhere, in wave-etched sands of beauty on a beach, in clouds with names like unicorn and griffin, in rocks pretending to be human faces staring yearningly down at us—as if wishing to be what we were, as if the inanimate stuff was trying on life without the spark of it, and finding it wanting.

There could only be one reason for all the experimentation--life. Life was the purpose of the universe, life for reasons we may not ever understand in this existence, life because it is capable of perception, life, because the inorganic image was not enough for the force that created the universe.

Life was the sole reason for it all.

And finally I began forming my humble understanding into words I could give to Betty, urging her to rise and look at the sunrise, to think of the source of that vision, and to go with Abigail and me toward the doorway that would lead to the rest of *her* life.

With feeble words I tried to translate this ten or fifteen seconds of thought into something that would reach Betty Wolftooth and move her forward.

"Betty, pay attention. Abigail's quilted Dawn Dragon is rising. Look, see it to the east?"

Remarkably, I watched as Abigail's face finally sloughed off the lethargy a night of terror had left behind and lit up with the same sense of urgency I felt.

And Betty turned away from death long enough for us to reach her. I'd spoken Abigail's childhood words, and somehow they had reached the child still alive within both of them.

And then the sun completed its part in this effort. It rose. It rose below heavy black clouds and above the dark, tree-broken line of the horizon in all its glory.

The clouds above the sun sprang to life with the reflection of its hot spirit, in reds, oranges and yellows, and turned the gray dawn blanket into a magnificent quilt of many colors.

I heard myself say, "You get two of these each day, one in the morning and one at night, Betty. They're worth everything that happens in between. We need you to fight to live, honey. We need you to help us get you to safety."

The words were whispered as we held her swaying between us, facing the rising sun. But I saw the change I needed, not just on Betty's face but on Abigail's as well.

Together we moved her off the couch, and finally toward the front door and her escape. But behind me Rosalia waited, and I knew Abigail could never manage to get Betty far enough away from this hell-bound house alone. I was suddenly torn anew.

In that moment, a second—or was it a third, Eddie being the first--small miracle of the night appeared in front of us. It was Zen Hannah and Glam Gerry.

My silly brain looked down at Gerry's sandled feet and saw that she'd found my spare pare of socks and covered them to protect her painted toenails from the underbrush on their trip down Snakebite Hill, and all the magic evaporated.

"Where's Rosalia?" Hannah barked. She was a guard dog, taking command.

"I don't know. I'm going back for her now. You two take them to safety. Matt's on the way."

At that second, the arriving army of rescuers broke from cover of the copse and came into view. The sunrise continued to amaze me by lighting them up to look like King Richard's Crusaders on horseback.

Another scream from the back of the house turned me around and headed me down the dark hall. I knew I was crazy. I knew I would get killed. I knew I had to find Rosalia.

So did Hannah and Gerry, who nevertheless called after me to stop. My heart was pounding in my breast again.

Before taking a handful of steps, I spotted movement at the other end of the hall. My gun raised up as if to face whoever was there, as if it had a mind of its own. A dragging, foot-stepping sound was making its way down the hall to the left. I waited in terror.

It was Eddie, standing only a few feet away now, still bathed in darkness, still all in grays and that ridiculous cowboy outfit, only looking much healthier than the last time I'd seen him.

He was almost handsome.

He was dragging and pushing two of the Mexican bandito's toward the back door. They looked terrified.

He took the time to flash me a grin. Then he dragged his two charges out the back door and down the steps.

My skin tried to run away from the sight of him but my mind had locked up. I must have stood there watching him for untold seconds, before breaking free of some demon spell.

It was uncanny to see him again, to be aiming a gun at him again.

Then I turned and rushed to help Rosalia, still not knowing who else was back in the small, bloodied den.

EPILOGUE

Sunday evening

Abigail's final words as she was being led away into the rising sun by Hannah and Gerry had been, "But will life be worth anything without Buddy?"

Words I didn't register at the time.

But they became the last worried thoughts that I'd carried into the land of sleep with me after returning home Sunday morning, along with one happy thought.

We'd found Wisdom healthy and sleeping soundly at the foot of our bed. He merely raised his great, gray head and looked at us reproachfully for having stayed out too late, and then returned to sleep.

Looks like we get to keep him for another day or two. One day at a time, as the saying goes.

A ringing phone woke me way too soon, but the sky was darkening again, so I answered the call, sighing loudly as I slumped back on my half-used bed, phone to ear.

It was Abigail. She opened the conversation by shouting that Buddy Zinzer had been found alive. Now I was awake.

I turned on the bedroom television and listened to a story already growing old in news-time, that indeed Buddy was alive. Unfortunately, another Pinto boy had been found quite dead and quite mutilated only twenty feet away.

Not that Buddy had escaped harm. He had been cut in many places. I told myself that if any of them had been life-threatening, they'd be saying so. But...

"How badly?" slipped from between my lips before I could stop it.

"I don't know. My mom just left for the hospital. She said she'd call. Of course he's in ICU."

But before I could grow too morose over the slaughter of innocents, Abigail switched mental gears and told me she'd just had the weirdest dream.

How like a teenager to say she'd had the weirdest dream, right after having lived through the weirdest nightmare. How quickly youth began to heal, I mused as I listened. And then I worried that she wasn't really healing, just suppressing.

"I think it was because of your dragon comment. You know, Dawn Dragon?"

I knew.

"I think that's why I was riding one in my dream, swooping across some bucolic landscape. But he wasn't a fire breather, my mount, he was a kind animal, a gentle hero. Maybe like the creature in the NeverEnding Story. Have I ever told you that I love fantasies?"

A good thing to love.

I told her no, but of course I knew. I'd just helped sew some of her first dragon quilt. I felt there would be others. And her magnificent flowers were fantasies.

"And...there were maidens, all kinds of them, all in trouble, tied to trees, locked in dungeons. They were in all kinds of situations. I was flying from one to the other and freeing them. Of course I know I was dreaming about what has just happened, but it seemed different. Like there was a truth in the dream that wasn't in the real thing. I told my mother. She actually listened to me this time."

Another good thing. But maybe she had her assumptions backwards. Maybe the truth was in the real thing, not her chimera-dream.

"I mean she didn't talk down to me like she sometimes does. So then we talked more and she agreed—*at long last*—that I could continue to go to Pinto Springs high school."

She stopped. I just listened.

"But now I'm not so sure. Maybe I'd rather not...of course I can't go back to the home school group...it's just that I don't have the warmest feelings about Pinto Springs high anymore."

"Maybe another school." Me, not just listening.

"Yeah, maybe. Anyway, I still can't let the dream go, you know? There's something there, me flying around, saving maidens in distress."

"Like a social worker might?" Me, just giving her feedback.

"Yeah, like that, I guess. Or maybe...a lawyer. Or a doctor. You know, not the ones just after money, but like a public lawyer, a doctor who works in a poor community. Or, maybe a cop."

"Or a tailor, or candlestick maker."

She giggled.

"Yeah. I guess it's too early to discuss careers."

"Or an artist."

"Of course. But there has to be more. I'll keep thinking about it. I did love riding that dragon, saving those maidens."

"Good thing to love."

I dressed and went to see where the boys were.

I found Wisdom on our back deck listening to his wilder spirit-buddies. Matt was soundly sleeping in his favorite recliner in front of an unseen and unheard television, so I took off for another visit with God.

It was getting to be a bad habit, me showing up at St. Peter's Church to sit and ponder and yes, even pray. I was hardly what you would call a regular churchgoer. I didn't even take communion I was so riddled with sin.

I was riddled with sin because I couldn't get up the nerve to confess. I'd never really felt comfortable with confession—the process by which you un-riddle yourself--having been a failed Protestant and all.

But the church was still a good place to think. Lots of nice thoughts hanging around you in the air. Sort of kept your musings from going too dark.

So what drove me there, you might ask, besides familiarity? Well, maybe it was the second call from Abigail, the one I'd illegally taken while driving to church, the one where she'd told me Buddy had been razor cut in so many places they'd just stopped counting. More importantly, he would survive and nothing vital had been removed, no missing parts. So, He-She needed to be thanked.

No, that hadn't been what sent me to church. I'd already been on my way. So I decided understanding why I have this urge to connect with God in this Catholic place could wait for another day.

Anyway, in church, thinking back on Abigail's trials and her indomitable spirit, I said a prayer for her, and thanked the unknowable force. The fates. The gods, or God, or whatever-whoever that makes the world come back together mostly okay when chaos lets loose its random confusion.

It's only one God. We know this because there is only one message.

I brushed aside the fantasy that this strong-willed thought had been from anyone but me. Me to myself.

Abigail was going to be okay. Definitely the best thing of the night had been finding Abigail and Betty, and helping them escape. Thank you, God, for that.

And then I thanked God for helping us find Buddy, by sending in the flies, who called the cops. It was their buzzing that attracted the searchers' attention.

My thoughts and I wandered and finally I found myself back home. Matt was still before the television, but this time listening.

"The locals are calling this final Pintos victim a hero. I concur. His name is Javier. I think he took Buddy's death. His mom and dad say he was like that, a brave and true believer."

I wished I was.

I wished I was a true believer and brave. But I wasn't. I was just driven to help others when the chips were down. Some random gene. Some....

By design.

My Marine continued as I wandered into the kitchen for some of what he was drinking and snacking on.

"Buddy's awake, but he can't remember what happened after they first started cutting him on his parents' bed," Matt called after me.

That meant Buddy couldn't explain why the Pinto boy had been killed.

"Gloria says Abigail only remembers being taken in another direction by the Hidalgo gang and listening to Buddy's screams as she was leaving. I think Gloria is going to need your help."

I reminded myself to call her.

"Anyway, Buddy's mom and Abigail are taking turns watching over him now, along with the Zinzers. They're talking about moving to Cardiff-by-the-Sea, for an extended stay with a relative there. I can't see how they'll ever sell that house."

Poor Abigail, find him alive and lose him to a move. I reminded myself that she was thirteen, and settled down on the couch.

But that thought brought my wandering mind back to early this morning, after I'd raced back into the house to find Rosalia. Fact is I didn't. But I found a room full of dead Hidalgos, three of them to be exact, at the end of the L-shaped house. One had had his left eye replaced with a bullet hole.

It gave me chills to know Eddie Stowall was now that good a shot, like it had given me chills to think about where he went with the other two bad guys, before I'd found out.

"And Harks called."

The Deacon.

"Guy has amazing connections. He's in awe of Eddie's capabilities, the ones that allowed him to confront and survive dealing with five drug terrorists. That's what Harks calls them, drug terrorists."

I was in awe of Eddie's capabilities as well, but probably with a different take-away.

"I wonder if the man is sane."

Matt looked at me, thoughtfully. "So do the FBI and cops. I'm on the fence."

"But he saved Rosalia."

"Right."

We stared at each other for a long time, probably sending the same conclusions to each other. A long marriage makes that possible.

I sipped my drink, decaf diet Coke--otherwise known as expensive, bubbly water. Ate two chips dipped in salsa.

As I ignored the television and mulled over Eddie's behavior, I decided that for me the most important part of Eddie's actions during the final hours of this event was the saving of Rosalia Fousat. She was found lying in a heap out next to one of the Hidalgo get-away cars— still alive. The Hidalgos had almost gotten away with her. They'd almost killed her before they tried to flee with her, and then they'd almost placed her into a car and fled south.

And it was Eddie who foiled that kidnapping, chasing the bad guys back into the house. Eddie saved Rosalia--and probably Betty, Abigail and me.

And no, it wasn't me who found her; it was the FBI, various cops and one Marine. Will was with me, dragging me out the front door and back to safety with Abigail and my unpaid apprentices, Gerry and Hannah.

Rosalia is in an ICU ward somewhere down in Chula Vista now. She'll survive, but she's terribly damaged, like Betty and Buddy.

Matt continued to catch me up on Harks' call.

As I said, the Deacon has amazing connections, which allowed Matt and I to know more about what was going on than we could have otherwise. Really amazing.

The Deacon's connections told Matt that about a hundred yards below the Mexican border the son of Antipapa, ContraCristo, had already been found eyeless, earless and noseless. And without hands and most of his teeth. Next to him was a similarly mutilated corpse, another Hidalgo gang member, who remains nameless as well as almost faceless.

I wondered aloud how they identified ContraCristo.

"Harks said he was wearing an upside down cross around his neck—that matched one around the father's neck."

I knew this to be the work of Eddie. Earier, when I was sitting in St. Peters Church, it occurred to me that I needed to say a prayer for Eddie's soul. I just didn't quite know how to word that prayer. I just didn't know what I thought about this man, who could shoot so well and torture so well, all in the name of justice. Or vengeance. Or personal rage.

Back with Matt, though, I only said, "I pray the world never hears about ContraCristo's death."

"So did the authorities in Tijuana. They're so terrified of the reign of violence that Antipapa would unleash against their population that they've buried the two in a pauper's cemetery outside Tijuana. Harks says there's no way of knowing who mutilated the two Hidalgos, Eddie or the Tijuana cops." Matt.

Again, we made eye contact.

"Unless the fool police chief has kept the cross as a souvenir." He grinned that Irish grin I love so much. I was thinking some rum must have found its way into his Coke.

"Anyway, a spokes-hole for the Feds has leaked that ContraCristo is still hiding somewhere in the US. Probably to keep his Papa searching. We think they're just helping out another terrified border town by floating this rumor."

Matt also told me that these same "leaks" had contained the information that the reason the authorities moved on the house when they did was that a white truck was spotted approaching the west side of the little house, and they believed it was the key get-away car.

Some of this he'd picked up from Harks, some of it he'd heard on television as I was sitting on a pew.

Which returned me to another question that had jigged around my mind: what might happen to me, Hannah and Gerry, because we rushed pell-mell down Snakebite Hill into the jaws of terror to help rescue the girls? My guess was nothing, based on what transpired in the final moments after the rescue.

Learner took custody of me, Gerry and Hannah and led us off to his vehicle in the mass confusion of all those rescuers. We were later quietly transferred into Matt's truck and driven up to Gerry's car.

You get the picture. We were spirited away before our names became known and our pictures were taken.

So probably nothing would happen to us.

Matt's final comments on the recent events, before slipping back to sleep, was that when he and Learner worked out the "a dress" Nana had given them, Learner was using an iPad.

"An iPad, for crying out loud. A cop. You can't believe what you can do with an iPad, Rache, in the friken middle of nowhere."

He was green. I almost reminded him Christmas was coming. But he knew that.

While he was dropping hints about Christmas presents, he slipped in his burning question.

"So, did you fire your gun today?"

I decided simple was best and answered, "No."

Again, our eyes locked, his slightly glazed. We both pondered the fact that Eddie had been the one doing all the shooting this morning.

Or was he still letting me know he was pissed because I'd gotten in the middle of things?

But Christmas was coming and presents can make lots of things better. The great American act of penance.

To the music of Matt's light snoring, I rose to join Wisdom on the back deck, wrapping a sweater around me against the Southern California November chill. The sun had set and still we could hear the gnus stampeding through the wild animal park. Wisdom was thinking about what it would be like to run with them.

I thought about my dogs.

Our first dog had been Joy. She was the shepherd of our twenties and early thirties. Our second was Prophet. Prophet had guided us through the rest of our thirties and well into our forties. Matt liked to spell the name *Profit* with an f.

And then had come Wisdom, who lingered with us now, not wanting to give up his little bit of spirit to the winds just yet.

We'd discussed it--out of earshot of Wisdom of course--and decided our next shepherd, since he or she would take us into our sixties, we would name Comfort.

A quilt can be called a comforter. The Holy Spirit is sometimes referred to as The Comforter. It fit for me.

And maybe after that one, Path.

As I pondered the evil I had rubbed shoulders with recently I wondered what Ruth's take was on all this. Last month she'd left me with the message to "Love them all, anyway."

A few minutes later, I heard the phone ring in the house and I turned to go answer it. Matt beat me to it, tossing over his shoulder as he entered the kitchen to get the phone, "Take a listen to this news."

It was CNN again.

"For those of you just joining us, fourteen-year-old Mary Kaye Barnacle has sent her parents a text message. I'm going to read it again now and if any of you have any information about this, please let the authorities know. Mary Kaye's text says, "Mom, dad, i've been kidnapped. i think they're taking me to mex. i keep telling them my name isn't abigail...."

My heart skipped a beat. Another girl was in trouble. And in the throes of fear again, Matt finally handed me the phone.

"Here, this is for you. I think its Hannah but she's not making any sense." I noted the sarcasm in his voice. He was still feeling conflicted about my new girlfriends.

I carried the phone back out to the deck.

"Hi Hannah, have you been watching...?"

"Rachel! My mom! She's awake! Rachel. *Ruth is back!*"

"What..?"

"She's come up from her coma. She's all there, talking with the kids, asking for coffee."

I heard Ruth's scratchy voice call out in the background. *"Tell her...,"*

I couldn't make out the rest.

"Hannah..?" Me.

Her kids were laughing and screaming so much in the background I couldn't tell what was happening.

"Wait. What mom? Oh, yeah. She wants me to tell you 'Sometimes you have to use tough love,' or something like that."

Tough love?

Then I heard Ruth call toward the phone as clear as day. "Like a gun! Use a gun on them. And you need to clear your thoughts. I can't get through to you."

The phone went dead. At first I thought Hannah had hung up, but then I saw that my cell phone had run out of juice.

I smiled. Ruth was back, and so was all her unbelievable magic. Of course, none of us admitted to any of this. Not openly.

And, of course the gnus weren't really stampeding. They were just kicking up their heels.

Characters

Lyons Investigations and Research, Inc (LIRI)
Rachel Lyons, Private Investigator, lead researcher
Matthew Lyons, lead Private Investigator, Rachel's husband
Marvin Luis Lewis, junior apprentice
William Townsend, senior apprentice

The Stowall Family
Victoria Stowall, matriarch of the Quilted Secrets
Mark, Luke, Martha, Anne, Mary, John and **Sarah**, children of
Jake and Victoria Stowall in birth order
Eddie Stowall, grandson of Victoria

Quilted Secrets Hand Quilters
Elizabeth (Elixchel) Chavez, adopted by Victoria Stowall at age
13 after her parents died in a car accident, now a bookkeeper
at an area Indian casino, in training to be a midwife
Andrea Kelly, was fostered by Victoria Stowall after her
parents rejected her for being a lesbian, now an artist in
Southern California
Hannah Lilly, daughter of Ruth McMichaels, husband is Peter,
home schooling parent and small-scale homesteader
Rachel Lyons, newest member of the quilting group
Ruth McMichaels, Victoria's sister, mother of Hannah
Geraldine Patrone, wife of billionaire Marshall Patrone, owner
of the San Diego major league soccer franchise
Abigail Pustovoytenko, daughter of Gloria, 13-year-old
homeschooler
Gloria Pustovoytenko, mother of Abigail, head nurse of
Cleveland General Hospital ICU
Anne Stowall, daughter of Victoria, filling in for Ruth
McMichaels at this bee
Victoria Stowall, oldest living Quilted Secrets member

Law Enforcement
Tom Beardsley, junior detective, Cleveland County Sheriff's
Department, brother of Geraldine Patrone
Robert Learner, senior detective, Pinto Springs Police
Department, aka Pestilence
Khoja Marana, Cleveland County Medical Examiner
Leslie Mosby, senior detective, Pinto Springs Police
Department, aka Famine

Proof

Made in the USA
Charleston, SC
10 July 2011